River's Bend

Charlie Russell

Also by Charlsie Russell

The Devil's Bastard

Wolf Dawson

Epico Bayou

River's Bend

A Novel

Charlsie Russell

Loblolly Writer's House
Gulfport, Mississippi

Loblolly Writer's House
P.O. Box 7438
Gulfport, MS 39506-7438
Visit our website at www.loblollywritershouse.com

First Edition: September 2011

This book is a work of fiction. Names, characters, and incidents are products of the author's imagination. Any resemblance to actual events or persons is coincidental. Any scenes depicting actual historical persons are fictitious.

Library of Congress Catalogue Number: 2011902232
Russell, Charlsie.
    River's bend: a novel

    ISBN 978-0-9769824-3-2
    1. Mystery – Fiction

Book design by Lucretia Gibson
Copy editor, Nancy McDowell
Cover design: Transformative work of an original 1860 drawing "A Midnight Race" between the Natchez and Eclipse by H.D. Manning for Currier and Ives. After, Francis F. B. Palmer lithograph of the same name featuring the Memphis and the James Howard (1875). Shown here is an adaptation of a Hulton Archive photograph of a Getty print.

Printed and bound in the United States of America.

For Lola,
who always loved my stuff, but never read
a thing I wrote

Guide to Characters

Rafe Stone - The mysterious new owner of River's Bend plantation home
Delilah Graff - Rafe Stone's reluctant bride, the price for River's Bend

Richard & Charlotte Graff - Delilah's deceased parents

Josephus & Ophelia Collander - Delilah's uncle and aunt, the previous owners of River's Bend
Bernadette Collander - Their daughter, fiancée of Douglas Champion

Douglas Champion - Bernadette's fiancé, with a romantic interest in Delilah

Markham & Emmaline Merrifield - Post-War owners of River's Bend
David & Raymond Merrifield - Their sons
Cecilia Merrifield - Markham Merrifield's second wife; both he and she were murdered inside River's Bend

Morgan Ward - Renegade Confederate officer wanted for murder and the theft of one hundred thousand dollars in Federal gold at the close of The War Between the States
Lorelei Richard (Ward) - Ill-fated bride of the notorious Morgan Ward. River's Bend was her ancestral home

Gil & Annie Douglas - Slaves/Freemen long associated with River's Bend
Simon & Lucianne Douglas - Gil and Annie's son and his wife
Belle & Bo Douglas - Simon and Lucianne's children

James Dexter - Private detective in the employ of Rafe Stone

Townsfolk (Natchez):
Mr. Grapple - Property agent
Harry Tyler - Coal gas expert
Henry Gifford - Newspaperman/Editor of *The Natchez Gazette*
Mrs. Howell - Housecleaner employed at River's Bend
Elvira Cutter & Constance Mack - Furniture saleswoman and her friend
Dr. Surrey - Natchez surgeon
Lee Broderick - Adams County Sheriff

Chapter One

"Mr. Collander is expecting me."

The primly dressed Negress took his card and nodded, at the same time swinging the door wide. Raeford Stone stepped into a broad entry with polished floors of heart pine and a staircase to his right. The young woman took his hat, then motioned to him. "This way."

They'd not taken two steps when a door several paces up opened on their left, brightening the dim foyer. A short, pleasantly plump woman with dark hair filled the portal. She didn't look his way, but focused her attention into the room from where she came.

"I want her out of here, Joe. Immediately. She's going to ruin everything, you know it as well as I."

If Joe responded, Rafe didn't know. The woman rolled her head on her shoulders and looked at the ceiling. Then, her back to them, she stepped into the foyer, slammed the door shut, and hurried away from him and the maid.

When the dark-haired shrew disappeared into the room at the end of the hall, the servant led him to the slammed door, knocked, then pushed it open and beckoned him inside.

A tall, middle-aged man, hands clasped behind his back, stood staring out a bank of floor-to-ceiling windows on the far wall of an opulent study.

1

"Mr. Collander, suh?"

"Yes, Stella?"

"Mr. Stone to see you. You was expectin' him?"

The man, stout himself by anyone's standards, pivoted with surprising grace. "I am indeed. . . . Ah, ha," he said, meeting Rafe's eye before moving around a large desk, "you're already in." He caught up with Rafe in the middle of the room and extended his hand. "Welcome to Mississippi. I trust you had a pleasant trip from Galveston?"

"I did, thank you."

"Stella?"

Her hand already on the doorknob, the black woman turned. "Lemonade or ice tea, Mr. Stone?" Collander asked.

"Tea, thank you."

"I will have tea, also," the man said to Stella. "Please sit, Mr. Stone."

And sit he did, in a fine leather wing chair strategically situated in front of that most impressive desk. Collander took his seat behind it.

"Dorian Tatum contacted me yesterday. Says you're interested in that old plantation house on the river, south of Natchez."

"I am, sir."

"It's a beautiful site. The house was once a showcase, I understand, looking down on that bend in the river. River's Bend. Do you know anything of the history?"

"Some. Actually, I'm an architect. I came across the house while studying pre-War homes in the Natchez-Rodney area. I believe it could be a showcase again."

Josephus Collander laughed. "The place has attracted its share of curiosity seekers in the past. For all intents and purposes, no one has lived in it for over fifteen years. I've seen it once, seven years ago. It was in a bad state then. However, Dorian assures me you are legitimate."

"I will tell you that I made a close inspection of the exterior before I ever started to trace ownership. I am aware of the condition of the house."

2

Collander sighed. "You must consider my lack of attention to it reprehensible."

Rafe looked around the rich room. Obviously the man had some means, but the upkeep of a house like River's Bend would prove costly.

"Not at all. I understand it came to you by way of inheritance?"

Collander nodded with wide-eyed exaggeration. "By way of my wife's grandaunt who herself acquired it by a fluke." The man waved the matter away at the same moment a knock sounded on the door. It opened despite the lack of a reciprocating *entrée*, and Stella came in, carrying a tray with two crystal glasses filled with chunks of ice and lemon floating in amber brew. Both men rose, and Collander took the glasses, handing one to Rafe, who nodded to his host and thanked the servant.

"Sun-steeped and sweetened with sugar," Collander said and took a big swallow.

Rafe sipped. Sweet was right, but it was also cold and wet, the perfect complement to this hot and humid late-October day.

Joe Collander took another swig, almost finishing his drink, then placed his mostly empty glass on Stella's tray and eyed her warily.

"What?" he said finally.

"Miss Ophelia wanted you to know that Mr. Champion has got here."

Collander's expression soured.

"She say she wants you to—"

"Watch them from the window."

Rafe could have sworn Stella smirked. "Yessuh," she said.

"Thank you, Stella."

The maid turned to Rafe, who put his empty glass on the tray. He smiled, she smiled, and then she left. Collander watched the door close behind her. "Only woman in the whole damn house who isn't a pain in my ass, Mr. Stone. And this is a house full of women."

Surprised, Rafe met the man's eye. Collander winked and,

turning his back on him, walked to the bank of windows. Outside, on the lawn, Rafe had already heard the sound of feminine
voices and high-pitched laughter, now interspersed with the boisterous shouts of a man. He walked toward the desk, from where
he could see what Collander was looking at.

A blonde woman sat in a swing, suspended from the stout
branch of a live oak tree. She was being pushed by a tall, dark-
haired man over whom a plump brunette fussed and, apparently,
gushed. Rafe was too far away to make out any of their features,
but the build and carriage of the man indicated he was around his
own age. The two women were probably younger, the brunette
not yet over the silliness of girlhood.

"After the War, the house passed to some Merrifield woman
up in Ohio. She was from the Vicksburg area, but had married
and moved away years before the unfortunate conflict. She and
the plantation's last master were half siblings, I do believe. The
family had been decimated by the War, so she was about the only
one left to inherit.

"She died a number of years later. Her husband remarried,
and he and his family were murdered in the house, as I understand it." Collander glanced briefly over his shoulder at Rafe. "A
sordid affair."

A double entendre? Patricide, matricide, fratricide . . . incest.
Shoot, sordid didn't begin to describe the tangled relationships
leading up to those murders. Rafe followed Collander's gaze back
to the threesome outside. The blonde jumped gracefully from
the swing and started away from the other two. The young man
followed, hindered somewhat by the pleasingly endowed brunette.

"My niece has become troublesome, Mr. Stone."

Rafe was sorry, but he really didn't care to know it. The
young man, hurrying after the willowy blonde, stopped when the
brunette tripped and almost fell trying to keep up. Well, yes, he
guessed she had become somewhat of a problem—more for the
dark-haired man than her uncle.

"The other young woman is your daughter?"

"Yes."

"The young man her intended?"

Josephus Collander tightened his lips and nodded. "That is our dearest hope."

"And your niece is displaying some affection for him?"

Collander turned on his heel and looked Rafe over.

"Are you married, Mr. Stone?"

"Not yet."

"You've an intended?"

Rafe hesitated before replying, "No."

Collander smiled, then stepped to his desk and sat, motioning for Rafe to do likewise.

"The house was sold again after the murders. Bought by a Missouri banker for his daughter and son-in-law as a wedding gift. They lived there for a few months and had, in fact, begun renovations when they abruptly abandoned the place. Subsequently, the Missouri banker tried to rent it out. The renters stayed only a couple of weeks. Shortly thereafter, the banker sold the place, at a loss, to my wife's uncle by marriage. The uncle died before he and my wife's aunt did anything with it, and her aunt withered away. They were childless, and my wife inherited the property nine years ago. I've had neither the time nor the compunction to do anything with it."

"Were repairs that daunting?"

"The property is reputed to be haunted."

Rafe laughed, and Collander cocked his head.

"Don't be too quick to scoff. That unique feature of the place apparently drove out the newlyweds and the renters."

"By whom is the place haunted, Mr. Collander?"

The man shrugged. "I believe the ghost ties into the murders following the War."

"So a more recent ghost?"

"And a dangerous one. Some speculate it is the ghost of the killer."

"That would make the specter quite ominous."

Collander picked up a paper weight, studied it, then placed it back on the polished surface of the desk. "Have you any prospective feminine interests, sir?"

Rafe frowned. "My feminine interest is restricted to women of an easy persuasion."

"Wonderful, Mr. Stone, and in my opinion, only a fool ever loses interest completely in women of easy persuasion." Collander leaned forward. "And now that we understand each other, how old are you?"

Josephus Collander might understand what the hell he was talking about, but Rafe sure the devil didn't. "I'm twenty-nine. I'll be thirty in January."

Collander nodded. "And have you given any thought to settling down?"

"I have not."

Collander leaned back in his chair. He was different now from the friendly man who offered refreshment and showed pride in and consideration for his servants. Collander was assessing him, weighing his options. He had a deal in mind, and that worried Rafe. Collander had turned into a businessman, which, in fact, is what he was.

"You have made a generous offer for the house. Much more than it's worth."

"I have the capital."

"Your offer tells me you want that property very much."

"I think I can do a lot with it."

"Desperately," Collander said, as if he hadn't heard him. "You've shown me your hand, Mr. Stone."

Rafe felt like he'd swallowed a brick. Despite that, he smiled. "I'm a damn lousy poker player, too."

Collander pursed his lips. "Either you know something I don't, or you are a fool, or 'lousy' is a gross understatement regarding your card-playing ability."

Damn. Rafe leaned back, hoping he appeared as nonchalant as Collander. "I didn't want to haggle with you over the price. I'd like to get started on the house before winter sets in. I hoped to make you an offer you could not refuse."

"Winters are mild in this neck of the woods, sir."

"I wouldn't know. I'm not from here."

"You're not from up north, either."

No he wasn't, nor was he about to tell the man where he was from.

Collander rolled himself into the desk's kneehole.

"I don't know why you want that property. I don't believe you're an architect. An adventurer would be my guess. The house is not for sale, Mr. Stone. . . ."

That brick in Rafe's stomach crashed into his lower gut.

". . . but I will give it to you as my niece's dowry."

The mad man continued to talk. Rafe stared at him, though he wondered why he considered the man mad. Proposals such as this were not unusual, historically. Still, he never considered himself a candidate for such an offer.

". . . my stepsister's daughter. She was orphaned when she was twelve and raised by her paternal grandmother. The woman died three months ago. Delilah's been with my family since then. The girl, young woman actually, is quite charming . . ."

If fawning over an inattentive man could be considered charming.

". . . and beautiful."

In truth, beauty was a subjective thing. Where he came from, the derrière of choice did have meatier hips, but he preferred a slender bottom, trim waist, and flat belly. Still, the little brunette, from a distance, appeared to have a pretty face, and a man could always find fringe benefits in a plump body.

"She's nineteen and very well educated."

Her youth was a good thing. Education was not necessarily a plus. Well-educated women often proved more trouble than they were worth. At least, that's what he'd been told.

"Mr. Collander?"

Collander stopped the sales pitch.

"You know nothing about me."

"I know you can support her."

And leave her, or beat her, or even murder her should he be

7

so inclined. "I would think you'd have more requirements on your list."

Collander made a sibilant sound. "I have an uncanny ability to size a man up within minutes." He waved his hand over the room. "A key to my success."

Still, were there no eligible men Collander did know upon whom he could foist his niece? But, of course, "knowing" worked both ways. There was more to this story than the girl's simply being a silly chit. "What's wrong with her?"

Josephus Collander sighed. "There's nothing wrong with her, except that she's penniless and. . . ."

"In need of a husband," Rafe said when Collander hesitated.

"In need of a refuge, most assuredly." The graying merchant laid his arms on his desk and leaned forward. "And you, Mr. Stone, have inadvertently provided me the opportunity to rid myself not only of a worthless piece of tax-draining real estate but also an unwanted guest."

Chapter Two

"No," she told Uncle Joe.

Josephus Collander took the seat next to her on his office settee. "Think about this, Delilah. He has—"

"I have thought about it. I've thought about it for seven long years. No, longer than that. For as long as I've been able to see and hear and understand." She fought for breath. He was out of his mind. "I do not wish to marry and certainly not a stranger."

"And what do you plan on doing with your life? Mooch off me?"

Delilah stiffened. She was still in control here. At least she thought she was, and she would not allow him to put her on the defensive.

"I want to be a seams—"

"Seamstress, my foot. You can't make a decent wage working as a seamstress."

"You told me you could help me establish my own business."

"That offer is off the table. Money's short right now, and I haven't time to waste."

"It's because of Douglas, isn't it?"

"Yes, it's because of Douglas, the whelp. He took one look at you, and Bernadette ceased to exist."

Delilah held out her hands in supplication. "I want nothing to do with him. I've told him so."

"When?" Her uncle rose and started pacing along the well-worn path in the Aubusson carpet. Back and forth. He always paced when he was agitated and determined. He didn't plan on losing this bout.

9

"From the beginning."

"And have you seen a lessening in his interest?"

No, she hadn't. Douglas Champion was rich, handsome, and full of himself. He had not believed for a moment she wasn't madly in love with him. "I've done my best to discourage him."

Uncle Joe stopped pacing. "I know you have, honey, but he will not have it. He's asked that he and his father speak to me in the morning. I'm sure they wish to renegotiate our tentative agreement regarding the 'proposed' proposal to Bernadette and ask for your hand instead."

"Tell them no." She tilted her chin defiantly. "And if they persist, the deal is off."

"Delilah, darling"—he enunciated clearly and firmly as if she were a dunderhead—"the nation is in recession. I cannot afford to gamble with the merger. To Douglas and his father, it is all the same, daughter or niece, the families are joined."

She opened her mouth to speak, and he held up a hand. "But, Delilah, honey, Bernadette is my baby, my only child. She has her heart set on the fickle son of a she-dog, and you are fouling up the works. And on top of it all, I have to live with her mother."

And she was an unwanted niece, not even blood, who didn't want anything to do with that fickle son, son . . . person. Poor, smitten Bernadette. Delilah squirmed in her seat. "If you could help me get established in New Orleans—"

"Even if I were willing to abandon you alone in New Orleans, which I'm not, he would follow you there. As long as you are on the market, he will continue to ignore Bernadette. And who could blame him?"

Delilah furrowed her brow, and her uncle scowled. "Oh, come now," he said. "I'm no fool and neither are you. Other than a well-filled body and a moderately pretty face, Bernadette has nothing to offer but my money. She's a spoiled, silly chatterbox with frivolous interests, concerned only with catching a sociably acceptable husband in order to please her mama. I was fortunate enough to find a man who met her mother's requirements as well as my own needs."

"But if he doesn't want Bernie—"

"The merger, my dear. The Champions are businessmen. The marriage between Douglas and Bernadette was ideal for both companies and families, but when you came on the scene, young Douglas saw the opportunity to have the best of both worlds. You are exceedingly lovely . . ."

Oh good Lord, this was the last thing she wanted to hear.

". . . demure, intelligent, and mature."

"And where does that maturity stem from, Uncle? You should be rewarded for protecting Bernadette."

"And I intend to continue protecting her from the realities of life as best I can."

But protecting his orphaned niece didn't matter. "And I commend you, Uncle Joe, but I don't want Douglas or his world."

Her uncle rolled his eyes to heaven, and for a moment she closed hers.

"But he wants you," he said, "and he is used to getting what he wants. That alone should be enough for you to help me thwart him."

Delilah's laugh bordered on hysterical, even to her ears. "I refused him. That should be enough."

"You agreed with me moments ago that has not dissuaded him."

She looked away.

"I am desperate for this merger between Champion and Collander, Delilah, and I am desperate for my daughter."

Stubbornly, she kept her eyes averted. She absolutely would not do as he wanted. She'd offered other courses of action, up to and including her leaving Mississippi City. How in the world had her life become so entangled with Bernadette's?

"The truth might dissuade him. Do you want to try that tack?"

She sucked in a breath. "You're threatening me?"

Remorse washed across his face, an emotion she rarely observed in Josephus Collander, primarily because her forthright uncle rarely did anything to elicit remorse.

"You owe me," he said.

Brutal honesty, however, was a different matter.

"I paid off Prudence Colburn and did more than my fair share to stifle your grandmother's ranting. I compelled her to take you in when she would have preferred you on the street, and I supported you financially through her. I kept the scandal to a minimum."

Yes, he'd done all those things, and finally, after all other options dried up, he'd brought her into his home. And she was sure Aunt Ophelia had fought and cajoled and nagged him every step of the way.

"It was all a lie. You know it."

"Probably."

She stared at him. "You *know* it was."

He held up a hand. "I do know it, but it doesn't matter. You have learned how people think."

Yes, she'd learned. Delilah closed her eyes tight and bent her face toward her lap. "The woman is always to blame."

She felt him retake his seat beside her, and she opened her eyes. "I swore that day I'd never be at the mercy of a man."

"You have always been at the mercy of a man, my dear. First your father's, and now"—he reached into her lap and patted her hand—"you are at mine."

She balled her hand into a fist, hoping to discourage his touch. Perhaps he sensed her anger, because he moved his hand away.

"What do you know of this person?"

He straightened, and she could sense the change in him, more light-hearted, relaxed. He smelled victory.

"You'll not find your plight so bad. He is, in my opinion, a very handsome young man. He is also well-spoken, smart, and solvent."

Her bottom lip trembled. "My father was handsome. I was hoping for something a little more meaningful."

Uncle Joe let out a breath. "Your father was a rare case."

She jerked her head to search his eyes, and her left shoulder numbed. The sudden movement had been foolish, and one she'd learned to avoid. Delilah tilted her head to the right and stretched

12

her neck. Scorching heat shot down her left arm, and she hissed in a breath. After a moment the discomfort was gone. She glanced at her uncle, watching her.

"My father was worst case," she said. "What else do you know of this person you are giving me to?"

"He transferred an exceedingly large amount of money to a bank in New Orleans from one in Brownsville, Texas. Apparently he sold his ranch."

Or robbed a bank, maybe worse.

"That's all you know?"

"Dorian Tatum assures me he is real."

"A real what, Uncle?"

Josephus Collander gave her a sheepish look. "Architect."

"Architect?"

"Yes. An architect looking for a wife."

"Am I to assume he came to you looking for me?"

"You can assume that."

Yes, she could, if that made her feel better. She didn't believe this man came to Josephus Collander in search of a wife—not unless Uncle Joe had advertised to give her away in the paper. She couldn't rule that out, but suspected she'd have heard about it before now.

Her fingers stung. She looked in her lap where she was wringing them and stopped.

"What have you told him about me?"

"That you are a beautiful orphan in need of a husband."

Chapter Three

"Joe says that you are a rancher turned architect," Ophelia Collander said to Rafe.

Rancher turned architect? He looked at Collander, standing nearby at a small, lacquered cabinet pouring wine. The man had taken his line and expanded it, but Rafe was curious as to how his host had come up with the rancher part.

Collander stepped forward, handing first his wife, then Rafe, a charged crystal glass. They were in the luxuriously appointed parlor of Collander's home, brightly lit by gas sconces and a fire in the hearth, which also served to chase away the subtle chill of the encroaching October night.

"It was my father's ranch. He died six months ago. Cows don't interest me much. I have a younger sister who recently married. My brother-in-law bought me out."

Ophelia Collander giggled. "And you studied architecture?"

"Not formally." He glanced at Collander. "I'm self-taught."

She wrapped a manicured hand around his arm and gently stroked the gray wool of his sack coat, before tittering again. "Josephus says you've acquired a plantation home on the river and you intend to renovate it."

He smiled at her and wondered when Collander intended to tell his wife he'd offered him her inheritance.

"I'm still in negotiations, Mrs. Collander."

"Ophelia, please . . . , Rafe." Her face was painted, and a touch of lip rouge showed on her teeth when she smiled. She smelled good though, and except for the hand placed possessively on his arm, Ophelia kept her body to herself.

14

"And are negotiations stalled?"

The servant girl Stella stuck her head in the door. The dark-haired man he had observed that afternoon on the lawn outside Collander's office loomed behind her.

"Ah, Douglas," Collander said, stepping away from Rafe and his wife. "Come in, son, come in.

"Rafe is waiting for the approval of his fiancée, Ophelia dear," Collander said, looking over his shoulder while shaking the new man's hand.

"Oh," Ophelia said, releasing his arm with a simper, "you are engaged?"

"He is in negotiations there also, my dear," Collander said. "Douglas Champion, Rafe Stone."

Rafe took Champion's hand and shook firmly. Champion reciprocated in kind.

"Where are the young ladies?" Champion asked.

Ophelia stepped toward the door. "I'll send Stella for them."

Douglas Champion immediately turned to Rafe and opened his mouth to speak, but before he got his question out, the pretty, buxom brunette stepped through the door. She was dressed in a colorful blue satin gown, decorated with frills and bead embroidery, the hem and bodice trimmed in fur. The color suited her. She was rosy cheeked and breathless, and from the way her gaze landed on Douglas Champion, it was obvious her uncle had yet to mention Rafe and his proposal to her at all. Rafe swore the girl didn't even realize he was in the room, and he felt as irritated over her behavior as Douglas Champion, despite his pleasantries, appeared annoyed.

"Bernie dear," Collander said, causing the girl to tear her gaze from Champion. "We have another dinner guest."

"Oh?" Her smile brightened when she found Rafe, and she looked him over, head to foot, then stepped forward, hand extended. "Hello, I am Bernadette."

"And I'm"—he cocked his head and frowned—"Rafe . . . Stone."

She laughed. "Are you sure?"

15

He was confused, that's for certain. He glanced at Collander, who wrinkled his brow at him, then back to the girl. "You're *Bernadette*?"

She smiled sweetly. "Yes, that's my real name. The family calls me Bernie. It's dreadfully masculine, I know." She giggled. "But I do answer to it."

Distracted as much by this girl's rapid-fire response as he was dumbfounded by her name, he said, "It fits you."

The smile froze on her face, and he tensed with the realization of what he'd said. He took her hand. "Your real name, I mean. Bernadette. I have always thought it beautiful. With your permission, that's what I'll call you, and you, please, call me Rafe."

She simpered like her mother. "A very handsome name."

Well, he figured he'd managed to extricate himself rather nicely from that most impolite bungle.

"And it is, indeed, very nice to meet you, Rafe." She looked back over her shoulder to Champion, and it occurred to Rafe, still holding her hand, that she hoped the man had noticed his interest in her. Champion, however, was moving toward the hall door.

"Ah, Delilah."

The willowy blonde Rafe had seen jump from the swing stepped into the room. She acknowledged Champion, then locked her eyes, a shimmering sea green, on him, and he sucked in a breath. Damn, he'd known this one was pretty, but he hadn't counted on blinding beauty.

Collander tactfully inserted himself between the blonde and Champion, who bumped the older man in an effort to get to *la belle* first. Collander took her hand.

"Rafe Stone," he said, kissing the golden-haired siren's fingers before giving her hand to Rafe. "I would like for you to meet my niece, Delilah Graff."

Chapter Four

The beautiful, trim-hipped blonde was the niece, and she actually looked like a Delilah. She was studying him with utmost intensity, but he didn't believe for an instant *she* thought Rafe a "handsome name." Without a doubt, Joe Collander had talked to this woman about the proposal, and she didn't like it.

He couldn't fault her. Like him, how was she to know what she was getting? Rafe narrowed his eyes, glanced at Collander, who was watching them with what was, by all indicators, bated breath, then returned his gaze to his proposed intended.

"Miss Graff," he said.

"Mr. Stone." She smiled with faux sweetness. "Could I have my hand back, please?"

He rubbed his thumb over her knuckles and felt her tense. Satisfied, he brought her fingers to his lips and kissed them. "For the moment," he said and let go of her hand.

Collander stepped closer to them, and Rafe looked over the older man's shoulder to watch poor Champion sandwiched between the two jabbering Collander women. Ophelia had apparently lost interest in him once she discovered he was about to become engaged. The glaring Champion hadn't lost interest in him, though.

Collander's stratagem was making sense now. Delilah Graff was the "wanton" woman, the home wrecker, or in this case, the proposal wrecker. Rafe had no doubt Champion was totally enthralled with Delilah, but at least in public, she gave no indication she reciprocated that affection.

He found those astonishing eyes once more and searched them.

17

After a moment, he pursed his lips. Delilah Graff wasn't particularly interested in bestowing any affection on him either.

A log, its mass condensed to glowing embers, fell into the flames amidst a spray of sparks. Delilah rubbed her palm over the brocade surface of the chaise where she sat, then glanced at Rafe Stone, talking to Uncle Joe about coastal shipping. Her uncle had surprised the poised Mr. Stone when he put her hand in his. Oh, he hid it well, but Delilah knew without a doubt she was not what Rafe Stone had been expecting. As for herself, she was unrepentantly pleased with the man's appearance and equally dismayed by his arrogance. Her knuckles still tingled from his kiss.

He was handsome by any standard, with neatly trimmed, tawny hair; clean-shaven, not sporting the popular mustache she found distasteful on both her uncle and Douglas. His eyes were dark, hazel, and wide-set. Her mother used to tell her wide-set eyes were a sign of intelligence. Her father had wide-set eyes. Rafe Stone's met hers, watching him. For a moment, she held his gaze, and his mouth quirked. An exceedingly handsome mouth between a strong chin and a straight nose. He had straight teeth, too. She'd noticed that earlier.

"More wine?"

She turned to Douglas, who'd come up to her chair beside the fire. Goodness, how had he escaped Bernie and Aunt Ophelia?

"No, thank you." She'd had two glasses, and they'd yet to sit down to dinner. She was nervous and needed to keep her wits about her. Douglas reached to take her near-empty glass, but she tightened her hand around the stem. "I'll finish this."

He straightened beside her. "I would like to talk to you in private."

"What do you have to say to me that should be conveyed in private, Douglas?"

He kept his hands behind his black dinner coat, but a subtle twitch of his shoulders indicated he wanted to reach for her arm, to touch her. Fortunately, he restrained himself. Delilah allowed her gaze to wander over his tailored suit . . . and tails. So formal for a simple dinner. She glanced down at her own teal-blue, braided gown, then to the satin gown worn by her cousin. Formality made Delilah uncomfortable. That and the fact she could not afford such extravagance with her own wardrobe. In fact, all she could afford depended on the money her uncle gave her, and she never asked for anything. Delilah closed her eyes. Her grandmother had though, repeatedly.

"You know how my feelings for you have grown."

Delilah blinked and looked at Douglas. "And I have told you I do not share those feelings."

He bent closer, and Delilah averted her face. "Please, let's speak in private," he said.

She let loose a little laugh. "We can hardly leave to—"

"We'll meet in the garden later, after dinner."

"I don't want to be alone with you, Douglas. You have"—she lowered her voice; Rafe Stone was watching them—"entered a loose agreement to wed my cousin. She regards it as a promise as do her parents."

"That," he said, "is precisely why I must talk to you. I fear you are spurning my affection as a matter of honor."

"I can assure you I do not need any excuse to spurn a man's affection. Now let me be."

He straightened abruptly when Bernadette called his name, then pasted on a smile before turning to his supposed intended.

"Miss Graff?"

She jumped. Rafe Stone had sneaked up on her other side, but though his words were for her, he kept his eyes on Douglas's retreating back. "Dinner's been called," he said. Now he looked at her. "May I escort you to the dining room?"

From where Bernadette was looping her arm through one of his, Aunt Ophelia the other, Douglas glared at the handsome Mr. Stone. This Stone person appeared to take no notice.

That was another thing about Mr. Stone, his confidence and cool lack of formality. He bent his arm at the elbow, holding it out for her. She rose and slipped her hand through the crook and laid her fingers against the rich wool of his coat. His ascot matched his eyes, and she wondered if he'd had it custom made.

She was on his right side, a tactical error on her part she realized when her shoulder touched his bicep and piercing pain shot down her arm. The world teetered, a persistent, but relatively recent phenomenon added to her affliction. He braced his arm for her support, and she steadied.

"Are you all right?" he asked.

"Too much wine before dinner," she said.

"A fortifier, Miss Graff?"

She turned to him and smiled. "Or a foreshadowing of things to come, Mr. Stone?"

He nodded agreeably. "Thanks for the warning. So you'll know, I had two shots of bourbon before I left my hotel tonight."

"*Y*ou are giving up ranching for architecture?"

Collander had placed the unfaithful fiancé across from him. The lovely Delilah sat on his left across from Bernadette, who sat next to the man she hoped to marry.

"I have given up ranching for real estate speculation." Now, that sounded impressive.

"Where was your ranch?"

Douglas Champion had completed his meal and sat back in his chair. Rafe washed his last piece of roast down with a glass of fine red wine. And it was fine wine.

"South America," he said and wiped his mouth with his napkin.

Champion frowned, then opened his mouth to speak—he was going to ask where in South America, but Ophelia Collander smiled brightly and said, "You don't sound like you are from South America."

"You sound quite Southern, Mr. Stone."

Delilah's words had been gently spoken, and he reached beneath the table and took her hand from her lap. "Thank you, Miss Graff, I've worked very hard on my accent."

She was studying him with those gorgeous eyes, her gaze as

soft as her skin in the candlelight. He wanted to touch her face. At the end of the table, Stella started clearing the dishes.

"What are you looking for, Miss Graff?"

"A forked tongue," she answered quietly, but the others would have heard.

Ophelia coughed. "Now stop your flirting with him, Delilah, dear. He has an intended."

Confusion washed over Delilah's face, and she turned toward her aunt. Rafe bent close to her ear.

"That would be you, Delilah, dear." No one else heard that.

Stella reached for his plate, and he screwed his head around to see the young servant over his shoulder. "Could you bring Miss Delilah's shawl, please. I intend to take her for a walk in the garden."

He rose, and Champion sat forward. Bernadette allowed her mouth to drop open, then she shut it, and a wide-eyed Ophelia dropped her knife onto her china plate with a clatter. Josephus Collander met his wife's eye and took a sip of wine. "It's all right, dear," he said.

Delilah pushed her chair back and rose as did Champion and Collander. Champion flexed his jaw. Rafe ignored the man and focused on Delilah, who stepped around her chair. She didn't look at anyone but Stella, who handed her a short cape.

"It's gotten cool out, Miss."

"Thank you, Stella."

He followed Delilah down the wide entry hall into what appeared to be a library, its books and furnishings spectral in the silver glow of moonlight cascading through French doors. Delilah pushed a latch down and swung the doors open, then stepped onto a brick patio. Rafe followed her out, and a cool breeze kissed his cheek.

"This way," she said, leading him onto the path, which led past the swing he'd seen her on this afternoon. In front of him, her skirt stirred fallen leaves, and in her wake, he crushed them beneath his feet. The air was chilly, heavy with the scent of pine and a hint of sea.

21

"There's a gazebo at the end of this path," she said. "It has a light. We can talk there." For sure, given her pace, he didn't want to try and talk to her any sooner than that.

The gaslight was on a pole outside the gazebo, and he reached and turned up the flame before following her inside the large structure, furnished with pillow-laden wicker furniture. She had already turned and was facing him when he stepped inside.

"Do you want to sit?" he asked.

"I'm all right."

The strain in her voice gave him leave to doubt that.

"Your uncle has talked to you, I take it."

"He has."

"Are you in agreement with this proposal?"

Suddenly, she turned and sank into the settee behind her, and his stomach tensed. He wanted River's Bend and knew Josephus Collander wanted to be rid of it. He also knew Collander wanted to be rid of this beautiful young woman, but he was troubled by the man's recklessness in achieving that end.

"Why would you take a strange woman, sight unseen?"

Ah, so her uncle hadn't told her he was bribing him to take her. A minor kindness under the circumstances.

"I did see you."

She laughed, more amused than unpleasant. "You thought you were getting Bernadette. I saw it in your eyes when I stepped into the room tonight."

"I was shocked by your beauty."

"There's that forked tongue wagging again, Mr. Stone."

He sat down next to her on the settee, closer than was necessary, and she leaned away.

"Would you like to see my tongue, Miss Graff?"

*H*is words held a double meaning, she could tell by the glint in his eye and the smirk on his handsome mouth.

"I would not," she answered.

His smirk grew into a grin, and light from the gaslight flashed off his teeth. Her shoulder had started to ache. It was cold out here, but her discomfort stemmed primarily from nerves. Rafe Stone watched her for a moment, then leaned back in his seat.

"You didn't answer my question."

"I said I didn't want to see your tongue."

"The question I was referring to was the one asking if you were in agreement with your uncle's proposal."

From somewhere near the house, Douglas Champion called her name. Beside her, Rafe Stone snorted, and she sighed. "I am."

Again Douglas hollered for her, his call more demanding, and she cringed.

Mr. Stone cocked his head in the direction of Douglas's hail. "Are you sure?"

"More than ever," she whispered and rose.

He looked up at her. "And why would a young woman such as you wed a man she knows absolutely nothing about?"

"I'm not welcome in my uncle's house, Mr. Stone."

"The question is 'why'?" he said and stood.

"You'd be better off with Bernadette."

"Bernadette would drive me to distraction."

"I could drive you to distraction."

"Oh, Miss Graff," he said, taking her arm and guiding her out of the gazebo, "I'm sure you will, but it will be a different kind of distraction. Now, let's go tell Champion that you are marrying me."

Chapter Five

Aunt Ophelia, arms akimbo, turned on Uncle Joe. "I don't see why this wasn't handled with more taste. Look at her. She didn't even buy a new suit. Why, she wore that same dress when she graduated from that private school *you* paid for."

Delilah pulled the bonnet from her head. It was a very pretty dress of white satin. If her groom found anything wrong with what she'd worn, he hadn't said so. He had told her she was beautiful.

She placed the bonnet on the petticoat table in the front room. The hat was years out of date, but served to keep her hair in place, and she'd taken very good care of it. "Uncle Joe has spent too much on me already."

Ophelia turned on her when she spoke. "And a civil ceremony. People will think you're in the family . . ." Her aunt's eyes widened, then she snapped her head back to Uncle Joe. "They only met last night. What is —"

"Ophelia, stop this right now!"

Delilah's cheeks warmed. She looked at her groom, standing coolly at the room's entrance. He hadn't said a word since shaking Uncle Joe's hand and thanking him for his best wishes.

Aunt Ophelia's reaction had proved quite the opposite. Why, Delilah wasn't sure. Appearances she guessed, because she was certain her aunt wanted her out of this house more than her uncle did. Or perhaps it was because Delilah had consulted neither her nor Uncle Joe. Rafe Stone had asked her what kind of ceremony she'd wanted, and he'd suggested a justice of the peace. Obviously he was in a hurry to wed.

24

The civil ceremony had suited her. The last thing she wanted was to cost Uncle Joe more money, up to and including the price of a fashionable tailored ensemble to wear before the justice of the peace.

"It's Halloween, Delilah."

She, and everyone else in the room, turned to Bernadette, who sat in the Windsor chair next to the cold fireplace. Up until now the girl hadn't said a word. Bernie shook her head. "Surely that's an ill omen for a marriage."

"Oh, for the love of Christ," Uncle Joe cried, and Delilah squelched the urge to burst into tears. She'd expected Bernie, at least, to be happy, if for no other reason than she was no longer competing for Douglas Champion's attention. Delilah rubbed her aching temples and turned to take the chair next to Bernadette's. Goodness, she wished she could take down her elaborate hair-do.

"Perhaps a reception, Delilah? What do you think, Ophelia? The weather is holding. A barbecue?"

Delilah dropped her hands from her temples. "No, Uncle. It's too much trouble, and I know few people here."

"That is fine with me," Ophelia snapped. "This escapade is simply another example of her lack of appreciation."

Delilah's heart skipped a beat, and she met her uncle's eye. She started to speak, but he held out his hand, patting the air.

"Ophelia—"

"I wanted the civil ceremony, Mrs. Collander," Rafe Stone said. "I also insisted we keep our plans secret. I didn't want you trying to talk her out of this. We've known each other such a short time. She swept me off my feet. I wanted the opportunity to do likewise."

Aunt Ophelia blinked at him, then turned with an aggrieved expression and looked down her nose at Delilah. "Well, I cannot believe she did not have the good sense or consideration to confide in Bernadette, at the minimum." Her voice had calmed, and she turned back to Rafe Stone. "And what will the young woman you led down the primrose path say when she finds out you've wed another?"

25

"In our conversation last night, Mrs. Collander, I was referring to Delilah."

Aunt Ophelia's jaw dropped.

"And I am anxious to leave Mississippi City and get up to Natchez."

His words tore through Delilah's aching brain like lightning furrowed the ground along the root of a stricken tree. She turned to her uncle and found him watching her. He knew. All along he knew this man meant to take her to Natchez.

"I've bought a plantation near there on the river."

Delilah turned back at her new husband's voice. He was watching her and no doubt had seen the silent accusation she'd directed at Uncle Joe.

"Oh, did negotiations. . . ?"

Aunt Ophelia narrowed her eyes, looked at Delilah, then turned to Rafe Stone, who said, "Yes ma'am, they did."

"You intend for us to live in Natchez?" Delilah asked him. Before her head had simply ached, now it pounded in step with her heart.

"In the Natchez area, yes."

For sure, she wasn't happy about Natchez, but that wasn't negotiable. He'd come to Josephus Collander for a house, not a bride. She was along for the ride, and she'd agreed to it. Surely Collander knew he intended to live at River's Bend. If his niece had some great opposition to the place, Collander should have considered it. But then, he'd shown her little regard from the start.

"We've got tickets on the 2:15 to New Orleans," Rafe said to Collander. "Delilah tells me she's packed."

"I'd like to change," she said, rising from the chair. "Once I've done that and packed this dress, I'll be ready."

Chapter Six

"We'll be settled in the hotel in time for supper," he said and handed her an opened headache powder. "Take this. It'll help you feel better, and you'll sleep before we get there."

The train rocked on the tracks. She didn't think she'd be able to sleep, and the real cure to this headache was getting the stupid bonnet off and her hair down. But she took the powder; he'd been kind to go to the trouble, and she hadn't once complained of pain. That meant he was paying attention to her, and she wasn't sure if she liked that or not. He handed her a glass of water he'd gotten from the dining car and settled beside her on the upholstered seat.

"Drink all the water with that," he said, after she'd taken a swallow.

She glanced at him.

"Those powders are bad for the stomach, and the water helps get them into your system faster."

"Are you really a doctor, Mr. Stone?"

"Rafe. And no, just experienced with headaches."

"You give them?"

He studied her, then smiled. "I acquire them, it seems, but I'm learning to cope."

Despite herself, she smiled in return, then finished the water. He took the glass and snuggled it into the seat corner behind him.

"How long will we be in New Orleans?"

He hesitated a moment, then said, "I'll be there overnight."

"And me?"

"I thought I'd leave you there for a few days." When she did

27

nothing but stare at him, he quickly added, "I thought you'd enjoy shopping."

She turned and focused upon acre after acre of scrawny pines passing by the window. A few miles beyond lay cypress swamp, then the Gulf of Mexico. Muddy water for as far as the eye could see. The sun shone on the desolate, tangled forest, bleak, abandoned, and forlorn, victim of the '93 hurricane. Forgotten. At least she'd been safe, if unwanted, in her uncle's house.

"The house where I intend for us to live is in disrepair. Hardly the place I would wish to take my bride right now. I'd have to leave you in town, and I know you have a dislike for Natchez."

"I never said I disliked Natchez." She kept her focus out the window.

"You didn't have to. I saw the look on your face when I told everyone I was taking you there."

She shrugged and tried to concentrate on something interesting outside, but if there was anything worth seeing, she didn't notice it.

She felt his weight shift.

"What happened to your parents?" he asked.

"They died." She kept her eyes locked on the window. "What happened to yours?"

"How did they die?"

"Yellow fever." That's what she told everyone who asked.

"I'm sorry."

She cocked her head his way, but didn't look at him. "Thank you." Momentarily she turned back to the window. He hadn't told her what happened to his parents, but she lacked the heart to pursue her question. And she wasn't sure she cared. His lie could be as big as hers, perhaps bigger.

"Are you going to tell me why you dislike Natchez?"

"I don't dislike Natchez."

But she didn't want to go there, and that was just as well. He didn't have time right now to deal with a wife, particularly one he had doubts about. She was a whole other problem, and he inwardly cursed being saddled with her. But without her, he'd not have River's Bend.

He took her hand, and she twisted to face him.

"I'll rent the room at the Grunewald for two weeks," he said. "By that time I should have made a place for you in Natchez, and I'll send for you."

She removed her hand from his, placed it in her lap, and returned her attention to the fleeting landscape. "It sounds like a lovely honeymoon, Mr. Stone. Thank you."

A *faux pas*, but he caught himself before he cursed out loud. "We've only just met, Delilah," he said quietly. "I considered you might want to know me better before we indulged in intimate relations."

She turned, then leaned away, startled, it seemed, by how close he'd brought his lips to her ear to keep others from overhearing their conversation.

"Indulged? Is that how you regard consummation of your marriage vows?"

He straightened and placed his arm over the back of their seat, but he didn't touch her. "It must be the excitement of the moment, I'm not thinking clearly."

"And what a wonderful way for you and I to get to know each other, me in New Orleans and you in Natchez. You are something, Mr. Stone. Dismayed, regretful, or plain disinterested, but hardly excited. Why did you marry me?"

He sighed. A lie wouldn't work with this woman and the truth would be downright cruel. "I had my reasons."

"That had nothing to do with me, did they?"

He narrowed his eyes.

"Uncle Joe paid you to take me, didn't he?"

"Not one red cent."

She furrowed her brow. She was angry, but beneath that anger, she was hurt. "Then he blackmailed you."

"He knows nothing about me."

"Wonderful," she said, turning back to her window refuge. "He married me off to a man he knows not the first iota about."

29

Well, hell, he'd talked himself right into that one.

"I suspected that's what he'd done. The whole thing happened too fast. He told me you'd approached him in search of a wife, but I can tell when he's lying to me. You confirmed my suspicions when you took my hand last night with that shocked-stupid look on your face and realized I was the one you were getting and not Bernadette."

"That 'shocked-stupid' look, as you so rudely put it, was one of pleasant surprise."

"Bullshit."

"I beg your pardon, *darling*," he said, at the same time, widening his eyes and looking around the car with feigned dismay. There was no one nearby. "We are in a public place. I do not wish my bride to make a spectacle of herself."

"Mr. Stone," she said, "you don't have a bride. You have something you are stuck with."

"I am not stuck with you."

"No, perhaps you're not. I don't know what form of coercion he used to force you to marry me, but all he would be concerned with is my name on a marriage document. That would abrogate his responsibility."

"I think your uncle has a little more feeling for you than that."

She scrunched her back into the corner of the seat and faced him. "Then how do you explain my being here with you?"

How indeed? He sure wouldn't have given his niece to a stranger who showed up on his doorstep, no matter how much money the man flashed.

"Your uncle seemed . . ." Hell, there was no way he could delicately state this. "Desperate to get you wed. Why?"

She sucked in a breath. "Don't you think it's a little late to be concerning yourself with that?"

Last night, when she had told Champion she was marrying another, the man hadn't said a word. Just puffed up like a fighting cock on that moonlit path, stared at Rafe, glared at her, then turned on his heel and stalked away.

"Mrs. Stone," he said, "I am willing to raise another man's

30

child. I accepted that possibility when I agreed to marry you. But I will not be duped into believing it is mine."

"And who do you assume is the father of my alleged child?"

"I assumed Champion."

"You are a fool, Mr. Stone."

He didn't like being called a fool. Given his hasty nuptials, lunatic would describe him better. "Your uncle?"

For a long moment, she simply looked at him. Then she raised her chin. "Actually, you are not a fool. You are a callous, disgusting ass, and I do not see any future for you and me."

Chapter Seven

He rented a two-room suite for them at Hotel Grunewald on Baronne Street near the French Quarter and paid in advance for seven days. He guessed their marriage had a future of seven days. Funny, he hadn't thought about a future for them at all until she mentioned they didn't have one. Not that he believed that. He simply hadn't concerned himself with it, with them. They simply were. Obviously, she had thought about their life together. But from his view, 'them' and building a future were all she should have to think about; he'd had other concerns. Now he considered the lovely young woman, with whom he truly was stuck, might have had other things on her mind, too, that hadn't included a husband, and she was as stuck as he.

Delilah hadn't initiated a conversation with him for the rest of the train ride and had, in fact, told him to leave her alone when he'd tried. He certainly didn't broach the reason for her agreeing to marry him again. She had told him in the gazebo last night she wasn't welcome in her uncle's house. If there were a more sinister reason beyond Champion's infatuation, he didn't know, but it did occur to him he might be mistaken about her being in the family way.

She hadn't gone down to the world-renowned dining room to eat dinner with him either. She had no appetite, she said. As it turned out, he didn't have much of one either despite an extensive menu of Cajun and European specialties. He opted for a steak, rare, and even that old standby weighed heavy in his stomach. The expensive bourbon in the bar was the only thing that helped him feel any better, and it was well short of a cure. When he got back to their rooms, she was sleeping (he was pretty certain she'd never shed that headache). So much for a wedding night, if he'd intended one to begin with.

*H*er husband wasn't in their suite when Delilah woke late next morning after a fitful sleep. A quick check of the outer room confirmed his bags were gone. She rolled her lips together, stopping their trembling, but she still felt her chin pucker. Quickly she blinked back the tears. Abandoned. Ever since he'd told her his plans on the train, she'd suspected that would be the case. Part of her had hoped otherwise. As best she could tell, he hadn't left her a cent, and she wondered if he had, indeed, reserved the room for two weeks as he said.

One week, the manager told her when she'd gone to the lobby in an effort to recoup the money. She needed the cash more than she needed a week in one of New Orleans' most luxurious hotels. Her effort was for naught. Mr. Stone had paid cash for seven days, the snotty little man told her, and he'd reserved the suite for seven more with assurances he might or might not need it for the additional week. The horrid person looked down his disdainful male nose at her and refused to give her the money.

She didn't even have money to eat, but thought she'd try to put a meal on Mr. Stone's tab and charge it to the room. She stepped to the sixth-floor window and looked down on the mid-afternoon hustle and bustle of Canal Street. Beyond stretched the French Quarter. There was a life of sorts here. Delilah shuddered. She needed to wire Uncle Joe. Under the circumstances, he might acquiesce and send her the money to get a start away from Mississippi. She could find work as a seamstress, surely, and Uncle Joe didn't want her back there. Lord, she'd pay him back every cent.

She laid her forehead against the cool glass. No, she could never repay him all he'd done, and now she should let him be. A tear slipped out of the corner of her eye and tickled her cheek. Behind her, the door to the suite rattled, and she swiped at the tear, then turned in expectation of a maid.

Her heart started to race when she saw it was him, his back to her as he closed the door. She'd stepped away from the window by the time he turned and found her. She tried to shield all emotion from him, whatever those emotions were. Anger, relief, pleasure, maybe all three and a hundred more. She swallowed. "You got a haircut."

He rubbed his chin. "And a shave. I've never been in a barber shop like the one here. Didn't know such places existed. You need to visit the ladies' parlor down there, too. It's nice." He stepped away from the door. "I've got my baggage on the ship and purchased my ticket."

Her stomach quaked.

"I'm going to leave you some money. I've paid for the suite for—"

"Seven days."

His eyes narrowed.

"I've already tried to recover your money."

"Why?"

God, whatever those one hundred and three emotions had been, only pain remained. She wasn't even angry; shattered hit closer to the mark. His return, her renewed hope, and now this kick in the . . . Stop it. He didn't want her, but he had come back to provide her some sort of sustenance. Perhaps . . .

"I need enough money to help me get started on my own."

"What are you talking about?"

Sweet heaven, she hated asking this strange man for anything, but short of going back to Uncle Joe or selling her body, she had no known options.

"Give me enough money to help me until I can find a job as a dressmaker. I'm an excellent seamstress. I hope one day to design dresses. New Orleans is perfect for me to—"

"Delilah," he snapped.

She clamped her mouth shut.

"You are married to me."

"We can annul the marriage. That's what you want, isn't it? That's better than abandoning me. It will relieve you of all moral

34

and financial responsibility and someday, when you find someone you want to marry, you won't be committing bigamy."

"Thank you for that legal assessment, Mrs. Stone. But I can assure you if I were the sort of man who would abandon you here in New Orleans I would hardly concern myself with the commission of bigamy. I came up here, after going to the bank, to provide you with fifty dollars in cash."

That would certainly assuage any guilt on his part. "I'll pay you back every cent, I promise."

He sucked in a breath, and his visage turned from confused to stormy. "You're not paying me back a damn thing, Delilah."

She started at the tone of his voice, at the anger in his eyes. "Of course, I will," she said.

His nostrils flared. "Delilah, get into your room, please, we're running out of time."

Trepidation almost overrode her mounting anger. Almost. "What?" she forced out. "Am I expected to earn that fifty dollars now? I do believe I probably lack the experience you expect of me, and if I wish to prostitute myself, I can do it on the street with a hundred men who will not care if I am carrying another man's child."

"They probably won't give a damn about your level of experience either," he said, grabbing hold of her left bicep.

Lightning struck, searing the length of her arm and blinding her with its light, and the fingertips of her left hand numbed. She would have tried to pull free, but the room was topsy-turvy. His hold was her anchor.

"What's wrong with you?" he asked, concern replacing the anger in his voice.

"Help me sit, please. You don't have to force me."

He eased his hold, but placed his hand on her opposite shoulder, keeping her steady as he looked for a chair.

"I'll never force you. I only meant you need to hurry and pack your bags. Our packet leaves at five o'clock, and I still need to check us out and buy you a ticket."

Chapter Eight

"Did you win?"

Rafe had his hand on the knob of their stateroom door, but turned at the sound of Delilah's voice. He hadn't seen her leaning against the rail, her head cocked toward him. She had on her traveling cloak, her beautiful blonde hair covered against the cold wind, which blew down the muddy road of water that was the Mississippi.

"I did." He dropped his hand from the latch and walked to her. He'd left her sleeping at noon after giving her another pain powder. She'd said she had a headache, but he believed it was that left arm he'd grabbed yesterday, almost bringing her to her knees, that really ailed her. His eyes glanced over the water, churning more than two stories beneath them.

"But not much. Spent most of the afternoon winning back what I lost when I first sat down."

"Are you a gambler, Mr. Stone?"

"Obviously, *Mrs.* Stone, but not so much at cards."

She turned back to the water, the stiff breeze teasing the edges of her hood and sending wisps of blonde hair dancing around her face. "I gave you the opportunity to be rid of me."

"And how am I to know I'd have been rid of you?"

"I could hardly see myself pestering a man such as you."

"Such as me? What sort of man do you think I am?"

She sighed. "I have no idea what sort of man you are."

"Not one to abandon you in New Orleans."

"I thank you for that."

"You think you thank me for that."

36

She glanced at him with a silly smirk. Yes, he'd guessed right with that one. He hadn't deserted her as she thought he was going to do, but now she wasn't sure what fate had in store.

"It's cold out here," he said. "Why aren't you inside?"

"This is my first time on a steamboat, and I've spent the entire trip sleeping in our cabin."

Rafe looked out over the river, his eyes tearing in the wind and late afternoon sun. They'd hit every little river town they'd come to upriver, then laid up four hours last night south of Baton Rouge, the pilot's visibility hampered by smoke from cane fires. The *Red River Princess* was, at present, scheduled to reach Natchez shortly before midnight.

"How is your head?"

She nodded positively.

"Your shoulder?"

She shrugged. "It's better."

"What happened to it?"

"I fell when I was twelve and broke it."

His lovely bride hadn't missed a beat, had known he would ask. "How did you fall?"

She straightened and clasped the cape at the neck as a gust buffeted them. "I tripped over a stool in my parents' bedroom."

"A freak accident, Delilah?"

She turned to him with her chin held high and her hand still gripping the neck of her cape. "A very unusual accident, Mr. Stone."

"Rafe, and you haven't eaten since breakfast. Would you care to find the dining room?"

"I would like that."

*H*e'd been solicitous since he'd inadvertently hurt her yesterday afternoon, and she considered herself a nuisance. Despite his consideration, Rafe Stone didn't want a wife.

"How was your étouffée?" she asked.

"Surprisingly good. How was your lamb and new potatoes?"

"Good, also. I've never eaten mutton before." And she was

proud of herself for talking him out of the roast. Her gut told her
he habitually ordered beef, and there was too fine a menu on this
boat for him not to stimulate his palate with something new.
There'd been one problem with her meat; it required both hands
to cut. Her left shoulder now throbbed much as it had shortly
after he'd grabbed her in the hotel.

"Dessert?"

"I'd like coffee."

He nodded and waved down their waiter, dressed in a white
jacket. The young darkie moved easily over the plush red carpet
of the dining room, mostly empty because they had dined early.
Rafe ordered two coffees and a piece of pecan pie.

"I think of baked bugs every time I look at one," she said
when the waiter brought their order and she had once again
declined a slice of pie for herself.

He took a bite. "Darn good bugs."

"I know it tastes good, I simply can't get the thought of bugs
out of my head."

"What kind of bugs?"

"I'm not going to tell you. You'd never eat another piece of
pecan pie."

"Honey, you'd be surprised what I've eaten and kept down."

She sipped her coffee, laden with sugar and cream. "Cock-
roaches," she said.

He stuck the last piece in his mouth, chewed, and swallowed.
"The great big dark ones with wings?"

"The smaller brown ones."

He smiled, then raised his cup. He drank his coffee black, she
noted.

Around them, waiters were lighting candles, and somewhere
in the room, silver clinked melodiously against china.

He set his cup back in its saucer and leaned against the table.
"We'll stay in Natchez tonight."

"In a—"

"The Natchez Hotel. I've a room reserved already, but I don't
know if I can get an adjoining one this late."

38

"That's all right—"

Gently he touched her arm, indicating sleeping quarters was not the reason he'd broached the topic of their accommodations.

"I will get up early and go to River's Bend, Delilah. You are not going yet."

Her heartbeat quickened, but she forced herself to remain calm.

"I will be back tomorrow afternoon. I promise you. It's only six miles from town. I am going to make arrangements to have enough of the house cleaned so that it's accommodating. I have seen the house, and I will not take you there until some scrubbing is done. Do you understand?"

She nodded.

"I am not abandoning you."

He was talking slowly and clearly, as if making a point to a child.

"I know you aren't."

"If you want to shop or—"

"I'd like to rest in our room and read, if that is agreeable."

He breathed in. "That is very agreeable to me. Do you have books?"

"Yes."

*T*he bright November moon passed behind silver clouds. The wind had stilled somewhat with the passing of the sun, leaving the night peaceful and quiet, except for the churning of the paddle wheels and the lapping of the water against the ship's hull. Out of the darkness, a leadsman called out a depth, his words repeated moments later by another hand passing the information to the pilot.

The *Red River Princess* steamed north, paralleling the fortress-like bluffs that dominated the easternmost extension of the ancient, meandering Mississippi. They would dock in Natchez within half an hour, and the side-wheeler was rounding the bend from which his home derived its name. He wished it were daytime so he could see the house from the river.

The full moon emerged from behind a cloud and silhouetted the crowns of pine and deciduous trees dominating the hill a half mile away. At his side, Delilah touched his arm.

"There," she said, and he watched as moonlight illuminated the eighty-year-old columns, then washed over the house. Small with the distance, but stately still, River's Bend glowed with a soft and pristine beauty. A lump filled his throat, and suddenly he was glad there was no sun after all, for daylight could have never conveyed the faded glory of the house the way the silver moon did. A lovely ghost from a bygone age.

"Is that it?"

"That's it," he told her. She turned to him, and he knew she was trying to read his face, sure she'd heard the emotion in his voice.

"It's beautiful, Rafe."

So wrapped up in the house he was, it took him a moment to realize she'd called him by his given name. He glanced at her and found her studying him, her face golden in the ship's light, her eyes bright.

"And I'm not sure what River's Bend means to you," she said softly, "but there is no doubt in my mind that it is more than a piece of real estate."

Chapter Nine

"The foundation is solid and the roof's still keeping the water out," Adam Grapple said. The agent smiled at Delilah, still in Rafe's arms. Her handsome husband set her on her feet, then helped steady her, slightly off-kilter from being swept up and whirled across the threshold.

"I warned you," he said to her. "You could have stayed in New Orleans or, at least, Natchez."

And forgone the unexpected thrill of being carried across the threshold like that? No, she was glad for the decision she'd made when Rafe returned to their room this afternoon and gave her the option of one more night in the hotel or the floor of their new home.

Rafe reached behind her and pushed the huge portal shut. It squeaked unmercifully, as it had when Mr. Grapple opened it, but it sat nicely in its frame, no warping or sticking.

"House was well built," Mr. Grapple said, "in all three stages."

"Three?" Delilah asked, out of politeness as much as curiosity.

"Three. The first as I understand it"—he motioned them across the foyer, replete with a double, curving staircase, through a short hall, and into a large interior room with a huge fireplace against its left wall. On the rear wall, another door led to a room beyond. This room was empty but for massive built-in shelves and cabinets. Delilah gathered her skirt and tapped her foot against the wood floor, its varnish thick and dark with age.

"Heart pine," Mr. Grapple said. "It's used throughout. This room constitutes the original cabin."

She glanced at the plastered walls and the fireplace with its rough bricks of varying size.

"Place was built before the Natchez Indians slaughtered Fort Rosalie in 1729. They killed the inhabitants here, too, according to legend. Sometime between then and 1740 another Frenchman, Eugene Dumas, moved in. Around 1760, Charles Richard married Dumas' only child. Richard built the series of rooms immediately surrounding the cabin, including a small second story.

"Charles's son made the major expansions during the 1820s and '30s, that's when one of Charles Richard's additional rooms became the foyer with that impressive double stairway we just passed. The wrap-around veranda with its Corinthian columns, spaced every twenty feet, was added around the same time." The agent nodded at Rafe. "You can get the exact dates on all the architectural changes and plans at the county clerk's office if you're interested."

They followed him through the room's back doorway into what proved to be the kitchen. To the right was a small alcove with a short hall and a rough-hewn door, which appeared to lead outside. "Servants' stairwell is back there," Mr. Grapple said, indicating the hall. He handed Rafe the ring of keys. "All new locks per your request, except the one to this door, which leads to the old cookhouse. This monstrosity" — he touched the rough-hewn door — "was apparently one of five matching doors Charles Richard added in the 1770's. This is the only one left. We speculate the other four were removed during the major renovations. They kept this one, I reckon, because it was on the back and out of sight. It's an odd size, not quite six feet high, by four wide. Folks were shorter in those days, I guess."

"And fatter."

He laughed with Delilah's words. "This door is three inches thick, Mrs. Stone, constructed of yellow pine panels. Given your love of old houses" — Delilah blinked at Mr. Grapple — "you might consider this thing a treasure."

"Indeed, I do," she said, then twisted around to better see her husband, who smiled at her.

42

"I knew this was the house for you, darling," he said.

"You have no idea, sweetheart, how much I appreciate your efforts finding this perfect home for me." With that, Delilah turned from him and stepped toward the overlarge door. She touched the lock, a six-inch square contraption with a keyhole big enough for a papa bumblebee to fly through.

"It's French manufacture," Mr. Grapple said. "Seventeenth-century, cast-iron. All five locks probably were. Old when Charles put them in, I imagine. This door is locked, and there is no key. Hasn't been one since who knows when. But"—and he smiled—"the door is no great mystery. It opens onto the breezeway that leads to the old cookhouse in the back, which you can access from the outside. Appears Mrs. Merrifield used the cookhouse as a larder. It was the Merrifields who brought the kitchen into the house proper."

Rafe moved closer to them, nodded approvingly at the door, then asked Mr. Grapple, "Did you check the furnace?"

"Except that you need to get some boys in here to clean it, it's good to go. You'll need coal, too."

"Ordered some today."

"Pittsburg Coal or Rutherford?"

"Rutherford."

"Delivering it by river?"

"Tomorrow."

"Has someone checked your landing?"

"I was hoping you would."

"I'll be happy to, but I imagine it's okay. Markham Merrifield had a new one built right before he died." Mr. Grapple's glance moved quickly over Delilah and settled on Rafe. "That was fifteen years ago. Life expectancy on the things is about twenty."

"Well, there hasn't been any upkeep as far as I can tell."

"Nope, inhabitants here have been few and far between since Markham and his wife died. But if the landing's no good, I'll go on down to Rutherford's when I get back and tell 'im he'll have to deliver by wagon."

"Thanks."

"Mr. Grapple?" Delilah said.

The kindly agent looked at her.

"What happened to the Merrifields?"

Grapple cast Rafe a furtive glance.

"It's all right. Would be hard to keep the story a secret from her for long."

Delilah's stomach tightened.

"They were murdered, Mrs. Stone."

"By whom?"

"Markham Merrifield's sons, we think."

"You think?"

"Both boys disappeared. Their father and stepmother were found in the master bedroom upstairs."

"Oh," she said and looked at Rafe. He was watching her, but didn't say anything.

Mr. Grapple laughed shortly. "Some around here say this place is haunted."

Delilah smiled, all the while wondering what the man thought was funny about that.

"But that's foolishness, Mrs. Stone." He turned to Rafe. "The work required on this house is all superficial. It's as sound as bedrock. Been all but empty for more than a decade, but you got here in time. All it needs is some care and love livin' inside." He smiled at Delilah and gave her a two-fingered salute. "Reckon a fine-looking couple of young newlyweds can provide both."

Chapter Ten

"You knew about the murders?" Delilah asked when Rafe entered the bedroom. She was on hands and knees, making a pallet on the floor.

He dropped wood beside the hearth and squatted. "I've heard stories, but it wouldn't have made any difference."

"And you told Mr. Grapple you bought this house for me?"

"I told him I got it for you, yes."

"Which is why you carried me over the threshold like you did?"

He twisted in his squat and found her still on all fours, watching him over her left shoulder. "It was all an act," she said.

"No, it wasn't." He turned back to the wood.

"Then why did you tell him that?"

"Delilah, it wasn't *all* an act."

"Ah, so subterfuge was part of it?"

"I prefer the term discretion."

"But why—"

"And what do you think of Mr. Grapple's ghost story?"

"Those murders," she said, "were so awful to have happened in this fine old house."

Relieved to have diverted her, he returned to his work. "Yes they were."

"What do you know about them?"

"Talking about this will probably give you nightmares," he said as he lit the fire.

"I have plenty of other things to give me nightmares. I'd like to know what happened here."

And he'd like to know what those other things were. The fire caught. "Merrifield and his second wife were found in the bedroom down the hall. A bedroom neither of us will use."

"And no one knows what happened to the two boys?"

"Speculation is, they ran."

"That's all you know?"

"Yes." Except for the gruesome details, which he wasn't going to relate to his bride. He took a last look at the fire now burning in the fireplace, then rose. For a long moment, she held his gaze, then she reached for the quilt on top of the pallet, and he stooped to help her fold the blanket back.

The room was relatively clean, if one were to overlook the dirty walls and dingy windows, easy enough considering the dim light. Like this one, another bedroom had been swept, as had the kitchen, which had also been wiped down, all on short notice, thanks to Mrs. Howell, the sixty-year-old woman Adam Grapple hired to do the job. She'd forged her two teenage granddaughters and three daughters-in-law into an effective cleaning team — for an impressive sum. She had assured Rafe that for tonight the chimneys were safe enough, but he needed to get sweeps in here soon. He'd hired the Howell crew to do the whole house. As far as he was concerned, Delilah could take over supervision at this point. He figured the entire job would take at least a fortnight.

He placed his palm in the middle of her pallet and felt the hard floor beneath. "We can still make it back to Natchez before it gets too late."

She looked up from where she'd laid her fluffed pillow at the head of her make-shift bed, then glanced at the two trunks pushed against a bare wall. "This is fine for me unless you want to return to Natchez, but all our things are here."

It was dusk outside. Rafe scowled at the garish gaslight overhead. That was one thing he hadn't taken care of today. The house's coke gas plant wasn't operational, but they had several coal oil lamps burning, and the room was relatively bright. "I'm willing to stay, if you are," he said.

She nodded and rose. She was still favoring that left arm, but had been using it. "Come," she said, "I'll help you with your bed."

He followed her into the adjoining room, wallpapered in a dark print, faded by years of sun and peeling in places. This room was bleaker than the one they'd left, despite the bright flames in the fireplace, which backed up to the one in her room. The two hearths shared a chimney. The entire house smelled fusty, and their every move echoed.

"Someone could have kidnapped the boys."

"They were seventeen and fourteen. If they'd been kidnapped, they'd have eventually come back unless someone killed them, too."

"That could have happened."

He had stopped near the door, and now watched her smooth the first quilt at his feet.

"I'm likely to roast in here."

She looked up. "I thought . . ."

He grinned. She wanted him as close to the door between their two rooms as she could get him. "We can share the floor in your room if you like."

Her nostrils flared slightly, and she grabbed a corner of the quilt and stood. "I would not wish to cause you any undue hardship, Mr. Stone. It is you who does not wish to be made a fool of, and I have no intention of asking you into my bed before your *maidenly* jitters have subsided."

"I'm not talking about sharing your bed, sweetheart, simply the floor." He leaned closer to her. "I know you don't want to sleep in that room by yourself."

She met his eyes, and he took the quilt from her. "Come on," he said, stepping back into her room, "this is silly."

Delilah didn't argue with him, thank goodness. She was proud, but not foolishly prideful. The story of the Merrifield murders had made her uncomfortable, and though he'd be willing to bet she'd never admit it, she wasn't averse to *de facto* surrender.

"Do you know why people say the house is haunted?"

"I have no idea," he answered. He shook out the quilt, folded it once, and laid it on the floor. She placed a second one over it.

"Do you think perhaps it's a very old ghost?" She put an embroidered case on a feather pillow.

"I've been told the ghost stems from the murders."

"Markham or his wife?"

"The sons or the family dog. Delilah, I do not know what was seen or heard in this house to make the locals say it's haunted. My personal belief is that people simply like to tell tales."

"Well, you and I are inside this place. I'd like to know why people say such things."

"Violent events happened here, that's why they say them."

She laid his pillow in place, then covered his mat with a sheet and another heavy quilt. Both she turned back, giving the pallet the semblance of a made-down bed. "Are you not concerned at all, then?"

"Thank you," he said, when she looked at him, "and no, I am not concerned. Not over ghosts anyway."

Her eyes widened slightly.

Senhor Bom Di. What was he thinking saying that?

"What are you afraid of then?"

He held out his hand to her, and she took it as he knew she would for no other reason than the comfort of human touch. "I didn't mean my words to come out that way. What I meant to say was if I were going to be afraid of anything, it would be a person, not a ghost. Now, are you hungry?"

"We have food?"

"Canned soup. Mrs. Howell's daughter-in-law, Sarah, put it up in September. Mrs. Howell says it's great, but we'll have to find the pot among the boxes in the kitchen."

"Is there enough wood for the stove?"

"If not, we'll cook it over the hearth, like we're camping out."

He swore she skipped once beside him as he led her into the broad, second-story hall and toward that magnificent staircase.

"Do we have bread?"

"We do, but I knew we didn't have an ice box, so there is no butter."

※

Vegetable soup and good. Rafe told her he'd also bought two jars of Sarah's corn chowder. They ate in the room that once comprised the original cabin, on a blanket Delilah spread out on the floor in front of the fireplace.

"I think this would make a good dining room," she said.

He wiped a drop of soup from his chin. His gaze darted from wall to wall, then returned to his speckled bowl.

"I think that's what it was, at least in modern times."

Delilah wanted to ask him if they'd be able to purchase furniture soon. One night eating and sleeping on the floor might be fun, but too many more would grow tiresome. She didn't ask, though. She had no idea what his financial situation was, nor if he were the type of man to discuss such matters with his wife.

"Are you finished?" he asked.

She nodded and started to push herself up with her free left hand. Ouch. She shifted her empty bowl to her left hand and put her weight on her right.

"Give me your bowl."

She did. Hands free, she easily pushed herself to her feet.

"Do I need to take you to a doctor about that shoulder?"

He was headed out of the room, and she smoothed the back of her dress and followed him into the kitchen. "A doctor has looked at it. I fear the injury is permanent, but it's not always so debilitating."

"I didn't grab you that hard."

"I think it was the angle you caught me."

She watched him place the dishes into the large cast-iron sink, its appearance worse for wear, but its functionality, Delilah was sure, as good as it ever was. She reached for the pump handle and started pumping. "Do we have water?"

Rafe's brow furrowed when the pipes coughed, then groaned. He took the handle from her and started pumping fast.

"Sure we do. Mrs. Howell used this pump earlier today."

Red-tinged water spit out, followed by a belch of air and a more even flow of water. Delilah placed the soup pot under the spout and rinsed it. "I'm not sure of the pipes."

"That's only rust. It'll clear."

"I'll boil water so I can wash the dishes. We need a kettle."

"We have one, packed away in these boxes somewhere."

The near-full moon was bright enough to illuminate the shimmering river half a mile beyond and below. Delilah stood with Rafe at a pair of French doors, which climbed from the floor and ended somewhere in the dark shadow of the room's twelve-foot ceiling. This was the far room on the first floor of the house's west wing. Matching floor-to-ceiling windows repeated themselves at intervals across the front and east and west walls of the house. No veranda column blocked the magnificent view of the Mississippi from where they stood.

This room was dark, lit only by the hurricane lamp Rafe carried, its wick shortened so they could see outside. He'd been the one to suggest a tour of the place, but now she wondered if he'd realized how dark the house would be.

"This room would make a wonderful library," she said, turning from the glass.

In the dim light, she saw his jaw flex. "It was the library once."

"In Mr. Merrifield's day?"

He shrugged. "I don't know."

She furrowed her brow, and his shadowy visage smiled. "The walls of built-in shelves give its function away."

"Do you have plans for it?"

He dropped his gaze and stepped closer to the glass. In the yellow light she could see his reflection, staring down at the river. "Great view. It would make a fine office."

Her stomach tightened. She wanted to be able to share the view, too.

He found her reflection. "I remember, you enjoy reading. It stands to reason you'd like libraries."

She, likewise, focused on his muted image in the glass. "I like books in private libraries."

His lips curled into a smile. "Does a private library mean yours alone?"

50

She moved closer. "Of course not," she said, "This would be our library."

He looked at her over his shoulder. "So you think we should make this room the library?"

"Yes."

"Sometimes you're so darn forthright, Delilah."

She couldn't see any reason for him to perceive an underlying motive in her wanting this room to be used as a library.

"Why can't you be as honest in telling me how Collander coerced you into marrying me?" he said.

"I've asked the same of you."

"You have."

"Well?"

"Are you asking again?"

"Yes."

"And if I tell you my secret, will you tell me yours?"

"Maybe," she answered.

"From forthright to coy."

"Are you going to tell me your secret?"

"Not without more assurance."

She pursed her lips. "Let's see who can figure out the other's secret first, shall we?"

"We could make a bet."

"What sort of bet?"

"This room as his or her own."

The thought of losing this room to him was not nearly as distressing as the thought of his learning her secret, at least learning it before he'd gotten to know her.

Goodness, who was she fooling? She never wanted him to know her shame. She bit her bottom lip to still its trembling. And because he knew there was a secret. . . . "Douglas Champion was attracted to me," she blurted out, "and my presence in the house was putting a strain on Douglas and Bernie's prospective engagement, an impending business merger, and even Uncle Joe and Aunt Ophelia's marriage. Uncle Joe wanted me out of the house. I am destitute. He offered me little choice, you or the streets."

"That's very flattering."

She gave him a shrug. "Your reason could not help but be more interesting than mine. Unless you are presently spending Uncle Joe's money, he didn't pay you to take me. You are obviously not interested in me for sexual pleasure."

She could see his dark form silhouetted against the window, his shadowed face studying her with what appeared to be amused interest.

"And," she continued, "you've told me he has nothing with which to blackmail you, so what in the world could have compelled you to take me?"

"What indeed? Why didn't you want to come to Natchez?"

Her stomach dropped with his question. The silence drew out, but she wasn't about to answer. Finally he smiled. "So, sweetheart, there is more to your secret than Douglas Champion?"

Delilah looked away and Rafe took her arm and guided her toward the door. "And I do believe we have, at your suggestion, placed the perfect wager for our hunt."

Chapter Eleven

Simon Douglas laughed. "Naw, Miz Stone, if there be such a thing, it be new. My mama worked in this house for more than thirty years . . ."

Rafe folded his arms over his chest and leaned against the doorjamb. Delilah and the tall black man had their backs to him and didn't know he'd snuck up on 'em. From the sound of this conversation, his beautiful bride (and she was beautiful even in worn cotton with her flaxen hair knotted into a kerchief-draped bun) was still looking for the origin of the alleged ghost.

". . . from the time Mama was sixteen till Miss Lorelei disappeared at the end of the War. Weren't no dead hauntin' this house."

Delilah bent at the waist, watching the man's progress. "Is that when your mother was freed?"

"No, ma'am," he said. He hit the brick with something hard and a cloud of soot billowed from the opening. Delilah stepped back at the same time Simon squatted low and bowed his head, then pulled the brim of his slouch hat over his eyes. After a moment, the soot settled.

"Ole massa, Frank Richard, freed his slaves when his last boy died in 1859. All that was left to follow him was a little granddaughter. He was gettin' old. Accordin' to my mama, ole massa said weren't no way a flighty girl woulda been able to handle his business. He worried she'd marry just to have a man to take care of matters. Weren't no way of knowin' what kind of massa his people'd git, so he freed us all. I was eight."

"And did she marry?"

He dropped his hat to the floor before sticking his head back into the chimney. "She sho' did."

"And was he awful?"

Simon was scraping against the brick, making a horrendous noise. After a moment he stopped, and Rafe figured the poor man wished Delilah would go bother the cleaning ladies down the hall. Goodness knows that's what Rafe wanted. But a moment later Simon's good-natured laugh bounced off the brick.

"Not so's I'd ever say it. Wild's what he was, lookin' back. And handsome in that gray uniform and sittin' on the back of a fine horse. I was twelve when first I recall 'im." Simon scraped the brick again. "He was the kind them young white ladies be quick to fall in love with and shouldn't."

"He left her?"

Delilah had bent again at the waist, trying her darnedest to see Simon Douglas, his head up the chimney. Of course, she didn't care a hoot about the progress of the cleaning.

"They was married in the fall of '63. That Morgan Ward was a major in the Confederate cavalry and a seasoned soldier. He come back to her a couple times. Last time he left was a month before Easter 1865, Mama says. He never come home again. Miss Lorelei took her life. Mama say the sweet girl just couldn't live without 'im."

Simon ducked his head and maneuvered away from the fireplace. Delilah took a step toward him. "Maybe he does come back. Or perhaps it could be Miss Lorelei still waiting for him."

The black man chuckled. "Maybe. Lots more to that story you ain't heard yet."

"What —"

Rafe shifted his weight and a floorboard groaned. Delilah half-turned, saw him, and jumped.

He grinned. "Thought you'd seen your ghost for certain that time, didn't you?"

She gave him a withering look.

Simon plucked his hat from the floor and wiped sweat from his brow.

"That be the last one inside, Mr. Stone. Still needs to check 'em from the top, but I can see daylight. They was cleaned by me and my daddy years ago for that newlywed couple. Don't think they spent many cold nights in this house before they moved out."

Simon dusted his soot-covered hat against his leg and settled it back on his head. He glanced at Delilah, then Rafe. "Sure hope that don't happen with you two."

"If there's a ghost in this house, Simon, we're living with it."

Simon grinned, displaying a mouth full of white teeth against his dark skin. "Yessuh." He tipped his hat to Delilah. "And don't you worry none, Miz Stone. If the ghost be Major Ward or Miz Lorelei, they'll be easy to get along with."

The black man ambled out of the room with a soft chuckle, and Rafe gazed at Delilah who watched him with a haughty tilt of her chin.

"I am not worried, merely curious."

"Curious, my ass," he said, moving into the room.

"You won't think me foolish if the thing haunting this house is the same thing that killed the Merrifields."

He leaned close. "What killed the Merrifields, my beauty, was flesh and blood."

She leaned forward in turn and placed an index finger on the bare flesh exposed at the open neck of his cotton shirt. Her touch was warm.

"Maybe the ghost is one of the Merrifields."

He fought the urge to kiss her. "There is no ghost." His gaze dropped to her lips. What would she do if he did kiss her?

She straightened and stepped back as if she'd read his mind. He straightened, too. "You're not far enough away, honey."

She batted her eyelashes in blatant provocation. "Far enough away from what?"

"From me."

"I wasn't aware I needed to be away from you."

"As a matter of fact, you don't."

Her expression hardened slightly, and she raised that defiant chin. "It's been six days since you questioned by integrity, my

55

honor, and my virtue. Nothing has happened to prove that I am not carrying another man's child."

"There is a way to confirm your virtue."

Her eyes widened. "Indeed, but I am denying it to you."

His mouth dropped open in faux shock. "You would deny me my conjugal rights?"

"I certainly would." She smiled brightly and turned toward the door.

"You said I didn't need to force you."

"And you said you never would. And I believe you." She stopped at the door and placed her hand on the jamb, then turned back to him with a smirk. "You hurt me, husband. I would have granted you everything without question, but you doubted my motive. Now, sir, you must woo me. Something you could have gotten away without doing."

"Woo you?"

"If you can manage to get me in the mood to be wooed, darling."

"I'm quite good at wooing, *darling*."

"Perhaps, with other women you've known."

Yes, "wooing" could hardly be considered an art when pursuing those to whom sex was either business or play.

Delilah stepped into the hall.

"Hey, check the women will you?" he called after her.

"That's where I was going."

"And, Delilah . . ."

She stuck her head back into the room.

"We've got hot water in the bathroom."

"Now that is good news."

"Later, maybe you can scrub my back, and I'll scrub yours."

"I'll be happy to scrub your back, sweetheart, but I'll wash mine . . . alone."

Chapter Twelve

"Mrs. Cutter is Mrs. Howell's sister-in-law, you do realize that?" Rafe said.

Delilah hadn't known that. "Meaning?"

"Meaning our oh-so-helpful cleaning lady could be filling your head with a bunch of bull to make some sales."

Her heart beat a little faster; she resented the fact he considered her gullible.

"You yourself asked Mr. Grapple where to go. He told you Mrs. Cutter had some fine pieces."

"And she probably does." Rafe helped her from the carryall. "I think Felicia Howell's long harangue about Mrs. Cutter getting the cream of the Merrifields' furniture at the estate sale may have been exaggerated. Besides, that was a long time ago."

"To tell you the truth, the fewer things we have that belonged to the Merrifields the happier I'll be, so I don't know why she emphasized that point."

"Ghosts don't live in furniture, sweetheart."

"You don't know that, but I believe it is safe to assume the Merrifields' things were out of the house before the newlyweds—"

"It was the bride."

"Who saw the ghost, you mean?"

"She didn't see the ghost. She heard and smelled it."

"Who told you that?"

Rafe pushed open the door to Cutter's Furniture Showcase near the west end of Main Street. "Mrs. Howell."

Delilah took in the huge warehouse advertised as the largest showroom of fine, imported, new and antique furniture north of

57

New Orleans. Whether it really was or not, she didn't know, but, looking at it now, she had her doubts. The place was one big cluttered mess of dusty, displaced pieces, some worn, chipped, and broken, others magnificent. Bull or not, largest showroom or not, she and Rafe were in desperate need of beds. She glanced at her handsome husband who was watching her with knowing eyes. He dipped his mouth to her ear.

"If we purchase two beds, Mrs. Cutter might suspect we are not sharing one."

"From what I've heard of Mrs. Howell's conversations with her daughters-in-law the past two days, I do not believe Mr. and Mrs. Cutter share a bed."

"I don't know what you believe you've heard, my sweet, but Mrs. Cutter is a widow, so you are correct, by default. They do not share a bed."

Delilah smiled. "And neither do we."

"And you don't want our associates to know it anymore than I do."

He was right. She didn't, but she would not grant him the satisfaction of admitting it.

"There are six bedrooms in that house, Rafe, and all of them are empty. No one will be shocked if you buy two beds."

"*We* buy two beds."

She stopped and turned to him. He stopped also.

"Can we buy a kitchen table?"

"And a couple of chairs while we're at it."

"Fourteen rooms in that beautiful old place and you've furnished seven of them." Elvira Cutter giggled and stroked Delilah's arm. Her right arm, Rafe noted. Mrs. Cutter was the effusive, gushy type of woman who was always hugging and squeezing the person she was talking to—and the woman was a merciless jabberer. She especially liked talking to Delilah. Half the time, he wasn't sure what she was saying, she talked so fast, and he thanked the Lord her gibberish was directed at his wife and not him.

"And all from your lovely showcase, Mrs. Cutter."

The woman placed her arm around Delilah's shoulders and squeezed her to her ample form. Rafe grimaced at the hand on Delilah's left bicep, but Delilah didn't appear to notice. "You're so sweet, my dear Mrs. Stone." The woman looked over her shoulder at him. "And you, Mr. Stone."

Yeah, they were sweet all right. He and Delilah had made Elvira Cutter's living for the next year. "Give all the credit to Delilah, Mrs. Cutter."

The plump, gray-haired woman stopped short, stared at Delilah, then turned to him, her mouth puckering.

Rafe frowned, but Mrs. Cutter had refocused on Delilah and gave a little laugh. "Delilah. Is that your given name?"

Delilah's questioning smile froze on her lips, and Rafe's gut tensed.

"It's unusual." Mrs. Cutter placed an index finger to her lips and looked at the floor. "I've heard it before."

Delilah nodded woodenly. Elvira didn't see, but he did. "She was the exotic enchantress who seduced the secret of Samson's hair from his lips, then betrayed him."

The woman looked up, twittered, and squeezed Delilah to her once more. "No, sweetie, I know that story already."

"What plans do you have for the house?" Delilah asked, then touched the spoon of her place setting and looked at him. She'd picked their table in a secluded corner of the Over-The-Hill Restaurant. The Victorian house, which Rafe knew had been a classy whorehouse after the War, sat atop the bluff near the south end of Broadway overlooking both Natchez' Under-The-Hill and the river. From where they sat, he and Delilah didn't have a view of the water, but he hadn't argued with her choice of tables, despite the host's frown when she'd refused his offer of a seat by the window.

"There's so much to be done cosmetically. Paint, wallpaper—"

"Kitchen modernization." He eyed her. "You do believe in cooking, don't you?"

She leaned over her plate. "Having food in the house would help."

"You need to make a list."

"I will." She poured cream in her cup and stirred her coffee. "The point I was trying to make is New Orleans has architects and a whole variety of establishments specializing in floor and wall coverings. That's where Aunt Ophelia goes. I can ask her the name—"

"Natchez has all those things, Delilah, including architects."

"Oh, and am I to assume you really are an architect?" She laid her spoon down, and he covered her hand.

"No more so than you want to go to New Orleans to buy wallpaper."

She removed her hand from beneath his and placed it in her lap. She wore a dark dress, the color of cabernet. It was velvet and had a wide satin sash, dating it. If he had time, he would take her to New Orleans and buy her a new wardrobe.

"Nor are you a real-estate mogul."

He studied those lovely green eyes of hers, weighing whether to speak or not. Despite his better judgment, he asked, "Is there something you wish to talk to me about?"

She straightened, but her bright smile was oh-so-obviously false. "Only if you wish to be equally forthcoming. I have no intention of simply handing over the Riverview Room to you."

"The Riverview Room?" Ah, there was an honest smile, which he quickly returned.

"It has a nice sound to it, doesn't it?" she said. "And I intend to make sure it's mine."

He wondered what progress she thought she was making in uncovering who he might be. They'd known each other ten days and had been married nine. Of those nine, she'd been with him day and night, so unless her uncle had uncovered something on him, and he was pretty sure the man hadn't even tried, she knew absolutely nothing about him. Her ploy, he surmised, was to divert his attention from her.

"You can't hide away at River's Bend forever. We live in

Natchez, Delilah. We will always live in Natchez." He watched her throat quiver subtly. "If it happened here, I'm going to find out."

She blinked and looked away, but not before he saw the combined fear and anger in her eyes.

"Tell me."

"I will tell you," she said, "but not before we know each other better. I simply would like to stay away from these people before you hear some tale from an ignorant stranger."

"If you are concerned about their telling it, then you tell me."

"Not yet." She wadded her linen napkin and placed it by her plate. "Thank you for lunch. I was so tired of soup, no matter how good it is."

He glanced at her half-eaten meal. "Do you fear I'd kick you out?"

"I"—she closed her eyes—"want you to know what sort of person I really am first."

He did know, basically. "Could it be worse than carrying Douglas Champion's child?" he asked.

"Or Uncle Joe's?" she snapped, then pushed away from the table. "This is so disgusting. Can we go?"

He sighed and rose. "I want to get your signature at the bank."

She looked at him askance.

"I might be traveling some, and I want you to be able to pay the workers."

"You're going to trust me with your money?"

"There's a limited account set aside for running the household. And yes, you could skip town on me should you so desire, but I'm trusting you won't. Pity you don't trust me as much."

"I'm trusting you with my life and my future, Rafe."

But not with her fears and her shame, whatever those might be.

Chapter Thirteen

"Jim," Rafe said and extended his hand to one James Dexter, private investigator, who took it with a firm shake. "Come on in. I've got an office where we can talk."

Rafe carefully shut the door behind them. The hollow click echoed across the near deserted foyer, and he glanced to the landing above them. "This way," he said and led Dexter from the foyer into the long hall, dimly lit with now functioning gaslights. "What have you found?"

"Not anything on your man Mizer."

"Did you check the navy records?"

"Oh, there's a few in the navy. Some during the War, too, but none of them were in this area or anywhere on the Mississippi or the Missouri. There are also records on 'Mizers' who served in the army during the War, but again, not in this area."

"The name could have been an alias."

"True. Any suggestions on where to go from here?"

Rafe rubbed the back of his neck. "No, I'll have to think about what to do next." Mizer or whoever he was could be dead for all he knew.

James Dexter slowed beside him and pulled an envelope out of his coat.

"This is what I found on your wife."

Rafe took the package without missing a step.

"Unlike Mizer, there's plenty of information on her. Mostly notes and newspaper clippings. I'd like to brief you if I could."

Rafe resisted the urge to stop and rip the envelope open. "You were quick."

"Miss Graff wasn't hard to track. She's been on this earth nineteen years. Spent the first twelve in Rodney, right up the road, and the next seven in Jackson before moving to Mississippi City a few months ago after her grandmother died."

Rafe opened the door to Delilah's Riverview Room, and he pointed Dexter in the direction of an upholstered wing chair. He then circled around his desk and laid the envelope on it.

"How about a whiskey?"

"Pleased if I do."

The furniture he and Delilah bought from Elvira Cutter had been delivered this morning, and Delilah had actually gone into town with Mrs. Howell and bought linens and curtains for the two occupied bedrooms. Delilah was in hers now, asleep, thank goodness. Her arm had been aching from all the activity this afternoon, and he'd coaxed her to take one of his pain powders. Lucky, because he hadn't known his agent was going to show up on their doorstep tonight.

Rafe handed the private investigator a crystal tumbler, half-filled, then poured one for himself.

"Tell me," he said, taking a seat behind his desk.

"Delilah Graff was the only child of Richard Lwelleyn Graff and Charlotte Wells, Josephus Collander's stepsister. Charlotte Wells Graff was apparently a striking blonde beauty . . ."

As was her daughter.

". . . Richard Graff was a handsome, somewhat successful businessman by Rodney's standards. He struggled like everyone else there of late, but financially he appeared solvent.

"Graff, however, had one serious flaw—jealousy." Dexter blew out a breath. "Extreme jealousy."

"Did he have cause?"

Dexter shook his head. "Don't know, but my gut feeling is that if Charlotte Graff had actually been unfaithful, her intent would have been to leave him for good. From what their neighbors told me, her life must have been pure hell. Mrs. Graff could not leave her house alone. She couldn't go shopping, to ladies' socials, any place where her husband could not, or would not, go with her. For the last several years of their lives, they would forgo any social engagements—dinners, dances, church functions. She could not talk to another man. Graff had gotten to the point where he would rant, rave, and even hit her after they returned from a public place, and his wife finally refused to accompany him anywhere."

Rafe leaned back in his chair, his heart beating faster. "Where was Delilah in all this?"

"In the middle, I reckon. According to the neighbors she was a sweet, quiet girl. She went to public school. They all three went to church together up till the last two years, when Charlotte Graff stopped attending with her husband.

"Seven years ago this past September, Mrs. Graff, by then six months pregnant with her second child, came to Natchez to see a Dr. Miles Colburn. Apparently her husband was not aware at the start that she went to see the man. According to the investigative report, she saw the doc only twice, three days apart. On her second trip, her husband was home waiting for her when she returned from Natchez.

"She told him where she'd been, that there was something wrong with the pregnancy. This guy Colburn was an expert in obstetrics. The next day, Richard Graff came down to see the good doctor himself. What happened at that time, no one knows. Graff apparently ranted and raved a few days and did some checking on Colburn."

"Was there anything wrong with the woman?"

Dexter nodded. "According to the doctor's record, Mrs. Graff was suffering from high blood pressure, kidney malfunction, and body swelling. It's a medical condition that sometimes occurs during pregnancy and is often fatal.

"Dr. Colburn was forty-eight years old, married with three children. He had come to Natchez fifteen years earlier from Jackson after an alleged affair with one of his married patients. All this was brought to Richard Graff's attention by someone in Jackson, probably his mother. Five days after his first confrontation with his wife, Richard Graff went back to Natchez and

64

shot and killed Miles Colburn—who was by that time a well-respected member of the community. Graff returned to Rodney where he shot his pregnant wife three times, killing her, and his twelve-year-old daughter once. He then, with one bullet left in his revolver, stuck the barrel in his mouth and pulled the trigger."

Rafe swallowed. "Let me guess. He got his daughter in the left shoulder?"

"The bullet's still there, small caliber, .22. The girl went to live with her paternal grandmother in Jackson. The old woman sold off everything she could of her son's estate, paid off his creditors, then squandered the rest. Delilah Graff's uncle, Josephus Collander"—Jim Dexter gave him a knowing look—"supported her via the grandmother for the next seven years. He sent her to the finest private girls' school in Jackson and basically kept her fed and clothed. You've got yourself a well-educated little lady there, Rafe. I also gathered the grandmother kept herself in high cotton by having the girl with her.

"The grandmother was, by all accounts, a witch. Her son was an only child. She had not wanted him to marry and move to Rodney, and my guess is she was a major source of the strife between the couple from the start. She fed Richard Graff's insecurities every chance she had." Dexter rubbed his chin. "The girl, your wife, that is, looks like her mother. According to neighbors, the grandmother was not nice to her."

Rafe swallowed—saliva, not whiskey. Damn. He could see why Delilah was ashamed, but couldn't understand why she thought he would hold all this against her. He played with the edge of the envelope, then opened it, spilling the contents onto the desk's surface.

"Everything is there. I wrote you a lengthy report, pretty much rehashing what I just told you. The police reports, doctors' reports, coroner, et cetera, et cetera, are all documented, too."

Rafe nodded. "What happened to the grandmother's estate?"

"There was no estate. Collander owns the house they lived in. He took good care of the girl financially. Can't say too much for her emotional well-being."

"I think Mrs. Collander probably had a lot to do with that shortcoming," Rafe said. "What about Douglas Champion?"

"Per your suggestion, I talked to the maid, Stella. She says the relationship between Delilah Graff and Champion was one-sided. He began courting the Collander girl back in May, then all but ignored her when Miss Graff moved in this past August. She says she overheard Miss Graff telling the man on more than one occasion that she was not interested in him and to leave her alone. Those conversations Stella relayed to her employer. From that, I gathered Collander had instructed her to spy on the two."

Rafe could believe that. "So Josephus Collander knew Delilah had no designs on Champion?"

"I would think so, yes. He probably also knows by now that you're checking."

Rafe smiled. "I imagine you are right, but that's okay."

Dexter finished his drink. "What's next, Mr. Stone?"

"The Union dead's widows and orphans."

A monotonous thump, thump, thump labored beneath Delilah's breast. Wet with sweat, she tossed back the quilt, then the sheet. Cold air chased away the foreboding of an unremembered dream, but not the darkness shrouding the room, and when she breathed, ripe-smelling air overwhelmed the now familiar scent of seasoned wood.

Night had fallen while she slept, and she rolled to her good side, from where she pushed up on her elbow in search of the window next to her bed. Not a hint of sunset remained. She dropped back onto the pillow and closed her eyes. The room teetered slightly. Darn that drug Rafe had talked her into taking.

She breathed the strangely scented air, then stiffened at a sound, which caused her to sit up and snatch back the discarded covers.

"Rafe?"

A soft tap clicked across the hard floor and screamed through her mind. She jerked her head in the direction of Rafe's door, unseen in the dark.

"Rafe?" she called louder.

Her blind gaze turned in the direction of the noise she'd heard, and out of the corner of her eye she caught, she was certain, movement in the reflective surface of the window's now pristine glass, but when she looked back, nothing was there.

She rolled to the opposite side of the bed, tangling herself in the sheet, then fell to the floor. She managed to brace her fall with both arms, but hit her shin against the bed frame and sent her now superfluous (given the functioning bathroom), and blessedly empty, chamber pot skittering across the floor and into the fireplace. The searing heat in her left arm eclipsed the racket created by her fall, then numbness and paralysis eased that suffering. The pain in her shin did not numb, but she struggled up anyway and lurched forward, reaching out with her right hand.

Brick, brick. The fireplace. She touched the smooth surface of the wall, and splaying her hand on the cool plaster, she felt her way . . . wood. The door, thank you sweet Jesus!

Cold air whispered against the back of her neck, and for certain she felt the touch of frigid fingertips on her spine, then she cracked her wrist against the knob, but having found it, no matter the pain, she turned it, pushed, and fell through the black portal. She whirled, anticipating resistance from whence she came, and slammed her body against the door, and it shut with a disconcerting bang. Fighting for breath, she leaned against it, but couldn't lock it. She couldn't see, and there was no key.

Careful not to make a sound, Delilah inched away from the ominous thing, and when she felt she was far enough, she turned her head and cried, "Rafe, wake up, something's in my room."

She quaked in the silence, but stumbled in the dark to where she knew his bed must be. She found it still made, then held her breath and listened to what she perceived to be scratching on her bedroom door.

Chapter Fourteen

Delilah almost bowled him over when he swung the door open. "There's something in my room!"

Rafe, settled somewhat by seeing her in one piece, drew in a breath. Her cries had sent his heart racing and, from the way James Dexter sprang from his chair, had left the cool detective shaken.

She was disheveled and pale and frightened. Wisps of flaxen hair, free of the rough braid that fell halfway down her back, curled around her face, and those beautiful eyes, bright and wide, stared at him.

Her gaze darted behind him, and she yelped, then jumped back into the dark hall. She covered the bodice of her flannel nightgown with both arms. She'd seen Dexter.

"I'm sorry," she said, backing away, tears in her eyes. Suddenly she covered her mouth with her hand, and he thought she was going to sob.

"It's all right, Delilah." He stepped after her and took her upper arms in a gentle hold. She grimaced, and he remembered that damn shoulder.

"I didn't know anyone else was here. I was so scared I didn't think about . . ."

She was talking fast, and he, more concerned with what had frightened her, couldn't think. "You're fine. We'll go back to your room, get your wrap, and make proper introductions."

Her head was shaking before he was half through trying to calm her.

"There's something in my room."

He placed a finger against his lips to shush her. James Dexter could not see them where they'd retreated in the hall, but he certainly could hear them, and though it was none of James' business, Rafe was self-conscious about another man's knowing he wasn't sharing a bed with his bride, a most deliciously lovely bride.

She nodded as if she understood, then leaned close and whispered, "There's s-something in my room."

He hugged her shivering body. It was cool in the house, but the furnace was operating now, and it wasn't that cold.

Lord, her teeth might be chattering, her bare toes probably frigid, but the rest of her was warm. He tightened his hold.

"Is she okay, Rafe?"

When Rafe glanced back, he found Jim, concern in his eyes, standing in the dim hall.

"I'll go up with you to check the room."

"Y-yes," Delilah said, "let him come."

"Come on," Rafe said, turning her down the hall. "We'll get the lamp going and see what's in there."

*D*elilah squealed and stepped back to the door, her hand on the knob. "Don't hurt it."

Rafe adjusted the noose one more time.

"Let's try not to let it get under the bed, this time," Dexter said.

"Delilah," Rafe called over his shoulder, "you come guard the bed."

"Poor thing," she said, inching toward the footboard, all the while stretching her neck to see the cornered raccoon in front of Rafe.

"Poor thing, my ass. If you weren't here to stop me, I'd have already shot the thing. Coons are mean."

Rafe glanced at her. She'd stopped at the bed, strategically placing herself to shoo the animal off should it try to find refuge there again. It hadn't taken long to find the culprit once they'd made it back to the room. Other than a wardrobe, a bed, and a dresser, there was nothing in the room and virtually nowhere for the beast to hide.

"I didn't realize they were so big," she said. "It's the size of a small dog."

"More like a medium dog," Dexter said.

"And they have hands like people."

Oh, she liked that. When that coon had grabbed the broom-stick Dexter was using to keep the animal in the corner, Delilah had laughed at the sight.

"Paws, Delilah. A coon has paws, not hands, and don't take any chances, if it starts toward you and acts like it's not going to back down, get out of its way. They also carry rabies."

She smiled, bright-eyed, watching the animal, not him. He hoped she'd heard him.

"Seems healthy enough," Dexter said.

It sure did. Healthy and angry.

"I don't understand how it got in the house without anyone seeing," Delilah said.

Rafe adjusted the loop a little larger and stepped forward. "Somebody probably left a door open at some point during the day, been so many of us in and out."

He motioned to Dexter. "Go." Rafe's big question was how it got into Delilah's room unnoticed. He found it hard to believe she missed the thing when she retired earlier, and he'd checked to make sure her door was closed before coming downstairs.

Dexter pinned it with the broom. Rafe, noose in hand, moved forward.

Ha, got it that time. The raccoon snapped, but Rafe avoided the teeth, then tightened the noose around its neck. Dexter, still holding the struggling beast with the broom, looked at him with a lopsided grin. "Now what? That thing's not going to simply follow you outside on its tether."

No, it wasn't. The moment Dexter moved the broom, that stupid coon was going to attack the rope around its neck—right on up to the person holding it.

Rafe wrapped the rope around his arm until the length was

relatively short. Then extending his arm, he raised the animal off the ground.

"Oh, Rafe, you'll strangle it."

"I don't care, Delilah. Get the door open and stay out of the way."

The coon swayed and struggled and even flip-flopped on the rope. Rafe was worried the thing might manage to get out of the noose, and he hurried downstairs and out the door. How the devil he was going to get the rope off it was the next question.

"Jim?" he hollered and stopped at the bottom of the porch steps, "you got a knife on you?"

"I do."

Rafe breathed in cold air, then exhaled a foggy mist against the black void of forest in front of him. "Leave the door open, Delilah."

She'd followed them onto the veranda, and now he admonished her to get back. He didn't want her anywhere close when he set this thing free. With a frustrated sigh, she stepped back from the porch's edge. Jim positioned himself safely behind Rafe and reached for the rope to which the coon now clung with its "hands" and teeth. It was relatively still, but Rafe wasn't sure if that were because it was near death, worn out, or calculating its counterattack.

"Cut out of reach. It can get the noose off on its own."

Jim laughed and started sawing at the hemp rope. "Yeah, with its little fingers."

A couple of frigid minutes passed before the coon fell to the ground with an unceremonious plunk. Both men stepped back, but the raccoon was gone before they stopped their retreat.

Jim Dexter shook his head. "One of those things got in my granny's kitchen when I was a kid. Got into a sack of flour. Lord, the mess."

Rafe frowned. "Well, we haven't checked our kitchen yet."

"If it's wrecked, I don't want to know." Dexter turned and found Delilah, who still stood at the top of the steps. He smiled at her. "You two are on your own."

71

Rafe slapped him on the shoulder. "Thanks."

"Anytime. By the way, I put those papers we were working on in your desk drawer."

"I'm sorry to have interrupted you," Delilah said.

"We were done, Mrs. Stone."

No, Jim was done. He still needed to read through that investigation, then find a safe place for it. He wasn't going to bring up Delilah's childhood and the death of her parents. He'd wait and let her do that.

"She's favoring that arm pretty good," Jim said softly, taking a step toward his open carriage.

"She fell on it when she got out of bed."

"Well, Mr. Stone," Jim whispered in the dark, "if I were you, I'd go take care of her."

Jim drove away, and Rafe started up the steps, stopping at the second from the top. She stood directly above him, her face shadowed in the light falling through the open front door.

"Yes, Mrs. Stone?"

She gave him a tentative smile. "Nothing."

Rafe considered she might expect him to be angry at her for greeting James Dexter in her very modest nightgown . . . or perhaps, for talking to James Dexter at all.

She turned to the front door. He caught up with her and wove an arm around her waist, drawing her right side against him. "We probably do need to check our kitchen."

"And all the doors and windows," she said.

Chapter Fifteen

Delilah ran her hand over the smooth surface of their break-front. It wasn't really new, but it was new for them, and the piece was still beautiful, in perfect condition, and Rafe seemed satisfied with the entire set she'd chosen. Truth was, he seemed happy to let her manage the house.

"We'll find china for it," he said, following her out of the kitchen, as neat as they'd left it hours ago. They'd eaten early, then he'd given her the pain powder. Even now, the hour wasn't late, and she was in no hurry to go back to her bedroom.

"My mother had china," she said. "Beautiful pieces. The set belonged to her grandmother and mother before her."

Beside her, Rafe had stilled, and she regretted saying anything about her mother. He was going to ask—

"What happened to it?"

Delilah yanked open a cabinet door, feigning interest in the inside so Rafe couldn't see her face. "Grandmother sold off everything to bury Papa." The horrible old woman had sold off her daughter-in-law's heirloom china to give the man who'd murdered her an extravagant funeral.

"What about your mother's funeral?"

She fidgeted with the button to her flannel wrapper. "Uncle Joe paid for that."

"Where are they buried?"

"Jackson."

That was partially true. Her papa was in Jackson; his overbearing mother was next to him now. Her mother, however, was a short way up the river from here, in Rodney. Alone.

73

"When's the last time you visited them?"

Delilah's heart started to pound. He was going to suggest they go to the site; he would naturally assume there was only one.

She and Uncle Joe, Aunt Ophelia, and Bernadette had visited her mother in Rodney this spring following her graduation ceremony in Jackson. She'd seen her father's grave the end of July. She'd even plucked a rose from her grandmother's casket to place on the man's grave. He had been a sick human being, deserving pity, not hate. And she did try hard not to hate.

"When Grandmother died," she told him.

She should go up to bed before he asked her more questions, but she was still anxious over her earlier fright and didn't want to go upstairs by herself. She dropped her hand from the neck of her robe and moved away from him. "I love this fireplace," she said.

She felt him beside her. Her interest in this ancient 'heart of the home' was not feigned. She'd been studying the rough brick and the wall around it for days.

"This fireplace was part of the original house," he said.

"I know." She knocked on the portion of wall between the brick and the deep-set west wall of the room. The construction of the wall and fireplace was similar on the other side. "Have you noticed this off-set? Look how far the fireplace sets in the room in relation to what must have been the back wall of the cabin." She knocked on the wall again. "It's hollow in there."

"I think you're probably right."

Delilah heard the mock seriousness in his voice and whipped around. "Am I amusing or boring you?"

"You are entertaining me."

What subtlety was he trying to convey with that? "All right, smarty pants, why do you think they built in that wasted space?"

He furrowed his brow as if giving the matter great thought, then said, "You know, Delilah, I've already admitted I'm not an architect."

She smiled. "Are we going to play guess the secret?"

"Only if your secret is open for discussion."

Her heart skipped a beat. "I'd rather talk about the fireplace."

"Well," he said, turning his attention to the blackened hearth and folding his arms across his chest, "my guess is that the cabin's original back wall was pretty much flush with the front of the fireplace."

She nodded and stepped closer, folding her arms under her breasts in mimicry of him. She saw his smirk, and her own lips twitched.

"Continue," she said.

"When the owners started expanding, they felt this room was too small and therefore, added two feet along the back wall by knocking out the original wall and making it flush with the back of the fire chamber instead of the front."

She pursed her lips and again studied the fireplace. "Are you sure you're not an architect?"

"I'm sure, and it would not take one to figure that out."

"You seem very confident about what happened."

"Well, what do you think happened?"

Again, she stepped forward, but this time flattened her palm against the wall alongside the fireplace. "I think there's a passage back there."

He made a sibilant sound, stepped forward, peered around the short corner that ended with the back wall, then looked the wall over from the floor to its crown molding twelve feet above.

"Delilah, this wall is in the middle of the house. There's a fireplace on one side, this room on the other, and another room behind it. What kind of a passage is that?"

She was making him anxious with this talk of secret passages, and her on edge with raccoons in the house and the cleaning and repair people volunteering information on ghosts. He wanted her to go to bed, so he could read the report Dexter had brought him, but he had a sinking feeling she wasn't leaving his side. She was frightened.

"There's a room above us," she said, "and who knows what's below."

Her words flew off her tongue like bullets from a Gatlin gun, and on top of that, she had managed to divert the conversation away from her parents and family, which was the direction he'd wanted it to go.

"So you think there's a stairway next to the fireplace?"

"There could be."

"Yes, I guess there could be, but it would be very narrow, and what would be the purpose?"

She waved her hands.

"The ghost walks it?"

"I doubt the ghost built it, but whoever did build it could be the ghost now."

"There is no ghost." Rafe looked up. "And the empty space should come out in your bedroom."

"Where my fireplace is."

He frowned at her.

She smiled. "I've already checked."

"And did you find a way in?"

"Not yet."

Thank goodness for small favors. "Delilah, if you ever find a secret passage, please don't explore it on your own. And with that thought in mind, I have to go to New Orleans."

He swore she paled. No, he didn't have to worry about her exploring dark passages, just finding them.

"When?"

"If we leave in the morning, we'll get there before nightfall."

She breathed out; she'd actually held her breath since asking her last question.

"You're taking me?"

"Of course." He hadn't wanted to. Not because he didn't want her with him, but because he didn't know what he'd do with her while he was working.

"When are we coming back?"

He started to say day after tomorrow, but she was so beautiful and excited—probably because he was taking her—and her dresses were so out of date.

"Three days," he said. "I've got work to do, but I should be finished Wednesday morning." That would give them the afternoon for china and silver, table linens and whatever else a woman needed for her dinner table; Thursday to look for wall coverings; and Friday with a seamstress and a variety of emporiums.

Chapter Sixteen

James Penworth, Charles Slade, Richard B. Wilson, Thomas Harrison, George Frothby. Dead, the lot of them according to the April 13, 1865 *Crescent City Gazette's* front page. Three men were missing (along with one hundred thousand dollars in processed gold) and believed drowned. That was a lot of money, and no one believed, not for a minute even then, that the gold was at the bottom of the Mississippi.

Known dead on the Confederate side were Harmon King, Billy Tulles, and Jeremiah Gifford. The number grew in the days that followed, and Lincoln's assassination usurped the front page, but as of the morning of the thirteenth, those were the only names known and that story topped the news.

> *. . . the converted side-wheeler* GILDED ROSE, *purchased by the War Department in 1861 and armored for riverine warfare, plied the waters of the Ohio, Missouri, and Mississippi Rivers engaging in duties from routine patrol and interdiction of smuggling to major battles against Confederate forces. . . .*

Rafe squinted, then trailed an index finger down the yellowed column. This was his third time through the article.

> *She fought her last battle after running aground on a sandbar off Carthage Point south of Natchez in the early morning hours of April 12.*

Rafe blew out a breath and stopped reading. Captain Zachary Scott Stowe, U.S.N., had been skipper of the ship, Major Samuel Prescott, U.S.A., the detail. . . . And heads would roll.

He'd found everything he was looking for in the *Crescent City Gazette* archives. That was lucky. Too many clerks and too many questions might draw the wrong person's interest farther north. That group of Yankees had been betrayed. He had a name, but it didn't fit . . . but hell, all he had were dead men's names anyway. He needed the names of the living, but where to find them? The name of every crew member on that side-wheeler, every man in the detail, every clerk from a Virginia City, Montana gold mine through every army and treasury office, through every port along the Missouri and Mississippi that shipment had passed. Without a doubt, the government had all the information. Had it and had gotten nowhere.

He double-checked the name of a Union army lieutenant he'd jotted down from an unrelated article. A curiosity actually, but the incident resulting in the lieutenant's arrest happened during the wee hours the same morning of the heist, at an isolated spot on the Mississippi River where Old St. Catherine Creek emptied into St. Catherine Bend, just around the corner, so to speak, from Carthage Point. In its broken, convoluted trek over land and across Butler Lake, Old St. Catherine Creek offered an alternative route linking the two navigation points. He'd give the name to James Dexter and see what came of it.

Rafe closed the volume of thirty-year-old papers and returned it to the clerk. Eventually he might have to go to Washington and check the names of the ship's entire crew, as well as the fate of the other members of the decimated detail, but the Carthage Point incident was still an open case, the gold still unaccounted for, and he didn't want to draw attention to his interest. Nor did he think he would have to. The conspiracy had developed closer to where the actual crime took place. Everything had happened quickly. Opportunity had knocked, and someone had been ready.

He pushed open the door to the newspaper building and the sun hit him full in the face. It was a beautiful, cool November day in New Orleans. A breeze caressed his cheek, and he breathed in a unique mixture of chicory and fried bread with a subtle hint of the river, an arguably clean, early morning scent in the air. The smell wasn't always so pleasing in New Orleans.

He pulled out his watch. Not yet ten. He hoped Delilah was still in bed, because he wanted to wake her, torture himself with the warm, sleep-soaked scent of her skin and the fragrance of her perfumed hair. He needed a woman, but no longer would just any woman do.

Growing up, Rafe figured he'd meet the girl of his dreams, marry, and live happily ever after, but a short-lived broken heart at the age of seventeen had resulted in a more pragmatic outlook on love—and on women. Then other interests had garnered his attention. Josephus Collander's offer of his niece for River's Bend had put that pragmatism to the test. The only question he'd had when he shook on the deal was what was so wrong with the woman that Collander needed to bribe someone to take her off his hands. Even not knowing the answer to that question, marrying Delilah was a price he'd been willing to pay for River's Bend.

Well, he had at least part of the answer to his question, and his pragmatism had begun to fade when he got his hands on the deed to the property, replaced by his growing interest in his bride. Curiosity had grown into desire, tempered (damn his soul) by tenderness. He'd felt guilty from the moment she'd turned that stricken look on him when he suggested she might be in the family way, and as a result, he welcomed her challenge to "woo" her. That suggestion held more promise than her initial assessment they had no future together.

The heavy panel door shut with a soft click. The suite was quiet, and the door between their rooms was open. He tossed his fedora on a chair and crossed the carpeted floor—

"Oh!" She caught her hand to her breast. "You scared me. You're done early."

"And you're up early."

"It's midmorning, and I wanted to be sure I was ready when you got back. I know how men detest waiting on women."

"There are other things I need to teach you about men."

"Really? Well, I know they do not like to shop."

"I volunteered, remember?"

She scooted around him. "I do, indeed, and I was pleasantly surprised. Did you accomplish what you intended?"

"Yes," he said, following her with his eyes as she moved away from him. She smelled like gardenia.

"Which was?"

"Which was what?"

"Which was 'what were you trying to accomplish?'"

"You bathed this morning, didn't you?"

She turned from the mirror where she was putting on tiny pearl earrings.

"I did, but I fail to see the relevancy."

"The relevancy of what?"

She dropped her hands and looked at him with a crooked smile. "Rafe, what have you been doing this morning?"

"Are you trying to get information out of me?" he said and pushed away from the door.

She closed her eyes and breathed out. "I asked the question initially to make polite conversation."

He looked her over, head to foot. She wore a dress of pale-blue silk with a high velvet collar and long sleeves. The garment fit tight around the waist, and he wondered what she looked like in just her corset. Damn, he was not the least bit interested in polite conversation with his beautiful wife.

She straightened at his approach. "Then it did occur to me, you might slip and tell me about the matter that brought you to New Orleans."

He stopped in front of her, and she tilted her head up slightly to see his eyes.

"Now it occurs to me you may have been involved in something . . . stimulating."

"Stimulating?"

She stepped back. "What *have* you been doing this morning?"

"Actually I've been giving you a lot of thought."

"If you'd been thinking of me, you'd have been here."
"I am here."
"Now you are."
"That's my point."
"You've made no point."
"You mentioned stimulating. I mentioned you."
"Would you please get to the point?"
"What point?" He touched her right elbow. "I really don't think there is a point."

He saw the tremor of her throat, and his eyes met hers, wide and bright.

"There's always a point," she said.

Gently he tugged on that captive elbow and dipped his head. "I remember now. Stimulation"—he brushed her lips—"and you. Stimulate you."

"I made no such—"

*H*is mouth, firm and warm, covered hers at the same moment he released her elbow to snake his arm around her waist and pull her to him. Her nipples, despite the layers of cloth, hardened, then tingled against the jersey webbing of her corset. Instinctively she circled her arms around his neck, and when his tongue probed her lips, she responded by parting them, but stiffened when he inserted said tongue into her mouth. The arm circling her waist tightened, as if he feared she'd try to get away, but now heat moved from her gut to her pelvis, and escape was the last thing she wanted.

Emboldened, she touched his tongue with hers and heard him groan. Immediately he released her lips and pulled her roughly against him. She felt his warm breath against her ear.

"You see, sweetheart, I stimulate you, you stimulate me."

She drew in a labored breath. "When I said stimulating, I was thinking more along the lines of some sort of catalyst."

"Me, too." He breathed in her ear and warmth filled the space between her legs.

"Gambling, alcohol, opium . . ."

He licked. She gasped and strained away, but he held her firm, kissing her neck below the lobe. She tilted her head back, giving him easy access to her throat.

"A woman, Delilah. One specific woman."

She grabbed his shoulders and pressed gently. "Are you wooing me, husband?"

Reluctantly, it seemed, he dropped his arms, releasing her. "Yes, wife, I'm 'wooing' you, but be advised at any given point my 'wooing' will turn into full-fledged seduction, and I do not intend to warn you."

She breathed deeply. "I think I'll know."

"Oh, Delilah, sweetheart, I don't think you will or you'd know the difference between my volunteering to take you shopping and the kiss we just shared."

Chapter Seventeen

"Do you know anything about the history of this house?"

Rafe swallowed. His heart had leapt into his throat at Delilah's fervent entrance into what they were both now calling the Riverview Room.

"Only what I've been told by people who lived around here." Pretending indifference, he sat forward in his chair, laid James Dexter's investigative report in front of him, then covered it with his forearm. They'd gotten back from New Orleans last evening, and she'd begun this day focused on their home, as if invigorated by the art and domestic designs they'd discovered while browsing the fashionable shops of the Crescent City. She'd been gone a good chunk of the day, and he thought she'd been putting their house in order.

"You sure spent a lot of time at the grocer's."

Delilah spun and closed the door. She whirled back his way, skirts flouncing, and struggled with the top button of her new Mackintosh. Her gray, kidskin gloves she held crushed in one hand. She was lovely with cheeks flushed from the cold outside, excitement, or perhaps both. She draped the coat over the upholstered settee on one side of his desk, set the gloves on top of it, then sat, the green and black stripes of her new silk dress contrasting favorably against the settee's red velvet. She tucked a wisp of golden hair behind her ear.

He focused through the fog created by her beauty. Obviously, she intended to stay, so he opened the desk drawer, placed the papers inside, then pushed them to the back left-hand corner.

"I have just come from the grocer," she said when he returned his attention to her, "but I spent the morning at the chamber of commerce and the library."

If this didn't give him a headache nothing would.

"Did you eat lunch?"

"No," she said with an impatient wave of her hand. "I'm not comfortable going into public restaurants unescorted."

He thought about the papers he'd squirreled away in the desk and considered they probably explained why.

"Did you get something to make for supper? I'm starving."

"Yes, I'm hungry, too, but let me tell you about this house." She pulled a journal from her reticule, and he sighed inwardly.

"The original cabin was built by one Maurice Dumas"—she looked up at him, and he smiled—"the older brother of Eugene Dumas—you remember, Mr. Grapple told us about him."

Rafe nodded.

"Well, he built it in 1726. He was a French colonist who came here with a land grant from the Mississippi Company. He had a wife and two small sons, all of whom perished in this house in 1729 during the Indian attack. His little brother Eugene came here after the subjugation of the Natchez. Eugene Dumas was one of very few French colonists who prospered in the area after the Natchez' uprising.

"In 1761, Dumas' daughter married Charles Richard, another man whose family had come over with the Mississippi Company venture." She again looked up from her notes. "Around this time, remember, Natchez came under British rule.

"Anyway, Charles Richard inherited everything when his father-in-law died in 1771, and Dumas' holdings were apparently significant on both sides of the river. It was Charles who made the first major changes to the house between 1779 and 1790." She found his eyes, then waved a knowing index finger at him. "That was while the American Revolution was going on, and there was an American raid—"

"The Willing Raid. I'm aware of it."

"Anyway, rumor has it that as a result of that raid, Charles Richard *did* plan a secret ingress and egress into his house so that

85

he and his family could safely avoid similar marauding pirates from the river."

"'Rumor has it', my beauty? Do you have any information describing the location of this alleged secret passage?"

"No," she said and squirmed in her seat. "But Charles added on the rooms surrounding the original cabin—all the way around the house—and he added two large rooms on top of the lower expansion. It was he who expanded the one-room cabin by knocking out and relocating the back wall."

"How did you find all this out?"

"At the Fisk Library. There's a section there on the houses of Natchez compiled by Samuel Winnisfree back in the 80's. He researched every conceivable record, apparently, to come up with his compilations. Our house, given the original cabin stuck in the middle of it, is probably the oldest in the area. But I digress.

"Charles had two children, a son and a daughter. The son, André, inherited River's Bend, and it was André who was the owner during the era when cotton became so lucrative. He further expanded the house, adding the rooms that make up the east and west wings." She glanced around the room, then out the French doors to the veranda overlooking the river. "That would have included this room. He added rooms upstairs at the same time, as well as the high wrap-around veranda supported by thirty-two fluted Corinthian columns. He painted the brick and wood white.

"André was apparently a businessman more than a farmer. He was also influential politically. According to the librarian, even in the heyday of the Cotton Kingdom, River's Bend never had more than fifty darkies at any one time. It was André's son who freed the slaves at River's Bend in 1859 when his only son died. A little over a year later he died, and River's Bend was left to his granddaughter Lorelei, the young woman who married the Confederate major who never came home from the War.

"But, Rafe . . ."

She sat forward so far and so fast he feared she was going to fall off the seat.

". . . there is more to that story."

"Yes?"

"It was Morgan Ward who reputedly led a raid on a Union shipment of gold headed downriver. The gold had been shipped from Montana and was headed for New Orleans."

"I know the story."

She widened her eyes. "One hundred thousand dollars in gold, Rafe, and it hasn't been found."

He curled his lips into a grin. "Maybe it's here, Delilah, in the secret passage."

"Make fun all you want, but the ship carrying the gold ran aground on a sandbar scarcely over a mile north of here."

"And the Confederates were waiting for it."

She started to speak, then stopped and pursed her lips. "That doesn't make sense, does it? How could they have known that it would run aground?"

He laughed. "Dumb luck or an inside job, my dear, and since the Rebs' luck was about used up, I doubt the fickle lady was smiling on them."

"On any of them," Delilah said. "Seven Yankees died during the robbery, and the five men who rode with Ward also died. Three were found the next morning, shot in the back. One Yankee was found dead on the north shore of Butler Lake"—she waved her hands to the east—"right in back of us."

"A good four miles in back of us, Delilah, and it was that dead Yankee that led authorities to conclude the heist was an inside job."

"Well, if that's so, Ward double-crossed them all, including his own men, all Adams' County boys, for the money. He murdered them and disappeared. Lorelei disappeared that same night. The clerk at the library told me Lorelei couldn't stand the shame of Morgan's treachery, and she drowned herself in the river."

"Or she ran off with him."

Delilah's eyes widened slightly. "Or maybe he forced her to go with him."

"Sweetheart, despite the romantic appeal abduction and submission may hold for a woman, in reality it would be extremely tiring for a man to try to keep a woman who does not wish to be with him—particularly if her subsequent escape could result in his being pinpointed for theft and murder. Under those circumstances, his most likely course of action would be to abandon her, which is what the locals believed actually happened, or to kill her."

Delilah smirked. "Or, for his treachery against the boys she'd grown up with, perhaps she killed him."

"And hid his carcass in the secret passage, where it smelled as it rotted, and *she* absconded with the gold."

Delilah looked around the room. "But do you think she would have left this place, her family's legacy? If she'd killed him, why not let authorities think someone else did it—such as a member of his group of thieves—hide the money, and stay at River's Bend richer than Midas?" She straightened, then nodded. "That would have been the smart thing to do."

"Delilah," he said, furrowing his brow, "have you considered she cared for him?"

"Oh, well, perhaps she did. That would have been a problem. Then if she did kill him because of his treachery, her subsequent suicide would have been the correct solution."

"Sweetheart, I do believe you have taken honor to a new sphere."

"No"—she grinned, and he was somewhat relieved to realize she was teasing—"Lorelei Ward did. I would have taken the money—"

"And opened a seamstress shop."

"Excuse me. I would have never worked again. But poor Lorelei's ghost roams these halls searching for the man she loved, but could never respect."

"I think it more likely she absconded with the money."

Delilah rose and pirouetted. "No. The only thing that would have taken Lorelei from these halls is the man she loved, and if he were dead, there would have been no reason for her to leave."

"And the disgrace?"

"Her family went much farther back than most around here. André Richard held on to this house long after the cotton that made him rich had depleted his lands. A lot of plantation owners took their gains and moved on, but he stayed and turned to other investments. River's Bend was home, a legacy, a history." Delilah beamed with conviction. "Lorelei would have held her head high and lived with the disgrace. She did not leave with the money. If she did indeed love Morgan Ward, whether she shot him or not, she died when he did."

"That's terribly romantic."

"I wish we had a more honorable hero for her."

He shrugged. "Well, I think I'm correct when I say no one knows his side of the story, right?"

"Hmm, that may be true." She pursed her lips. "Are you suggesting I write my own ending?"

"If you want. Is that the end of your history of the house?"

"No," she said, and plopped back onto the settee. "I found more on the Merrifields—"

"I thought we were talking about the house."

"There have been no significant architectural changes to the house since André Richard's day. What we were talking about was the heinous events that occurred within these walls."

Well, her frightening herself senseless might drive her to him in the darkest part of the night. Despite the appeal, he didn't want her to be afraid here.

"Markham Merrifield's bride, Cecilia, was pregnant," she said.

"Who told you that?"

"Desmond Taylor, the grocer. He says it's a common belief the boys killed their papa and stepmother because they feared losing their papa's estate to his bride and her children."

"What happened to Merrifield's money?"

"I don't know."

"Well, now, let's think about that. Unless the boys abandoned River's Bend and took Merrifield's money, and he was an astute businessman, who I'm relatively certain kept the bulk of his money in a bank, the boys could not have gotten their hands on anything the man owned without being caught and hanged." He cocked his head, inviting a response.

"Which begs the question of another motive for the murders," she said finally. Again, she waved that just-suppose index finger at him. "Well, what if the boys or their father found the money?"

"The hundred thousand dollars in gold hidden in the secret passage?"

"Yes, and it could have been hidden anywhere, Rafe. That is not important. What if they found the gold and the sons decided to keep it for themselves?"

"And cut the father and wicked stepmother out, you mean?"

"Yes. . . ." Delilah frowned. "Was she wicked?"

Rafe shook his head. "I don't know anything about her. You are the investigator here, but I did hear something about an illicit affair going on here in the house."

"Cecilia had a lover?"

"One of Merrifield's sons."

"No one has brought that up to me."

"Probably because you're talking to men and not women. A man would be reluctant to discuss such things with you."

"Hmmph. Perhaps you're right. Mrs. Howell will be back on Wednesday. I'll ask what she knows."

"Someone else could have killed the Merrifields for the gold shipment."

"Do you think so?"

"I'm adding fuel to your fire, Delilah." He grinned and rose. "But . . ."

She followed his progress around the desk.

". . . your investigation into the deaths of the Merrifields is really not the fire I wish to feed."

Her pretty mouth curled into a smile, and he saw the tip of her tongue touch her top lip. "All those things happened, Rafe. You can tease me all you want, but there's a reason for what has occurred in this house, and there are too many things left un-explained."

He reached out, and she laid a palm in his. With a gentle tug, he pulled her up.

"Such as?"

"The robbery, the murders of the Confederate soldiers, the disappearance of Lorelei and Major Ward, the killings of the Merrifields, and the disappearance of the two boys."

"And the missing one hundred thousand dollars in gold," he said and raised her hand, turning her slightly one way, then the next. "You are beautiful in your new store-bought dress." He'd bought her five ready-made dresses at the Emporium and ordered nine more from the seamstress.

"Thank you." Her glance darted to his lips, then back to his eyes, and with that silent invitation, he pulled her closer. She flattened her free hand on his chest. "You desire something from me, sir?"

"I do."

"And what is that?" she said, gently running her index finger along his jaw from his ear to his chin.

He dipped his head so that his lips almost touched hers and he could smell her sweet breath. "Supper."

She furrowed her brow.

"You want me to kiss you, in return I want you to cook me supper."

Her mouth dropped open at the same time she pushed at his chest and struggled to free her captive hand.

Planting his palm against the small of her back, he locked her to him, and when she managed to yank her hand free, he immediately wrapped both arms tight around her waist and crushed her breast to his. A poof of air escaped her lungs. She slapped at his shoulders. "Let me go, you oaf."

"It's a perfectly fair trade, Delilah. How can you fault it?"

"It is you who wishes to —"

She whimpered when his lips covered hers, but then surrendered, with ardor, and he knew she'd turned the tables on him. But he didn't care, relishing each stroke of her tongue against his. Heat flowed to his manhood, and he hardened. The little

91

witch. She hadn't known how to kiss a few mornings ago in New Orleans, but had been game to learn, and he'd spent the next three days helping her perfect the technique. She'd mastered it now, better than any whore on Bourbon Street, and he was eager to teach her more in the way of a whore's tricks.

His cock pressed against the crotch of his pants, and he stifled a groan. She wouldn't let him, he knew. She wasn't ready to let him off the hook on which he'd skewered himself on their wedding day. That was okay, he had ways of getting . . .

He cupped a breast and moved his thumb. She pushed him away with a ragged breath, but not before he'd felt the hardened nipple beneath the silk dress and underlying corset.

Lips tight, she stared at him in mock anger. She was still within arms' length. He didn't reach for her, but eyed her body, foot to head, with appreciation.

"Be careful how you tease me, sweetheart. You may get more than you bargained for."

"Your idea of seduction, *sweetheart*?"

"Anyone's, however, you were doing a good job yourself."

Delilah straightened and jutted her chin out just a bit. Her cheeks were flushed again, her hair in wonderful disarray around her face. "Thank you." She smiled smugly, then reached out and grabbed the collar of his shirt, and she tugged him to her. His heart skipped a beat, and he caught her right bicep and yanked her closer, wondering how many workmen he'd have to pass as he carried her to the bedroom upstairs.

A loud knock sounded on the door. They both turned to it in tandem. He dropped her arm. "Saved again, my beauty."

"Ha, it was merely my intent to make you suffer more."

"Suffering works both ways," he said, tapping her pert nose with an index finger. He started toward the summons. "So does relief." He grinned at her over his shoulder. "And I have no intention of forcing you to suffer."

"You're such a thoughtful man," she said, moving to the back of the room.

He opened the door. The gasman stood there.

"I'm done for now, Mr. Stone, but I need to show you some-thing."

Rafe glanced at Delilah, who stood near the French doors, looking down at the river, then back at the man. "Three, right?"

Delilah turned their way, and the man tipped his hat. "All done for now, Mrs. Stone. I'll check back with you. Need to show you, Mr. Stone. Some of those lines need to be changed."

"All right." Rafe glanced back at Delilah, who looked at him with a silly smirk. He winked. "Could you write me out a voucher for three dollars?"

She nodded. "Tyler, correct?"

"Yes ma'am."

Chapter Eighteen

"These lines have cracks in 'em, so I went ahead and shut the gas off at the valve. And you got termite damage," Harry Tyler continued, "but the termites are gone. Too wet for 'em I reckon at this corner of the house. Had a leak once, down the chimney."

Rafe could see the damage now that Mr. Tyler had torn out part of the crown molding. Termites and rot.

"I'll need to have the whole house inspected."

"This is the oldest part of this place, I suspect," Tyler said. "All wood beneath the plaster, but from what I can see, she seems solid. But I ain't no pestilence man, I'm a gasman, so I reckon you do need to get an expert in.

"That little wife of yo'rn wants lights put in on either side of your hearth, but that's gonna cost you. New lines are gonna have to be run."

Cost him what? He could afford it, but he knew that what his sweet beauty really wanted was to get on the other side of that panel. If she thought a passage was back there, she should be trying to find the door, not knock holes in the wall. "I'll talk to her about it, Mr. Tyler, and try to figure out what she wants to accomplish."

"I've done about all I can till those new lines come in. I'll be back in a few days."

Rafe nodded and looked toward the door of what was once the original cabin and what was now his and Delilah's dining room. "Let me go see what's keeping her with your voucher."

94

When he opened the door to the Riverview Room, his heart crashed to his pelvis and crushed what was left of his erection. Delilah didn't even look up, though he knew she'd heard him enter. Without a word, she placed James Dexter's report back into the drawer and closed it. She nudged the chair, rose as it swiveled, and walked to the French doors from where she stared down the sun-warmed hill, which stretched silently into the river.

He moved to the desk. From a side drawer, he pulled out the voucher book and wrote Harry Tyler his payment. The man saluted in thanks and started down the hall to the front of the house. Rafe quietly shut the door and turned.

He was angry, not at her for reading the papers, but at himself. He should have never left them there for her to find, but he'd been so wrapped up in the feel of her wet tongue and warm breast that the existence of the report hadn't crossed his mind since he'd tucked it away.

He stopped at the desk. "Delilah?"

"Do you intend to beat me for rummaging through your desk?"

It wasn't really his desk, though she'd known the papers were his. Still, he was fairly certain she'd found them by accident because he'd asked her to write the voucher. And if the situation had been reversed, he'd sure as hell have read the report.

"I think you know me better than that by now."

"Well, I wish you would, because it would make it so easy then for me to punch you back."

For all the emotional abuse she'd suffered, she'd obviously never been hit by a man. "I won't hit you, Delilah, not ever, but if it will make you feel better, I'll let you hit me."

She laid her forehead against the glass. "It's black and white. The report, I mean. So cold. Stories are about people. People who know pain and sorrow and love and happiness. Flesh and blood exists behind the base facts. At least with my histories, which you regard as silly, I try to make the people real. Look at them as humans, with feelings."

"I know," he said. And she did speculate on the emotions driving the Richards and the Merrifields, no matter how unlike the

95

people she imagined might be from those who had actually lived. Each person had possessed a human passion. Passion lost with death.

She inclined her head his direction, but didn't look at him.

"My mother was not an adulteress. She was a beautiful, caring woman who wasted her life on a madman. The child she carried, the one he murdered when he killed her, was his."

Rafe didn't say anything.

She straightened, wringing the hands she'd clasped in front of her.

"Dr. Barette sent her to Dr. Colburn. She was very sick. Papa was concerned, but felt Dr. Barette could care for her despite his advising them to seek a specialist. He was in his seventies. He'd been Mama's doctor for years. Papa felt he was safe.

"Papa was always like that, jealous, full of distrust, as if she looked for any opportunity to give herself to another man. He was offensive and disgusting in the things he said to her. Every year she spent with him, she grew more miserable. She couldn't go anywhere or do anything without him. By the time she died, she couldn't go anywhere with him either. If she talked to, even looked at another man, he would rant and rave when they got home."

"Why didn't she leave him?"

Delilah, her face stamped with disbelief, turned to him. "How? Where would she have gone? Her parents were dead, and Aunt Ophelia would not have wanted Uncle Joe to take her in. She didn't become a whore till she died, Rafe. Had she left him, if indeed he would have ever allowed it, she'd have been marked for having abandoned him, and she would not have been able to take me, you know that."

No, he really didn't know much about such laws in this state, but thinking about it now, he imagined Delilah was right. And on top of the legalities, there was the social code.

"I swore I would never marry. Never allow myself to be at the mercy of any man."

But she was now, and at the mercy of a stranger, no less.

"Your uncle forced—"

"I owed Uncle Joe."

How could she have owed him her freedom? And her uncle hadn't known a thing about what sort of person he was.

"I begged him to give me enough money to get started as a seamstress, but he said he couldn't do it, for my own good. What he really feared is that as long as I was free, Douglas would hold out hope I'd marry him and would never bring himself to marry Bernadette. I said I'd leave town, but he said Douglas would follow.

"The only hope I had left was you didn't want me either. And when you first looked at me in shock, and I knew you had believed you were getting Bernie, I thought I had a chance. I don't know what he offered you, but you didn't even hesitate to switch brides."

"I told you I was pleased."

She bridled. "I think you're horrid. What did he promise you that you would have willingly taken a girl you believed smitten with someone else, possibly carrying his child, and promise to spend the rest of your life with her?"

"I had my reasons. Love is not a prerequisite for marriage, Delilah."

"Love is not a prerequisite for anything."

He felt a bit nauseated, but since they were already in the middle of a hurtful confrontation, he asked, "Did your father say anything before he shot you?"

A strange sound emerged from her throat, and she covered her mouth, but couldn't quite stifle her cry of anguish. She turned from him, her gaze again on the muddy Mississippi glinting in the late-afternoon sunlight.

He stepped toward her, but she looked over her shoulder, and he stopped.

"He said, 'You are your mother's daughter, but I doubt you are mine, Delilah. I won't have that whore's child live bearing my name.' Then he turned the gun on me and fired. The impact knocked me against the wall. I fell to the floor, half-conscious.

There was another shot. I thought he was gonna keep shooting me like he had Mama. I didn't know he'd fired his last bullet."

She rolled her lips together. "They'd been married over two years when I was born. He was out of his mind, and had been, I know now, for years. Looking back, it seems to me he had everything a man could have wanted. My mother loved him once, I'm sure of that. In the end, she feared and despised him. To him, she was a piece of property, a treasure to keep only for himself. My grandmother hated my mother because my father wanted her, and I think she hated him, too, a little, for that same reason. She would have hated any woman he chose to love.

"I hate myself for hating him, he truly was so pathetic, but I do. . . ." She shut her eyes tight. "Everyone in Natchez thinks my mama caused what happened. After everything else he did to her, he left her with that final, eternal disgrace."

"I'm not sure people think that, Delilah."

For what seemed endless seconds, she was quiet. Then he watched her lift a hand and swipe a tear from her cheek.

"I think I'll plant roses next to the veranda over there. Mrs. Howell says this house used to be covered with roses, all the way around. Why, I bet they climbed that column there."

"Cherokee."

She turned to him.

"It was the Cherokee rose that grew. Blooms covered the house. Somebody told me that during summer, long before the Richards ever painted the wood and brick, the house looked white to the boats passing on the river."

She leaned her back against the French doors. "Why didn't you wait?" she said, her voice breaking. "I would have told you."

"I initiated the investigation the same afternoon your uncle proposed I marry you."

She blinked back tears. "James Dexter brought you the report the night that raccoon got in the house?"

"Yes."

"I would have thought it prudent to wait on his report before marrying me."

98

"That had been my intent. Then I met you, and we talked at the gazebo."

"Flattery, Mr. Stone?"

He took a hesitant step toward her, but again she stopped him with a look.

"It is the truth," he said.

Her laugh was without joy.

"Why would you think I'd hold the events regarding your parents against you?"

"What do you mean? You didn't know me at all. Do you think I wanted you to know you'd married the daughter of a man who'd disowned her, the daughter of a woman alleged to be responsible for the death of two men?"

"Your grandmother's words."

"And the daughter of a madman, Rafe. Those aren't my grandmother's words. Those are my words and Uncle Joe's and Aunt Ophelia's, and they are true."

Without a doubt, her Uncle Joe and Aunt Ophelia had taken Charlotte Wells' side in support of Delilah. Nevertheless, despite Richard Graff's cruel, final words to his daughter, she was his progeny, and she was no doubt both ashamed and fearful of his madness and people's belief that madness could be passed to the next generation. Well, madness was one thing, but as far as Rafe was concerned, Richard Graff's obsession had been fueled by his hateful and possessive mother, not by insanity.

Delilah's gaze moved around the room before falling on him. "Well, Mr. Stone, it appears you have won your office. Despite the fact you cheated."

"Delilah, honey, we aren't playing the game right now."

"Yes, we are," she snapped back. "Of course, I am at a disadvantage, being unable to hire my own private investigator to uncover the secrets of your past." She moved toward the door, keeping her distance from him. "Perhaps what I should do is use some of that household money you've turned over to me and do just that."

He grimaced, but he doubted she noticed. And he was glad

she was fighting back, using anger to hide her hurt. She sucked in a breath, but never stopped moving.

"That would be poetic justice, wouldn't it? Investigate you at your own expense." She yanked the door open, stepped into the hall, then looked back. "And I have no intention of cooking one darn thing for supper tonight."

She closed the door, too loudly, but didn't slam it nearly as hard as she could have. Rafe drew in a breath and looked over the rather meager furnishings in the room, its walls covered in worn, dark wallpaper and accented with gloomy green moldings. He needed to write Collander.

And as far as supper was concerned, he'd pretty much lost his appetite anyway.

Chapter Nineteen

Delilah yanked on a vine, a vicious, gangly thing. Roses had indeed grown here once, but those had been overtaken by blackberry, which, she was sure, had been green and vital and full of fruit as recently as this past June. Roses, she was equally confident, hadn't bloomed here in years.

The afternoon sun was warm, despite a chilly breeze, but its rays were fading, and she considered putting on the jacket she'd removed earlier.

She'd gotten so angry at Rafe, but what had she expected? Would his lack of interest have boded better for them? Of course not. In truth, she respected him more for bothering to find out what he could about her. She had questioned his soundness when he'd agreed to marry her sight unseen. Trouble was she couldn't apply that respect to herself. She didn't even know where the devil he hailed from, and the fact he remained evasive about his origins hadn't been lost on her.

A spiky tendril snagged her thin cotton dress. She reached for the shackle with a gloved hand and pulled it away. He'd come out about a half hour ago and told her he would help, but she'd told him to leave her alone. He said tomorrow he'd hire hands to clear the rough area, but she'd firmly told him the point was not to clear the area, but to take her mind off his treachery.

He'd told her that if she really wanted to work off her anger, the kitchen would be a good place to do it, and he'd finally retreated back through the French doors when she stopped responding to him completely.

A hornet buzzed around her head, and she swatted at it, then paused before wiping a wisp of hair from her brow. The river flowed lazy and peaceful this afternoon, and beyond, the setting sun silhouetted the darkening forest of Louisiana. She breathed in, and the combined scent of humus and river, spiced with the tang of evergreen, filled her nostrils.

She waved her arm at the persistent wasp and checked the ground. The things should be about gone this late in the year. She found a rotted log where she feared they nested, and prudently turned to an ancient azalea, interwoven with blackberry, which had, over the years, shrouded a marble statue of Saint Francis in leafy shadow. With her right hand, she pushed aside verdant foliage and stepped closer . . .

A flash of orange struck her boot, and she jumped back, then kicked out, but caught more of her skirt than the snake. Her heel caught on unkempt ground, and she sat hard on her bottom from where she pushed away with her feet, stirring up leaves and scrunching her back against the scraggly limbs of the azalea. She no longer saw the snake, but she could feel the blackberry pricking her back and shoulder. She hissed at the sharpness of the stickers, and as anxious now to escape the briars as she was the snake, Delilah looked over her shoulder.

Low drones drowned the beating of her heart, and her hornet-covered shoulder eclipsed the threat of the snake. A sharp sting pierced her temple, and she rolled away with a soft yelp, swatting at the insects. One stung her cheek, another her neck, and she struggled to her feet as she tried to brush the vicious beasts from her shoulder. She glanced quickly in the direction of the azalea. Another angry insect stung her head, and she spun toward the house.

He'd watched her off and on since first spying her outside, changed from her new dress and ready for work. She was clearing that spot where earlier she'd said she wanted to plant roses. He'd made a feeble attempt to make up, knowing even then it was too soon and she was not in the mood. He'd learned some things about women over the years. She was mad. Worse, she was hurt.

Wait until she uncovered the fact that Josephus Collander had thrown her in as an unwanted rider on the house. Rafe had feared she already knew when she began the long harangue on what she'd discovered in Natchez today, but remembered, when she failed to bring up his acquisition of River's Bend, that Samuel Winnisfree's compilation on the houses of Natchez had only come up to the 1880s. That bought him a short respite. Unless she was totally devastated by the fact a private investigator had divulged her darkest secrets, it would only take her a matter of time to uncover her uncle's wheeling and dealing at her expense.

Rafe pulled out his chair and sat. Damn, he was going to hire a cook. He might have to do without sex whenever he managed to make his beautiful wife angry, but he shouldn't have to starve on top of it. He glanced at her once more, bent now and searching beneath a bush.

He wanted to read through Dexter's report again, but he sure didn't want her to catch him doing . . .

Céu Doce! He surged up, almost toppling the swivel chair, and grasped the handle of the glazed door, which he slammed against the inner wall. Cold bit his cheeks and hurt his nostrils. He leapt from the porch and almost collided with Delilah, who was now yelling his name. He tried to pull her to his right, away from the apparent source of the hornets, but she tugged him toward the house crying — and she really was crying now — something about a rattlesnake pilot.

Reversing direction, he slapped at the handful of insects still on her shoulder. "Did it bite you?"

"No," she whined.

"They're almost gone, come on." Rafe propelled her up the stairs and onto the veranda from where he pulled her into the Riverview Room. He reached for the door, but was distracted by Simon Douglas hollering at him from the yard. Simon's fifteen-year-old son, Bo, deviated from his father's path and picked up Delilah's hoe. Rafe waited, door open.

"I done seen that copperhead, Mr. Stone. Was she bit?"

"She says not. Got in a hornets' nest though."

"Yessuh, I done seen that, too. Me and Bo was comin' over to he'p her with the clearin'. Could I look at her?"

"Do you know anything about their stings?"

"Not so much me," Simon said, removing his hat and stepping through the French doors. He dipped his head politely at Delilah, who nodded back with a tear-stained face.

She was breathing hard and holding that arm close to her body.

"Let me see them stings, Miss Delilah. We might'n need to put somethin' on 'em."

Rafe stomped on a lingering hornet Delilah knocked to the floor. "Sit down," he said, guiding her into the swivel chair. She was trembling terribly and awkward, clumsy even, on her feet. But though her breath was ragged, her tears had stopped.

Simon handed Rafe his knife. "You needs to cut that cloth away."

Delilah was quiet, pliant.

"Are you breathing all right, sweetheart?"

Her gaze found his, and she nodded, but her breath hitched.

"Do you feel any swelling in your throat?"

She shook her head as he unbuttoned the top two buttons of her cotton dress, then cut through the dress and chemise exposing the red, welting skin of her neck and right shoulder. In a number of the welts, tiny specks of blood were visible.

"Oh, shoot, they done got her good." Simon bent forward and said softly, "Got her in the head, too."

"And the hand," Rafe said and motioned to a welt on her finger, which clutched her injured arm.

She grimaced, and he saw.

"What's wrong?" he asked. He'd once seen a man die within twenty minutes of a single wasp sting.

"The pain comes in waves."

"It do that, Mr. Stone. Come in waves like she say when a body's had this many stings."

Rafe touched her shoulder. "You're sure your throat is all right?"

104

Again she nodded. "I've been stung before."

"Ain't never good to have this much poison in your body, Miss Delilah. My mama, she makes a poultice of buttermilk and snuff spit to help draw it out."

Simon stood. Outside, Bo Douglas tapped on a pane in the glazed door, and Simon opened it. Rafe took Simon's place beside Delilah.

"Couldn't find that old copperhead, Daddy. Miss Delilah, she done scared it off, I 'magine."

"Want you to run on over to your grandma's, boy. Tell her you needs that bee-sting poultice."

The young man glanced at Delilah, then Rafe. "She bad?"

Simon turned to Delilah, carefully moving the shorn fabric. "She be swellin' up pretty good. Lots of poison in this arm. You run on to your granny's now and come straight back."

"Yessuh."

"How far is she, Simon?" Rafe said, rising.

"She be close. Never been far from River's Bend. Old massa, he made sho' all us he freed had a place to live close by. Just a handful of families left by then. We still worked here for pay and trade. Bo, he won't be mor'n quarter hour, half at most."

Damn, a lot of swelling could happen in that much time. Rafe turned on his heel. "I'm going to get her a cold cloth while we wait."

Chapter Twenty

"She gonna be sore a while, but take the poultice off in a bit. Them welts'll itch when they start healin'. Keep witch hazel on 'em, missy, that'll he'p some."

Annie Douglas twisted from where she sat beside Delilah on the bed. "She be all right," the old woman said to Rafe. "If'n she ain't dead now, ain't gonna be. Not from them hornets, anyways."

Rafe knew that now, but nodded his thanks to the Negress. She was eighty if she were a day, and she'd come herself, her grandson Bo driving them in her rickety buckboard. Rafe suspected what had drawn her here was more than a desire to help River's Bend's new mistress. Annie Douglas wanted to see the inside of this house again, to see the new owners. A lot of her history was tied up in this place. Rafe knew the Richards had kept their slave families together, generations of them raised here side by side with their white masters until the latter finally freed them. Even then some had stayed.

"Thank you, Miss Annie. I'm feeling better now."

The old woman, her gray hair covered by an orange kerchief, pushed herself up with thin arms and stood. She was stooped and frail, but her brown eyes were bright and her mind appeared as sharp as those yellow jackets' stings.

"You ain't had no suppa, have you, son?" she said, starting for the door. Rafe thought she might be talking to Simon, until she looked at him.

"I have not."

"Yo' wife might eat broth. Doubt she be wantin' much else."

He could provide that from a jar.

"You needin' a cook?"

"You lookin' for a job?"

She cackled. "Not anymore, suh, not anymore. But I got a granddaughter is a fine cook."

"When can she start?"

On the bed, Delilah moved. She wanted his attention. Well, she wasn't going to get it. If she'd been in the kitchen where she belonged, fixing him something to eat, instead of in the yard doing a hand's work, she wouldn't be in the situation she was right now.

"How 'bout mawnin'?" Miss Annie said.

"That means I'll have to eat soup again tonight."

The old crone laughed at that, too.

"Belle and her mama Lucianne fixin' fried chicken tonight, Mr. Stone," Simon said. "We'll send you a basket."

"Oh, Lawd," Miss Annie said, and Rafe turned her way. She had stopped at the door and now held to the frame while she looked him over. "Should've seen yo' face just now when he said 'fried chicken.' Some things they never change. Fried chicken, black-eyed peas, and collard greens—"

"With hot pepper sauce," he finished.

"And the softness in a man's eyes when he looks at the woman he loves."

Rafe followed Miss Annie's gaze to Delilah who was watching the black woman.

"Some men's eyes, they talk," the Negress said to him.

"So I've been told."

"One way or other, all things keep goin' on and on. Ain't nothin' can stop it." The woman smiled. "Welcome to River's Bend, Mr. Stone." She bowed her head and disappeared through the door.

"I'll send Belle over d'rectly with that basket," Simon said. "She be my daughter Mama's talkin' 'bout workin' for you, if'n you serious about hirin' a cook."

"I'm serious." Rafe looked at Delilah. "My wife will do the hiring though."

"Yessuh, I hear that." Simon nodded to Delilah and left.

"Miss Annie seemed quite taken with you," Delilah said.

He snorted and sat beside her on the bed. "Let's hire the cook."

"You might want to taste her chicken first."

"I'm so hungry anything would taste good."

Delilah looked down and traced the stitches in the patchwork quilt on her bed. "I'm sorry I was so upset with you earlier. You bought me all those new clothes, and I wouldn't even fix you supper."

Hurt, then sorry for the fight. Well, that was okay as long as she kept up the struggle. He smiled. "You had a right to be angry, but I still think it is within my rights to learn all I can about you."

"There are better ways to learn them than by hiring a detective, Rafe. I feel spied on, violated."

"I'm sorry, and you're right, there are better ways." He dipped his head and gave her a kiss. "Can we hire the cook? I don't want you cooking anyway. I want you managing the house."

Managing the house.

"I know it's not the same as having your own dressmaking business, but it is a big job." He leaned away. "I can pay you in new dresses."

She settled into her pillows. "Is a housekeeper all you're looking for, Mr. Stone?"

"I believe we already have a marriage contract specifying your other obligations, *Mrs.* Stone."

"Touché . . . however, you have not acted on any of those entitlements."

"I asked you to cook me supper."

She rolled her eyes. "Oh, really, Rafe, do go away."

He laughed and rose. "I'll send . . . what was her name . . . ?"

"Belle."

"Belle up when she gets here."

His mouth covered hers, and he forced her back into the pillows. Her body warmed right down to her toes, but before she had a chance to respond properly, he'd pulled away. "And I intend to take full advantage of those entitlements, sweetheart, but the only way I can be sure I get my money's worth is to wait until you're ready."

"You're the one with doubts."

"What I lack in the way of trust," he said, "you might very well make up for in lack of judgment."

"So you're suggesting we continue our charade until I uncover who you really are and what you're doing here?"

"Hardly." He glanced at her injured shoulder and wrinkled his nose. "The only thing I'm waiting for is you to get that snuff spit off your body so I can continue 'wooing' you. I don't know whether to be happy or unhappy about that hornet nest you got into."

"I beg your pardon?"

"It might have been days before you spoke to me again."

She'd stayed mad at him for less than two hours. "Or cooked for you again."

"Cooked for me again? You mean cook for me ever. I've done all the cooking up to this point."

"Soup and beans. One can hardly call that cooking."

"And I also bought you meals at the finest restaurants in New Orleans and Natchez."

She pushed up. "Well, sir, you have me at a disadvantage. I do not know what I brought you in this marriage, but obviously it was something other than my mere self. So perhaps all things are equal after all." She flounced back onto the pillows as a look of honest contrition moved over his face.

"God, Delilah, I truly am ashamed."

Her heart skipped a beat. "For what?"

"For my hopes regarding you, darlin'."

She breathed in. "And those are?"

"I'm hoping you won't feel like eating, and I'll get all the chicken for myself. I'm going downstairs now and wait for my new cook to get here."

Chapter Twenty-one

"What is it?" Delilah asked.

Rafe pushed the front door shut and turned. "Came by ship on your uncle's line." He walked over to where she was examining the crate near the foot of the stairs.

She was lovely this morning, dressed in a satin—what had the saleswoman called it?—oh yes, dressing sacque. He'd talked her into the expensive one, trimmed in lace. It was a modest piece of clothing yet decidedly feminine at the same time. He'd had no idea the effect modest femininity would have on him.

"A wedding present, perhaps?" she said. He didn't miss her stealthy sarcasm, and he smiled when she looked at him.

"I don't think so." He handed her the letter that the Collander minion had delivered to him. "It's for you."

She yawned, then stretched when she reached for the missive.

"You're feeling all right this morning?"

She nodded, opening the envelope. "My shoulder is sore and hurts to the touch."

"Swollen?"

"Not much. I think the poultice helped."

Her face was all right, too. Well, maybe that cheek was a tiny bit puffy, but all that remained of the sting on her temple was a small red bump. Her hair was up, held in place by faux-pearl encrusted combs. She unfolded the letter, and as she read, she sank to the third step. After a moment, she raised the fingers of her free hand to her lips, her concentration riveted on Josephus Collander's written word. When he saw her blink in quick succession, he turned away, feigning interest in the crate.

I retrieved it from the auction block. She had no right to put it there. I remember when Abigail bought it for Charlotte on her tenth birthday. Charlie was so proud of it, and Papa built several pieces of furniture for it. He was quite fond of your mother, you know, him never having had a daughter of his own. And I know for a fact, because Charlie told me so, that you and she often worked on it together.

You should have it, I thought, so I brought it to Mississippi City with me to make sure your grandmother never got her hands on it again.

Ophelia and I stuffed it away in the attic and quite honestly, I had forgotten it was there when you arrived in August.

I was in the attic with a roofer (we have a leak) a fortnight ago, and I saw it and determined I should get it to you. I am certain you have more room for it in that enormous house of Mr. Stone's than we have here.

Enjoy the precious memories, my dear. Your mother would have wanted you to, as she did in memory of her mother. Perhaps one day, Mr. Stone will bless you with a little girl of your own, and you will find it in your heart to forgive me your rushed nuptials and unfamiliar groom.

With much love,
Uncle Joe

Delilah thought at that moment the pressure behind her stinging eyes would cause her head to explode. Rapidly she blinked back the tears and rose on shaking knees. Rafe turned to her, and she met his eyes. Immediately she dropped the hand she'd held over her mouth, but waited a moment to speak.

"It's . . ." She averted her eyes from his questioning gaze, and Rafe, bless him, didn't push her.

"It's my mother's dollhouse," she forced out, then closed her eyes tight when he rubbed her back.

"I'll move it to your room as soon as Simon and Bo get here. Is that where you want it?"

She nodded quickly. "Yes. Thank you."

"You ain't said nothin', but I'm thinkin' you might wanna add lights to either side of this fireplace, too. Might as well do it if we're gonna run lines down below."

Delilah pursed her lips and walked over to where she'd discovered Mr. Tyler studying her fireplace wall. He pointed above and to the right of the heavy mantle. "We could put one globe here and run the line thisaway to the other side. Probably have to go right behind the fireplace mantle."

Harry Tyler turned on his heel and looked at her. He was a wiry man of medium height, gray around the temple with an abundance of silver in his several days' growth of beard.

"They make some pretty etched-glass mantles for these things. Collier's can order them out of Chicago. Will take a little time to get them, but shoot"—he shrugged with a smile—"it's my understanding you and Mr. Stone are planning on staying awhile."

She nodded, folding her arms under her breasts and moving to the side of the fireplace. "Does Mr. Collier have samples of those mantles?"

Tyler grinned. "He does."

"And do you get a percentage of what he sells?"

"No, ma'am. Hopefully, I get the job, though. Not too many around here who deal with gas short of going direct to Natchez Gas, and they charge you an arm and a leg."

Given what she knew of Rafe's expenditures, Delilah figured he could afford Harry Tyler, who had come highly recommended by Mr. Grapple. He was, in fact, an employee of Natchez Gas Works, but worked the myriad of private coal gas plants on the side.

"I would like wall sconces in this room, Mr. Tyler, and in the room next to mine and in the dining room below, but I'm afraid Mr. Stone has left me strict instructions not to mount them on the fireplace walls."

"Oh." He scratched his neck. "Where would you like 'em, then?" he said, looking around the room.

She turned with him. Where indeed? For decorative effect and beauty, the fireplace wall was the only sensible location. Her eyes returned to the mantle.

"Let me talk to him again. I don't know why he's against putting them on this wall."

But in truth, she did. Rafe was thinking the only reason she wanted to add the gas lines was to gain her the opportunity to get behind the wall. He was right about her wanting to get behind the wall, but wrong about it being her only reason, and she also knew Mr. Tyler wouldn't knock out the wall to run the lines.

". . . easiest here," he was telling her, and he knocked on the wall to the right of the mantle. "See, this wall is hollow."

"Is it?" She kept her voice steady, but her heartbeat had quickened.

"Yes, ma'am. Both sides. We could drill here and here." He pointed to the opposite side of the fireplace. "Then run the line behind this mantle."

He slid the block of wood away from the chimney.

"It moves?"

"Yes, ma'am. All these mantles just lay on their braces. Big and heavy as the things are, they ain't gonna move without some effort, and they're so thick, a body can't find a nail long enough to hold 'em without messing up the surface."

The mantle was almost the size of a railroad tie. Well, perhaps a small tie, but the thing was bulky, and doubtless, heavy as well.

Mr. Tyler studied the exposed brick a moment, then pointed with a knotty finger. "I could run a quarter-inch galvanized line along the brick here, then cut a dado along the back of the mantle, so it would sit flush with the brick. You'd never even know the gas line was there."

"You did work for the Merrifields, didn't you?" she asked, following Mr. Tyler into Rafe's bedroom.

He studied the wall behind her fireplace. "Yes ma'am, I did. The first mister and missus and the second.

"See here," he said, and he again pulled out the mantle. "Now in the newer parts of the house, or the parts renovated by the Merrifields"—he forced the piece of wood into place and waved her toward the hallway—"the mantle and molding of the entire fireplace are one big finished piece."

He pushed open the door at the west end of the hall, which Delilah knew had been the Merrifields' master bedroom. The room overlooked the river and was bright with afternoon sun, and Delilah rued the fact the Merrifields were murdered here. It really was the finest of the bedrooms.

"You see," he said, running his gnarled hands along the fluted sides of the fireplace. For a moment, he allowed them to linger on the flat, white surface of the mantle. "This mantle is made of one by six. To move it, you'd have to move the entire piece, which is sitting against a rough, brick-lined hole.

"The Merrifields put this piece in?"

Tyler shook his head. "I reckon not. My guess is all this construction was done before the War. You can tell as these folks got richer, their tastes got richer, too."

"You seem to know a lot about this house."

He started at that, then said, "I run all the gas lines when Merrifield moved in. A person payin' attention can see which phase of construction belongs with what."

All major construction she was aware of had indeed occurred before the War. "What did the Merrifields do?" she asked.

"Other than install gas?"

"Yes."

"Mr. Merrifield and his first wife added that second bath down the hall for their two boys, running water and all. Shoot, two baths when one is a luxury tells me he had money to burn. They also turned what was, way back then, the children's dining room into a kitchen.

114

"Anyways, Merrifield was getting ready to put in a gas stove when he and his second wife was murdered." Tyler nodded at her. "You need to be thinkin' about a gas stove."

Belle cooked, and she was good at it, too. Still, making a constant chore easier for the young woman was worth considering.

"Do you have any theories about who killed the Merrifields?"

He wasn't looking at her, but at the gas pilot beside the fireplace. "There's them that say old Markham Merrifield murdered his first wife for that young thing he brought into this house without grieving six months. Always are some likes to tell tales."

"Do you know the official cause of her death?"

"Pneumonia." He looked at her then and shrugged. "Could as well've been a pillow over 'er head for all I know."

A subtle chill moved over Delilah. "What was the second Mrs. Merrifield like?"

"She was a ripe young strawberry, Mrs. Stone, to put it delicately. Eighteen, but she knew she was the topping on his dessert. Markham, he was pushing fifty and rich as sin itself. Just twixt you and me, she was sin itself. He brought that gal into this house with them two boys having just lost their mama. With Miss Cecilia here, and I guarantee you she wasn't after nothin' but the money, those boys stood to lose their inheritance as well."

Delilah moved closer to the window and looked out on the Mississippi, bluish-gray in the autumn sun. Across the river, red and orange and gold of deciduous trees splashed against the evergreen blanket covering Louisiana's flood plain. "Where did she come from, Mr. Tyler?"

"Natchez. Her grandpa was a banker, took hefty losses with the War. Her mama's daddy was a merchant, and Cecilia's daddy inherited the store when the old man died. They was all prominent, but fell way short of aristocracy, if you get my meaning. Course, so did Merrifield. First wife inherited this place through Lorelei Richard's husband. Merrifield weren't nothin' but an opportunist with the heart of a carpetbagger. Folks from this house were legend in these parts, but it's not like he stole the place from its rightful owners. That Ward gal, Frank Richard's

115

granddaughter, up and disappeared after her husband stole the gold shipment and killed off his men."

"What do you think happened to her?"

"Now, I reckon I don't know about her. I moved here myself after the War, but most say she killed herself after her man murdered his troop and abandoned her."

Delilah looked out to the river. "I wonder what happened to that gold?"

He laughed at that. "Lots of folks would like to know that, including the Federals, but I reckon it's long spent."

"Of the three missing men, Seth Abernathy and Micah Ziegler were members of the army detail. Both were regulars. Ziegler's remains washed up weeks later near St. Francisville. Abernathy's body was never found, nor was Morgan Ward's." James Dexter slid the open leather pouch and papers across the table to Rafe.

So, odds were Abernathy was Mizer, if any of them. Rafe glanced at Jim's report, but didn't pick it up. Despite his and Jim's seats near a west-facing window, the quiet tavern on the north end of Silver Street was dark. It was noon, and the sun was straight up. Rafe rubbed his chin. "You saw the local records?"

Dexter shook his head. "Researched the army's investigative reports. I can confirm those local records if you like."

Rafe nodded, and James Dexter leaned forward and sipped his beer, which was lukewarm, Rafe knew.

"Funny thing," Dexter said. "When I talked to Ziegler's wife, she said the effects sent home included a pocketknife and a gold watch with the initials S.A. on its case. She remembers the initials because she immediately thought of 'shit ass' in relation to her dearly departed."

"Didn't think much of him, did she?"

"From what I saw of her, I'm thinking the affection, or lack thereof, was mutual. Probably the reason he joined the army."

"Did you see the watch?"

"I did ask. She sold it right after she received it."

Rafe narrowed his eyes.

"She says it wasn't his and neither was that pearl inlay pocket knife, which she also sold. Says he wasn't above coming by such things using 'unethical' means."

"And why did the United States Army have a man of doubtful character escorting one hundred thousand dollars in gold?"

"He could have taken those items off a dead Confederate, for all we know. But no matter, then Private Micah Henry Ziegler, whether through dumb luck or natural predilection for duty, was a war hero. He was cited for briefly rallying a failing Union flank at Sharpsburg in '62, turning a rout into a tactical retreat, saving his unit as well as his unit commander. In so doing he probably averted the loss of a general officer. He was gravely wounded for his efforts, and as a result of his 'selfless devotion,' he requested and was awarded an assignment to the Montana territory. He was with the gold shipment from the time it left Virginia City."

Rafe grunted. A large, concentrated shipment consigned to the U.S. Treasury, then shipped to the Department of the South in New Orleans in anticipation of the presentation of U.S. bonds from South American creditors—not to mention compensation to countries that suffered periodic abuse from U.S. Navy ships pursuing Confederate blockade runners into sympathetic South American ports.

"Was there anything on his body that did identify him?"

"Two letters from his mother and furlough papers to begin the twentieth of April, after the detail arrived in New Orleans."

"His widow was left destitute when he died?"

"I think they were probably destitute before he died. She's an old woman now. Owns a boarding house on the seedy side of Cincinnati, but I think more than boarding goes on in that place and has for a long time. I don't believe she misses Mr. Ziegler."

He guessed that was good to know. "How about the others?"

"The others?"

"Widows? Orphans?"

"You mean, are they struggling, or in high cotton?"

James was putting two and two together and his figures were adding up to five. Rafe breathed in. "Either."

117

"Of the seven Federals killed, only two left widows. Another had been married, but his wife died the year before, in childbirth. The other widow belonged to George Frothby. She died three years ago at the age of sixty-five. He has two grown sons, both farmers in Pennsylvania. Comfortable, not wealthy."

Rafe's eyes met Dexter's, and Dexter's gaze held his. He could assume anything he wanted. Rafe liked James Dexter, but the man was an employee, not a friend.

"You don't want me to talk to the Confederate widows?"

"Or orphans."

"A hundred thousand dollars in processed gold disappeared off that ship."

Rafe took a sip of beer and glanced out the window at the river glinting in the sun. They'd spoken on this subject as much as they should for now.

"There's been searches made for thirty years by men who know more than you and me."

He turned back with Dexter's words, and Dexter shrugged. "Than me, at least."

Rafe reached into his pocket and removed the folded note paper he'd annotated days ago in New Orleans. "Here, see what you can find on this fellow. I found his name in an old newspaper article in New Orleans while I was researching the heist."

James squinted. "Lieutenant John Thomas Thompson."

"He and a civilian postmaster were arrested on the Mississippi at the mouth of St. Catherine Creek, same night as the *Gilded Rose* raid. They'd apparently requisitioned the mail packet and were awaiting the arrival of stolen cotton."

"St. Catherine Creek flows out of Butler Lake."

Rafe smiled. "The death site of Charles Slade, I know. Did you get a chance to review the Merrifield murders?"

"Not yet."

"I'm interested in what authorities speculated happened to the two boys."

Chapter Twenty-two

Delilah lay so rigid her muscles ached. For now, quiet prevailed.

Beneath the covers, she carefully rolled over, shivering when her skin touched the cold sheets not already warmed by her body. Her eyes were open and had been since muffled sobs woke her minutes ago. Now facing the wall separating her from Rafe, she curled into a fetal ball and stared into the darkness shrouding the fireplace.

Tense, she waited. A similar, short-lived reprieve had occurred moments earlier. She licked her bottom lip, then raised her arm to . . .

Delilah's heartbeat quickened as the mournful weeping resumed. With a whimper, she threw back the covers, sat up, and drew her legs over the edge of the mattress. Her feet dangled above the floor while she groped the foot of her bed for her dressing sacque. She found it, its satin fabric cold against her fingertips, then she slid off the bed and gasped when her bare feet hit the freezing floor. After thrusting her arms into the gown's sleeves, she pulled the bodice around her and tightened the belt so fast she all but cut herself in two.

More secure now, she fumbled for the matches beside her bed and lit the coal oil lamp.

The welcome light radiated into her room, warming it, if only its atmosphere. From the corner of her eye, a shadow danced on the wall beside her, and she spun around, startled. Her shadow.

Delilah drew a deep breath and stepped toward the fireplace, from where, she was certain, the crying emanated. She stopped where the wall turned from the chimney proper and continued at a ninety degree angle to the back wall. The corner was dark, despite the lamp, and she frowned as she reached out to touch the wall. It fell backward, which caused Delilah to careen forward before catching herself on an ancient two by four. Heart in her throat, she whirled from the black chasm (and from whatever lurked within) and scrambled toward the room where Rafe slept.

His door was ajar; she'd kept it that way since the night of the coon, and he had not protested. Heart and head pounding, she pushed his door wide, and the light from her room cast an eerie glow over his domain.

The masculine scent of his soap filled her nostrils, the soft intake of his breath, her ears. Her loins tightened, and Rafe Stone eclipsed the haunting next door.

"Rafe?"

His name, her lips, and the scent of gardenia seeped into his sleep-soaked consciousness. He groaned and rolled toward her voice. Snuggling deeper into the pillow, he reached for her beside him to pull her close and cuddle her within the warm cocoon of quilts. That should shut her up. Hopefully he wouldn't even have to open his eyes.

"Rafe?" she whispered, shaking him at the shoulders. Being a damn pain in the . . .

He opened his eyes, then surged upward, the covers falling away as Delilah jumped back. Without thought he reached for her, grounding himself in the reality of her warm body beneath her silky bed clothes.

With his tug, her palms flattened against his bare chest, and his penis swelled.

"Are you awake?" she whispered against his lips.

Hell, yes, he was awake. He blinked, adjusting his eyes to see her, a softly muted beauty in the dim light, and from the look on that lovely face, she wasn't playing a game.

"What's wrong?"

"Shh! Listen. Can you hear it?"

120

He cocked his head, then wrinkled his brow. "I can hear my damn heart pounding in my chest. What am I listening for?" Truth was she'd about scared the shit out of him.

"Come on," she said, wriggling against his loose hold.

Immediately he let her go. "Where," he asked when she took his hand, "are we going?"

"The wall is open. I hear someone crying."

He locked his jaw to stifle another curse. The wall was open?

Even if he'd been unable to see the beautiful golden disarray of hair, the scent of her skin would have wreaked havoc on his senses, which irritated him to no end. Darn it. He wouldn't be having this problem if he had her sleeping where she belonged.

"Delilah, I need to find my pants," he said and reached for the covers with his free hand.

She let his one hand go and caught the other. "You are nude?"

He looked her in the eye. "Asked the lady who invaded the gentleman's chamber in the middle of the night. Why she would ask, the gentleman wondered, because it shouldn't matter."

She straightened and huffed. "Are you?"

"If you'd come into my bedroom in July you'd have found me in the buff, but tonight I've got on woolen drawers."

"That's fine. I've my dressing sacque—"

"Delilah," he got out, "it's colder than a Republican's heart in here, and for all I know, you're leading me to my doom. I refuse to be found dead in my drawers."

"Oh, for Saint Peter's sake, Rafe, where are they?"

She followed his nod to the wing chair, over the back of which he'd draped his pants. She grabbed them and returned to the bed, thrusting the trousers beneath his nose. "Please hurry."

Tossing them to the foot of the bed, he rose, then sucked in a breath. "Darn it, Delilah, why haven't we bought rugs?"

Her response was a much-put-upon sigh. Well, if the panel was open, the little witch had found the latch. He reached for the pants with one hand, the tie to his drawers with the other, and at the same time looked up to find her watching him. He grinned despite his mood.

121

"I'm not putting these pants over my underwear, sweetness. Do you intend to watch me disrobe?"

She rolled her eyes heavenward and turned her back.

"I was hoping you'd watch," he said, dropping his drawers.

"And what perverse pleasure would you gain from that?" she asked over her shoulder. "Please hurry up."

"Done."

"Are you sure?"

"I am." He stepped around her and pulled a long-sleeved wool shirt from his dresser drawer. "I'm putting on shoes, too."

"Oh, please, Rafe, it's going to get away."

It was going to get away? Well, he'd hurry, but he absolutely refused to believe anyone, or thing, was going to get away.

"Were you crying in your sleep maybe?"

"Do I look as though I've been crying?" She leaned to where he sat on the bed pulling on socks.

He glanced at her briefly before putting on a shoe. "I can't see you well enough."

"Well, I haven't been, and why would I be? I am so deliriously happy living here with you."

"I'm glad to hear it." He moved in back of her, and she turned, watching as he lifted the shoulder holster, replete with pistol, from where he'd draped it over the same chair that had held his pants. When her eyes narrowed on the weapon, he said, "Don't think it will be much defense against a ghost, but then, I don't believe in such."

"I didn't know you—"

"I wear it all the time."

"But why?"

He shrugged. "You never know what you might run across in a strange land."

"Or house," she said, watching him secure the gun to his side.

"Or house," he agreed, offering her his hand. She took it. His mood was improving by the second. If he were smart, he'd forget the damn panel, toss her onto the bed, and make them both deliriously happy. He closed his fingers over hers. "Let's go."

-ᴥ-

"*I*t was open."

He could hear the tears in her voice, but his concern for her frustration was compounded by frustration of his own. If she'd opened the panel earlier, she should be able to find the latch instead of stumbling around, helplessly studying each brick in the fireplace and the moldings on the adjacent wall. Finally, she held up the lamp and kicked the wall.

"You don't believe me?"

He did consider the possibility she'd dreamed the open panel and the crying, but he also had to weigh the consequences of her finding the latch on her own and exploring the innards of this old house alone. That wouldn't do. He rose from where he pretended to study the floor next to the panel she said she found open. Her glistening eyes watched as he moved close to her, not bothering to get out of his way. It occurred to him that she expected him to kiss her—for comfort perhaps, if for no other reason. Well, he wouldn't mind kissing her, but that was not his intent.

"Hold the lamp close to the mantle."

Eyes on him, she did as he said.

"Watch carefully now." He pulled out the heavy mantle and removed a brick, then glanced down when he felt her beside him. "Look inside," he said, and when she did, he reached into the rebate and pulled the hidden latch. He winked at her, then stepped around the corner of the fireplace and gently pushed. The wooden panel gave. He heard Delilah's breath catch, and she skirted around him to peer into the dark recess beyond. Cold air, drenched with the musty scent of old timber, washed over him, and Delilah turned with eyes full of question.

He shrugged. "You were right, there is a passage beside the chimney."

"How did you know about it?"

"I started searching for it after you put forth the idea it might be there."

"And you found it?"

"Obviously. I'm an architect, remember?"

123

"You are not. I am beginning to think you are a treasure hunter. And why didn't you tell me you'd found it?"

"To tell you the truth, sweetheart, I didn't want you to know about it."

"You didn't want to acknowledge I was right." She pushed the panel wide. A rough floor lay at their feet; all else remained dark.

"It's a landing for a stairwell, and my not telling you had nothing to do with eating crow."

"Have you been in here?" she asked, stepping forward, but hesitating to test the void. He didn't blame her; it was very dark, and her bedroom, lit by the single lamp she still held, was dim.

"I have."

"Where does it go?"

"The stairs go up to the attic, again discreetly hidden by a wall surrounding the chimney. And they go down, eventually to a basement beneath the house."

Her slippered foot touched the unfinished flooring, and her face turned to his. Her breasts rose and fell at an accelerated rate, and he wished like hell that was because of her interest in him and not this dark, dreary hole.

"Let's explore it," she said, her breath hitching.

"Now?"

"I know it's dark, but we can't wait. What about the crying I heard?"

"Are you having trouble breathing?"

"Of course, I am. I'm excited. Now, please, let's go."

Under the circumstances, he should check not only this secret stairwell but the entire house. He reached inside the landing and took a lantern from a hook. Its light when he lit it cast an eerie glow over her beautiful face, and he knew she was witnessing a similar effect on his. "I know what lies ahead, my delicate beauty. You do not. Are you sure you want to come with me?"

She narrowed her eyes. "I'd like to know how you really knew about the panel and the lantern hanging inside the wall."

"I told you. I found the release for the panel, and I found the lantern hanging right where you saw me get it just now."

"Did it have oil?"

"Dry."

"I wonder how long it had been hanging there?"

At least fifteen years, he reckoned. "It's wet, nasty, and cold beneath the house, Delilah."

She wrapped her hand around his bicep and turned him toward the opening. "I don't care."

"All right, bring the lamp, too."

*S*he watched him turn back, the lantern he held hanging from his fingertips. He'd ventured a good distance into the tunnel, and she'd kept her eyes fixed on the glow of his lamp. "Nothing down here," he called and started her way. Goodness, what would she do if something jumped out and grabbed him?

"You went to the end?" she asked when he got closer.

"I went far enough to see the end. The tunnel's closed about sixty paces down. I went to the end the other day. I wanted to confirm there was no longer a way to get in the house from outside this tunnel."

She stepped aside when he reached the opening, glad he was again within reach. He hadn't wanted her to go with him, telling her she'd ruin her slippers. From what little she had seen of the man-made tunnel, it was a most uninviting place. The dirt base was sinking and muddy, and roots from the plants growing in the clean air above hung in mats of hairy tendrils for as deep as she could see into the darkness. The dank smell of earth clung to the tunnel, and the combined glow of their lamp and lantern had revealed rivulets of shimmering water hugging its muddy sides. In places he had to bend at the knees and scoot forward.

"There has to be a way." She turned her back on the cavern and studied the faded white-wash covering the brick walls beneath the original cabin.

"Delilah, are you certain you heard crying?"

During their descent, on what was for all intents and purposes a sharply angled ladder, Rafe had shown her the simple mechanism for opening the first and second floor panels from inside the passage. The one for accessing the attic worked the same way, but they'd gone down, not up, and she hadn't seen it. That particular entry was irrelevant anyway, he'd told her, since no one would enter the house from the roof, three stories off the ground.

"And I imagined the open panel, too?"

He moved into the room where he could stand full height, if just barely. The floor was brick, set in sand, but it was damp. The square footage was the same as that of the original cabin, now their dining room, but this space looked smaller, a combination of the low ceiling and the simple fact that their lamps left the four corners in darkness. He stomped to get the mud off his feet.

"I'm still not sure you didn't hoodwink me into showing you the latch."

"And why would I have done that, husband, never suspecting for a moment you believed there was a secret passage." She found his eyes. "And I'm still not sure you didn't know about the hidden stairwell all along. What are you really, Rafe Stone? A thief or an adventurer?"

"A killer, lawman, soldier of fortune. An avenging angel, perhaps?"

"Maybe all," she said softly.

"And maybe none."

He was toying with her again. He wasn't going to answer her question. Feigning interest in the subterranean room, she turned and stepped into one of its dark corners and tentatively touched a place where the two walls came together.

"If the tunnel is blocked, then there is another way into the stairwell."

"There are three other ways, Delilah. I told you."

"But to use one of those ways, the intruder would have to enter the house another way."

"A door, a window, the chimney itself. Christmas is coming."

"You're comfortable," she said, continuing to run her hands along the rough brick, "with something entering our home during the night, ensconcing itself in that secret stairwell, and opening the panel into my bedroom?"

⇒·⇐

*N*o, he certainly was not. In fact, the open panel, assuming Delilah hadn't opened it, and it was looking pretty certain she hadn't, disturbed him greatly.

"It could have been Lorelei."

He drew in a steadying breath. "This house is not haunted."

"And you're a medium on top of all your other abilities?"

He held the lantern up and started checking the wall adjacent to the corner where she'd begun, moving opposite her.

"In this case I am."

He heard her soft snort. "Mrs. Merrifield, perhaps?"

"Why would you think her?"

"Mr. Tyler says some believe her husband killed her so he could wed Cecilia."

Rafe stopped in his tracks. "I thought she died of pneumonia? Why couldn't it be Cecilia? We know somebody murdered her."

"Or Markham Merrifield for that matter."

"Sorry, but I still don't believe in ghosts."

"I'm sure that must rule them out."

Three minutes later they met on the other side of the room. "You do know these walls are built against packed earth?"

"I figured," she said and scanned the floor. "There are footprints all over."

"Ours, sweetheart. Here, see along the walls we just finished checking. Your slippers aren't leaving much, but over here are my muddy ones. But I looked when we first came down. Other than you and me, no one else has been in this basement, at least not since I was here a few days ago."

"No one who could leave a track, you mean."

The hair on the back of his neck stood up. At the same time, he felt her touch his arm.

"Let's get out of here, Rafe." She looked back toward the dark abyss of the tunnel. "This place gives me the creeps."

It gave him the creeps, too, but not as much as her open panel. "Come on," he said and draped an arm around her shoulder. "Let's go check the real ways to get in and out of this house."

Chapter Twenty-three

She'd dozed off, finally, at dawn. As far as she knew, Rafe had started his day at that time — or perhaps he'd considered his day started when she woke him in the wee hours.

They'd checked every ground-level door and window. All remained bolted. There was no evidence anyone had entered the house, nor any indication anyone accessed the stairwell via the dining room — not that there would have been, even if the access had been used. He'd checked that section of the secret stairwell leading to the attic alone. The stairs weren't safe, he'd told her.

Delilah turned from her bedroom window where she'd been watching Rafe with Simon Douglas in the yard below. The panel was innocuous in the morning light, the room pleasant and by all appearances, safe. Either Rafe would have to break that mechanism, ensuring no one, or nothing, could enter her room while she slept, or she was going to find another room. But as for today, she had other things to keep her happily distracted. Tomorrow River's Bend would host its first Thanksgiving in many years.

"We'll probably never know what went on in that house. I've heard those rumors about his killing his first wife, but place little store in them. He had his dalliances on the side. He didn't need to marry one of them. He had a wife of good family. From where I was standing, it would seem more likely that Emmaline would have killed him, but she and her sons were secure. Merrifield was wealthy when she married him. He was a good businessman and quick to smell a potential profit, and there was plenty of legal thievery going on then, Mrs. Stone, you know that."

Henry Gifford kept eyeing her funny, and she suspected, by the way he placed the emphasis on "Mrs. Stone," that he knew who she was. He was a distinctive man, short and stout, with a decided limp. He had a head of coarse, silver hair and piercing gray eyes. He was publisher of *The Natchez Gazette*, in the front office of which they now sat, discussing the brutal events of fifteen years ago. He'd been a reporter then and had progressed after a few more years to senior editor. He knew what had happened to the Merrifields a decade and a half ago, but he didn't know why.

And without a doubt, he knew what later happened to Miles Colburn and Charlotte and Richard Graff, but in that particular case, he thought he knew why. Well, he was missing some facts, but Delilah had no intention of trying to set him straight. Her clarification of events surrounding her father's commission of a double murder, an attempted murder, and his subsequent suicide would sound like excuses to this man's ears, and she wasn't making any excuses.

"If Mr. Merrifield were unscrupulous—"

"And he was."

"Then he must have had enemies."

"Some for sure, but not bitter ones. The only home he inserted himself into, he inherited through his wife. For sure, River's Bend was a prize status symbol and perhaps would have been available for the taking by others of his ilk had it not fallen so fortuitously into his hands as the War ended, but that would have been, at most, a matter of irritation between jackals. Besides, the murders didn't occur until years later."

"Do you think it was because of the gold?"

"The gold shipment stolen by the Confederates?"

"Yes."

"I think that. . . ." He drew in a breath, then let it out. "Is that what's gained your interest, madam? One hundred thousand dollars in gold?"

"Things that go bump in the night are driving my interest, Mr. Gifford."

129

"Well, I don't think it was a ghost that killed Merrifield and his wife." He moved around to her side of the table, where she'd placed herself about an hour ago to research the old newspaper articles relating to the Merrifield murders. "What was reported here"—he pointed to the column she'd been scanning when he'd ventured from his office and joined her—"is only part of the story. The Merrifields were mutilated."

He might as well have punched her in the gut. "How?"

He hesitated only a moment. "To avoid being clinical, suffice it to say intimate parts were cut."

Oh, goodness.

"There was nothing to indicate someone broke into the house, and Merrifield was known to keep his doors locked."

Delilah wondered if Mr. Gifford knew about the tunnel and the secret stairwell.

"There were valuables still in the house. His first and second wives' jewels, works of art, and so forth."

"Was anything taken?"

Gifford gave her a satisfied smile. "There was no inventory, so we don't know. We do know plenty was left. Myself and others, the sheriff at the time included, have long suspected the sons."

"Because of Mrs. Merrifield's pregnancy and the inheritance, you mean?"

"In a way. The boys were very close to their mother. Both, particularly the youngest, Raymond, took her death hard. Then Merrifield turned around and brought Cecilia Wilkins into that household. She was scarcely a year older than the older boy and she was a pretty, flirty little thing. The first Mrs. Merrifield had been dead less than six months. There was resentment, the servants said so."

She looked down at the likeness of Raymond Merrifield, which had quickened her heartbeat when she'd first seen it a short while ago. The drawing had been published in the paper fifteen years earlier, and it was the familiarity of Raymond's eyes that drove her anxiety.

"What happened to the boys if they had no money?"

"Don't know. They'd be either side of thirty now, if they survived."

There went that foolishly fluttering heart again. Thirty. Grown men. "Do you know if any photos exist of them?"

"Mementos such as that were sent to the family in Ohio, I believe." He nodded to the picture in the paper. "That drawing was made from a photo found in the house. We reckoned he was about twelve when it was made."

Darn it. She would like to have seen the actual photo of Raymond at twelve. Again, she studied the drawing. The defilement could have been the sons' way of desecrating their father and what he held dearer than them.

"Jealously and betrayal," Gifford said slowly, "can provoke bizarre and violent acts in a seemingly sane man."

Though gently said and without malice, his words sucked the moisture from Delilah's mouth, and she steeled herself. "Jealousy in a weak man, Mr. Gifford, invites the unwarranted delusion of betrayal."

For a moment, the man studied her, then he nodded to the picture she pondered. "I was referring to the Merrifield murders, Miss Graff."

Heat washed over her, and she closed her eyes. She felt his hand close over hers. "My mother was innocent," she said.

"I know, but Cecilia Merrifield, I fear, was not."

She blinked him back into focus, then smiled, a silent thank-you for bringing their conversation back on track. He smiled in return.

"If the boys did kill their parents," she said, "they had to survive somehow."

"Indeed, but remember we have no way of knowing what they might have taken with them when they left."

"The gold?"

He shrugged. "I doubt it. That gold was in a number of strong-boxes, each one heavy. They couldn't have simply walked away with it. Taking it would have required planning."

"And do you believe Morgan Ward had a plan?"

131

"I'm sorry to say I do."

"But what if Lorelei killed him before she killed herself?"

He squinted at her. "Do you have reason to believe that happened?"

"No, I'm just supposing."

He watched her, the look in his eyes clearly saying he doubted her denial. "I'll grant you, Mrs. Stone, if that were the case, the gold could still be hidden nearby."

$\mathcal{D}$elilah closed her eyes and blew out a shaky breath. The chancery clerk's office was dim, chilly, and quiet as a tomb, but for the occasional stirring of a county minion. She still needed to stop at the general store and the butcher. That's what she told Rafe she was coming to town for, and by now he was probably wondering where she was.

Let him wonder. She'd lost all heart for Thanksgiving. She should pay Belle a double wage to forsake dinner with her own family and cook the meal Delilah had planned on making for her new husband.

She closed the record book. For the past nine years, her Uncle Joe had been paying the taxes on River's Bend, a property Aunt Ophelia had come into by inheritance. The plantation home had switched hands three times since the murders of Merrifield and his wife. The two owners between Merrifield and her aunt had held the property only a matter of months. She'd known about the newlyweds who claimed the house was haunted. The bride's father had eventually sold the property to Aunt Ophelia's childless aunt and uncle, both of whom had died within a short time without ever having lived in the house. Those last details weren't part of the county record. The old clerk had remembered.

Rafe had wanted the house; he was tied to it . . . somehow. She'd known that since the night on the riverboat when they watched it materialize beneath the silver moon. What she hadn't known that night was that Rafe had gone so far as to marry her to get his hands on it.

※

$\mathcal{J}$ames Dexter maneuvered his chair to avoid the afternoon sun shining through the Riverview Room's French doors, then he sat. "I went over the coroner's report and the investigation. It wasn't a pretty scene. Their bodies were butchered."

Rafe laid a forearm on the surface of his desk and reached for the papers Jim Dexter held out to him.

"You don't seem surprised."

Rafe looked at him, then returned to the report. "People tend to tell me the gruesome details when they find out I'm the new owner of this house. Do you think the boys did it?"

"Sheriff concluded the killer or killers were already inside the house. The two sons were never seen or heard from again. It was all guesswork, if you want my opinion, but my gut tells me the guess was right." James nodded at the papers Rafe held. "Sheriff Lee Broderick was a deputy at the time. Said they figured the boys killed their parents and ran off, but regular folks around here feel David Merrifield would have taken Cecilia with him, not killed her."

"Yeah, I've heard that rumor, too."

"Gossipy old women say Cecilia had set her cap for David before Markham made her a better offer. Personally, I believe that presents an argument for his having killed them both."

"But did David reciprocate her prenuptial interest?"

"No one knows for sure, but if he weren't interested, he was the only young man around who wasn't." Jim had lowered his voice; now he leaned forward. "Broderick provided me details on the mutilations. Merrifield's cock had been cut off as had his balls. The dick was stuffed into Cecilia's vagina, and the balls slit, then placed over the wounds where Cecilia's nipples had been. Those were found inside Merrifield's mouth. Whoever killed them was mad, literally and figuratively, and a killing like that clearly indicates rage, which is usually personal. That's why authorities think the boys did it. But I gotta tell you, boss, I'm no expert on the psyche of killers, but I can't see two men cooperating in that kind of ritualistic defilement."

"So, you think only one of the boys killed the parents?"

"If they were involved at all, yes, and I can't help but conclude, if that's the case, there's another body buried somewhere."

Rafe laid the papers on his desk, then looked at Jim and said, "No attempt was ever made to access Merrifield's accounts?"

"His creditors were paid off, his properties sold. He had a hefty mortgage on this house—had used it to invest in a railroad venture out west. What little is left is still sitting in the bank waiting for those boys to come back and claim it." Jim narrowed his eyes on Rafe. "Of course, maybe the boys don't need it."

"You're thinking they have the Yankee gold?"

"Not me, but the Federals considered that possibility all those years ago, this being the last known home of Morgan Ward. They didn't turn up any more than the locals did, which brings me to that name you asked me to check a few days ago.

"First Lieutenant John Thompson, who was reprimanded by the army as a result of the incident in the paper, had recently been recruited by a civilian, a local, working for the army postmaster. The man's name was Peter Steward. Both were arrested that night along with two darkies.

"Of the lieutenant and Steward, the latter is the most interesting. Thompson was apparently just beginning his career trafficking in stolen cotton. Steward had a history. Seems little over a month before, he'd been caught moving cotton taken from a Federal warehouse. Steward was in the calaboose overnight, then all charges against him were dropped. The order came from an officer at district headquarters in Vicksburg whose purview included contraband. Steward's release did not go unnoticed by the adjutant who launched a brief investigation of his own and subsequently concluded that it was the same individual who released Steward who had provided him the stolen cotton."

Jim's pause was by design. "Charles Slade," Rafe said.

"The same Charles Slade found dead at Butler Lake. Looks like you might have had a good hunch there, boss. His seniors were bringing charges against him; his career was over, not that he had much of one left anyway. West Point class of '55. He graduated third from the bottom, but tried to make up for his shortcomings in combat. At the time he was relieved and moved to a desk job, his unit had one of the highest casualty rates in the army. Stealing cotton during early Reconstruction ran rampant among Federal officers. Truth is, Slade's seniors didn't like him."

"When Steward was arrested, he didn't implicate Slade?"

"He did not, and no one seemed eager to follow up with him; too busy with the *Gilded Rose*, I guess. Plus, with all those dead Yanks, Steward probably didn't want authorities thinking he was in any way associated with that plot."

"Do you think he was?"

"Hard to tell. Two bales of cotton were found stashed south of Butler Lake. Somebody was supposed to move them, and that somebody never came. That's why Thompson and Steward got caught, they lingered too long. I'm thinking the cotton could have been a ruse. If Slade were planning on moving the gold down the Mississippi, he'd have wanted to disguise his cargo somehow."

"That would have been hard unless the crew was made privy. That gold was heavy."

Dexter shrugged. "We'll never know. The investigative report indicates Thompson believed he was moving cotton. The man Slade might have provided details was Steward, and he died in '88." James Dexter slapped his thigh and rose. "That's all I got, boss. By the way, I saw your lovely bride leaving the *Gazette* office as I was going in."

So that's what was keeping her, trying to find a story to fit her blubbering ghost. Rafe stood, too. "Did she remember you?"

"Being inconspicuous can be an advantage in my line of work, but I hope pretty women don't find me that unmemorable. She'd been researching these same cases." He grinned at Rafe. "Could save you some money if you trusted the little lady's investigation."

"She's looking for ghosts. I'm looking for a killer."

"I was willing to bet you were looking for gold."

Rafe stepped away from his dual-pedestal desk. "I'm trying to rule out a link."

Jim opened his mouth to say something, but Rafe said, "Did Delilah speak?"

"Sure did. Was a bit standoffish at first, but warmed up when she got to talking about what she was working on."

"She knows you investigated her."

"Oh."

"She said she was going grocery shopping. I was wondering what—"

"She told me she was on her way to the chancery clerk's office to find out how many times this house has switched hands since Merrifield died."

Merda! She might not be coming home at all now, and unless she got sidetracked, he'd bet his river-front property she was no longer in a good mood.

"Look," James said, "if you'd like, I'll follow up with Markham Merrifield's extended family. If those boys survived, could be they've made some sort of contact with their kin in Ohio over the years."

"Go ahead. And find out what you can about Cecilia. She was young, pretty, and liked men and money. She could have gotten under the skin of the wrong man."

"Merrifield was a Yankee businessman."

Rafe nodded. "I agree. He might have run afoul of someone, too."

Jim hesitated, then flexed his jaw. "You know, boss, it'd be nice to know if I'm looking for the same killer you are."

Rafe studied his investigator a long moment, then said, "Depends on that particular killer's link to the gold."

"Mrs. Howell, I'm going into Natchez to meet my wife." He wasn't about to tell her he didn't know where Delilah was. It was getting late, and he was anxious.

"She was in the kitchen with Lucianne putting groceries away a few minutes ago." Mrs. Howell pulled a glove over one hand. "We're about done today. That kitchen is scoured good." She giggled. "You'll not have to be worrying about catching anything untoward in your food unless she decides to poison you."

He stifled an urge to ask if Delilah had said something to that effect in the kitchen, but the twinkle in Mrs. Howell's eye told him the answer was "no." The plump, effervescent woman pulled on her second glove, then situated her hat on her head. "She's a bit quiet though. I think she must be tired. She's let Belle go for tomorrow."

Delilah planned on denying him Thanksgiving dinner.

"Don't know if she should've done that, but I think she wants to make her new husband his Thanksgiving dinner all by herself." The woman shook a glove-covered finger at him. "She'll learn the fallacy of that in time, but for now, enjoy her effort no matter how awful it is."

Rafe stared at the woman. Delilah was a good cook. At least, that's what he'd been told. She'd learned in that fancy school her uncle sent her to. She wasn't going to cook, *that* was the problem.

"Belle has already left?"

"Probably. Looks like rain back to the north, so Miss Delilah was shooing us all out of the house."

Rafe blew out a breath, then opened the front door with a short bow.

"Oh, my"—and the woman twittered—"thank you, Mister Stone."

"You're welcome, Mrs. Howell. Have a happy Thanksgiving."

"You also. We're gonna start on that front room Friday. Your missus says she has painters coming next week."

"She does." Actually, he did. He closed the door behind the giddy Mrs. Howell and started across the foyer. Moments later he stuck his head through the kitchen door.

"Hello."

Delilah looked up from where she was pouring measured cornmeal into a large wooden bowl. "Hi," she said and dropped her gaze, at the same time pushing a wayward wisp of hair behind her ear. "Could you get the oven going?"

He nodded, then squatted and opened the wood box. Loaded. He rose and reached for the box of matches. She seemed all right, but her glance was furtive, her actions jerky. Delilah wasn't hiding her hurt in anger this time, but in work. Actually, she'd done the same the day she'd gotten into the hornet's nest. He'd have to stay with her to make sure she didn't catch herself on fire.

It also meant the anger was there, below the simmering surface. A smart man would leave. But he wasn't smart, at least not where this woman was concerned.

"What are you doing?"

She turned to the icebox and pulled out a pitcher. "I'm making the cornbread for the dressing. I need to make it and the biscuits tonight, so all I'll have to do in the morning is get the turkey on and finish the dressing."

All she'll have to do? He knew enough about cornbread dressing to know she'd be in the kitchen all day. But it did look like she intended to cook for him.

"You have cranberries?"

"I do. That's something else I can do tonight."

"You've had a long day." He wanted to ask what Belle made for dinner tonight, but thought that might be a tactical error.

"I went to the newspaper office, into the archives. I wanted to research the Merrifield murders."

He rose, cautious. "Still looking for a ghost?"

She looked at him, then back to the batter she was stirring. "I'm trying to piece some things together. Would you get the big skillet out of the drawer, please?"

"Where's the lard?"

"In the bottom cupboard. Here," she said and pushed the sack of cornmeal his direction. "When it's melted, sprinkle a little of this in the skillet. How's the oven?"

"Heating faster than the burner." He carefully lifted the skillet and turned it, allowing the dollop of lard to spread across its surface. Surreptitiously, he glanced at her, pretty in a dress the color of a pumpkin, trimmed in black piping. She'd found that dress at the Emporium, but ready made or not, it fit her perfectly. She broke an egg into the batter and stirred, then turned quickly and caught him watching her.

"Is the skillet ready?"

"Let me get the meal in."

"It needs to be good and brown."

"I know."

"So wherever you come from, the people make cornbread?"

"Some of us." He dusted the cornmeal from his hands. "Did you learn anything at the newspaper?"

"Nothing new, really," she said, curling her arm around the wooden bowl and stepping toward him. "Except that Markham and Cecilia Merrifield's bodies were mutilated."

"That wasn't in the newspaper."

Her eyes met his. "I had the pleasure of discussing the case with Henry Gifford, the *Gazette's* publisher for the past five years. He reported the case fifteen years ago."

"Ah."

She motioned for him to level the skillet. "You already knew?"

"I did . . . do."

She pulled the oven door open, frowned, closed it again and straightened. "For how long?"

"Jim Dexter gave me a detailed report this afternoon." True, if not the whole truth.

Her lips tightened. "I saw him in town."

"He mentioned that."

She poured the batter in the skillet. Immediately, he joggled the pan to and fro over the burner, leveling the viscous substance across its bottom. Delilah opened the oven door, and he shoved the heavy skillet inside. With an agitated movement, she whirled away from him and returned to the table. "I'll be so glad when our gas oven gets here. Belle will, too, even if she doesn't know it. They make cooking so much easier. The temperature —"

"Delilah, I know you know."

She lightly hit the table surface with the wooden spoon she'd picked up, then dropped the thing with a clatter. She didn't look at him, but started toward the cabinets.

"What are you doing?"

"Looking for the damn oleander."

Now was not the time to reprimand his bride on her choice of language. "You put oleander in cornbread dressing?"

"I put sage and poultry seasoning in cornbread dressing. I was being facetious."

"Oleander would ruin it, wouldn't it?"

Her shoulders heaved with her sigh. "Oleander is a poison if used to excess."

"Listen to me —"

"I don't need to listen to you. I've known all along Uncle Joe offered you some compelling reason to take me, and I've known from the start that reason was not me."

He watched her stretch and reach for a can on a high shelf. He snagged it before she did. "He needed —"

"I need the one next to it, too."

He handed it to her, and she turned back to the table. He wanted to explain the situation, so that her uncle's passing her off wasn't as demeaning as . . . as it was. Anything he said to her now would sound patronizing.

He moved away from her, toward the ancient door leading to the breezeway. "I need to remove this thing and make you a proper pantry."

She whipped around. "My treasured door?"

He turned on his heel and watched her approach.

"Never. The reason André Richard did not replace that door was not because it was on the back of the house and couldn't be seen. He could afford it. He kept that door because it truly was a treasure and still is. It's a historical reference for the house." She jutted her chin and turned back to the table. "Like me, it came with the property. It stays, whether you ever open it or not."

Another double meaning? She wasn't looking at him, and he wasn't sure she realized what she'd said. His gut told him that, yes, she did. "Your Uncle Joe —"

"Needed to be rid of me." Calmly she placed the two cans on the table. "I was his terms for the house."

She sounded calm, but the set of her mouth and the pucker in her chin belied that. He cocked his head, discreetly trying to read the labels on the cans.

"To a stranger," she said, looking down and touching the top of one. "I thought he cared more, if not for me, than for my mother, to do such a thing. Good Lord"—her voice broke at the same moment she stretched her hands out in front of her—"you could have been a monster." She dropped her hands and stared at him.

"Delilah, honey—"

"Sweet heaven, you could still be a monster."

For Christ's sake. "Sweetheart, your Uncle Joe does care for you."

"Oh, that's right," she spat out. "He let you have this great big house, then sent me my little, bitty one. No doubt he found the parallel amusing."

"You don't believe that. He needed to settle you in a home away from his. He offered me the house—"

"Oh, bullshit, Rafe Stone."

"That's exactly what happened."

"Exactly my foot. You make it sound like he approached you in a bar and offered you the deal. I'm no fool. You wanted the house. You found him. And *you* were compelled to take me or not get this place."

"I wasn't going to deny it."

"You weren't going to bring it up, either."

No, he sure wasn't, but she had it figured out. "Well, now we both know why one married the other."

"No, we don't."

His head was starting to hurt. "I admit I wanted the house."

Delilah thrust her chin. "Fine, but the truth is this old house is as emotionally important to you as my little dollhouse is to me. But why, Mr. Stone?"

Further protest was foolish; Delilah wasn't stupid.

She smiled sadly when he didn't answer. "And there, sir, lies the true mystery."

Chapter Twenty-four

Soft crying wove seamlessly into his dream, but there was no place there for the almost soundless click of the door.

Rafe opened his eyes. His room was relatively warm, the embers in his hearth still glowing. Not much time had passed since he'd fallen asleep. He rose on an elbow and listened. Quiet now, but he saw light beneath the bedroom door joining his room with Delilah's. She was up, her door closed. He lit the coal oil lamp on the bedside table and opened his father's enameled watch lying beside it.

His gut tensed with the creak of a floorboard, and he reached for his woolen undershirt and donned it. He was wearing the woolen drawers. Damn, if Delilah had heard the crying and was about to enter the hole without him. . . . He couldn't believe she would, but she'd been so upset this evening, it was possible she was reluctant to wake him as she had last night.

He crossed the freezing floor. Dammit, he was visiting Cole's over on Commerce Street this coming week. Carpets were next on his list—after the painting. Careful not to make a sound, he turned the knob and pushed the door open, keeping his hand on it all the while. Her room glowed with golden light, dim and peaceful, inviting. Delilah stood at the window, her back to him, holding the lace sheers to one side so she could see out. Her golden tresses, free now of the braid, hung in thick waves to her waist and his groin tensed at the sight of her slender body, draped in cotton flannel trimmed in eyelet and ruffled gathers. Her arm moved, and she swiped a cheek.

The tears he'd heard cried were hers.

He saw her stiffen, then heard her draw a breath. After a moment, she allowed the curtain to fall into place, and she turned to face him.

"I'm sorry," he said, "but I heard crying and feared you'd gone chasing after your ghost again."

Her breast rose gently. In the lamplight, she was the most beautiful thing he'd ever seen in his life.

"But I find the tears are yours, sweetheart."

"I did not mean to wake you."

He stepped into her room. "Why can't you sleep?"

"I'll need to get up soon to get the turkey on."

"Delilah, it's midnight. Do you plan on our eating the turkey for breakfast?"

She smiled.

"And though I believe the fear of someone entering that panel might keep you awake at night, I do not believe that same fear would cause you to cry."

"I'm not crying," she said, her glistening eyes locked on his approach.

He stopped in front of her and raised an index finger to her cheek. Her skin was soft, and wet. He licked his finger. "Salty."

"So is your skin."

Gently he cupped her face with his hands. "You should have woke me."

"Why?" she asked, turning her cheek into his palm and closing her eyes.

"Because sometimes a person needs to be with another."

Tears squeezed between her closed lids. "You must have been the answer to his prayers."

He wanted to be the answer to her prayers. "Sure," he said, "can't you just see your Uncle Joe on his knees beside his bed in his nightcap, praying for some fool to come along and take his beautiful niece off his hands?"

She giggled, despite the tears. "He used you horribly, foisting me on you."

"So you do consider me a fool?"

143

"I believe he took advantage of you."

"Honey, if he took advantage of me it's because I allowed him to. I don't believe for a moment you are mad, nor do I believe you ever will be. I told you my main concern, and I no longer consider that worry valid."

Her soft laugh surprised him. "Don't you see how desperate Uncle Joe was to find me a husband? I'm not a good catch."

Inwardly, Rafe sighed. Josephus Collander had humiliated her. He didn't believe the man realized it or he'd have never done what he did, but nevertheless, that is exactly what Joe Collander had done by compelling a stranger to marry her.

"That fickle, dandy Champion thought you were a fine catch, Delilah. That's why your uncle wanted you out of the house." He squeezed her to him. "You were, in fact, in too great demand."

"Douglas didn't know about my parents." She snuggled her nose against his breast and heat shot from his nipple to his manhood.

"Would you scratch my back, Rafe? Where the hornets stung me? I can't reach the spot, and they've itched all day."

Oh, yes. His John Henry was stirring, and he wasn't about to miss any opportunity to caress any part of her she wanted him to touch. He placed his hands on her shoulders and pushed her far enough away so he could study her face, gauging her thoughts, her needs. Her mouth was beautiful, full lips gently parted, her eyes filled with wonder and laced with anticipation. Good signs. He tugged the bow securing her gown at the neck, and he heard her soft intake of breath. His hand moved inside the gown, over her collarbone and around the back of her neck, then down over her back and shoulder. The insects' stings had almost healed, but he found the clusters of small bumps. She moaned in pleasure as he gently rubbed the spots, and she lay against him.

"Better?" he murmured into her hair.

"That feels so good."

His manhood suffered, stricken with a delicious pain. He knew other tricks of hand, fingers, and tongue that felt good, too.

"Do you dance, Delilah?"

144

She pulled back, but not far. "I know how to dance, if that's your question?"

"School curriculum?"

"Most assuredly. Reading, writing, social graces. You've a properly educated wife."

"Properly, or one that can survive without a husband?"

"Both, should she have to."

He took her right hand in his left and raised it to his breast, then humming the lilting tune of the ballad *Lorena,* he drew her from the window into the dim interior of the room.

"Is that what you still want?" he said, adeptly turning them with a graceful twist.

Her eyes filled with tears, and he realized his tactless error.

"If that's what you want, I will set you free."

"I didn't say I want to be free, Delilah." He drew in a long breath and sang, "*We loved each other once, Delilah*" — she smirked at his change in the lyric — "*More than we e'er dared to tell.*

"Answer me, Delilah."

"I'm no longer sure what I want."

He pushed her back far enough to see her face, and he grinned in triumph before spinning her around in his arms. "*Oh what yet might be, Delilah, if but our loving prospers well.*

"In that you're no longer sure you want to live out your life as an old, unhappy spinster."

"I never wanted that," she said.

"Well, my beauty, you are at a great disadvantage."

"Why?"

He squeezed the hand he held and pressed his free one against the small of her back. His lips found the lobe of her ear, and his tongue traced her jaw until it met her chin. He pulled back. Damn, he wanted to press his hard-on against her belly, but he restrained himself. Two days, a week from tonight, yes, but right now he needed to proceed with more finesse.

"Because I know exactly what I want," he answered.

Her breath had quickened with his tongue's caress; now her eyes widened.

❧❧

"Are you wooing me again, husband?"

His tongue filled her mouth, and she closed her eyes with the force of him. Immediately, she weaved her arms around his neck, drawing him to her. He responded in kind, pressing her breasts against his. Her nipples burned and warmth pooled between her legs.

"Rafe?" She clung to him as he lifted her in his arms and started toward his room.

"Yes, but I'm going to 'woo' you in my bedroom. I've still got a fire going, and I've got that big bed you talked me into."

Then from atop that same bed, she lay watching him stoke the fire, and as ominous shadows danced across his handsome face, he straightened and turned to her, then peeled his undershirt up his chest.

For a moment, his torso was all she could see, his face covered by the shirt. His chest was broad and muscled, his stomach firm. Large, flat nipples filled her senses and her gaze followed the path of dark body hair down to his navel and the waist of his drawers . . . and to the bulge below.

The shirt cleared his head, and his eyes met hers. He'd caught her watching him, and he studied her with an intensity she'd never seen in his eyes. She shivered, a pleasant tremor despite her anxiety, and mustering courage, she leaned back on her elbows.

"It's called an erection, sweetheart."

She glanced again to the bulge between his legs and licked her dry lips. She heard him laugh and immediately jerked her gaze to his face.

"Oh, darlin'," he said, laying his body over hers and pushing her into the feather mattress, "do you have any idea what a temptress you are?"

"You are the one with the 'erection'."

"Yes, but you're the one who put it there." He kissed her deeply, and she felt his hands on her nightgown, then her breasts. Her stomach quaked as his free hand moved over her hips to her thigh. She wriggled beneath him, and he released her lips and

146

worked his hand underneath her flannel gown to tug it over her calf.

"You've moved beyond wooing."

"Ah," he said, his voice husky, "you do recognize the difference." And he kissed her again as his other hand trailed down her opposite side.

The angry resolve she'd first known on their wedding day regarding sexual intimacy with him was gone. So was the contrariness she'd felt over the days that followed. Now she willed away the doubt she harbored this afternoon when she looked at the likeness of Raymond Merrifield's eyes. Her body was on fire and painfully alive, craving his touch. She wanted to feel his calloused fingertips on her breasts, to suffocate beneath a blanket of heated flesh covering her, with nothing between them.

He pulled her up, and at his urging, she raised her hips. He yanked the gown over her head, and beneath his scrutiny, her desire dissipated, and she covered her breasts with folded arms.

"It's all right," he said softly, "I've seen naked women before."

"Not me."

"Not you," he said amicably, pulling her arms away, exposing her breasts to his view. He kissed her lips and her nose. "Delilah, I've only been with easy women, and I'm trying like the devil not to embarrass you, but I'm going to look at you, and I'm going to touch you, and I want you to enjoy it."

Her heart was pounding, and she wondered if he'd spoken by design, knowing the desire his words would engender.

His rough thumb slid over the nub of a nipple and her body arched. "The tongue is better, I'm told," he said and dipped his head. Soft, slick wetness covered her other breast, then the tip of his tongue teased her nipple. She closed her eyes and twisted her body, coaxing him to take the other. And he did.

Instinctively, she bent her knee and rubbed her thigh along the fabric of his drawers. He forced his 'erection' against her pelvis, and a groan escaped her lips. Shocked, she opened her eyes and raised her head, and he wrapped his arms around her and kissed her lips.

Delilah twined her arms around his neck and drew him closer. The strength in his corded muscles enticed her, and her hands explored his shoulders, then his back. She found his hard biceps, strained from holding him off her, and she struggled to sit up. Reluctantly, it seemed, he pulled away. His handsome face was directly above hers, his wide mouth, lips parted to accommodate his intake and exhalation of air, was mute, and his green eyes watched her in question. She pushed him back so he sat on his knees, and she managed a sitting position.

"Afraid I've changed my mind?" she asked.

"You haven't got a prayer."

She blinked, determined to match his ardor, wanting to please him, but not sure how. The tip of her tongue touched his nipple, raw and salty. He sucked in a breath, and she pulled back to see his face, while he caressed her arms with the palms of his hands.

"Yes," he said, watching her, "I like being touched, too."

Resolved, she tightened her hold on his biceps and drew in a breath. "Take off your pants."

"Take off my pants?"

"You have to take them off, don't you?"

"Eventually."

"Do it now."

He furrowed his brow, but he was already off the bed and searching the waist band of his drawers. She reached out and helped him find the drawstring. Before he pulled it, his gaze found hers. "We won't look the same. You do realize that?"

She smiled, calmed somewhat by his levity. "I know."

"Ready?"

She nodded, and he pulled the string, allowing his woolen underwear to fall. She'd never seen a male member before, much less an erect one, and she clutched her knees to her breasts and breathed a little faster. No doubt his manhood was the most dominating feature of his body, and her eyes locked on it. She raised them to find him watching her. He wanted to say something she was sure he considered funny, and when he didn't, she said, "It's very nice."

148

He laughed, and her bravado fled. "Hold me, Rafe, I'm —"

"Shhh." His hands were on her shoulders, and he pushed her gently. She fell to the mattress. Again, his lips found a breast and in quick succession, he splayed his hand over her belly, then lower to smooth his thumb over her womanhood. Need, as hungry and demanding as it was sweet, filled her pelvis and spread across her belly, then her limbs. She pushed against the heel of his hand, and when she whimpered, he cursed, and stroked her until sensation overpowered her body, and she found herself swaying with wave after receding wave of pleasure that left her limbs languid and her skin damp with perspiration. She reached for him, and he pulled her into his arms.

"I had no idea," she whispered against his throat.

"Delilah, I don't think a man's ever felt as good as I do now."

"Did you feel what I —"

He pecked her lips. "Short of coming, that is."

Given the way her body trembled and the faint sheen of sweat on her skin, he'd made her happy, and that made him very happy. He sat back on his knees.

"Lie down," he said. "It's going to be harder getting my nice thing inside you."

She draped her arms around his neck, and he drew her knee up and pushed. She tightened her hold.

"Are you sure —"

"Hmm," he said, repositioning himself and pushing again. He made little progress and frowned. "I wonder what's wrong? It's always fit before."

She raised her eyebrows, and he winked.

"It will fit, Delilah. I swell, you stretch." He placed a hand beneath her buttocks, then thrust. Her one arm tightened around his neck as she pushed herself up with the other and pressed her head against his, ear to ear. A struggle of sorts, which he eased by holding her to him.

"It's only because it was the first time, isn't it? It won't always hurt like that, will it? I heard girls talking at school. . . ."

149

Gently, he extricated himself from her strangling embrace. "That's right. Only the first time."

He relegated the apprehension in her eyes to the back of his mind. He was hardly an expert on virgins, but boys talked, too, and his arousal stifled any desire to mull over her question. He pulled back, then pushed forward, increasing his pace, her helping him now, until he climaxed with a mild oath. Drunk on sex, he prolonged the moment, pushing against her pelvis as the pleasure subsided. She touched his shoulder, and he looked at her, questions in her eyes.

"You did magnificently," he said.

"I didn't do anything."

He chuckled, then fell beside her and drew her into his arms. "You gave yourself to me."

"If you were an avenging angel, who would you be an avenging angel for?"

She lay in the crook of his arm, her naked bottom snuggled against his hip. He frowned in the dark. "I am a guardian angel, and I'm protecting you."

"I'd hardly call what you've done protection."

Rafe rolled onto his side, freeing his deadening arm and pulling her rump against his pelvis. "Is too, and I think I'll protect you some more."

He felt her head move, and she said, "Could whoever you're avenging be a brother?"

He raised his head to kiss her—it was a cheek his lips found. "Yes, if I had a brother to avenge, a brother would be good."

"A mother?"

"Or a father, or—"

"A stepmother?" she said quickly.

He lay back on the pillow. "If she were worth being avenged."

Delilah tried to roll over, but her movement only snuggled her closer to him. He tightened the arm he'd draped over her waist.

"Sweetheart, who do you think I am?"

She freed herself, and though he couldn't see her in the dark, he knew she hovered over him. "You have Raymond Merrifield's eyes."

"I have Raeford Gavin Stone's eyes."

"I saw a—"

He tangled her in his arms, then swallowed her words with a kiss. She stilled completely, and he pulled back.

A long moment passed, then a hand touched his shoulder. The second followed suit, and Delilah pushed her arms around his neck and pressed her naked breasts against his chest. His body warmed.

"Trust me, Delilah."

"Rafe," she whispered against his lips, "I don't think I could say that I trust you any louder than this."

Chapter Twenty-five

Overhead, the ceiling creaked. Delilah rolled onto her back and pulled the heavy covers beneath her chin. She reached for Rafe, longing for his heat. The place beside her was warm but abandoned, and she opened her eyes.

Daylight. She sat up, holding the quilts to her naked breasts, and turned to the window behind her. Early morning and a dark, dreary day outside.

Again a joist groaned.

Delilah squirmed closer to the pillow where Rafe had laid his head and breathed his scent, then closed her eyes with the subtle tingling of her stomach. He'd not gotten far, given the warmth of the sheets.

A muffled knock emerged from the wall near the fireplace and her heart skipped a beat. He could be in her room next door. She looked around for her nightgown and spotted it on the floor next to her side of the bed; a ruffled sleeve blew gently in the air coming through the vent. He had the furnace going. Delilah reached awkwardly over the side of the bed, grasped the gown, and pulled it over her head before throwing back the covers and wriggling the rest of herself into it.

He'd drawn her spine against his chest after he'd made love to her a second time, and they'd talked about Thanksgiving dinner, Christmas, and long-term plans for the house, the riding horses he wanted to buy, and her plans for a summer flower garden. She'd not broached the subject of avenging angels again. All she'd wanted at the time was to lie in his arms forever, with him content to have her there.

Outside the wind gusted, and the house moaned. Again the wall, now at her back, spoke, and she slid off the high bed and stood on the floor. A very cold floor.

"Rafe?" she called softly, rounding the foot of the bed.

A barely perceptible squeak answered. She touched the wall and leaned through the door into her room, cold and dim in the overcast dawn. "Rafe?"

She heard a click and frowned. He'd gone through the panel. A game, perhaps? She didn't like it. The house was too dark, too cold, and too creaky, but she stepped into the room anyway and made her way to the secret panel.

"I'm not going to follow you."

But perhaps he hadn't planned for her to. He wouldn't have known she was awake, and by all earlier indicators, he'd been in the attic when she woke and had high-tailed it when he realized she heard him. But why? And therein lay a compelling reason to follow him.

She reached for the heavy mantle, pulled it out, and found the latch inside the brick rebate. Done, she pushed the panel open. A blast of cold air swept beneath her nightgown. She hesitated, but only a moment, then steeling herself, she reached for the lantern on the peg, an action that required her to step into the stairwell. Upon her entry, the wild, unpleasant smell she recalled from the night of the raccoon caused the hair on the back of her neck to stand on end, and a silent voice threatened her in the darkness.

Delilah choked back a sob, uncertain as to whether the thing crouched above or below her on the ancient risers, and she stumbled backwards into her room. Mustering all her courage, she forced herself to reach once more into the menacing void from where she yanked the panel toward her. It closed with a click.

"What are —"

She yelped and pivoted toward Rafe's voice.

". . . you doing?" he finished. He stood at the corner of the fireplace.

"You were in the attic?"

"What's wrong, Delilah? You look as if you did see a ghost."

153

She rushed into his arms, wanting to feel his warmth, his strength, to breathe his scent and let it wash the unfamiliar smell from her nostrils. Soap and musk and sweat. Rafe, Rafe, Rafe.

He held her tight. "Were you going in there?"

She jerked her head up, and he cried "ouch" when she hit his chin.

"Were you in the attic?"

"I was in the kitchen, then the furnace room getting the heater going. We've got bad weather this morning."

She looked out the dingy window and noted the intermittent rain from last night had begun again.

"I heard something in the attic," she said as he led her back to his room.

The wind howled around the side of the house and, as earlier, the structure moaned. Above them a rafter creaked. Rafe looked up, helping her back into his bed. "It's only the wind." He fluffed pillows and stacked them against the Louis XV headboard. "I've brought us coffee before we get to work on that giblet gravy."

She could smell the fresh brew and now noticed the service on his bedside table. Lord, she was such a fool scaring herself silly.

"You thought I was up there?" He'd moved to the fireplace and started to stack wood. He was dressed in yesterday's trousers and his same white shirt, partially buttoned and untucked. He had shoes on, but prudence dictated that, venturing into the furnace room.

"I called for you, you didn't answer."

"I would have answered."

"I thought you were teasing me."

Kneeling now on a knee, he turned to her. "I would never lure you into that passage, sweetheart. I don't want you in there. The stairs are weak in places, especially leading to the attic. The stairs at the end of the hall going up, on the other hand, are good."

"Why does the passage go to the attic, you think, if there's no way to exit the house from there?"

"It's not practical as an ingress-egress, I admit, and with the obvious entry to the attic just down the hall, it's not as if anyone would retreat there to hide." He lit the fire. "Of course, you could lead a pursuer astray, going up the obvious passage and —"

"Disappearing down the hidden one."

He rose, unbuttoning his shirt. "What frightened you?"

Her eyes lingered on his beautiful chest, then she heard him slip the shoes from his feet. "I don't know for sure. One of those uncomfortable feelings that comes over a person from time to time." She watched as he pushed his pants over his hips and thighs. He wasn't stiff now, but that only made him less ominous, not less appealing. Her breathing slowed.

"I hope, my beauty, you are not experiencing one of those uncomfortable feelings now."

"Nothing that being held by you would not chase away."

Chapter Twenty-six

"She make the dressin' separate," Simon told Delilah. "Uses chicken. Don't believe I ever ate a real stuffed turkey. Mama say it takes the turkey too long to cook."

Careful in the sodden grass, Delilah moved around the bush, which Simon, in front of her, skirted.

"Mr. Stone suggested we do the same thing. We'll be eating dressing for the next week."

"Yes'm. Most folks will, I reckon, and that be fine with me."

He stopped and pointed to a mound on the side of a shallow hollow.

"Tunnel come out here, but that be years ago. Merrifield's boys found it. He filled it in. Didn't trust havin' another entrance into the house." Simon looked up at the clear November sky and shrugged. "Don't matter none now, I reckon. Don't think there'll be any more river raids, and we won't be fightin' them Yankees for a while."

"Forever, let's hope."

War's destruction, if not its long-term consequences, had bypassed Natchez, and explained, in part, why River's Bend still stood. Delilah looked up the sloping hill to the sun-drenched house, its white columns bright, imposing still, against the azure sky. A cold wind blew and leaves still clinging to the branches of deciduous trees shivered, while others scattered across the unkempt lawn. Visibly untouched the house might be, but within its walls, its soul was scarred. The War, in a more subtle way, had taken its heritage, the progeny of those who built it, those who loved and nurtured it as much more than a house. With Lorelei

156

Richard's demise had come interlopers, and they had brought with them greed and lust and death. Not unlike what the hateful Yankee Republicans had foisted upon the South.

A frigid gust of wind howled from the north. Delilah wrapped her arms around herself, glad for her wool coat, and with a shudder recalled the terror she'd experienced yesterday morning when she opened the panel in her room. Inwardly, she cursed and closed her eyes, then warmed with the memory of Rafe's adept touch. He'd kept her with him through another night, and she hoped he intended the move to his room permanent.

She opened her eyes, momentarily blinded by the reflection of sunlight off the white-washed brick. What had River's Bend's present occupants brought with them?

Simon spread the rain-soaked grass and dead brambles with his booted foot.

"You're sure there were no other entries?" she asked.

"I'm sho'. I were in that basement hole as a boy myself, Miss Delilah. You saw for yourself there was only that one tunnel."

"Could the tunnel have branched off?"

"Didn't then. Come straight on out to this place here. Can't rule out that someone added another tunnel after, but that ain't an easy thing to do, and I reckon I'd of seen somethin'. Besides, your husband told me a few days ago he went down that passage to where it was closed in."

"He's talked to you?"

Simon chuckled. "Yes'm. 'Stead of you two talkin' to me, one of you needs to be talkin' to the other."

So Rafe had worries of his own; worries he wasn't sharing with her, though he had told her he'd been down that tunnel from the inside. He'd also not wanted her to explore the tunnel that night he'd taken her down the passage stairs. She had only his word for what was inside.

To trust or not to trust? And what was she trusting him with? She wanted the truth regarding this man with whom she now slept at night, but he was reluctant to divulge it.

"Do you remember the Merrifield boys, Simon?"

157

"Some. I was older, so we didn't play together, and I weren't on River's Bend much after Miss Lorelei disappeared. Mama, she worked here at first, cleanin' and cookin' and he'pin' the first Mrs. Merrifield, but they hired themselves young white women. Mama, she say Miss Emmaline, she be the first Mrs. Merrifield, was born on a slave-holding farm up on the Big Black outside Vicksburg. Miss Emmaline was real young when her mama died. By the time she was thirteen, her papa expected her to manage the house. Most young misses don't get that job till they wed. She say the house servants was more trouble than they was worth, always fussin' and not doin' what she say. Easier to do it herself. Said she was happy to wed a man from Ohio didn't own no slaves, and she left her daddy's house."

Simon nodded toward the river. "All that's growed up now, but come spring you'll see the woods full of azaleas of every color. Japonica, too."

He started that way, and Delilah followed.

"Now, my mama she didn't like Miss Emmaline not hirin' her full-time, but"—he turned to her and grinned—"Mama she knew River's Bend too well. I know with out no doubt in my mind that she made Miss Emmaline mad tellin' her how to do things—like her darkies when she was but a girl tryin' to be mistress for her papa.

"Now, Mama, she say the mister was the one didn't want her. She said a pretty young white woman was more temptin' for a ruttin' man with a wanderin' eye than some old, bent, negra woman. Said he didn't like darkies at all."

Mr. Merrifield seems to have had a reputation for fornicating, and Delilah could readily believe either story. Perhaps there was truth to both, and Emmaline Merrifield may well have turned a blind eye to her husband's diddling, happy he left her alone.

Simon stopped and pointed to a naked tree.

"Crepe Myrtle," Delilah said.

"Yes'm. Brightest pink you ever gonna find." He waved a finger along the ragged edge of the woods leading down to the river. "Whole row of 'em all the way to the water."

"It must have been beautiful once."

"Still is," he said, "only in a wild, sad way now."

... in a wild, sad way. ... She wondered if she and Rafe should even touch this yard given Simon's words. "What did the boys look like?" she asked.

"Tow-headed the both of 'em. Tall for them's age."

"Eye color?"

He stopped and frowned at her. "Don't recall if I ever took notice. You need to talk to Mama. Boys visited her a lot when they was growin' up. She filled them's heads with tales of River's Bend and Morgan Ward, who was kin to 'em, and them's bellies with pound cake and divinity. They liked her, and she liked them, and she took extra special pleasure in ruinin' dinnertime for Miss Emmaline."

Delilah came up alongside him, and they moved on together. "Do you think the killers killed them, too?"

"Don't make sense to me, Miss. Why not leave them's bodies like the daddy and stepmama?"

"Maybe they had something the killers wanted."

"What could them boys have had?"

"Yankee gold."

"Confederate gold. Them Yankees didn't hold on to that gold, ain't nothin' says it belongs to them."

A pleasing, if mercenary viewpoint, and for a moment, Delilah wondered if Simon had the gold. She looked over his worn work clothes. If he did, he certainly wasn't spending any of it.

"No, if I had to guess, them boys killed them's daddy and stepmama or they knowed who did. Maybe they saw who done it and didn't want to be dead themselves. Anyways, they run off."

Her heartbeat quickened. "If they saw the killers maybe—"

"Things weren't right in that house after the first missus died, Miss Delilah."

"Please continue."

"Boys weren't happy when them's daddy wed again."

"He married too soon after their mother passed on."

"Too soon and too young a gal, I reckon."

❦

*H*mmph. Wonder if he kept his pretty young maids after he married Cecilia?

Delilah swept into the warm kitchen; it smelled of sage and lye. Turkey soup warmed in a cast-iron pot on the stove. She shivered lightly, then removed her coat and smiled at Lucianne, stirring the white tablecloth Delilah had started boiling before she left the house to find Simon. She'd dropped cranberry sauce on it yesterday and hadn't wanted to risk waiting till washday to try and get it out.

"Has Mr. Stone left?"

"Yes'm. Said he'd be back before dark."

He'd told her before she left the house he'd be gone for the day. Delilah hung her coat on a peg near the back door, then rubbed her hands together. Lucianne opened the icebox door and took out cloth-covered bowls, which Delilah knew contained dressing and gravy. The black woman lifted the cloth, stuck her finger in the latter and tasted it. "Miss Annie been by to see y'all, ain't she?"

"Not in days."

Lucianne frowned. "You made this?"

"Mr. Stone made the gravy," Delilah said on her way out of the room. "He surprised me actually. But don't you worry, Belle's job is not in jeopardy. Neither of us has any great desire to cook, and yesterday reconfirmed that."

*F*rom the northwest corner of the veranda, Delilah studied the oak. Its higher limbs, thirty-five feet off the ground if she were to guess, touched the eaves. She'd certainly never climb out on such limbs to access the roof, but it was not inconceivable that someone would.

To her back, the sun had set over the Mississippi and the air, cold to begin with, had become frigid. Delilah's gaze drifted from the tree to the darkening woods, and she shuddered. Over the years, the forest had encroached on the house, and on this north-west corner, gangly pines and tangled blackberry grew not more than a stone's throw away. She breathed in, studying the dense area in front of her, and her skin crawled.

"It's cold out here, sweetheart."

His voice was soft and seductive, and she almost cried out with happiness at hearing it.

"Rafe, we need to cut down this oak."

She turned and watched him come to her. He stopped beside her and looked at the tree.

"This oak?"

"Yes. It's too close to the house."

"That tree is at least two hundred years old. It's always been too close to the house, and it will remain so."

She stepped closer to the porch edge. "Look way up. Its limbs are damaging the roof."

"Wouldn't hurt to cut back some of those limbs," he said momentarily, then turned his gaze to her. "You still thinking about yesterday morning?"

"Yes."

"Sweetheart, even if someone could get up on the roof, how would he get into the attic?"

"Have you checked it for trap doors?"

"No, but I have for leaks."

She rubbed her arm vigorously with one hand. "I can't shake the feeling something was up there."

"Something could still be up there."

She spun and faced him, and he laughed.

"Honey, it's a bugaboo to keep you in my bed."

"You don't have to frighten me to get me into your bed. All you have to do is touch me."

"Touch you?"

She circled her arms around his waist and laid her ear over his heart. Her smile was for herself alone. "Yes, touch me and I want more of you."

His arms pressed her tighter. She could see the black shadow of the woods, but beneath Rafe's vest, his heart beat steadily. And he smelled good.

161

"Do you ever have the feeling you're being watched?" she asked.

"Sometimes."

"I have it now."

"Something in the woods, you mean?"

"Yes."

"Sweetheart, you are scaring yourself. I don't have that feeling."

"It's not watching you. It's watching me."

Chapter Twenty-seven

ctually he'd had that disconcerting feeling of being watched for days, albeit he hadn't had it tonight on the veranda with Delilah. Further, he doubted whoever watched him, watched her. But even the remotest possibility someone was shadowing Delilah, for any reason, concerned Rafe far more than his being spied upon.

"Our bath awaits."

He turned from where he squatted, tending the fire, and his groin tightened. She was in a chemise, cut-low and gathered beneath her breasts from where it fell to her ankles. The sheer garment was of some delicate, white material and laced at the shoulders with pink ribbon. She wore nothing beneath it; he could see the faint shadows of her nipples and the wedge of her pelvic triangle.

He rose, at the same time twisting his body so he faced her. "Did you buy that in New Orleans?"

"I did."

"I don't remember it."

"You weren't paying attention."

He coughed to soothe his prickling throat. "Honey, I have always paid attention to you."

"To my clothes, then." She looked down at the chemise and fluffed its skirt. "You like my nightdress?"

Damn. He fought the urge to rub the erection pressing against his trousers. "I do. What's it made of?"

"Lawn."

"I'd have guessed silk."

"I have one of silk, too, but it's not quite as"—her gaze locked on his, and she smiled—"revealing as this one."

"And where has my modest bride gone?"

"You prefer prudence?"

"Modesty, and no, I prefer this, but only for me."

The sudden change in her expression threatened his erection, and he would have cursed himself out loud had she not been standing there. What he'd conveyed was her father's attitude toward her mother, though he had not meant to.

"Who are you, Rafe Stone?"

If insane possessiveness had been what she'd heard in his words, she gave no indication. "I'm Rafe Stone," he said and took a step toward her.

She backed into the hall, a silly grin erasing the brief concern on her face. "Tell me who you are."

"I just did." He reached for her.

She giggled, avoiding his grasp. "Tell me what you're doing here."

"You mean to tempt me beyond endurance," he said, stopping and folding his arms across his chest, "then deny me?"

"Deny you what?"

"You."

"Only if you refuse to answer." She'd stopped in the center of the hall. It was dark here despite the gas globes illuminating the corridor's walls. She raised her chin in haughty challenge. "I think the trade fair, my body for information."

"Fair I don't know about, but I'm sure your tactic has been used since the dawn of time. By your namesake, for instance."

Her grin widened, curling her lips that by hook or crook, or plain physical superiority, he was fixing to capture.

"So do we have a deal?" she said.

"I'm your husband, and I live here with you." He dropped his arms.

She watched, and he saw her poise, ready to break. "Why did you want to live at River's Bend?" she asked.

"I like the view."

"Fiddle-faddle."

He furrowed his brow. "You don't like the view of the river from here?"

"Your liking the view is not the reason you wanted River's Bend."

He shifted his weight to his right leg.

She looked down, then up to his eyes. "Tell me the truth."

"Getting worried, aren't you?"

She touched her tongue to her top lip. "Anticipatory only. Tell me."

He sprang.

She yelped, but had barely gotten turned around before he snagged her around the waist and pulled her hard against his chest.

"No," he said, then breathed out gently before tasting the inside of her ear. She arched back against him, part struggle, part surrender. "Now tell me truly that the only reason you presented yourself to me tonight, dressed as you are, was to seduce information out of me." He kissed her neck, and she moaned.

"Actually, the thought of—"

He spun her in his arms and covered her lips. She melted against him, her warm breasts pressed to his chest. He relaxed his firm hold and caressed her bare arms, then pulled back, and she opened her eyes. "Actually," she said demurely, "the thought of seducing you didn't occur to me until I saw that glint in your eye when you turned and looked at me."

"Ah," he said, "learning your power as a woman, are you?"

She moved, bringing a delicately boned hand up to play with the buttons on his shirt. "Yes, I am, but I fear I'm more a victim of my abilities than a master."

"Oh, I'd say you are doing very well."

"I've no more information out of you than when we started this game."

"You'll have to plan better next time." Again he pulled her to him for a kiss. "Which brings me back to my question."

She frowned, then brightened. "Oh, yes, my original motive."

"Does it have any link with anticipatory?"
"As a matter of fact, it does."

At some point—night before last, perhaps, when they'd consummated their marriage—his lack of trust had evolved from frustration to hurt. But she wasn't going to let that spoil this moment. The hurt was too new and his lack of trust too old to hold it against him yet. Besides, she'd started to burn for him the moment she'd looked into his smoldering eyes as he built the fire in their bedroom.

On trembling legs, she stepped back out of his arms, and he let her go. The large Victorian bathroom with its claw-foot tub and dolphin toilet was old and in sore need of a full remodeling, but it was functional, and right now it waited for them, heater churning, the tub full of hot, scented water.

Sure she held his full attention, she brought her hand up and pushed the nightgown off one shoulder. She did the same to the other, then gently pulled the bodice down, baring her breasts, belly, and hips until the delicate fabric pooled around her feet.

His breath was labored, and her pelvis warmed with the excitement evoked by her wantonness. Gracious, she must trust him, mustn't she? That or she was delirious on the thought of sex with him, and nothing else mattered. A delicious shudder coursed through her, partly the cold, partly "anticipation." She loved the way he ravished her with his eyes. Sexual games were proving to be a lot of fun. She gave him a smile, then kicked the gown free of her feet, pivoted and started down the dim corridor.

She heard him move, and placing her hand on the door jamb leading into the brightly lit bath, she looked back. Rafe had knelt to pick up her nightgown. He brought it to his face.

"I am cold and naked in this dark hall, darling. Please do stop your dawdling and hurry up."

He held the gown wadded at his side when he rose, and he started her way.

A floorboard creaked, and she whirled to peer down the hall in the direction of the stairs leading to the attic. Dim light vied with shadow, and her heart skipped a beat. Perhaps there'd been movement, perhaps not. A moment later she was in Rafe's arms. He slammed the bathroom door behind them, shutting the cold and the shadow outside.

Chapter Twenty-eight

"Oh you remember, Elvira, the stories going around about her and that Peters boy, Roy?"

"This is the one, dear," Elvira Cutter said to Delilah before looking over her shoulder to a woman she'd introduced to Delilah as Constance Mack. "I do know, Connie. You remind us—"

"Broke the poor boy's heart."

Elvira sighed. "She was only fifteen then, if I remember."

"I recall the things his mother said of her, and other young men's mamas, too."

"No doubt she was a shameless flirt."

"Married that lusting old man for his money." Constance, her pinched face nodding knowingly, stepped to where Delilah and Elvira Cutter stood. "Oh, I always thought him awful. Ever since I heard about him and the Barwick girl."

"The Barwick girl?" Delilah could keep her mouth shut no longer.

"She worked as a maid in his house." Constance Mack raised her brow and nodded. "He handpicked her."

"Loose," Elvira Cutter put in.

"And she wasn't the only such in his household either—"

"Constance, no one ever knew for sure about Nancy."

"Hmmph. *I* knew about Nancy. She was my cousin."

Elvira stopped stroking the wooden footboard on the bed she was trying to show Delilah and glared at Constance. "She told you for certain she had carried on with Markham Merrifield, and you've kept it a secret all these years? Certainly you do not expect—"

168

"Oh, for the good Lord's sake, Elvira. I said I *knew* her. I knew how she was. She didn't confess anything to me."

Elvira rolled her eyes to the ceiling, obviously much put out, and returned her attention to Delilah.

"She didn't have to tell me, Elvira," Constance persisted, raising her voice a pitch.

"Oh, pooh, Connie . . ." Elvira Cutter waved her hand in dismissal and took Delilah by the arm. "This, my dear Mrs. Stone, is a Louis XV low bed. Perhaps he would like this one better than the one you have already purchased. It's mahogany. It is part of a full bedroom set, but I would consider a partial trade-in if you wished to return the tester bed.

Delilah bet she would, and the piece was beautiful, but she had come here looking for a Belter bed, because according to the description of the furniture given to Delilah by Miss Annie, and subsequently passed to Elvira Cutter by Delilah, a Belter bedroom set had graced the master bedroom of Lorelei Richard Ward's grandfather. Delilah surmised that after the old man died and Lorelei wed, she and her rogue husband, Morgan Ward, had shared that bed.

Despite the beauty of this particular piece, she had her heart set on the Belter bed. Mrs. Cutter didn't have a bed in that style, and Delilah was now much more interested in the escapades of Markham Merrifield, his servants, and his wives, than she was in looking for another kind of bed.

"The house is so large, and Mr. Stone is tall, this bed looks like him."

Delilah contemplated the massive piece of furniture with its central finial in the headboard and carved flowers on the side-pieces. Rafe already had a Louis XV tester bed and this one did not look a bit more like him than that one did. Both were too ornate. Perhaps the Belter bed would be, too—until she actually saw one, she wouldn't know—but the latter had been an intimate part of River's Bend, and that is what she wanted.

"Can you find a Belter bed, Mrs. Cutter?

The woman nodded. "It may take awhile."

"There is no hurry."

Elvira Cutter smiled, hugged Delilah, then said, "Oh, that is so good to hear, my dear. That means you two plan to be there for a while." She stepped around Delilah and weaved her way through the furniture-laden warehouse to her desk in the back.

"Did your cousin Nancy continue to work for Mr. Merrifield after he married his second wife, Mrs. Mack?"

"Miss Connie," the gaunt, older woman corrected, "and no, Nancy was long gone before the first Mrs. Merrifield died. The mister, it seemed, tired of women quickly." She folded her arms beneath her modest breasts. "He liked variety."

"Do you think he continued to practice infidelity after his new wife moved in?"

Connie shrugged her narrow shoulders. "Oh, I would imagine so."

"Did you know the boys?"

"They were handsome," Elvira Cutter said. She had quietly rejoined them. "Their father was not a bad-looking sort, though he'd grown rather stout by the time of his death. But I imagine the boys' good looks came from their mother's side. She was a beauty. Younger than Merrifield, too, though not as much as Cecilia."

"And you don't think Cecilia was forced into the union by her family?"

Elvira cocked her head in what appeared to be feigned shock. "Cecilia got what *Cecilia* wanted. She could have had any man—"

"Not one with a brain in his head," Constance said.

Elvira sighed. "Could have had any number of men—"

"Foolish men."

"Lord's sake, Connie, her father was wealthy. Any 'intelligent' young man could see the benefit in that."

"I have always suspected," Connie said, ignoring Elvira and placing an arm around Delilah's waist, "that one of her numerous suitors killed them."

"Suitor before or after she married Markham Merrifield?" Elvira said.

Constance coaxed Delilah to take a seat on an upholstered settee for sale on the showroom floor, then sat beside her and glared at Elvira Cutter. "Lover then, Elvira, if you prefer."

"And which one would that be?"

Apparently much taken aback, Connie Mack stared at her friend. "How would I know? I can assure you, Elvira, that had I known who killed them, I'd have told the authorities long ago."

"I was under the impression you were speculating."

"I am."

"Speculate, then. Give us a name."

Elvira Cutter was obviously put out. Delilah wasn't sure why, but it might well have to do with too much talk and not enough in the way of furniture sales.

"Well, it could have been Roy."

"You've been trying to blame Roy for fifteen years."

"Where is he now?" Delilah asked, turning to Elvira.

"He's married to the daughter of Connie's nemesis. Connie has been trying to convince herself all these years that the only reason Roy Peters married Sarah was to soothe his broken heart when Cecilia left him."

"And why else would he have married the pitiful, horse-faced girl?"

"Because her father owned a general store and eight hundred acres of black-soil bottomland, and Roy Peters didn't have a pot to pee in. He never had a chance with Cecilia despite his good looks."

"Well, I—"

"Now as for me"—Elvira sat down on the other side of Delilah, drawing her full attention—"I have always said the sons did it."

"But under those circumstances, they couldn't get their hands on their father's money," Delilah said.

"They did it out of hatred, or they found that Yankee gold. Maybe both."

Delilah's heart skipped a beat; Elvira had leaped from fifteen to thirty years back in time. "Morgan Ward's money?"

171

"Hmmph," Elvira Cutter said, pulling a comb from her hair to tack up a wayward wisp. "More than Ward took that money. He'd have never done it without his men and the only thanks he gave them was a bullet in the back."

"Dog," Constance Mack said under her breath.

Well, at least she had these two back on common ground. "Do you two think Lorelei killed herself?"

Elvira snorted. "Her old darkies, loyal to the end, started that rumor, but the ring Morgan Ward gave her when they wed was found on the ship's landing, atop a creosote support post sticking up out of the water two days after she disappeared. For sure she'd divested herself of it before she jumped into the river."

"But why would she have killed herself so soon after the robbery? She couldn't have known he'd abandoned her."

Connie tapped Delilah's arm. "She'd have known if he'd come back through and told her so, and some think he did after he killed that Yankee at Butler Lake."

Delilah started to ask about Butler Lake, but Elvira peered around her to Connie and said, "Someone got killed in that house that night, for sure." She sat back to better see Delilah. "It's common knowledge the kitchen smelled of lye when the authorities got there the next day—all bleached down. Annie was out on the back porch doing laundry of all things. Lorelei was gone, never to be seen again. Now, tell me, what was she doing laundry for?"

Constance nodded in agreement. "Cleaning up and hiding evidence that's what. I think he got as far as River's Bend with the money. When she found out what he'd done—"

Elvira leaned forward. "She probably tried to stop him, planning to turn him in, and he killed her."

Delilah frowned. Rafe had indicated such a scenario, although that was only one of his ideas. Of course, these ladies didn't appear to have a firm idea between the both of them either.

"Then how did her ring get to the dock?" Delilah said. "And do you really think Miss Annie would have hid evidence to protect Ward if he killed Lorelei?"

"Of course, Mrs. Stone is right, Elvira. Miss Annie would

have been the first to see him hanged. I think Lorelei killed him, then couldn't live with herself. That's when she threw herself into the river."

After taking off the ring, of course. "Then where is Ward's body?" Delilah asked.

"She disposed of it," Constance said.

"I don't know if a grieving woman on the verge of suicide would have taken time—"

"Then Annie or her man Gil buried him."

"Or threw him in the river," Elvira said.

Delilah was getting dizzy twisting her head back and forth between these two. "Then does Miss Annie have the money?"

"I doubt Miss Annie or any of hers has the money, given their manner of living," Elvira said.

Constance nodded, then reached across Delilah with a bony index finger and waved it beneath Elvira Cutter's chin. "But you know, Elvira, they always paid their taxes on time, even in lean years, and never once did they run up a bill at Hubert's though he ended up with lots of folks' property, negra and white." She retracted the finger, leaned back, and patted Delilah's hand. "Plenty of folks speculate Morgan hid the money somewhere at River's Bend. If Lorelei did kill him, perhaps it's still there."

"Or years later," Elvira piped in, "the Merrifield boys found it, killed their parents, and ran away with it."

Delilah said, "I've thought about that very thing—"

"You and plenty of others."

Constance Mack harrumphed. "It could have happened a hundred ways. I am telling you that what happened to the Merrifields had nothing to do with the gold. Think about what was done to Cecilia and that randy old man. That was the act of a betrayed lover." Constance sat back, then gave Elvira a quick nod. "Recall what happened to Miles Colburn, what was it, five or six years ago? That lunatic came down here and shot him, then shot his own wife and daughter. Miles might have had it coming, certainly the wife, but why shoot the poor . . ."

Delilah had felt the blood start to drain from her face the

moment Constance Mack spoke the name Colburn. Now, still as stone and just as cold, she watched Elvira, eyes wide and fixed on her, raise a palm to quiet her friend's harangue.

". . . daughter," Constance finished more slowly, then followed Elvira's gaze to Delilah. Poor Connie's eyes widened, as if she understood.

"A wanton woman is at times nothing more than the creation of an insanely jealous man," Delilah said.

Elvira reached forward and grabbed Delilah's hand. "Oh, my dear, indeed. People here never believed that poor woman guilty. Prudie Colburn herself said there was no truth to the husband's accusations."

"Oh my," Constance said, "I'm so sorry, I had no idea. And Elvira is right, people here all agreed that the husband was quite insane."

"Connie, for heaven's sake," Elvira snapped, "shut up."

Constance sucked in a breath. "Mrs. Stone, I could cut out my tongue. If only you'd told us you were"—she wrung her hands and peered at Elvira—"that child?"

Elvira Cutter gave her friend a quelling look, and Delilah stifled a sob with a tear-filled laugh. "A reputed adulteress and a lunatic, ladies. Forgive me for not bragging on my parentage." Delilah rose. "My mother never betrayed my father. She was a good woman and a wonderful mother who wasted her life on a misguided tyrant, because she vowed she would when she wed him. I am proud to be her daughter."

Elvira rose to stand in front of Delilah. "Of course you are, my dear."

"As well you should be," Constance said and also stood.

"My mother was Charlotte Graff," Delilah said. "My father's name was Richard."

Chapter Twenty-nine

Rafe knocked on the front door of the big Fort Adams Victorian. A tall, elderly man opened it.

"Uncle Will?"

Without warning, the man lurched across the threshold and embraced Rafe, the hunger so strong in his frail arms Rafe's eyes filled with tears, and he returned his granduncle's hug. Reluctantly it seemed, the old man released him, then stood aside. "Get on in this house, boy. I've been wondering when you'd work me into your schedule."

The good Dr. William Gavin Stone's house shouted well-to-do. Nothing on the par of River's Bend in size, but certainly the upkeep had been better. Besides, there was only Will Stone, now. He'd been alone for many years.

Rafe had sat in the house for hours, soaking up Uncle Will's bittersweet memories and filling in the old man's missing years with remembrances of his own. More than once the old man had swiped an eye and blown his nose. There'd been a time or two when even Rafe had almost broken down and blubbered.

"When was the last time you saw the place?" he asked.

The old man sat forward in his chair. "August. Stopped by on a trip back from Warrenton. Always do. It was your mother's parting request of me. Just the outside, mind you. Haven't been inside since Emmaline died."

Rafe swallowed. "Uncle Will, about that. I've heard lots of rumors since I've been back. Do you think he killed her?"

Will Stone's eyes narrowed. "Those rumors are bull. Don't

you listen to 'em. Despite everything the man did, every indiscretion he made, Markham cared deeply for her."

Rafe nodded, relieved, and Will Stone cast him a thoughtful look. "I take it you haven't been up to Warrenton yet?"

"I know I need to go," Rafe said and rose. "But I haven't made time."

The old man pulled himself out of his chair. "Well, when you decide to go, take me with you. It's gettin' harder and harder for me to make the trip, and I think you'll find comfort having me there."

"We'll make a day trip out of it."

The old man smiled. "Excellent."

He couldn't imagine needing that comfort more than he'd need it in the next few minutes. "I have made time for one grave, Uncle Will, if I could. If I miss the four-thirty packet, I'll have a three-hour wait till the next boat." Even then he might not make it home before dark, and Delilah would be alone in a house she feared haunted.

Tight-lipped, the old man nodded, then rose. "Yes, you've got to get back to that bride you're saddled with."

"The bane of my existence." He caught his granduncle's eye, bright and blue, and grinned.

The old man snorted. "Your eyes talk, son. Whatever she is to you, 'bane' ain't it. Does she know who you are?"

"She does not, but she's pretty sure I'm not who I say I am, and that's a problem."

The old man frowned, and Rafe shook his head.

"I told you, 'the bane of my existence'."

Rafe followed his elder along a brick walk, which eventually gave way to a worn dirt path well behind the house. "Forgive me for letting it grow up back here," Uncle Will said. "I used to walk here daily and sit in the evenings." He pointed to the west with his chin. "Used to could see the river before the trees took over. Nice quiet place. Helped me relax."

The loneliness probably drove the old codger near insane, but from what Rafe understood, William Stone had had a thriving medical practice, a beloved place in the community, and a taste for the ladies. He'd been spry and handsome in his early and even his middle years, and though he'd not remarried after great-aunt Alice died, he'd not wanted for feminine companionship.

He brought them to a bluff where a proud oak stood sentinel over a quiet plot, its surroundings chilly and barren this deep-fall afternoon. With his foot, the old man brushed grass from the marble marker in the ground. "Always kept this site discreet, you understand."

To protect them all, Rafe knew.

"I need to tell you . . ." The old man looked away, then wiped his nose with a handkerchief. "That was a terrible, terrible night. There are times when things have to be done, decisions made, that may not seem right." He looked at Rafe, watching him, then smiled and blew out a breath. "Next visit, perhaps?"

Unsure what to say, Rafe nodded. His uncle, pensive now, motioned him forward; and swallowing the lump in his throat, Rafe kneeled and read the marker. *Unidentified* was all it said, and Rafe's vision blurred.

"I'm going to find justice for him," he said, then choked.

"He'd only want you to be happy."

"Justice for him will make me happy."

"Home and a good woman to love is what he'd tell you. You get on back to River's Bend and that gal that makes your eyes glow like a demon's. Breathe new life into that old hulk. You won't find happiness avenging ghosts or finding stolen gold."

"And what did the youngest boy look like?" Delilah asked.

Miss Annie blinked and took a sip of the steaming coffee. "Raymond was his name."

Delilah knew that. "What did Raymond look like?"

"Like a beanpole. His hair be light. Can't remember the color of his eyes."

Delilah had returned home from Natchez fifteen minutes ago to find Miss Annie, Lucianne, Simon, and Bo in the kitchen with Belle, all of them watching Harry Tyler and one other man place a new gas stove upon the raised floor, where the woodstove had sat for . . . what?

Only twenty-five years, Mr. Tyler told her when she commented. The Merrifields had put it in a few years after they moved in.

Belle turned to her father and beamed. "Ain't never cooked on a gas stove before."

"It's so little," Lucianne said.

"Ain't got a reservoir or a firebox. Don't need 'em. See here"—Harry Tyler opened the bottom door on the stove—"you got yourself another oven."

"Got only four burners," Belle said.

"All you need," Mr. Tyler said and closed the oven door.

Lucianne skirted around Belle. "What you know? You ever cooked for a house full?"

Harry Tyler snorted. "I know that if you got more than four burners goin' at a time, Lucianne, you need to find yourself an extra cook. And I know enough about cooks to figure y'all'd be stumblin' all over one another."

"They'd be hittin' each other upside the head with fryin' pans, Mister Harry," Bo said.

The helper laughed, and Harry Tyler winked at Bo. "Damn right, boy." The gasman looked at his audience. "Judging from this crew, looks like y'all are gonna be fightin' to use this thing."

Belle smiled and raised a hand. "No suh, Mr. T, I be River's Bend's cook."

"You know, baby chil', that new stove gonna take gettin' used to. Burn things up if you don't watch it."

"Yeah, Mr. Stone, he be sendin' you home to stay."

"You hush up, Bo," Belle said, still beaming, and she turned to Delilah, sitting by Miss Annie at the kitchen table. "I just think this be wonderful, Miss Dillie."

Belle had started calling her Miss Dillie shortly after starting work. The round-about familiarity hadn't bothered Delilah— it had, in fact, given her a feeling of belonging. What did bother her was the name itself, evoking images of a fat pickle. Worse yet,

178

it rhymed with "silly." "Silly Dillie" she imagined people calling her behind her back, if for no other reason than her fascination with the mysteries of this house.

"I'll be real careful, and I'll get used to it quick, I sho' will." The young black woman moved over and hugged Lucianne. "A gas stove, Mama. Ain't we somethin' now?"

Weren't they all. Delilah had learned to cook on a gas stove in her home economics class in school. Many women, particularly from the older generation, her home economics teacher included, didn't like the things, but the school administrators considered the institution advanced, so gas stoves were installed. Once she got used to how much faster gas cooked than wood, Belle would have no problem. What surprised Delilah most about these people's reaction to that stove, was the fact they regarded it as theirs, the house theirs, River's Bend itself theirs. Even Rafe Stone and "silly Dillie" belonged to them.

Delilah sighed, surprisingly content, and turned to find Miss Annie watching her.

"Why you worried 'bout them boys, missy?"

Because this house held secrets, and Delilah wagered Annie Douglas knew the answers to at least some of them.

"What do you think happened to them, Miss Annie?"

The woman gave her a long and thoughtful look, then poked out her bottom lip. "There were some ter'ble goin's-on in this house. I don't know what, but that oldest boy, David, he left the day before the killin's."

Delilah frowned. "I thought both boys disappeared the night their father and stepmother were murdered?"

Miss Annie's head was shaking before Delilah finished her question. "I found Raymond in the woods the day before. He was by hisse'f, wild and red-eyed. They was most always together. I asked him where David was. He said David was gone. Wouldn't tell me nothin' else. Didn't utter another word. Walked off, down toward the river. For all I know, he left then, too."

"Did you tell the authorities?"

"Tol' the sheriff what I seen after. Never did know if he placed

179

much sto' in what I said. By then, old Merrifield and his wife was dead and both them boys gone."

"Do you think David found the money and left his brother?"

Miss Annie narrowed her eyes. "You mean that stolen Yankee gold?"

"Yes."

A smile creased Miss Annie's face. "Don't believe them stories 'bout that gold."

"It was taken." She'd researched it.

"Oh, it was taken, all right, but them boys didn't find any gold in this house."

Delilah studied Miss Annie who watched her with similar interest. How could she know that for sure? And *did* she know it for sure? Delilah squared her shoulders. "The boys were seventeen and fourteen when they disappeared."

"Round that, yes'm."

"They'd be around my husband's age today."

"What you thinkin', gal?"

Delilah drew in a breath. "Do you know who my. . . ?"

Discernment registered in Miss Annie's old eyes, and Delilah silently cursed herself. "I mean—"

"Mrs. Stone?"

Delilah looked up to find Harry Tyler at her side.

"Right now you are without a stove."

"Oh?"

"Got to run a new line for the tank. I need a half-inch fitting vice three-eighths. I gotta go into Natchez, but Collier's is closed till mornin'."

Delilah looked at Belle.

"Got cold ham and potato salad, Miss Dillie. Butter beans are in the pot, still warm."

Good, she'd be able to feed Rafe, who'd gone to Fort Adams this morning to see a surveyor. Dusk was falling; the days were growing short, and suddenly she wanted him here, to have his hard body and adept hands thwart her questions and wash away the recurring doubts his lack of trust engendered.

Chapter Thirty

"Are you sure there's no trap?" Delilah asked.

"Well, no," Harry Tyler said and took a respite from checking the attic ceiling above their heads. "I ain't sure of nothin', but never seen nor heard of a trap, and I've done a lotta work in this house."

"From time to time, they've had to have access to the reservoir on the roof."

"They'd have used a ladder—from the outside."

Of course they would, but the house was so high up. "Who has a ladder that high?"

"Lyle Kendrick has one, . . ."

Well, she conceded a painter probably would.

". . . and Dixie Paul, the roofer, has one, too."

"And these people were around—"

"Miz Stone," he said, "I don't recall who provided the ladder way back then. I don't even know if Merrifield ever had occasion to get someone on that roof. The rainwater reservoir predates Merrifield. He put in the second bathroom." Tyler flexed his jaw, then nodded in apparent acquiescence. "Okay, I reckon someone was up there in his day to run new pipes. The first bath goes back to 1846."

"How in the world do you know that? You'd have been just a boy in 1846?"

He appeared to calculate, then said, "I was thirteen in 1846, but don't matter none. I ain't from here, remember? My point is I researched this house when I started my work for Merrifield. Records are kept anytime a license is purchased."

181

"Oh." She hadn't searched *those* records. In fact, she'd never given them a thought.

"County keeps up with such." He stepped around her with a grimace. "Property taxes, Mrs. Stone. Improve your lot, any part of it, and you're gonna pay for it. Sometimes I think its better to do nothin'."

She drew in a deep breath and followed him. He seemed to be making an effort to find a trap door for her, but he, like Rafe, said a trap in the roof was a ridiculous (neither used that word, but she knew they wanted to) concept because the thing would leak like a sieve.

"When was the last time the tank was checked? Surely those things must be replaced periodically."

"I reckon, but what an engineering feat that would prove. I imagine them that came before you as well as you and yo'rn will patch the leaks for as long as you're able, and I have no idea when it was last checked. Ah, here it is."

And there it was, a brick pillar roughly five feet by five feet square, up against—she looked around the dark, vast space to orient herself—the interior east wall of the house. That would put the water tank, which the pillar supported, well away from the roof's edge, the roof extending over the wide porch. Given the height of the house from the ground, Delilah hadn't seen the water tank and had only Mr. Tyler's and Rafe's words the thing actually existed—that and water in the upstairs bathrooms.

She touched the rough and oddly-shaped brick. "Well, this explains that strange protrusion in the two rooms on this end of the house."

"'Salient' I believe that's called."

"You sound like an architect, Mr. Tyler."

"No, ma'am, just grew familiar with some of the terms over the years. Now as I understand it, the first water tower was alongside the house. 'Ugly' was how I once heard Miss Annie describe it. Apparently, a big storm blew it down sometime before the War and the last Mr. Richard, who must have agreed with his cook, moved it to the roof where it couldn't be seen."

"And he built the pillar?"

"In 1856," he confirmed and moved farther into the attic. "Water's heavy, Mrs. Stone. Roof wouldn't have held otherwise, and adding that pillar wasn't much different than adding a chimney given its position on the outside wall."

"Is it hollow?"

He kept moving away. "Solid. Everything about this old place is solid."

She followed, unsure if she were relieved or not at the absence of a roof access. Either she was hearing only the creaks and groans of old joists, or there was another way into this house she didn't know about.

That or — she stopped and looked into the dark recesses of the extensive attic, and her skin crawled — something lived between these walls all the time.

"Houses are easily broken into from a window or door," Mr. Tyler said as if reading her mind. "Ain't no reason for a fella to risk his neck climbin' up on this roof, even if there was an entry."

He stopped and raised his lantern. The rafters sloped gently here at the center of the house, just enough to ensure rain-water runoff. Golden light wavered eerily over a dark, wood wall. He craned his head around one corner, then stepped around the other, again holding the lantern high, creating a dim and disconcerting amber atmosphere in the huge, musty space. "Nothin' but a big wooden box, looks like, Miz Stone. That chimney would be behind it. Wondered for years what possessed 'em to close it up that-a-way."

Her heart was beating like the hooves of a spooked stallion as she stepped closer to what Mr. Tyler obviously considered an aberration, and she prayed her face affected the proper degree of curiosity. Harry Tyler's knowledge of this house was uncanny, and she found it hard to believe he didn't know about the hidden stairwell, a thought suddenly eclipsed by the possibility the secret stairwell housed the trap to the roof.

"Maybe we should find a tall ladder and check out that roof."

He reemerged from around the back corner of the box and

looked at her. "If'n you're determined to see up there, that would be what I'd tell ya to do. You gonna climb it?"

She thrust her chin. "I just might."

He smiled at her. "Well let's not do it tonight, please ma'am. It's pitch dark now and I need to be gittin' on home. You and me need to talk to that husband of yo'rn 'bout gradin' that drive from the River Road. Dang hard to pick my way at night, and it's done got so narrow over the years branches hit my face when I'm sittin' in my wagon."

They did hers, too. "Mr. Stone is talking to someone in the Woodville-Fort Adams area today, I believe, about surveying the road."

"Fort Adams, you say?" He opened the door to the main attic steps, and she started down to the second story.

"Yes, why?"

He shook his head, pulling the door shut behind him. "Just curious as to why he'd go all the way down yonder."

"A friend of a friend, I believe."

Mr. Tyler stopped at the bottom step and blew out the lantern. "I thought your husband was new around these parts?"

"He is. . . ." Sweet heaven, who did he know in Fort Adams? "But he's made acquaintances. Someone recommended someone." Who recommended who, Delilah? She felt awkward and stupid, and curiously vulnerable.

Tyler handed her the lantern. "We all know how that works."

"We do," she said, "that's how we came by you."

"And I'm sure I come highly recommended."

She nodded, leading the way to the curving stairs and the foyer below. "You did indeed."

"Where'd you and your husband come here from, if you don't mind me askin'?"

She turned, hoping she'd forced her expression into some modicum of composure. "I'm from Jackson, he's from Texas," she said brightly. "He had a ranch in Amarillo." Lord, she hoped Rafe hadn't told Mr. Tyler more than he'd told her. "Now, would you like a cup of coffee to send you on your way?"

-⋙·⋘-

$\mathcal{D}$elilah pulled open the top, left-hand drawer of Rafe's dual pedestal desk. Nothing. She slammed it shut and jerked open the one below it. She didn't figure he'd be so foolish as to leave anything in here after she'd inadvertently stumbled across the investigative report on herself, but she couldn't *not* search.

Ah, letters. Four of them. She reached up and increased the gas flow to the gargantuan lamp hanging above the desk, then plopped into the swivel chair, turning so that the light shone on the documents. She faced the Riverview Room's French doors overlooking the dark river.

Mr. Tyler hadn't known the Merrifield boys well. The eldest, he couldn't immediately bring their names to mind, but Delilah knew that David would have been four or five, Raymond barely a year when they moved in. David was fair-haired, Mr. Tyler told her, Raymond bald. David's eyes had been green, and he reckoned Raymond's had been, too. Funny Mr. Tyler could remember the color of a five-year-old's eyes, but not recall the boy's name. But the eyes had been remarkable, Mr. Tyler told her, a golden brownish green. He'd looked at her and smiled. "Till the day I die, I'll recall the color of your eyes, Mrs. Stone. Ain't never seen eyes quite your color."

That had elicited slight discomfort, as if the kindly man were flirting with her, but her interest in David's "hazel" eyes held sway and diverted her worry. Still, she did feel a little better when he left. Belle and the others were long gone and, older man or not, entertaining him alone in this big house, after dark, with her husband who knows where, couldn't be considered prudent. Thank goodness Rafe was not her father.

But who had she married?

Three of the letters were from James Dexter. She snapped one open with a flick of her hand. Obviously, the man was checking other matters for her husband, but from the three short letters, each soliciting a meeting in Natchez at some establishment called Clooney's, she couldn't decipher what. The most recent of the letters requested a meeting four days ago.

185

The fourth was from Uncle Joe. That got her heart racing, though she doubted she'd learn anything from it about the man she'd married, rather more of what Uncle Joe was telling him about her.

But no, the short letter appeared to be a response to one Rafe wrote him. In it, Uncle Joe told Rafe he had sold the Victorian house in Jackson where she and her grandmother had lived, but that Delilah's bedroom had been decorated in white and lavender, wallpapered with a flower print. Ophelia remembered, he assured Rafe. She and Bernadette had gone up to Jackson and stayed a week to help Delilah plan her room.

Yes they had, she remembered, folding the letter and stuffing it back in the envelope. Her parents had been dead six weeks, her grandmother rued her very existence, but despite the fact that Aunt Ophelia and Uncle Joe had not felt compelled to take her in themselves, they'd gone to some trouble, and expense, to make sure she knew some degree of happiness.

Now they'd given her to a stranger and despite an inclination to be the happiest she'd ever been, the nagging question as to Rafe Stone's objectives, or his hazel eyes, wouldn't let her be.

The chair squeaked when she stood to shut off the light. In the dark, she turned toward the French doors, ready to maneuver around the large desk and out of the room. The moon, unseen at the moment from this end of the house, shone on the not-too-distant water.

Outside, the north wind blew, creating a soft wail around the corner of the darkened portico. She shivered, but slightly, and moved to the door to better see the peaceful night. There was nothing to fear; she knew what made the haunting sound.

The gentle breeze stirred the treetops, sparsely dressed in late fall. Folding her arms beneath her breasts, she watched the shimmering river. Rafe was always home before nightfall.

Above her head, a floorboard creaked in tandem with a gust of wind. She looked up to the fathomless darkness of the ceiling. Nothing to fear, if she gave the minor protests of the aging walls no thought. Much, probably all inside her head, if she did.

Her gaze searched out the hall door. She was far from the hidden stairwell where she stood. A creeping dread told her she should check to make sure it was secure, but what would she do if it weren't? And how the devil was she to secure the thing anyway? According to Rafe, the ingress and egress from outside was closed years ago, and Mr. Tyler had assured her there was no entry from above. Again, she considered the possibility of roof access from the hidden passage.

And if by chance there was—her heartbeat quickened with the low wail of the wind—where would she find the panel open? The dining room, her old room, or the attic?

Delilah wrung her hands. Perhaps she would not find it open at all. Perhaps the nefarious someone had snuck within, closed the panel, and now hid within the house.

And maybe, just maybe, whatever moved inside that narrow, twisting stairwell actually resided there, entering and departing the house proper at will, never going outside.

The wind rose in a violent gust, and the bare limbs of the ancient oak cackled against the house. Behind her, the wind whipped the door, and it rattled, giving her cause to face the glass.

With primordial precision, her hackles rose along her spine. On the edge of the porch, silhouetted against the river, loomed a dark form, facing the place where she stood, as if it could see her in the dark. Then the specter rushed the portal with ominous ferocity, blocking out the silver glow of the river, the yard, and the white Corinthian columns. With each step it took, she stumbled one backwards until she collided with the swivel chair.

A snarl escaped her lips as she shoved the wheeled chair away. She rounded the desk, hitting her hip on its sharp corner before sprawling to the floor. Behind her, the door clattered violently in its frame. One palm slipped from under her when she tried to push herself up, and she cracked an elbow against the wood floor. On her second try, though, she managed to find her feet, then she yanked her skirt to her knees and ran.

Chapter Thirty-one

Frantic footsteps clicked the length of the west corridor. Rafe pivoted on one heel as Delilah rushed into the foyer, stopped abruptly, then choked before crying out, "Where were you?"

Good Lord, people did turn as white as the proverbial sheet. "I'm sorry I'm late. The riverboat had—"

"Were you in the back?"

"The back where?"

"The back of the house," she railed. "On the porch, outside the Riverview Room?"

"I've just come in the front door."

"Did you land at our pier?"

"I came up that footpath along the river, by horse I might add. My boat had a fire, it's stranded south of St. Catherine Bend."

Waving her arms in front of her, she took a step toward him, her eyes filled with tears. "You weren't out back?"

Damn, he knew she'd be apprehensive here alone after dark, but he had no idea she'd be terrified.

"No."

She licked her lips and looked back down the dimly lit hall, then started toward him.

"There's something out back."

He wasn't liking the sound of this. "What do you mean, something?"

He would have wrapped her in his arms, but she brought herself up short of him. Worse, she resisted when he took her forearm and tried to pull her to him. Dammit, her eyes were shimmering again.

"It was on the porch, looking in."

"What did it look like, Delilah?"

"Big and black."

A bogey. "Man, animal, or what?"

She curled freezing fingers around his thumb.

"I think it came onto the porch from the yard. It was taller than me."

"Come on," he said, taking her hand in his. If it was taller than her, no doubt the specter was a human male.

"Did you lock the front door?" she said, resisting his pull.

"Yes." That was something he'd made a habit since moving in here, but that was due more to his own paranoia than fears of phantoms lurking in the woods. What was frightening Delilah at the moment couldn't be stopped by a locked door, but he figured more harm than good would come from telling her that. Then again, was the phantom, if indeed she'd actually seen anything, hers or his?

Whichever, she appeared to relax somewhat with his answer and, he hoped, his presence, and now she followed his gentle tug.

As they neared the cavernous door at the end of the hall, she placed her free hand on his bicep, at the same time situating herself behind him. "It came up to the door. It was trying to get in."

His gut tightened with that. Her seeing shadows in the dark, especially stuck here by herself with an imagination running wild, was one thing, but if there was more. . . . "You saw it at the door?"

Her steps slowed. She was keeping very close, but her hand was growing warmer as he held it. "It wasn't just at the door, Rafe. It was rattling the latch, trying to get in."

He patted the hand on his arm. "Maybe it was just the wind rattling the door. It's blowing a gale out there."

"The wind was what caused me to look around to begin with, Rafe. I know the difference. This thing was on the steps coming onto the porch. Then it crossed it like it was going to walk right through the glass. It didn't though. It tried the handle."

"An indication it was somewhat civilized, don't you think?"

He felt her tug on his arm. "Is that supposed to be funny?"

189

"No, honey, it was supposed to imply the thing was probably human."

He was, in fact, working hard to keep even the hint of amusement out of his voice, first because she was so scared, second, because he wasn't positive there was nothing to be concerned about. He didn't believe for an instant this place was haunted, but his presence here alone could mean "someone" was casing River's Bend.

"You were in the dark?" he said and stepped over the threshold.

She followed him in, hindering him only slightly. As much as he wanted to rush to the veranda door, he wasn't about to shake her off.

"I was getting ready to leave," she said. "If the light had been on, I don't believe I would have . . .

"Oh, God," she wailed and squeezed his arm. "It was probably out there in the yard all the time, watching me."

He felt her breath against his cheek and knew she'd turned her face up to his. Quickly, he tilted his head and pecked her on the lips. "But it didn't get in?"

She moved beside him, and he could only assume she was scanning the dark room. That's what he was doing. If anything were in here, it wasn't moving.

"I don't think so. The door was locked. I took off running, but it would have had to crash in and I never heard anything. By the time I got down the hall, you were coming through the front."

He found the door still bolted and unlocked it, then pushed it open. She clutched at him.

"No, you're not going—"

"Shh, do you see anything?"

"It could be hiding."

The near-empty porch—they'd yet to buy furniture for it— was dark, but he could see. He stuck his head out, but didn't venture farther. In truth, he didn't know what the danger was.

He looked at the woman hovering beside him. He could not see her well, but he could feel her anxious touch, smell her gardenia scent. With a grimace, he pulled his head back inside, shut the door, and relocked it. He'd acquired a vulnerability he was better off without, but there was nothing he could do about that now.

"There's no one out there."

She sucked in a stuttered breath and let go of his arm. "No one or no thing?"

He moved to his desk and reached up for the light. The room began to glow, then brightened mightily.

"Why were you in here?" he asked.

Her mouth dropped open. Immediately she clamped it shut and jutted her chin. He almost laughed at her sudden transition from terrified to defiant.

"I was searching your office."

He sat behind his desk and winked. "I've stopped investigating you, sweetheart. Anything else I wish to learn, I'll learn on my own."

"I wasn't looking for information about myself, Rafe."

He glanced up from the drawer he'd opened. "Oh?"

"I was trying to find information about you," she said and kept her gaze on him.

"Were you?" He opened the bottom drawer and pulled out the letters he'd placed there. "You read these?"

"I did."

"Did you learn anything of interest?"

"Only that you are interested in the color of my childhood bedroom."

He tossed the letters back in, shut the drawer, and leaned back in the swivel chair. "Well, I told you how, from now on, I intend to find out more about you. How do you intend to proceed with me?"

Ah, she couldn't quite hide that smirk.

"You were rather vague," she said.

His response wasn't a carefully couched smirk, but a full-fledged grin. He feared she stood a little too far away, but when he reached out and she jumped back, she wasn't quite quick enough. He did have to get out of the chair to rein her in, but once he had his arm securely around her waist, he sat back down. The chair squeaked and rolled a few inches.

"I'm going to sweet-talk it out of you." He kissed her ear.

She had struggled only a moment, more shocked by his sudden movement, he figured, than a real desire to get away. Now she situated herself more comfortably in his lap and turned her face to his. "Ask me anything else you are curious about. You already know my secrets."

Subtle bitterness tinged her words—he studied her eyes—more superficial than anything. "Historical information isn't what I want to know," he said and kissed her. She was slow to part her lips, but eventually she did and even caressed his tongue with hers. Her eyes were open when he pulled back.

"But historical information *is* what I'm looking for on you," she said.

"Then you have your goal."

"And as you suggested just last night, I should withhold sex from you until you answer my questions."

"I suggested no such thing. I was hoping you'd take the same course I'm taking."

"I do believe my tactic will prove more effective."

He tightened his hold when she struggled to get up, then dared to laugh when he almost came out of the chair trying to keep her. Being outsmarted by the little wench was one thing, being physically bested was absolutely out of the question. He yanked her into his lap, then took the offensive and clamped a hand over her breast.

"And you," he said, feinting to avoid a blow to his head, "are the one who confessed that all I had to do to get you in my bed is to touch you.

"Ouch." He freed her breast to take charge of the hand tugging at his hair, then pulled her arm down and around, snagging her wrist with the hand he'd woven around her waist.

She tried to kick his leg with the heel of one booted foot, but managed to kick only the chair. He returned his free hand to her breast.

192

"The devil take you, Rafe Stone. Stop it and let me up."

He kissed her ear, then removed his errant hand and helped her sit up in his lap. He didn't let her go.

As he watched, she closed her eyes, whispered a "woo," then laid her head on his shoulder.

He released her captive wrist. "Are you all right?" He hadn't thought about that old injury when he started playing with her, and now he feared he'd hurt her.

"I'm dizzy."

"And your shoulder?"

She sat back and looked at him. "It hurts a little," she said, then placed an index finger to his lips when he started to speak. "You didn't do it. I fell trying to get out of this room earlier."

"We need—"

"To continue our discussion on information-gathering."

She obviously didn't want to discuss that injured arm, so he said, "What I had in mind was your gorging me with sex, not denying me."

"Oh, you'd like that, wouldn't you?" She wriggled in his lap.

He cursed through clenched teeth and closed his eyes at the unexpected pleasure provided by her fanny, and when he looked again, he found her studying him. She glanced down to where she sat atop his private parts, then looked up and met his eyes. With blatant premeditation, she wiggled again, a smile sneaking across her pretty mouth.

"You little witch."

She giggled and would have moved against his now engorged cock once more had he not dropped an arm across her thighs and stopped her.

"You see, sweetheart, keeping me sated is the better ploy."

Her eyes met his, and she bubbled. "I am certain I will gain better results with denial."

He pulled her close and breathed in her ear. "I think not, for both our sakes."

She closed her eyes and raised her chin to expose her neck to his tongue.

"And you think sexual gratification will stop me from asking you questions?"

He could hope.

"Why don't you trust me, Rafe?"

He relaxed his hold. Dammit. This had been a hard day for him, and all he'd thought about since leaving Fort Adams was losing himself between Delilah's legs. But there was more to her than that. Darn her and darn Josephus Collander for giving her to him. She was causing him to shift his priorities, and he didn't want to do that.

She placed her palms against his chest and pushed. He fought the urge to simply let her go, which was what he should do. "You need to trust me, too, Delilah."

"I do trust you."

"Then why do you ask?"

She blinked at him. "For the same reason you had your Dexter friend investigate me."

"But I didn't trust you."

He'd hoped to elicit levity with this convolution. Instead, she turned her face away.

"Have you eaten?" she asked. "We've ham and potato salad."

He sat forward and rubbed his chin on her shoulder. "There are things I feel you're safer not knowing at this time, sweetheart."

Momentarily she nodded — unsatisfied, he knew — and pushed herself out of his lap. "I'll get us something to eat."

Chapter Thirty-two

"Sweetheart," Rafe said, taking Delilah's arm and guiding her toward the attic stairs, "this staircase and the secret stairwell are the only entries into the attic. No one is getting in from the roof." He closed the attic door behind him. "You didn't tell Tyler about the secret passage while y'all were up here, did you?"

"Certainly not, but he knows so much about this house."

"Let's assume that if he hasn't brought it up, he doesn't know about it, and let's not tell him."

She'd dragged him up here after supper, insisting he show her how to open the panel. The attic access was different from those below since there was no fireplace mantle behind which to hide the mechanism. Up here that device had been secreted in a small space carved-out of the joist closest to the chimney. The space itself was discreetly hidden by a square plug fitted to the hole. Once they got inside the hidden space, she'd been visibly disappointed to find the stairs only went down. From that, he'd gathered Delilah had expected them to go up to the roof despite his repeatedly telling her there was no roof access.

"Something is coming and going from somewhere," she told him, "or it's here all the time."

"Someone, more than likely, Delilah. You're giving us both the willies. And where did you come up with Amarillo?"

She was three steps ahead of him, and she stopped and looked back with an exasperated expression. "I had to tell him something. I didn't want him to know I had no idea who the devil I married or where he came from."

195

"Language, sweetheart."

She turned and continued down the hall. "Oh, shut up."

"But Amarillo? That's in Texas isn't it?"

She'd stopped at the stairs leading down to the first floor. "Of course it's in Texas. Where *do* you come from?"

"Well," he said and blew out the lantern, "I guess it had better be Amarillo since you've gone and told the town's biggest gossip that, but I told you and everyone else at the dinner table the night we met I came from South America."

He moved past her. That should keep her quiet for a while.

"South America is a big place," she said at his heel. "That's like me saying I'm from North America. Besides, you speak with a Southern drawl. We all thought you were lying about that. My uncle indicated you were from Texas."

"That's because I transferred money through a bank in Texas. Your uncle had me checked out far enough to know my offer on the house was good."

"How much did you offer him for the house?"

Uncomfortable with this discussion, he stopped, and Delilah ran into him.

"Suffice it to say I offered him a lot of money and in so doing, I gave away how much I wanted it, and we have already covered this ground."

"Yes, we have. Where in South America?"

At least they were off the subject of his marrying her for the house. "How well do you know South America?"

"The only place I know is Mississippi and not much of it."

"I took you to New Orleans."

She rolled her eyes. "All right, I am slightly familiar with New Orleans and the Mississippi River between New Orleans and Natchez."

"Someday I'll take you to my old home in . . ."

Wide-eyed, she waited.

". . . South America."

She tightened her lips, tilted her head, then moved around him. "Goodnight, Mr. Stone."

196

He laughed. "Goodnight?" It wasn't so funny, though, when she stepped into her old room and closed the door in his face. Moments later he stuck his head through the door joining their two rooms. "You're going to sleep in here alone with that thing roaming around outside?"

"Whatever is inside is worse," she said, pushing him back and pulling the door shut.

"Do you mean me?" he asked through the door.

"I didn't," she hollered, "but now that you mention it, you too."

He grinned at the portal. "Delilah, honey," he sang out in a lilting tone, "if you need me during the night, all you have to do is open the door."

"Thank you," she responded pleasantly, "but I think I'll play the game my way for a while."

Her way, hell. She'd already given her hand away. All he had to do was touch her. He turned to face the lonely bed and considered doing just that.

Instead, he stepped away from the door separating them. Tonight he'd let her have her pride. Besides, there was plenty of darkness left before dawn.

𝒟elilah smacked her lips and tasted laudanum. For days after being shot at the age of twelve, she'd lived on the stuff. You've drugged me, she said to him. Yes, he answered in her dream.

Rafe had knocked on her door at midnight, a cup of tea in hand. She'd been awake — she had no intention of falling asleep in her bedroom, and she'd been determined to keep out of his.

Drink it, he'd told her. Her arm was hurting, he knew that, and the tea would help the pain. She'd never heard of tea easing pain and now, in her dream, she told him so. She lolled her head on the pillow and whimpered as his hand closed on her breast. He kneaded it and hurt her when he did. "No," she heard herself say. Rafe wouldn't touch her like this.

"Stop."

This time she was sure she'd spoken out loud. She felt him

197

crawl astride her. Now both his hands squeezed her breasts. She squirmed, then pushed with her arms trying to shove his hands away. He kneaded harder.

"No," she cried louder.

"This is how you like it."

The voice was muted. His breath filled her nostrils, foul and warm, close to her lips.

"Get away!" she cried and struck out. He grunted, but didn't get off her. She screamed, then twisted beneath the covers, which were suddenly light and free. She sat up, awake, drenched in sweat and breathing hard. Her heart and head pounded. Her left shoulder ached; her breasts stung.

The hall door burst open.

The room was dim with dawn's first light. She looked around, then at Rafe, frozen in the doorway.

Delilah released the breath she held and brought her hand to her throat. "What did you do?" she choked out.

"Yes, I put laudanum in the tea."

"And you didn't tell me?"

Rafe raked a hand through his hair and stopped his pacing at the foot of her bed. "No, I didn't tell you," he bellowed at her and immediately regretted it because she flinched, but dammit, she'd scared him witless.

She stiffened her spine, forcing herself to sit straighter. She was dressed in her flannel nightgown, the bedcovers now around her waist.

"Why not?"

He bent down close to her. She didn't, thank goodness, move back this time as she had when he first approached her. "Because I knew you wouldn't drink it."

"Why did you give it to me to begin with?"

Accusatory, and that made him mad as hell all over again. He closed his eyes. Patience, Rafe. "Because your arm was hurting."

"You knew I wouldn't fall asleep in this room of my own free will. Why did you try and make me?"

He hadn't tried, he'd succeeded. He sank to the edge of the bed. "Because I couldn't get you to sleep in my bed. I knew you were hurting from the fall. I gave you the laudanum."

"Knowing there's something in the walls."

He knew nothing of the sort. "Knowing you believe there is something in the walls."

"You drugged me and left me alone in this room. . . ."

"Sweetheart, look at the other side of the bed."

She looked that way, then back at him.

"Well?" he asked.

He saw the movement of her throat when she swallowed. "It looks like it's been slept in."

"I slept by you all night. I would never leave you in here by yourself."

"I was alone," she cried out. "Unless it *was* you."

She drew the covers over her breasts. "Did you have relations with me?"

Lord in heaven, what was she thinking. "Delilah," he said, "I like you to be an active participant in our lovemaking. I like to touch and be touched." He scooted a little closer, his face level with hers. "I like the way you moan when I do something you like."

That didn't draw even the hint of a response. She was watching him, wide-eyed, and he wasn't even sure she was listening to what he was saying. She craned her face closer and breathed in. He frowned.

"Kiss me," she said, her eyes focused on his mouth.

"Kiss you?"

She parted her lips, sucked in a breath, and nodded.

He wanted to ravish that lovely mouth, but kissed her gently, not even touching her with his hands until she placed hers on his shoulders.

"You know how messy sex is," he said against her lips. She now appeared to be living and breathing every word he spoke. "You'd know if a man had intercourse with you."

"Where were you just now?"

199

"It was dawn. I got up about twenty minutes ago. Isn't Tyler coming about the stove?"

"Yes, but he has to get to Collier's first, and Collier's won't open until eight."

"Seven, I imagine." He stood and winked. "The early bird gets the worm." He would offer her the worm, but didn't think she'd be enthralled at the moment. Suddenly, his stomach swelled with bile, and he glanced toward that closed panel.

"I'm going to run you a bath. You check your body at the same time."

Chapter Thirty-three

ood, Miss Annie had joined her.

From his bedroom window, Rafe had seen Delilah come around the northeast corner of the house and walk toward the woods and the hollows, past the spot where once, long ago, that man-made tunnel had provided a safer escape route forty yards closer to the river.

He watched as the old black woman pointed to the egress, closed for decades, which Simon had shown him days ago, and he watched Delilah, hands gesturing and head nodding, searching in every direction beyond that spot, and Miss Annie's graying, cloth-covered head shaking patiently, telling her—he was sure—there was no other way into that tunnel.

He watched them two more minutes, Delilah skirting back and forth across the area, Miss Annie, drawn and hunkered in her heavy woolen coat, following more slowly. Finally, Delilah placed a hand on the old Negress's shoulder. The woman nodded and started for the house. Delilah turned around and headed into the woods.

All right, he thought, turning to the bedroom door, this he wouldn't abide. He bounded down the steps, then to the back of the house and the kitchen where Harry Tyler was installing the new stove, his every move studied by Belle and Lucianne.

Rafe almost ran into Miss Annie at the door, and her mouth dropped open in surprise.

"Where is Delilah going?" he asked her.

"Down to the river, she say. I done told her to keep to the path. Dern, but it turned cold again."

Rafe looked back into the kitchen, then pulled the door shut. "She was looking for the tunnel exit?"

Miss Annie rolled her eyes in consonant with a sibilant sound. "She know where the tunnel come out, she lookin' for another one. Don't know what's wrong wif you and her, lookin' for another way into this house. Why don't you talk to that girl? Tell her what's hap'nin'?"

"Miss Annie, I fear there's more happening than I know." He opened the door and stepped out of her way. "Go on in and get warm."

"Delilah!" Rafe called, and she spun. "Wait up."

He'd closed on her pretty fast, but didn't want to overtake and risk scaring her. Now, her watching, he loped over a worn trail he knew to be an old cow path.

"Where are you going?" he said, stopping next to her.

"To see the river."

"Via the woods?"

She looked at her feet, then around them. "The path is clear."

"Don't care. You're venturing farther into the woods, and I don't like it."

"Rafe, I can see the house and the river from here."

"But I can't see you from the house."

"I didn't know you were watching me."

"Watching you lead poor ole Miss Annie in circles."

Delilah shrugged. "I didn't ask her to come outside, she came because she wanted to. I finally sent her in. She was freezing."

He followed Delilah's gaze up between the bare branches of the deciduous trees. "It's clouding up, too," she said.

"Yep, rain's coming, and it's gonna get colder." He pursed his lips. "Well, what did she tell you?"

She sighed and, him in step with her, started down the path. "I don't care what y'all say, something is getting in that house."

"Have you considered a door or window?"

"We've kept them locked and checked them after every incident, and it's coming up the secret passage."

It, it, it.

She stopped and turned on him. "And if the tunnel into the basement is closed for good, there is either another way in or the thing lives in that stairwell."

The hair on the back of his neck prickled, and his ensuing shudder was not the result of the sudden gust of cold wind.

He caught her hand, as much comfort for himself as her. "Delilah, you told me you were okay. There was nothing to indicate anything was in the room with you this morning, right?"

$\mathcal{P}$hysically there was nothing to indicate something had been in the room with her. Her right breast was bruised, but she'd not told Rafe. She could have done it when she fell in the Riverview Room last night.

"I know it wasn't you, Rafe."

He raked his free hand through his hair. "Delilah, you said —"

"But, do you know who it could be?"

Shock, anger, or was it merely surprise that washed over his face? "I'm sorry?" he said.

"Not that you're a part of it, I'd never believe that, but maybe you know something you're not telling me."

"You already know there's plenty that I'm not telling you, and if I knew for a fact someone came into your bedroom this morning, and if I knew who that someone was, I'd kill the son of a bitch."

Despite the chilly day, she warmed from the inside out.

"But I don't think there was anyone —"

"Or —"

"Or thing, Delilah. I regret giving you the laudanum. That was an error on my part. I only wanted you to get some sleep, and I knew you'd hurt that arm again. But until first light, I was with you all the time, and not once did I touch you in any way that could be considered taking advantage of you, if a man can take advantage of his wife."

She squeezed the hand holding hers. He was angry and defensive, but sweet despite it all.

203

"And I'm finding it hard to believe that you, having seen whatever it was you said you saw on the porch last night, have come wandering down here by yourself."

She looked around at the same time he leaned close to her ear.

"What if 'it' doesn't live in the house, sweetheart? What if it lives in the woods and only comes up to the house at night?"

Goodness, he was right. What had she been thinking?

She whirled around, and he jerked back to protect his head. "Rafe?"

"What?"

"I've got to see inside that tunnel."

"I've been to where the thing dead-ends, Delilah."

"I've got to see for myself."

"You don't believe me?"

Her bottom lip began to tremble, and she bit it. She did believe him, she did. But maybe there was something he missed. Her vision blurred, and she closed her eyes.

"Darn you, Rafe Stone, it's you who doesn't trust me. I have to see for myself there is no way in."

"You are not going to see a ghost, sweetheart," he said, "even if—"

"Stop it!" She freed her hand. "I'm scared to go down there by myself. I'm scared to enter that stairwell." She swiped at a tear. "For the love of heaven, I'm asking you to go with me. I'm willing to enter the bowels of that dungeon with you. If that's not some sort of trust, what is?"

"Quit crying." He reached for her, but she slapped his hand away.

"I'm mad. If I'm mad, I cry."

He didn't look angry anymore, but rather contrite. "All right, I'll take you down there after supper."

It was mid-morning. "But it will be dark by then."

"Sweetheart, even if we went right now it would be pitch black."

"But I saw the thing after—"

"Another good reason to go then—to better our chances of finding *it*."

She blinked at him, and he smiled. He again reached for her hand, and this time she let him take it.

"I have a reason for the time and conditions to my going with you."

She felt his thumb caress her knuckles. "And those are?"

"It's nasty down there. You can't wear one of those new dresses I bought you."

"I have an old dress."

"You can wear a pair of my trousers."

She frowned. "I can't—"

"We'll roll them up and tie them with a rope belt. They'll be okay." He maneuvered closer. "After we get out of that hole, you have to take a bath with me."

She clamped her mouth shut, but couldn't keep the corners of her mouth from turning up. The first time they'd bathed together had been her idea, and it was one he'd actually questioned the practicality of. But he'd been hooked the moment he sank into the warm water and pulled her in on top of him.

"Afterwards," he said, drawing her to him, "you have to sleep in my bed with me."

Before she could answer, his lips covered hers.

"Do we have a deal?" he whispered against her ear after he'd completed the kiss.

"I suppose."

"Just say yes, you witch." And he kissed her again. "Come on, I'll walk with you down to the river."

Chapter Thirty-four

"You believe me now?" Rafe asked her.

The tunnel wasn't really nasty, not the way he'd led her to believe. It was dark and cold and narrow, very cramped in a couple of places, and smelled like freshly dug dirt, despite the fact this ground had originally been disturbed more than a hundred and ten years ago.

Delilah held her lantern up and checked the sealed exit. Water seeped in from above, dripping in places. It was pouring down rain outside. Tangled webs of roots hung from the roof, supported in places by heavy beams. The beams, Rafe told her, were not original. The tunnel, not far beneath the ground, had been shored up periodically over the past century and was dangerous, Rafe said, subject to cave-in, and Merrifield would have been wiser to fill the whole thing in twenty years ago instead of only closing the egress.

"It's not that I thought you were lying to me, but I did hope you were mistaken."

"You thought you might notice something I didn't?"

"Two eyes are better than one."

"Yes, they are, but I used both of mine the first time."

"I meant—"

"I know what you meant. A second check is always wise. However, I find my view is somewhat distracted this trip."

Her stomach quaked, not so much at his words, but the hoarseness of his voice. Heart beating faster, she turned to where he stood. At her back was a wall of dirt, the end of the passage. In front of her, blocking the pitch-black exit, Rafe stood at full height, his face and body disquietingly ominous in the lantern's glow.

"What?" he asked softly.

"You look like a devil."

His eyes glinted in the amber light. "A good devil or bad one?"

"A very handsome, bad devil. There are no good devils."

"Well," he said and set the lantern he held at his feet, "that depends on how you use the word good."

"Good is good."

"Good as in ability, my beauty?"

He took a step toward her, and she resisted the urge to back away. There was nowhere to go.

"What kind of ability?" she whispered.

"Sexual." He stripped off his jacket.

Warmth moistened her pantaloons.

"I intend to make you scream, Delilah."

This morning's nightmare eclipsed her fledgling desire. "You planned this all along." Heart racing, she stepped back. Part of her wanted to bolt; the other part wanted to spring forward and hide her face against his chest.

"I planned for our bath and bed upstairs. I didn't decide to ravish you down here until just now." He snagged her arm and yanked her to him. She dropped her lantern. Its chimney broke, and dripping water extinguished its meager flame, leaving his their only source of light. Then his lips, hard and demanding, closed over hers, and his hands reached for the buttons of the shirt she wore, his shirt, by his design. He tore his mouth away. "Thank goodness," he said, pulling the shirt from the waist of her pants, "I don't have to fool with all those stays and petticoats." He pushed the shirt off her shoulders.

"It's cold. . . ."

He yanked the chemise down and bared her breasts. "I'll get you warm." He pressed her against a wooden brace, then dipped his head and drew on a breast. He nipped gently, coaxing her nipple into a bud, and she fought to control her fear, to enjoy this game.

Then the dark, unseen end of the passage, the end that housed
the subterranean room with its brick floor and rickety stairwell,
gave up a barely perceptible sound, unlike any she'd heard this
old house make.

Rafe, his head bent to her breast, stilled. Then he straightened
and turned, his body rigid, his movements cautious, and she felt
her skin creeping.

She touched his shoulder. "Something's there, isn't it?"

"Shh." Head locked forward, he stooped and found the lantern, its halo lighting only a few feet beyond them. "Get dressed."

Chapter Thirty-five

He didn't rush her, not wanting to give credence to her fears, or his. Cautiously entering the underground room, he held the lantern head-high, paying attention to the dim recesses and corners, particularly that space behind the stairs. He'd about decided the only thing that frightened him was her reaction to a muted sound that probably had more to do with an old house and the wind outside, than a lurking danger within. That and the realization there was only one exit out of here meant he might have allowed them to be trapped in this awful place.

With a quick backward glance, Delilah scooted around him, strategically placing him between her and the now abandoned tunnel.

"I'd come get you," he told her.

She blinked at him. "I'm sorry?"

"You're thinking something is about to grab you and drag you back into that hole, and I'm reassuring you I'd come get you."

She pulled him toward the stairs. "I don't want it to get you either."

Above them a floorboard creaked; Delilah's hold tightened. "It's upstairs."

"It's the wind and the rain outside. That central chimney well creaks all the time. It's probably what we heard in the tunnel." Pressing his arm to his side, he squeezed the hand she'd wrapped around his bicep. "Do you see anything unusual in here?"

Again wood creaked above their heads, and she pressed closer to him.

Briefly he extended the lantern to arm's length and perused

the brick floor. It was an indecipherable mess. "Let's go," he said, guiding her up the first step.

"I know something was watching us. I could feel it."

Inexplicably a shudder passed through him. A sixth sense. Perhaps he really had felt it watching, too.

They checked the entire house room by room, including the attic and the hidden stairwell. She wasn't convinced whatever it was had not climbed from the dank hidden room, then exited by the back door, despite the fact it was locked from the inside, and that, indeed, had been the creaking they'd heard in the basement. Rafe had neglected the furnace after supper and the house was cold. By the time they were done, she was shivering and her teeth were chattering so loudly Rafe said he could dance to the tune. She wondered what that would look like.

He gave her wine and ran their hot bath. Outside, the wind-ravaged rain and dead tree branches beat against the bathroom window, and though Rafe had seemed more concerned with getting her warm than accepting his agreed-upon payment, she did manage to coax him into the tub with her.

"What exactly were your plans for us down in that tunnel?" she asked much later, them in his bed.

"A little game of dominance and submission came to mind."

"You always dominate, and I submit."

"I think that's probably because I'm the male, but may I remind you that you were on top in the tub."

"You put me there."

"Anytime you want to be on top, you let me know."

"And you'll give me permission?" She raised her head from his shoulder and looked at him. His eyes were closed, but he smiled.

"You've already learned how much power a woman wields when it comes to sex."

On a whim, she kissed his nipple and felt him draw a breath. "It was different down there tonight. You frightened me."

Eyes open now, he pushed up on an elbow. "I didn't mean to."

With her entire body, she pushed him back onto his pillows

210

and snuggled next to him. "I know. I feel foolish now, and I was 'warming' quickly when we heard that noise."

"I planned on touching you a lot."

"I should have never told you that."

"I had it figured out."

She rolled over in the crook of his arm and nestled her rump against his thigh. He'd locked the hall door to their room and placed a chair beneath the knob of the one leading to her old bedroom. At her back, she felt him reach to douse the lamp, and the room went black.

"Do you think locked doors will stop it?" she asked.

$\mathcal{N}$ot if it were a phantom, but Rafe wasn't near about ready to accept it being a ghost. A corporeal haunting was a different matter.

He spied James Dexter at their back table in Clooney's.

"Been busy?" Rafe asked when the man stood and extended his hand.

"I have." Dexter dropped Rafe's hand and sat back down. "Got all the way up to Columbus, but that trail has been traveled more than once. All that's left of the boys' people on their daddy's side is Merrifield's sister, her husband, and their three sons, 'bout the boys' ages, who say they never knew the Merrifield brothers. And before you ask, I did confirm those three boys were all born to the aunt and uncle. My guess is the two boys didn't go back to Ohio and no one has seen or heard from the family down here since Markham and Cecilia Merrifields' funerals." James locked his gaze on Rafe. "The aunt showed me a photograph of Raymond Merrifield, taken when he was twelve or thirteen, she told me."

Rafe didn't like the way James was studying him, speculation in his eyes and an unasked question on his lips. But James didn't ask, and after a moment, Rafe said, "What did he look like?"

James shrugged. "Like a normal adolescent. It's interesting to speculate, though, what he would look like today."

"He couldn't have changed that much in fifteen years."

"Maybe not. The real disappointment is she had no photos of David. None were in the belongings turned over to the family."

"Maybe the authorities have one."

"I checked with the sheriff. No photos of David were found in the house following the murders, but he says Emmaline's friends claim there was one. She kept both pictures of the boys on a table in the front room."

Chapter Thirty-six

"Jubilee Parrish, that be my guess," Simon Douglas said in response to Rafe's telling him about Delilah's fright in the Riverview Room the night before last. That was after he'd shared his concerns someone might be coming and going at will from his house.

"Ah." Rafe drew in a long breath. "Jubilee Parrish."

"Yessuh. Old hermit. Been around since long before I was born."

Simon forced the front window up. The sash had rotted, and he shook his head. "Lookin' like you needs to change out a whole slew of these windows, Mister Rafe, but if you be worried somebody breakin' in, don't think this is how they doin' it. I checked. All the catches is still holdin'."

"Mama she knows mo' 'bout Jubilee than me, but ole Massa Frank used to he'p him out. Story was, he shot hisself in the head on accident." Simon moved to the next window. "Didn't kill him, jest made him crazy, but Mama, she say he crazy long before that."

"I've heard of him. The Richards took care of him."

"Yessuh. Fed him, give him old clothes to wear, odd jobs to do. Warm spot to sleep on cold winter nights. He weren't dangerous. Miss Lorelei and us continued to look after him when he come around. He grieved terrible when ole Massa Frank died—refused to believe he was gone. Was always askin' after him. Missy, she finally give up and told him ole massa was feelin' down or just away for a spell. He come around less and less durin' the War, and after Miss Lorelei disappeared he mostly did, too. He'd come back months, sometimes years later. Mama, she say he still wanders up and down the river from Baton Rouge to Vicksburg, maybe farther, beggin' and doin' odd jobs." Simon shrugged and gave up trying to push open the adjacent window.

"This here's painted shut. I'm gonna break it if I keep tryin', but it be rotted too," he said, pointing to the sill. "You needs to change 'em all to make the house look right."

"And I do want it to look right," Rafe said, leading the way to the next room. "I imagine ole Jubilee would be doing his share of stealing."

Simon nodded. "Prob'ly, but just food, maybe some clothes. Imagine he be curious when he saw lights up here at River's Bend. He was real partial to this place and to the ole massa." Simon poked out his bottom lip. "Things changed for him with the Merrifields, though. Mr. Merrifield was particular who he 'lowed around him and his. He run po' Jubilee off mor'n once."

And had Jubilee, years later, reacted with anger? Given what he knew of the mutilations, Rafe didn't think it the work of a sweet-natured, if feeble-minded vagrant. Still, the thought of the off-kilter recluse watching Delilah from outside a brightly-lit house made him a little queasy. Years ago they might have all considered the man harmless, but that didn't mean he remained so over the years. He could be crazier than ever.

*M*organ Ward would be close to sixty today. Delilah flipped a page of the musty volume. What had become of him? Had he died or simply gone mad from losing the woman he loved and now wandered aimlessly, haunting River's Bend?

Here he is. Delilah pressed her index finger beneath Morgan Ward's name in the index, then turned to the cited page. Adams County, Seventeenth Horse Soldiers, C.S.A. Quickly her eyes skimmed over the names of the other men in the company. Twenty-four names, including one she knew—Henry Gifford.

"*B*y the summer of sixty-four, the company was decimated. Only nine men were left, and the unit had gone through more than that twenty-four you found in the Historical Society's archives. What's listed on page twenty-nine is the charter muster. In the years following, many fine men joined while others died in battle from Virginia and Tennessee across north Alabama and Georgia. That's not counting the men lost to the elements and disease." Mr. Gifford sighed softly. "Many a battle is listed on the regimental flags under which the Seventeenth rode. They were back in Mississippi by the War's end."

"They?"

"My name is on the original muster, but I was wounded in a little skirmish back in '62. Spent months in a hospital in Atlanta. Lost my right leg. I was removed from the roster and sent home."

"According to Miss Annie, Ward wasn't from Adams County."

"Not originally. He came to town in '57 like a whirlwind. A likeable, charming rogue and young. A gambler. Poor poker player, but loved racing horses—that he was good at. Won a small horse farm southeast of River's Bend. Didn't win Miss Lorelei till after the War started, though. She was too young, and he was too wild. War sobered us all.

"His horses supplied the Seventeenth early on. He was a real good friend of Jeffrey Talmidge, who formed the unit and served as its first commander. Jeff was killed in Virginia the spring of '63. Morg took over command then." Mr. Gifford shook his head. "Everybody liked Morgan, and he was a natural leader. Those who were left by the time the War was over would have risked anything for him." He slapped his thigh. "Anyway that's what Jeremiah told me when he snuck home on furlough, Christmas 1864."

"Jeremiah?" Delilah repeated the name tentatively, for she'd heard the affection in Henry Gifford's voice.

He smiled and tapped at the corner of his eye. "Jeremiah Gifford. One of those names added later—not on the original roster. My baby brother."

"He didn't survive the War?"

"He followed Morgan Ward that last night. Turned out to be one too many times."

"I am so sorry. Are any of the men left who were with Ward on that heist?"

He shook his head. "Authorities found them all the next day. Bushwhacked by a man they would have died for."

A lump filled Delilah's throat. Though the break in his voice had been barely perceptible, she'd heard it. "They all participated in stealing the gold?"

"Yes. At the time, authorities believed the betrayal originated all the way up the Missouri in Virginia City, Montana with the shipment of the gold. Lots of Confederate sympathizers out there, but I believe, as do most researchers today, that the idea to steal that shipment came from someone in the Federal detail.

"The robbery itself was well-planned and plotted. I'm not as sure about the double cross. Twelve men are known to have died on both sides. Ship's company suffered some wounded. In addition to Ward, one Federal is still missing, technically. He was a member of the detail, but he was seen in the water that night. Authorities are pretty sure the river took him. Took another one, too, but his body was found way down river weeks later."

"The betrayal doesn't seem to fit Morgan Ward, Mr. Gifford."

"The Yankee leader himself was found murdered at Butler Lake. Ward's the only one left."

"Do you think Lorelei left with him?"

Mr. Gifford closed his eyes. "I can't believe Lorelei Richard would have left River's Bend with a man who betrayed everything she believed in, but then I thought as highly of Morgan."

"You believe she might have killed herself, then?"

He opened his eyes and leaned forward, a sad smile replacing the grimace on his lips. "Lorelei was a feisty little thing, and she loved Morgan Ward, perhaps even more than she loved River's Bend."

"Did he come back to the house following the robbery?"

"Always been speculation. Miss Annie had scrubbed down the back mud porch by the time the authorities got there that afternoon. There'd been a brief shower before dawn that day. Nothing was found to indicate which way he'd gone, but most figured he moved that gold to the Piney Woods. That would have been his best bet. All they found at River's Bend was Lorelei's wedding ring on the boat landing. I've always believed Morgan came back through there that night to retrieve her or to tell her good-bye. I don't know what happened after that."

Miss Annie would know if Morgan Ward had come through River's Bend that night, and no doubt she did, but hadn't volunteered that information to Delilah. She squirmed in her chair.

"Could someone else have been involved and betrayed them all? Someone no one knew about?"

He studied her, as if she'd hit a mark, but she wasn't sure what damage she'd done with the strike.

"What compelled you to ask that?" he said momentarily.

Discomfited, she shrugged. "Not only is the story incomplete, it's passionless. I sometimes imagine Lorelei, mistaken about what Ward was alleged to have done, took her life and now walks the halls of River's Bend weeping for him, and him alive, mad with grief, roaming the river a broken man."

Henry Gifford, no longer dumb-struck, smiled at her. "Starcrossed lovers?"

"Yes, but my story doesn't work if Lorelei's love is a coldblooded killer."

"It doesn't work for you," he said, "because you're a romantic, but I can assure you even killers fall in love."

Yes, she guessed they did, and she felt foolish. She started to rise. Awkwardly, he rose, too.

"Mrs. Stone," he said, and she looked at him. "In answer to your question about someone else being involved — I've always hoped."

"Another romantic?"

"For you. Today."

She felt better, and she was sure that had been his design, and his only one. "I thank you for talking to me, Mr. Gifford."

"My pleasure, Mrs. Stone."

She didn't quite believe that. Her questions had dredged up bitter and painful memories. "Please call me Delilah."

217

"Miss Delilah then."

That would do. She turned to the door of his office.

"Miss Delilah?"

She pivoted to face him.

"I've done a lot of investigating on the *Gilded Rose* heist over the years. The presence of you and your husband at River's Bend is a curiosity to me."

"How so?"

"After Morgan Ward's disappearance, River's Bend passed to his closest relative, a younger half sister whose maiden name was Emmaline Sturgeon."

"That is correct."

"Emmaline had married one Markham Merrifield of Ohio, and they had two sons."

Delilah nodded in agreement.

"You are a charming young woman, Miss Delilah, but I am no longer sure you realize what you are involved with."

Her head was beginning to hurt. Two weeks ago she had attributed Henry Gifford's interest in her to the fact her name was Delilah and he knew she'd once been Delilah Graff. Suddenly, she wasn't sure Delilah Graff had interested him at all.

"I did some checking on you and your husband and this most recent sale of River's Bend to one Raeford Stone. I conclude, from what I was able to deduce from the chancery clerk's office, River's Bend was your dowry as part of your wedding contract." He smiled apologetically. "Rather archaic, but I have another piece of the puzzle that explains why your husband might want the house."

She held her head proudly despite the sour feeling in her stomach. Besides, weren't pieces to this puzzle what she was searching for?

"Morgan and Emmaline shared a mother," he said. "Have you uncovered her in your research?"

"No, I haven't looked in that direction."

"I suspected you hadn't, but I think you'll be interested to learn the woman's maiden name was Rachel Stone."

Chapter Thirty-seven

tone. Rachel Stone. William Gavin Stone was her brother Gifford had told Delilah. W. G. Stone raised Morgan Ward after his mother died. W. G. Stone had also had a son and that son's name was Raeford Gavin Stone, born too long ago to be *her* Raeford Gavin Stone, but Raeford Gavin Stone nonetheless.

Emmaline Merrifield had been buried with her people up on the Loosa Chitta River south of Warrenton. Mr. Gifford had been kind enough to pull out the obituary from nearly seventeen years ago, and they'd checked the name of the church, the Big Black Baptist as it turned out.

She opened a dresser drawer, rummaged through it, then slammed it shut. There had to be something here somewhere.

She reached for the drawer beneath it.

"You're putting my laundry away?"

She started, then straightened. Rafe leaned casually against the doorjamb, his arms folded across his chest.

"I'm searching your things, if you must know." She bent down again over the drawer. Behind her, she heard a floorboard creak and knew he was approaching. She slipped her hands beneath his starched shirts anyway. A moment later, she heard the mattress springs squeak. Darn him, he'd sat down on the bed.

"What are you looking for?"

She pivoted, and he cocked his head as if waiting for a response to a perfectly reasonable question.

"I'm looking for something to tell me who you are."

"I'm Raeford Stone. I am—"

"When were you born?"

He frowned. "January 2, 1866."

"Where?"

He hesitated a moment. "Biloxi, Mississippi."

"Biloxi?"

"Yes."

"Why?"

"Because that's where my mother was when she went into labor."

She sucked in a breath so fast she had to fight to suppress a cough. "I hadn't thought about your having a mother." She turned back to the dresser and pulled out the bottom drawer.

"Well, I did. A very nice one, and everything you would want to see I have safely stored away in a place where you can't get to it."

"Why won't you tell me?" she cried, slamming the drawer shut and straightening.

"I answered both your questions just now."

"What was her name?"

"Mrs. Stone."

She narrowed her eyes and ground out, "Her given name?"

"Mama."

"Darn you, Rafe Stone. Why was your mother in Biloxi? I knew you weren't from South America. I knew it."

"My mother would not allow me to be born outside the state of Mississippi."

"Is your birth recorded?"

He frowned. "I would imagine so."

"You don't know?"

"I do not. I've never seen a birth certificate, but she did put my name in her Bible."

"Where is the Bible?"

"My sister has it."

She breathed through her nose and took a step toward him. "And where is your sister?"

He stood up and took her hands, clasping them tight. Then he leaned his face close to hers so that their lips almost touched. "In

220

South America," he said very softly, then proceeded to hold onto her hands when she fought to free them.

He chuckled. "I'm not going to let you hit me, Delilah."

She growled in frustration and finally tore her fingers free. "I would never hit you," she said, then socked his left bicep. Picking up the hem of her dress, she skirted around him.

"You think you are so clever, Rafe, well, I'm no dunce either."

"I never thought you were," he said, rubbing his arm.

"Yes, you do."

"On the contrary, I do not. In fact, I fear just the opposite."

She stopped her retreat. "What are you hiding?"

She saw he almost spoke, but then must have thought better of it. Denying he was hiding something was futile. Finally, he said, "I don't want you involved."

"I'm your wife. I am involved."

"What you don't know won't hurt you or me."

"You think I would betray you?"

"Not purposefully—"

"Accidentally? You must think me a twit."

"Quit saying things like that."

She could hear the anger growing in his voice. Good. Better that than his cavalier attitude regarding her attempts to uncover his past. "What are you ashamed of?"

His eyes narrowed. "I'm not ashamed of anything."

"Oh?" she chirped shrilly. "Is that so?"

"Yes."

"I think you are."

"Fine, Delilah. Think whatever you want."

He turned away, and she bristled.

"Does it have anything to do with the money?"

He laughed, but there was wariness in the sound. "That's it. I'm after that Yankee gold."

"Bullshit," she said and stepped toward him. "What links you to this house is more than the prospect of hidden gold."

"What's for supper?" he said pleasantly.

Her nails dug into her palms. "Look at me."

221

He sighed and turned. "Let it be, Delilah."

She thrust her chin. "Who is William Gavin Stone to you?"

His eyes glinted, but despite her quickened heartbeat, she held her ground.

"You see," he said, taking a step toward her, "this is exactly why I don't tell you anything. You blurt out information you would be better off keeping to yourself."

He stood before her, so close his pleated shirt touched her breasts. His green eyes were stern and cold with anger, his body rigid. Her bottom lip trembled, but she drew it firm. "He's Rachel Stone's brother," she said. "Rachel Stone, also known as Rachel Stone Ward and later Rachel Stone Sturgeon, was Morgan Ward's mother as well as the mother of Emmaline Sturgeon Merrifield, Markham Merrifield's first wife." Delilah rolled her lips to still her puckering chin. "You see, Rafe, I trust you with the information I gather."

His arm circled her waist and crushed her to him at the same moment his lips covered hers in a brutal kiss. She placed her hands on his shoulders, to steady herself as much as anything else. He broke the kiss and hugged her close, bringing his lips to her ear. "You're a reckless woman, Delilah Graff Stone. How well do you think you know me?"

His warmth permeated her wool dress to sear her skin and scorch her soul. "I know that when you hold me like this I feel safe and wanted. I never thought I'd feel that way again. I don't want that to turn out to be a lie. I want it to be real, and I want it to last forever."

He shifted and placed his hands on either side of her face. "You're so damn passionate and so damn stubborn, Delilah." He kissed her before she could protest. "Hush now. W. G. Stone had a son, Raeford Gavin Stone, but I had a special name for him."

She breathed out a stuttered breath. "Which was?" she asked, though she was sure she already knew the answer.

"Daddy."

Chapter Thirty-eight

Rafe stepped into the Western Union station. He was siccing James Dexter on Gifford. Even without the man's showing interest in Delilah, it was past time to get to work on that loose end. Rafe had no way of knowing Gifford's present interest in the *Gilded Rose* raid, but thirty years ago he'd played an important role and lost a brother. Shoot, Delilah was making as much progress bungling around in the dark as Dexter was making under clear directives. Maybe, as James Dexter suggested, he should save his money and set his lovely bride to work on the problem.

But he didn't want her involved. Obviously Henry Gifford thought Rafe a potential threat to Delilah, or the newspaperman would not have insinuated the link between the Merrifield boys and the Stones. Of course, Gifford could be fishing. Gifford had no way of knowing how little Delilah knew about her husband, and she had assured Rafe last night, over a dinner of rice and black-eyed peas, that she had confirmed nothing for the man. But, she'd warned sheepishly, with every question she asked or every one asked of her, she risked divulging her ignorance of her spouse to the townsfolk.

Rafe knew she resented that fact, but he told her the solution was to quit asking questions. She'd responded by snorting like a horse.

Truth was he wasn't sure what was worse, keeping her in the dark or arming her with a cause. He knew determined women too well. A prudent female might keep herself from harm's way, but prudence wasn't a Delilah trait. And then there were the legalities. He despised being indecisive, but he wasn't ready to take on an impassioned partner, not yet. For now, he would work at his own pace.

"*He* was out there on the back porch, poundin' the door and hollerin' her name. I knew somethin' was wrong. With the War, we locked the doors, but she'd given him a key."

Delilah dropped her eyes from Miss Annie and glanced at her own hands twisted together in her lap. Consciously, she relaxed them and leaned back in the rough chair, which sat on the porch of Miss Annie's two-room cabin. Miss Annie had offered her the rocker, but Delilah knew instinctively it was hers and declined.

"Missy beat me to the door. He fell through when she opened it, right onto the floor, knockin' her over 'cause she tried to catch him. Lawd, he were a bloody mess, and my sweet woman chil' gathered him in her arms screamin' for me to get the doctor and him all the time fightin' her with what little strength he had, so she'd know to do no such thing.

"She loved him so. Had since she was a young girl when he first come here from up in Warrenton." Miss Annie chuckled. "He paid her no never mind, 'ceptin' to flirt and tease her. She was only a chil', and he was a young man, a bit of a rascal, but sweet as cane sugar. He raised fine horses on a farm to the south of us. Not long, though, 'cause the War come, and all the young men was anxious to fight them Yankees.

"Morgan left with the Seventeenth Horse Soldiers, and ole master he died. My missy, she all alone, but for us darkies who cared for her like we was her family.

"Spring of '63, them Yankees was fighten' to take Vicksburg. Federal ships come up the river; a slew of 'em stopped at River's Bend. One stayed. The captain and some army officers on that gunboat bivouacked, they called it, in the house. Weren't nothin' my girl could do, so she played the gracious hostess. Oh, her mama would've been proud the role she played.

"Two months later, they left us in peace." Miss Annie found Delilah's eyes and smiled. "Come fall, the handsome Morgan Ward and five of his men rode up and summons my missy. What was

the truth, he asked, to a tale he'd heard she'd been entertainin'
Yankee soldiers beneath the roof of her granddaddy's home?

"Oh, Miss Delilah, you should have seen my Lori's eyes flash.
True, she told him, to save her granddaddy's house. All the fool
men gone playin' war on them's fast horses and in them's pretty
uniforms, leavin' the womenfolk to fend as best they could while
foreign armies did whatever they pleased on their men's land and
in their homes.

"Well, he sat high on his horse, and he looked her up and
down—and I can tell you he weren't seein' no li'l girl when he
looked then—and he asked her how did she *fend* off that Yankee
dog puke." Miss Annie rolled her lips together. "My missy knew
'zactly what he meant with them words, but I'm here to tell you,
there weren't nothin' untoward happened 'tween them Federals
and my girl. I even heard that Union navy man tell one of him's
officers Miss Lorelei was a charmin' young woman and reminded
him much of his daughter back in Rhode Island." A smile wrinkled Miss Annie's old eyes. "Morgan Ward, he knew it, too, I
could tell by the way he watched her. He was tryin' to rile her.

"She told him to get his 'arrogant ass' out of the saddle and
into the house, and she'd show him how a woman fended off a
maraudin' soldier.

"Oh, Lawd, Miss Delilah, I was ready to wup her butt, sayin'
such to him and in front of his grinnin' soldiers. Why she pushed
Billy Tulles out of a tree when she were seven and broke his
arm." Miss Annie shook her cloth-covered head. "Course all them
boys knowed her, had teased her 'bout Morgan for years. They
egged him on like they was schoolboys, and all the while, I held
my tongue. I knowed how long she'd loved him, and we'd all
learned how short life could be with war happenin' all around us.
She went on in the house, and he followed, and the rest of 'em
shut them's fool mouths, like they suddenly realized how serious
things was. Two hours later Morgan come out and asked my man
Gil to fetch Father O'Toole in Natchez. Morgan Ward weren't
Catholic, but all the Richards was. Father O'Toole married 'em.

"He snuck back only twice before that terrible night. Spring of '64 on furlough, then in March of '65. Seventeenth was back in Mississippi for good then, renegades for General Taylor more than anythin', I reckon."

Miss Annie swiped her cheek. The old woman had glanced away from her, and Delilah knew she was having trouble talking.

"He was her life, she couldn't live without 'im. Me and Gil he'ped her move Morgan to the river bank and give him to the water. Ole Mississippi was swollen with the spring run off. Last time I seen her, river was takin' her away, too, bobbin' in the current. Didn't see her disappear, it still be night."

"Morgan Ward is dead for sure then?"

This time Delilah saw the tear before Miss Annie could wipe it away. "Oh, yes ma'am. For sure I can tell you he be dead. So is my sweet Lorelei."

"But did you—"

"I didn't say anythin' to them Federals come lookin' for 'im. Didn't tell the sheriff or any of them lawmen come later, either. Shoot," Miss Annie said before picking up her tin can and spitting brown snuff residue into it, "just look at you, gal. Been over thirty years and still you come today." The old woman's eyes shone bright against her drawn skin, and she nodded. "But I told you what I never told them."

She spit again, then placed the can beside her rocker and sat back, rocking in the cool, late-morning air.

"I think they all knowed I weren't tellin' everythin', but they thought me a stupid ole slave woman, too scared to talk to 'em, like Miss Lorelei done threatened me some way.

"As if she could, even if she wanted to. I was more her mama than anythin'. Same for my man Gil. We be the only two knowed for sure Morgan Ward come here that night."

Delilah leaned forward, pulling her jacket tighter as a north breeze swept the porch and unfurled Miss Annie's laundry, drying on a line at the side of the house. The tiny cabin faced north, connected to River's Bend, half a mile to the west, by a dirt road barely wide enough for a wagon.

"You don't believe he double-crossed his men, do you?"

"Don't and never did. Neither did my Lorelei. He was full of wild oats, but he weren't a cheat, and he weren't no murderer. Morgan Ward cared as much for his men as they did him and if any one of 'em was alive this day and standin' before you on my porch, he'd tell you so. They was betrayed, ain't no doubt of that, but not by Morgan Ward. That boy was a gambler if ever there was one. War over or not, he'd of gone for that gold. Win or lose wouldn't have made no never mind to him. The War, and losin' it, gave him added purpose. Endin' up rich and givin' his men somethin' to bring home with 'em, especially if it was taken from the Yankees, was butter on their wormy cornbread."

The brisk breeze died, and Delilah turned her head to better see Miss Annie. Something wasn't right. . . .

"Her ring."

Miss Annie's brow furrowed, and Delilah straightened in her seat.

"Lorelei's removing her wedding ring and leaving it at the landing is part of the evidence supporting her having killed herself because of Morgan's betrayal."

The old black lips pursed.

"If she knew he hadn't betrayed her and his men and the South, why did she remove her ring? It represented her eternal love for Morgan Ward. She would have taken it to her watery grave."

Miss Annie turned to the worn, dirt yard in front of her house. "That be part of the myst'ry, I reckon."

Delilah leaned forward. "Do you know the answer?"

The old woman smiled.

"And the gold?"

"What does your husband think of the stories 'bout River's Bend, Miss Delilah?"

Delilah watched Miss Annie study her with knowing brown eyes. "He just listens to mine."

The woman nodded as if she understood, then she rose. "Walk must've made you hungry."

The walk along the narrow, sunshine-mottled path had been

a pleasant distraction. Belle had given her directions to her grandmother's house, and Miss Annie had appeared happy to see her
walk up.

"You get up and come have dinner with me. I've had fresh collards in the pot since the sun come up, and the cornbread is still
warm."

"I didn't mean to—"

"Don't say no to me now. My baby Belle be a fine cook, but I
taught her and her mama, too, after my Simon wed her. I done
forgot more 'bout cookin' than either of 'em will ever know."

Simon Douglas pulled the mules up at an old plank bridge.

"Old St. Catherine Creek," he told Delilah.

She was out of Miss Annie's buckboard before he could come
around to help her. Twenty yards south of where they stood, the
creek flowed into Butler Lake. A mile to the southwest, it flowed
out again, meandering for roughly three miles until it emptied
into the Mississippi.

Delilah had spent the noon meal with Miss Annie speculating
on the gold. If Miss Annie knew anything, she didn't share it with
Delilah, but she insisted she knew nothing. Appetite whetted,
however, Delilah had prompted Miss Annie for a detailed account of the Carthage Point heist, which led to a reference to
Butler Lake. Simon had just stepped through the door of his
mother's cabin, and he offered to bring her here. She'd accepted.

The day had maintained its beauty, the afternoon even warming somewhat. It was cooler here, where they'd stopped, shaded
by cypress, gum, and loblolly pine, the air scented with evergreen. She stepped onto the wide bridge, which felt stable, but
she looked at Simon to make sure. "It's safe?"

"Oh, yes'm. This road still used some." He nodded to its eastern progress, and she followed his eyes. A short distance beyond
the bridge, the weed-choked road disappeared around a bend,
itself shrouded by woods. "Not like the old days, though, when it
was kept graded. Down the road apiece was lots of workin'
farms. That was before the War. River's Bend had a gin, and come

228

late fall, darkies moved wain-load after wain-load of cotton over this road."

"Where is the gin?" she asked from the other side of the creek. He followed her on across.

"Burned a few years after the War ended. Some thinks it was a vindictive nigger gettin' even at we's not sure what, others say Merrifield hisself burnt it for the insurance. Weren't as much cotton to gin then, fields was fallow, no one to work 'em, so it didn't prove as valuable as the insurance."

"You own your land, don't you?"

"Yes, ma'am. Ole Massa Frank give all him's people their patch in the quarter when he freed 'em. I got my daddy's now."

"Do you raise cotton?"

"No, ma'am. All that land round River's Bend cottoned-out long time ago. We raise food crops. Little extra for barterin', but come spring, I'll sharecrop for Mr. Billy"—he waved on down the rough road. "Don't know how much longer that will be though. Mr. Billy, he's havin' a bad time. He ain't, by habit, a cotton farmer. Makes for a long year. But these days it's the only crop that will pay the bills and buy seed for the spring. Last couple of years he cain't get ahead of the store. Jest have to do the best we can, I guess, in the world the Yankees left us."

"You're not in debt to the store are you?"

"No, ma'am, but lots of River's Bend's old darkies been forced to leave in the last ten years. Mr. Hubert, store owner, he's gettin' more and more patches of what used to be River's Bend. My mama and daddy told me never to buy nothin' on credit I don't need, cause it done add up to mor'n I'll get come settlin' time."

"Mr. Billy, he's—"

"Mr. Billy James. He an old white man. He give two boys to the Confed'racy and fought hisself. Held on to his place through the Republican times, but didn't matter. Republicans is gone, but they done them's damage. The old massas are gone now and too many mean men have the power, and they done took up greedy, Northern ways. Ain't nobody lookin' out for the po' folk, black or white.

229

"You be careful now, Miss Delilah," he said when she stepped off the road. "That bank gets real sedgy, and wif the rain we had, you gonna bog up."

"I wanted to see the lake."

"Come on thisaway," he said, then took her hand and guided her along the creek. They didn't fight their way through the marsh grass and willows all the way to the bank, for the spongy ground had become waterlogged; but she got a good view of Butler Lake through the clearing made where the creek emptied into it. The sun was just above the treetops to the west, and a gentle northwest breeze pushed the sparkling water against the wooded eastern bank. Shadows loomed over the western side of the lake, its blue-black surface appearing deceptively still. Beyond where the towering cypress thinned out in the middle of the lake, she could see the gray haze of the southern shore. Come summertime, Simon told her, when the sun goes behind the trees, the katydids drown all other sounds with their song. It was a beautiful place.

"Where was the Yankee found?" Delilah asked when they'd slogged their way back to the wagon.

He pointed to a grassy spot next to the road. "Creek was full and flowin' fast with the spring freshets. The wagon was prob'ly here at the bridge. Daddy said they figured them two had just finished off-loadin' the skiff when the shootin' happened." He nodded in the direction of that bend in the road. "They think Morgan Ward moved the gold east to the Piney Woods."

Delilah turned and looked back down the road from where they'd come, back in the direction of River's Bend. Simon had never been told that Morgan Ward had not gone east, but had, in the dark of night, trekked west, on this road he no doubt knew well, to die in the arms of the woman he loved.

Chapter Thirty-nine

Delilah had preplanned her escape this morning. Rafe told her last night he was leaving at daybreak and would be gone most of the day, and she'd known Peter Howell would be bringing his mother Sarah to work early; she'd hired the woman to do the weekly washing and ironing. Peter took her as far as Natchez.

She desperately wanted to get home before Rafe did to preclude having to tell him where she'd gone. He was downright aggravated the afternoon before when she told him she'd been to Butler Lake. She couldn't understand his irritation. The sojourn had been lovely, and what had it hurt for her to see the spot where Morgan Ward had allegedly shot Charles Slade?

He'd responded rather tersely that he didn't like her wandering around in the wilds, even if Simon was with her, and besides, he'd confessed, he'd like to go, too. She figured he'd added that last part when, in the course of his little tirade, he realized what a horse's butt he was making of himself. At any rate, his reaction had been so negative she'd dropped the whole subject of Morgan Ward, Lorelei, and the gold. Anything she got away with today was "butter on *her* cornbread," and she'd keep it to herself.

Well, her worm-infested cornbread had burned in the skillet—as black as the headstone in front of her.

April 4, 1837 – July 18, 1852.

The boy beneath it had lain here more than forty-three years. The marker stood three plots over from Emmaline Sturgeon Merrifield's, his first cousin, she knew, from piecing together what she'd already been told. Rachel Stone Ward Sturgeon and Alice Jackson Stone, the boy's mother, lay between them.

231

A chilling wind buffeted her, and she drew her Mackintosh tighter. A withered bouquet of wildflowers decorated Emmaline's grave, left awhile ago but certainly more recently than the seventeen years since she passed away.

Emmaline's was the grave she'd come to see, more to learn who lay around her than anything else. The name on this boy's marker had been the last thing she'd expected. Drawing a long breath through her nose, Delilah looked up and watched the brittle limbs of a naked oak shiver against a dull, gray sky. The lovely morning had given way to a cold, blustery midday. The temperature was dropping. Rain would follow. She blinked at Raeford Gavin Stone's marker and smiled sadly. Weather to fit her black mood.

"Miss Delilah?"

Her heart lurched, and she almost twisted her ankle when she pivoted to face the voice. "Oh, goodness," she said, placing her hand over her heart, "you frightened the daylights out of me."

Henry Gifford glanced at the headstone. "Seeing too many ghosts, perhaps?"

Heart slowing, she momentarily closed her eyes. "I can assure you the man I live with is not fifteen, Mr. Gifford."

He smiled, and she watched him, using some care, shift his weight. "Nor is he dead, I imagine."

"But who is he?"

She immediately regretted speaking aloud, but Mr. Gifford didn't seem in the least surprised.

"I don't know."

"He told me Raeford Stone was his father." Delilah studied Henry Gifford. "You knew about this grave?"

"I did."

"Why didn't you say something?"

"For the same reason you are being discreet with me, Miss Delilah. I don't know how much you know nor whose side you are on."

Rafe's, I'm on Rafe's side. Why, she didn't know. She blinked rapidly. Yes she did. She knew why, damn his black soul. So Mr.

Gifford was right to be prudent, but she couldn't believe Rafe was the bad man here.

"Could you guess as to who my husband might be?"

He smiled. "I would not."

Meaning he wouldn't, not that he couldn't. "Does he have a connection to these people?"

"I assure you, my dear, I do not know that either. He could be a relative. The only immediate way to confirm that would be to approach Dr. Stone himself. In my opinion, that would be a blatant indiscretion."

She stared at him, and he frowned.

"In case your husband is related to him."

"Yes, of course."

"The other possibility is —"

"He's David or Raymond Merrifield."

Gifford pursed his lips. "Yes, that could be the case, but I was mulling the possibility the man is an adventurer who has knowledge of the money and is after it."

"Would that be so bad?"

Gifford started to speak.

"I mean, if he's a fortune hunter, it's not as though he's a killer or anything. Surely there's a reward —"

"Finder's fee, yes indeed. But why take a percentage of the gold when he could have it all?"

"He could be an officer of the law searching for the money, or a detective, or —"

"He could be any of those things," Mr. Gifford said, holding up a staying hand. "But would a man with a legitimate purpose have married a woman to get possession of the house?"

Delilah's gut twinged. Of course not. Such lengths smacked of a confidence man, and once a bamboozler had achieved his goal, and his wife's usefulness expired, what then?

Mr. Gifford touched her arm. "I'm sorry, Miss Delilah. I did not say what I did to cause you distress. My point is that whoever your husband is, something brought him here. That something is a clue. I want that clue."

❧❧

"℘ere it is. You could probably look at the volumes covering the next several years and find an article on that event."

The weathered old clerk for *The River-Port Times* laid the bound volume in front of her and tapped the yellowed headline with a gnarled index finger. "You take your time, Miss Graff, and let me know if there's anything else I can pull for you."

"Thank you," she said, then laid her hand across her stomach when it growled. She'd caught the eight-o'clock packet out of Natchez. It was lunch time now, and she'd yet to eat. Not that she felt like eating, given what she'd found in the graveyard of the Big Black Baptist Church.

The April 1865 robbery of that Federal gold shipment led by Warrenton's native son, Morgan Ward, had been big news here. The revelation of his treachery had made the event bigger still.

A separate article detailing the life of Morgan Ward repeated the information Delilah had gleaned minutes ago from Raeford Stone's obituary:

> *The nephew of the respected and much-loved Dr. William Gavin Stone came to live with his uncle in 1847 following his mother's death from yellow fever. . . .*

Delilah skimmed the column.

> *Morgan grew up and went to school in Warrenton with his cousin Raeford Gavin Stone. The two were inseparable, closer than many brothers. Both boys symbolized everything Warrenton held dear and were a joy to their parent and guardian, teachers, and neighbors alike. Renewed tragedy struck the lives of Dr. Stone and his family on July 18, 1852, when the esteemed doctor, his son, and nephew, partaking of a quiet fishing expedition on the Loosa Chitta, were caught in a summer thunderstorm. Their small fishing vessel capsized, and fifteen-year-old Raeford drowned.*

234

The article continued, but she stopped and read the part about Raeford Gavin Stone's death by drowning one more time.

This Raeford Gavin Stone certainly hadn't sired her Raeford Gavin Stone before his death in 1852. Her Rafe wasn't born until 1866. Perhaps there'd been another boy, but another with that unique given name linked to Rachel Stone—and Rafe had confirmed that link himself two nights ago—seemed remote.

Mouth dry, she looked up. The clerk was alone, working at his desk across the room. Quickly she glanced around the office. No one here, but him and her.

"Do you know if Dr. Stone is still in Warrenton?" she said loudly enough for the man to hear.

He looked up. "He left before the War."

"Do you know where he went?"

"Fort Adams. Been retired for years now."

Rafe had visited there.

Delilah rose, shutting the huge volume of bound newspapers with a slap. "Where would I find the death records?"

Raeford Gavin Stone was dead. He had been since 1852 when he was fifteen. She'd confirmed that four hours ago at the Warren County seat, Vicksburg. Dooley Moon had taken her up in his old flat-bed buckboard drawn by two mules. She'd asked him to wait for her outside, in front of the courthouse; she figured she'd be an hour at most. She was in and out in fifteen minutes.

Dr. Jacob Fisher, the coroner in 1852, had signed off on Raeford's death certificate. Death by drowning, it said. She'd considered talking to Dr. Fisher, but on a hunch, she had checked the county record of death for his name and found him in 1863. So she took the record of Raeford's death as gospel, and why not? Why in 1852 would anyone fake the death of a fifteen-year-old? Who would have even anticipated losing a war then, much less the theft of all that money?

So Rafe had lied to her about his father, and she wondered if he held any blood relationship at all with Raeford Gavin Stone, or William Gavin Stone for that matter. Had he made it all up to more easily insert himself into an old tale replete with a hundred thousand dollars in gold?

Or was he more intimately involved? And to what part of River's Bend's history did he belong?

She closed her eyes and conjured Rafe's face behind closed lids; relived the first time he had kissed her, made love to her; and recalled his tender touch when she'd broken down at the arrival of her mother's dollhouse. She opened her eyes and cursed herself for a fool, but unless someone proved to her that her Raeford Gavin Stone was a cheat, a cold-blooded killer, a lunatic, or all three, Henry Gifford wasn't going to get any "clue" from her. Assuming she even came up with one.

Alongside, a steamboat whistled as it backed from the Natchez wharf. Delilah's little ferry echoed in refrain, signaling the departure of its own passengers and its haste to get underway. Delilah clutched the railing as the gangplank rolled gently with the river, and a Negro ship hand reached out to steady her until she'd stepped ashore. Night had fallen. Delilah was much later returning than she'd planned, and she still had to make the trek down the river road to home. She looked about for a carriage or wagon to rent.

"Hungry?" Rafe said, stepping in front of her.

She met his eyes. If she swallowed now, she'd swallow her heart. That would fill her up.

He took her elbow. "I am. I was thinking a nice supper at The Pearl restaurant."

"I've not eaten all day." She stopped and freed her arm. "But I fear I've lost my appetite."

"Well, recover it, sweetheart," he said softly. "I'm not angry with you, though I was until I found out where you were."

"And where was I?"

"You went to Warrenton. You're distinctive, my beauty. The ticket agent remembered you. I've met every steamer and ferry since two o'clock hoping you'd come back to me."

"And if I hadn't?"

He smiled. "I would have come and fetched you home."

Strangely, those words warmed her. "Would you?"

"Yes, ma'am. If you ever decide to leave me, Delilah, don't sneak off—tell me to my face. I want a reason."

"I wasn't sneaking off. I didn't want you to know I'd left."

"You should have made a point of getting home sooner."

"I became . . . preoccupied."

"With?"

"My research."

"Looking for Morgan Ward's grave?"

"Why would I go upriver to find the grave of a man thrown in the flood-swollen Mississippi south of here?"

"Right you are. You should have gone south."

She rolled her eyes. "There is no grave."

He laughed. "I can't understand why Miss Annie told you that bizarre tale."

"You don't believe she was telling me the truth about that night, then?"

He again took her arm and led her toward the waiting carriage. "Oh, I think there could be some truth in what she said, but I fear Miss Annie might be purposefully leading you astray."

"Why would she?"

"Because you're too clever, and if someone doesn't divert you, you might find out too much."

"Why would she care? If her precious Lorelei and Morgan Ward are dead, who or what would she be protecting?"

He turned swiftly, placed his hands on her waist, and lifted her onto the carriage seat. "Who or what, indeed."

She narrowed her eyes on him, not sure if he was being cavalier or not. "The gold?" she asked.

He grinned and started around the carriage.

She breathed deeply through her nostrils, then looked forward over their horse's head. Next to her, the carriage gave a little as Rafe climbed on board.

"You?"

"I wouldn't think so." He picked up the reins. "If you weren't looking for Morgan Ward's grave, then what did you do all day?"

"I told you. I did research."

"On what?"

Raeford Gavin Stone. Oh, she wanted to say that name, but bit her tongue, instead. She was not as comfortable tonight as she was last with trusting Rafe Stone, and odds were good, if he were pretending to be the son of a man too long dead, he already knew that man was dead. She turned and looked at him, and he looked back. When she didn't answer, a grin spread across his face, and her heart began to pound. A handsome face and a teasing, boyish grin. No, she wasn't sure of the stakes in the game they played, but she was sure she was willing to risk them.

"So, we're back to that, are we?" he said.

"On even ground, you mean? You tell me nothing, I tell you nothing."

"There's a blanket on the floor."

Delilah shook her head. She was cold, but wasn't ready to pull out the cover. It wouldn't take them long to get inside the restaurant. The ride home would be different.

He glanced over his shoulder for oncoming traffic. "Would you like to ask me something bearing on your research today?"

This time, she was the one to smirk. "Yes, you'd like that, wouldn't you? I'd tell you more with the question than I'd get back with your answer, if I got one at all. What I really want to know is what is on the menu at The Pearl. I'm famished, and I have my appetite back."

He flicked the reins and maneuvered the carriage onto Silver Street. "Granddad moved out of Warren County well before the War."

Granddad. So he was persisting with this charade. She should tell him that she knew the Raeford Gavin Stone "Granddad" had sired died over forty years ago, and "Granddad" had no grandson. Wonder what her handsome husband would do then?

"I know that. He's at Fort Adams."

She watched as he flexed his jaw. "Did you know that before you went up to Warrenton?"

"I did not, but so you are comforted my trip was not wasted,

I went up to find what I could on Emmaline Sturgeon's people, not William Gavin Stone."

"William Gavin Stone could be considered one of Emmaline Sturgeon's people."

"That is true, however, I was looking for her father's people."

He frowned at that. "And did you find any of them?"

"I did not."

"They're gone?"

"I wouldn't know. As I said, I became sidetracked."

"With what?"

"I am not going to tell you."

"Fine," he said, adeptly driving the carriage around a buckboard mired in the muddy street at the top of the hill. "Then let's get something to eat. We're both going to need our stamina when I start seducing information out of you."

"Do your worst, darling. You won't hear me complain."

As long as she was in the game, she intended to enjoy it.

Chapter Forty

"He approached her. Either he followed her up or he was as surprised to see her as she him. I don't believe it was a pre-planned meeting."

Rafe rubbed the back of his neck. He had a slight headache. Too much of the wine he tried to ply Delilah with last night. It had all proved for naught. When it came to seduction, she proved as formidable as he. What he'd ended up with, though exceedingly pleasant, wasn't information. Unfortunately, James Dexter had shown up around eight and roused him from bed. Delilah still slept.

"They only talked about ten minutes. Then she left the cemetery. I continued to shadow Gifford, like you told me to. Do you know what she was doing in that cemetery?"

"I guess she was looking for Emmaline Merrifield's grave."

"Why?"

Dammit. Rafe didn't want Dexter guessing about what Delilah was up to.

"I think she might be trying to solve the Merrifield murders."

A slow grin spread over James Dexter's face.

"Don't say it, Jim. She's my problem." Truth was he suspected Delilah was trying to rule him out, or in, as one of the Merrifield boys, and he didn't want Dexter thinking along the same lines. "You stick with Gifford."

"Gifford was involved with the heist?"

Rafe had hoped Jim would be the one to tell him that. Hell, Delilah might be making headway in her ad hoc investigation of him, but his own had floundered.

240

"He was, and he lost a brother to boot. Henry Gifford was the point of contact between Mizer's co-conspirator, Charles Slade, and the Seventeenth." Rafe held his breath, anticipating Dexter's asking him how he knew that.

"So Gifford never saw Mizer?"

Inwardly, Rafe sighed. "No, but he knew there was a Mizer. He wouldn't deal with Slade until the man told him how he knew about the shipment."

"Gifford approached his brother?"

"And his brother approached Morgan Ward."

"And the double cross?"

"Gifford thinks Ward was part of it, and he doubtless feels guilty for being the instrument by which the Seventeenth was drawn into the plot, then slaughtered."

"I can't help but feel my presence distresses you, Mrs. Stone."

"I would not be concerned if I were privy to the surreptitious meetings you conduct with my husband, Mr. Dexter."

Rafe watched Jim smile at her. "Such elucidation, ma'am, I will leave to the discretion of my employer." The man stopped short of clicking his heels, and Delilah withdrew the hand he held. Jim tipped his hat, turned, and exited through the front door, which Delilah shut so fast Rafe tensed, sure she was going to hit the man in the ass. She whirled on him.

"Was he here because of me?"

"Your name came up."

She glared at him. He was sure she was waiting for him to elaborate, and when he didn't, she raised her beautiful chin along with the hem of her pale blue morning dress and started across the foyer.

Darn it. He almost had Dexter out the door when he spied her on the stairs. She'd stopped in her flight down, her bright smile frozen on her face. The smile faded, but after the brief hesitation, she'd continued her descent, at a much slower pace, and offered Dexter a cool good morning. Until she'd whirled around a moment ago, she hadn't looked his way.

Rafe turned as she stalked past him, watching her departing back. "Don't you want to know why?"

"Are you passing out free information, or are we dickering?"

He touched his tongue to the corner of his mouth and sauntered after her. "We can dicker if what you have to barter is as good as you provided last night."

She stopped. "What I provided last night was offered unconditionally."

"What you offered last night was a well-thought-out diversion, a successful feint to distract me from my objective."

"So you are reversing strategy, thinking to divert me from my objective of gaining information?"

Close to her now, he seized her arms in a gentle hold and tugged her to him. "Under those conditions, I am sure my lips would not be available for talking."

She pulled free and again started for the kitchen. "So you get something for nothing."

"Nothing," he cried in faux distress, "you didn't think it was nothing last night."

She waited on him in the dining room. "Yes, last night it was I who got something for nothing. Your attempts to get me drunk on wine—"

"Resulted in my becoming intoxicated on your honey pot." He spoke as he grasped her waist, and she, looking over her shoulder at the open passage to the kitchen, pushed on his chest.

"Hush."

He looked over her head. "Belle's the only one here," he whispered, holding on to Delilah despite her feeble protest, "and she's gone to gather eggs."

"Still," she said, pushing hard enough this time to free herself, "you've no call to be indiscreet, or crude."

He followed her into the kitchen.

"Would you like some coffee?" she said stiffly.

"I've already had some."

She stared at the plates stacked neatly by the sink. "So you fed him, too. How long was he here?"

242

Rafe shook his head. Her animosity toward James Dexter was misplaced. "I will take some coffee." He pulled a ladder-back chair out and sat at the kitchen table. "Do you want me to make you some breakfast?"

She set the blue-speckled mug in front of him. "No, thank you."

The coffee steamed, and he blew on it, then carefully sipped. Delilah stepped to the sink and started pumping. The pump spat and coughed like it always did, then settled down to an even flow.

"How's your head?" he asked.

She turned to face him. "If you must know, I was in a fine mood until I saw Mr. Dexter at the foot of my stairs."

So, they were her stairs, now? "He had something to report to me."

"Oh?" she said, straightening and folding her arms beneath her breasts.

He squinted painfully and took another sip of the brew. "My head hurts. I think I have a touch of a hangover."

She turned and reached for a high cupboard from which she pulled a bottle of bourbon, then set it on the table in front of him. "Hair of the dog."

He took the bottle, uncorked it, and poured whiskey into his black coffee. "Thank you," he said, meeting her eyes. With a frown, she filled her own cup with coffee, sat next to him, and poured a good ounce of the amber brew into her morning solace.

He expected her to drink it then. Instead she reached for the cream. He blinked, but recovered sufficiently to catch her wrist when she raised the pitcher. "Delilah, what are you doing?"

"Putting cream in my coffee."

"You're going to put sugar in it, too?"

"That was my intention."

"Have you ever drunk that concoction before?"

Tentatively, she looked at the steaming cup, then back at him. "I've never had it with whiskey before."

"If you put sugar and cream in that whiskey and coffee you will make me sick, if not yourself."

"Have you ever tasted it fixed like that?"

"I have not."

"Then how do you know it's bad?"

"Delilah, sweetheart, trust me, you don't want to mix that whiskey with cream and sugar."

Her nostrils flared subtly, and she let go of the pitcher. "Trust you? Or trust my own judgment?"

Okay, he caught the double meaning. "And what does your judgment tell you about trusting me?"

She raised her haughty chin, then picked up the cup and sipped. The taste probably would have been better if she'd stirred in the whiskey. She hissed, but to his utter amazement, she didn't cough.

"You know what really bothers me, Rafe?" she said, setting the cup down hard and spilling the coffee. "You hold your little rendezvous with your hired lackey right here in our house and share information about me, and you do not even consider first talking to me about whatever it is."

"I beg your pardon, what was last night all about? Besides, until I talked to him, I didn't know what to ask. And what makes you think you were the subject of our conversation, anyway?"

Her jaw dropped. "You said my name came up."

"You were an aside."

She stood so fast the ladder-back chair almost toppled behind her. "Fine."

He rose too. "You could be a little more forthright yourself, darling."

"You already know everything about me."

"What did you talk about with Henry Gifford yesterday in Warrenton?"

She visibly paled. "You had Dexter follow me?"

"He was following Gifford."

"Why?"

"Why did you meet him?"

"I didn't go there to meet him. He was checking on something and inadvertently . . ." She blinked and looked down at the table. At least she assumed his arrival had been inadvertent. ". . . saw me there."

"In the Big Black Baptist Church graveyard?"

"Yes."

"Why were you there?"

She narrowed her eyes. "I told you, I was looking for information about Emmaline Merrifield's people."

"Her *dead* people?"

"Yes, specifically the man you called Daddy." Ha, see what he would make of that.

"His grave isn't there. He died six months ago in Brazil."

He said those words without hesitation, but he must know by now that she knew Raeford Stone hadn't died six months ago in Brazil. She sucked in a breath, ready to fling his lie back in his face, but again that growing doubt seeped into her consciousness. "Well, how was I to know that, Raeford Gavin Stone, *Junior!*"

His brow furrowed. She stepped away from the table and made a beeline for the dining room. She had to get away from him long enough to reassess what she'd learned, before she said something she shouldn't.

As, she suddenly realized, he had.

"Brazil, huh?" she tossed over her shoulder. "That's something new."

"Delilah, darn it," he said, closing in on her, "what did you and Gifford talk about?"

"You tell me why you feel compelled to have him followed," she said, still moving away, "and I'll tell you what we talked about."

"Delilah, I want—"

He snagged her left arm, and searing pain shot to her collarbone. With a snarl, she grabbed the rapidly numbing limb with her right hand.

Rafe's curse sounded as if he'd cried out from the bottom of a barrel. Her world spun. Perhaps she was the one in the barrel. He was on her right side now, guiding her toward a dining room

245

chair. The pain in her shoulder was lessening, and she closed her eyes to fend off the awful spinning, but that worsened it, causing her to stumble, then veer to one side. Rafe steadied her and settled her into the chair.

"I'm sorry, honey, I forgot about that shoulder."

Her arm was numb now. He hovered close, concern and guilt written in the strain of his lips and his gaze.

"Rafe, I'm going to be sick to my stomach."

"*I* asked you not to get up by yourself?" Rafe said.

Delilah looked up from spitting toothpowder in the sink.

If she felt only half as bad as her pale skin indicated, she was miserable. Somehow she managed a wan smile, and he handed her a towel. Shifting her weight so that the sink supported her body upright, she took the terry cloth in her right hand. She still wasn't using her left.

"Do you have feeling in your arm?" he asked, turning the faucet off.

"Pain."

He lifted her in his arms, and she stiffened. "I can walk by myself."

"I like carrying you. . . . Is that why you're not using it?"

"When I move it, it feels like it's on fire."

He figured those symptoms must be better than no feeling at all. He had feared, at first, her arm was paralyzed. He turned deftly to maneuver them through the bedroom door.

"Rafe, please put me down. I'm afraid I'm going to be sick again."

She'd been cool toward him since he hurt her this morning, and her persistent irritation with him bothered him to no end. Now, she laid her head on his shoulder. The action would have made him feel better, but he suspected the reason to be something other than snuggling with him. "You're still lightheaded aren't you?"

"It comes and goes."

"Which is why I don't want you walking around by yourself."

He laid her back in bed, then bracing on both arms, brought his face close to hers. "What if you fell on that arm Delilah?"

She averted her face. His question didn't need an answer and he neither expected nor did he get one. He'd talked to his granduncle about her affliction. One day she was going to have one of these spells, and she was going to lose feeling and use of that arm. Dizziness had not come up in that discussion, and she'd told him earlier that vertigo was a recent aberration associated with her old injury.

"I want to talk to the doctor who treated you in Rodney."

"I've lived with this for so—"

"Why have you lived with this?"

"Grandmother considered the operation a waste of money."

"Your uncle wouldn't pay for it?"

"He would have, I imagine, if she'd asked."

He heard something unspoken woven in her words. Irritation at his persistence? Anxiety?

"Why didn't *you* ask?" he said.

He followed her eyes to the window. Outside, the day lazed in mid-afternoon sunshine. Until she'd gotten up just now, she'd been in bed since he helped her upstairs four hours ago. "The operation is dangerous, Rafe."

Fear. That's what he'd heard. She was genuinely frightened of the procedure, and he didn't know if it was because she knew it was perilous, because a doctor told her so, or because she was letting her imagination run wild, and he cursed himself for not having found out more about that injury before now.

"Why wasn't the bullet taken out at the time?"

She faced him. "There was a lot of swelling. Dr. Barette was afraid to do it. He said I needed a surgeon. The bullet is lodged between a bone and a nerve. He was afraid he'd sever something not meant to be severed. "

Rafe rose. "I'm going to Rodney and see Dr. Barette."

She had started shaking her head when he said the word Rodney. "I'm not ready to—"

"I'm just going to talk to him."

"It's already late. You won't be back before dark."

Gently he laid an index finger against her lips. "Belle is here."

Delilah sat forward. "She's not in this room, Rafe."

"Shh," he said and sat back down. He would have drawn her into his arms, but she lay back on the pillows, and he let her be. He didn't want her upset, but her reluctance to move that arm frightened him. Every moment it lay limp by her side, despite her claim of feeling, he grew more apprehensive.

"I don't want you to go."

That was the nicest thing she'd said to him in the past four hours. A shadow moved over the room. Only a cloud passing across the sun, but with the darkening, a cold chill wracked his body. Inexplicably, he turned and looked at his fireplace and imagined it gaping at them.

Natchez had a number of good doctors, surgeons included. He looked at Delilah, watching him. "I'm going to get you some laudanum," he said.

Her eyes widened, but he raised his hand before she could protest.

"Belle is in the kitchen tatting. She can do that right over there on the settee. I'll go see Dr. Surrey. He can talk to Dr. Barette."

Chapter Forty-one

"It's the banner of the Seventeenth Horse Soldiers, Adams County," Henry Gifford said to Rafe. "Presented to the unit by my cousin, Felicia, and the young ladies of the First Episcopal Church of Natchez in June of 1861."

The unit colors, constructed of cotton bunting and patterned after the first national flag of the Confederacy. In its right hand corner a blue field boasted a circle of eleven stars enclosing *17th Horse, C.S.A., Adams Co.* Above the circle of stars, *Honored Sons*, below, *Beloved Home*, the numbers and letters pieced with what was once yellow cloth. The flag was dirty, frayed. . . .

"The worse for wear I'm afraid."

Rafe blinked, then glanced down at Gifford, sitting behind the desk over which the banner flew—tacked to the wall actually, but "flew" was the proper attribute. "I was thinking proud."

Gifford studied him a long moment, then said, "It was returned to me nine years ago by a fella in Indiana. Abner Polk. Farmer turned infantryman, then back to farmer. Seems we'd inadvertently left it behind in Tennessee when making a quick sortie and an even quicker retreat."

"I'm sorry."

"No need. We regrouped"—Gifford smiled—"unfortunately not around our flag, counterattacked, and regained our ground and then some, but by then those Yanks from Indiana had their trophy. Probably even told the folks back home they won the day, which they didn't. Not that day, anyway."

Henry Gifford watched him still. Disconcerting, to say the least.

249

"Ole Abner and I continue to exchange war stories. Now, sit down, Mr. Stone, and tell me what's brought you to my office this afternoon."

Rafe didn't sit. "I want you to leave my wife alone. Delilah has become embroiled in my business, and I don't want her hurt."

"And what exactly is your business, sir?

Rafe leaned over the front edge of Gifford's desk. "Why, that would be whatever it is you assume brought me to Natchez."

Gifford snorted. "I know nothing about you, Mr. Stone."

"I beg to differ. You know my name, which you linked to Rachel Stone and her daughter Emmaline Merrifield, then you graciously pointed out their relationship to my wife."

"Actually, I was hoping she was aware of the kinship and she might tell me something."

"Is that why you met her in Warrenton?"

"Rest assured your wife is innocent. When she confirmed her ignorance of your reputed tie to the Merrifields, I considered she might follow up. She's quite the amateur detective, you know. I followed her to the Big Black Cemetery."

"The more she knows, the more danger she's in."

"And why would that be?"

"Because one hundred thousand dollars in gold is an awful lot of money." Rafe cocked his head at the man. "Men have been known to kill for a sum like that."

"I figured that's why you were at River's Bend. I'm surprised you're just now making your way to my office. Most folks scrounging around for that gold start their search here at the paper."

"The irony being most people don't even know the editor's role in planning the raid. Think of the questions they might have asked."

For the first time since entering the newspaperman's office, Rafe sensed more than curiosity in him. Gifford sat forward in his chair. "There are those who have asked the questions to which you refer."

"The Federals, no doubt. I assume you lied to them, or you'd have ended up in prison."

250

"I'd have risked prison if that would have resulted in Morgan Ward's hanging."

"I'm curious about that, Gifford. Miss Annie doesn't seem to share your animosity toward Ward."

"Miss Annie didn't lose a brother."

"She lost her Lorelei."

Gifford's gaze softened. "Yes, she did, and she was quite fond of her Lorelei."

"To hear her tell it, she loved her like a daughter. Do you ever wonder if you're wrong about Ward?"

"An innocent man would have come back and made things right."

"Not if he were dead."

"There'd have been a body."

Rafe drew in a breath. "You and I both know Ward's not the only man missing from that night."

The subtle change in Gifford was more sensed than seen. "Do I?"

"Slade knew you. He approached you about recruiting the Seventeenth, but you knew where he worked at district head-quarters and doubted he'd be privy to the gold shipment. More likely it was a trap; so you refused to deal with him until he convinced you he was dealing square. He told you he had a contact on the detail escorting the gold. That contact's name was Mizer."

"I've researched the *Gilded Rose* case for years. I don't recall that name among the dead or missing."

"Or living. It was an alias."

Gifford poked out his bottom lip. "Of a man who might very well have died at Carthage Point."

"Except that the crimes committed that night don't fit Ward."

"And why do you say that?"

Rafe shrugged. "You're right. I never knew the man, you did. Would the Morgan Ward you knew have killed off his men for that gold?"

"He killed Slade at —"

"Have you considered maybe Slade fired first?"

251

"For the past thirty years I've considered just about everything, but the scenario you've presented makes no sense. The plan"—Gifford smirked—"as best I've been able to determine, mind you, was to move the gold to the Pearl. The Piney Woods was brimming with renegades and deserters. Ward had contacts there, he knew the area. Slade needed him—"

"Mizer needed him."

Henry Gifford squinted at him.

"Slade wasn't the ringleader," Rafe said, "Mizer was, and they needed the Confederates for only two things, to help steal the gold, then take the blame for the theft. Think about it. It was your and Ward's plan to move the gold to the Piney Woods, was it not?"

Gifford's visage had become inscrutable, and he said nothing.

"Slade agreed with the plan, but in reality, he and Mizer had already arranged to move the gold across Butler Lake and down St. Catherine Creek to the Mississippi. Mizer planned the double cross from the start, Gifford. Slade was his partner, not Ward. Ward was a victim."

"Where's his body?"

"Long buried."

"Then where is Mizer?"

"I hope he's still searching for that gold."

Gifford furrowed his brow. "Are you telling me that gold is still here?"

"I'm telling you to keep away from my wife."

"You need to tell her who you are."

"But then she might tell you."

Henry Gifford studied his face, and Rafe fought the urge to blink. Finally the newspaperman said, "I'm curious, Mr. Stone, have you ever visited the Big Black Creek Cemetery up in Warrenton?'

Rafe frowned at the man. He really wasn't sure how to answer that question. "Why do you ask?"

Gifford shrugged. "A hunch spawned by your lovely wife. What was it that brought you back? Gold, vengeance—"

"Maybe both. What keeps you going?"

"A need to know the truth. My gut feeling is you could use a small dose of truth yourself."

"I already know the truth, Gifford."

"I think you just might know most of it, sir."

Rafe's burning gut told him Gifford suspected who he was, so what did Gifford suppose he was missing? No doubt he'd see the man again, and soon.

The door clattered shut behind him. The day had become blustery, its now leaden skies weighing as heavily on him as his worries. He had known better than to approach Gifford, but Delilah's persistence was pushing him forward faster than he'd planned.

Two city blocks later he opened the door to Dr. Surrey's Main Street office and stepped in.

Chapter Forty-two

"You're up," Rafe said when he opened the back door.

Delilah turned from the cast-iron skillet on the stove, but it was Belle, beside her, who said, "Yessuh, she been up since 'bout three. Heard Mr. Tyler in the next room puttin' in those new lights, and she got plumb scared. Told her weren't nothin' to worry 'bout, but she was determined to get outa bed."

Rafe stepped farther into the room. "What's for dinner?"

"Fried chicken," the girl began again. "Miss Delilah, she he'pin' me get used to this new stove." Belle smiled brightly. "Lawd, it be nice not havin' to throw on wood and poke up the fire."

"It's working well?" He stepped closer still to Delilah and savored the aroma of the crispy meat.

"It is," Delilah answered, then looked over her shoulder at him. "You saw the—"

"Here, Miss Dillie, you let me do that now," Belle said and took the two-pronged fork from Delilah. "Sit down over yonder and talk to Mister Rafe. I can finish."

"I did," he said, leading her to the table. "Dr. Surrey will be by tomorrow to look at you. He's going to do the surgery."

"Not before he talks to Dr. Barette."

Rafe blinked. "Dr. Surrey is a surgeon, Delilah. He's familiar with your case from seven years ago." He reached across the table to take her right hand. "He and Barette are friends. Doc Barette discussed your injury with him. The reason they didn't take that bullet out when you were shot was as you said. They both felt the bullet could be removed easily once the swelling had gone down in your shoulder. By then, of course, your grandmother had moved you to Jackson and never followed up with anyone."

She looked away, and he squeezed the fingers he held. "I told him your symptoms, sweetheart. He thinks he should operate as soon as possible."

"I want to talk to Dr. Barette."

"We don't have time—"

"*We* don't?" she said, turning on him.

She might as well have slapped him. "What is that supposed to mean, Delilah?"

He watched contrition wash over her face, but she held her head proudly. He straightened, too, studying her all the while, then his gut knotted. "You don't trust me."

She blinked rapidly. "I'm sorry," she said, her voice heavy, "but for the first time in years, I wake up looking forward to the day, and my first waking thought is to seek you out." She closed her eyes, then found his. "I'm just wondering how much you really have to lose."

She started at the opening of the kitchen door, and he, not having taken a breath since she started talking, looked up. Simon stepped in from outside, and Delilah rose.

"You 'bout done here, baby girl?" the man said to Belle, still tending the chicken. Simon turned to the kitchen table and offered them a big grin as he wiped his brow. "Done warmed up mightily, Mr. Rafe. Sky's dark. Got us some weather comin' in."

Rafe fidgeted. "That's what the paper said."

Simon stepped up behind his daughter. "Um-um, girl, that chicken do look fine, and it smell even better."

"Miss Dillie done most of it."

"That so?" The man turned to Delilah, who'd joined them.

"She needs time to get used to the gas, Simon."

"Granny say she ain't never gonna cook on anythin' but a woodstove," Belle said. "I told her chicken is done in half the time, but she say that be her point. Got to fry chicken slow."

"Take some with you, Simon," Delilah said. "You can compare. We've fried a whole chicken. Rafe and I won't eat it all."

255

Rafe, in fact, didn't know if he'd be able to eat the first damn bite. "Is Tyler still here?" he said and stood.

Simon's head swiveled. "Yessuh. He be back up d'rectly. We was down yonder by the road, tryin' to figure how hard it would be to run a gas line to you."

"Too far, I imagine."

"Naw, gas lines goin' in all over the county now. He's sayin' your upgrades will take too much gas for River's Bend's plant, but I'm thinkin' he's drummin' up business for his boss at Natchez Gas. That Mr. Tyler liable to improve you into the po'house."

$\mathcal{D}$elilah exited the kitchen with a cup of coffee in each hand. Her feeling better, however, did not lessen the heaviness of her heart or alter the grim reality that she had to make a decision, possibly in opposition to Rafe, about the bullet in her shoulder.

Thunder rumbled, and she hurried past the dining room fireplace, but moving down the dim hall to the Riverview Room and Rafe held a foreboding of its own. Ever since Simon had pulled the door shut behind him and Belle an hour ago, she'd dreaded the coming confrontation with her husband. Her doubts regarding his motives had created a chasm between them, which, so far, he'd shown no interest in crossing.

Above her, a floorboard creaked, and she slowed to listen. The storm had moved in with vengeance only minutes ago, and now the old house rumbled, inside as well as out.

Rafe had been attentive to her efforts to get the meal on the table, and they had endured a quiet supper, the betrayal she'd implied of him gathering over them like the heavy skies outside. While they ate, she'd caught him watching her, as if he wanted to say something, but was unsure what, and at meal's end, he'd cleaned the table and washed the dishes while she dried. But he'd done scarcely any damage to that platter of chicken Belle worked so hard on, and Delilah wondered if he were trying to make her feel guilty. He needn't have forsook his meal; her own recollection of what she'd said had proven sufficient.

Still, they had to talk. Doctor Surrey was, after all, coming tomorrow. So when, after the dishes were done, he told her he wanted to check something in his office, and for her please not to climb the stairs alone, she'd told him she'd make them coffee.

The door to the Riverview Room was ajar when she got to the end of the hall, and she pushed it open with her good shoulder. Rafe looked up from behind his desk at the same moment lightning rent the darkness outside and thunder rocked the house. She saw he was reading the report James Dexter had written on her, and tonight he did not appear compelled to hide that fact.

"Do you want to be alone?" she asked when she set his cup in front of him.

"No," he answered.

The overhead creaked, and she fought the urge to look up, but did glance over her shoulder to the shadowy hallway. They were the only ones in the house now. Night, quickened by the stormy skies, was long on them. Harry Tyler hadn't returned from his survey for a gas line, and Delilah assumed he'd gone home.

Again thunder rolled. She looked at Rafe, watching her with unspoken questions in his eyes. Lord, but it was quiet in this room between the thunder's jolts, and finally, unable to bear her self-disgust, she braced in front of his desk.

"I'm sorry for what I said."

"For being happy when you wake up in the morning or for questioning my motives?" He leaned back in his chair, expecting an answer.

"I know you never wanted a wife."

"At what point do we start *never*, Delilah? I hadn't planned on a wife now, not 'never wanted' one. Your uncle's forcing you on me has caused me to reset my priorities, and part of me does resent that, though my reasons are muddled. But I don't resent your being a pain in my ass as much as I resent what you implied of me earlier, as if I didn't care or even hoped you'd die. Maybe even plotting your demise. Why would you think that?"

He blurred through her tears. "I knew he'd forced me on you, and I knew you considered me a bother. But when you wouldn't let me go, it seemed the only thing for me to do was become your

257

wife, but part of me's always feared I'm not the one you want to share your life with. I mean, you don't, do you? And the lies. . . ."

"I don't lie to you."

But he had, and she knew he had, and lost as to what to do next, she turned to the door. Behind her, she heard him rise.

"It's the light-headedness," he said, his voice rife with anguish.

She stopped, his words sinking in along with the tremor in his voice. Heart racing, she turned to face him. He stood behind his desk with glistening eyes.

"The dizziness and your trouble breathing," he said, and his voice broke. "I'd give up my quest—and my secrets—without a second thought, sweetheart, if that would keep you safe, but it'll make no difference. Dr. Surrey says the bullet's moved and is pressing against a major vessel carrying blood from your lung to your heart. It's got to come out, and it's got to come out now. And yes, the operation is risky, a fact I didn't want to burden you with, but you *will* die if we don't do it. And just so you know, I'm happy when I wake up in the morning, too." He looked at the ceiling. "Share my life with you, Delilah? You have become my life."

"Oh, Rafe!" Unable to hold it back, she sobbed.

"Now, would you please come over here and sit in my lap," he said, "because I really need you to."

Lightning crackled when she stepped his way, drawing her eyes to the preternatural landscape revealed in the flickering pink-hued light outside.

Ten feet behind her unsuspecting husband, a creature loomed against the insubstantial glass of the French doors. Thunder clapped, and Delilah choked out Rafe's name. Darkness snuffed the image, but not before she'd seen the hatred glittering in its eyes.

Rafe, who had twisted to retrieve his swivel chair, now shoved it out of his way. "I saw him," he cried.

Delilah staggered one step forward, her right hand at the base of her throbbing throat as Rafe swung one door open. The wind caught it and slammed it against the wall, drowning Delilah's denial; and Rafe disappeared into the wind-ravaged night.

Chapter Forty-three

No!

The frigid air swirled through the room, bringing with it a wet spray filled with withered oak and yellowed gum leaves.

Lightning lit the yard and illuminated the river, gray and roiling in the distance. The trees shrouding both sides of the house churned helplessly in the roaring wind, and a cold rain drenched Delilah's body and dripped into her eyes, and nose, and mouth, hindering her ability to see and breathe. One foot sank in the spongy grass when she cleared the porch. The earth rumbled beneath the thunder, and in the near distance, Rafe tackled whatever it was that stalked River's Bend. The yard went dark, but for the feeble halo of light cast from the Riverview Room, encapsulating the battle in shadow, and leaving her unable to distinguish the wind-tossed movements of trees and shrubs from those of man and monster. She tripped on her soaked skirt, and she raised the heavy wool and struggled in the direction of the fight.

Lightning again. The thing rose and turned, a tree limb in its hand. Half standing, Rafe reached up, it appeared, to bring the beast back down, but instead had to use that arm to ward off the blow. Delilah screamed as the light flashed out, but she was close enough now to see the black shadow strike with its club once more. She heard Rafe's grunt, saw him fall back, and watched the monstrous form raise its arm over her husband. . . . Lightning flashed, then reflected off an object in the creature's hand.

Thunder drowned her cry, and she forced herself faster. The thing looked up. . . .

Light and noise fused when a gunshot tore through the night.

She scrunched down beside Rafe, then sat on the wet ground, and between feeling around in the dark and seeing by the flickering lightning, she lifted his bloody head into her lap. Behind her, she heard a voice bellowing, "Git outa here. Git, you damn bastard. You go on and git!"

Tears and phlegm and rain mixed poured into her mouth. She touched Rafe's cold skin and smoothed the freezing rainwater over his face. Once she cried his name, then screamed it when he didn't answer.

Someone stooped beside her, and she clutched Rafe closer to protect him.

Harry Tyler's voice penetrated the storm. "He's gone, Miz Stone."

"My husband's been shot," she cried back. She searched for Mr. Tyler's face in the darkness. Lightning flashed, and she saw him, squatting beside her on one knee. "We've got to help him."

"He ain't shot," Tyler said loudly and leaned over Rafe. "Was me fired that gun to scare the bum off. Mr. Stone is knocked out. I'm just hopin' that person didn't stick him."

In the flickering light, she made out Tyler's hands searching Rafe's body for wounds.

"Come on," he said, rising. "Let's see if we can bring him to."

Newfound hope fed her strength, and she wrapped her good arm around Rafe's chest and kissed his cheek. Harry Tyler was shifting his own position, bringing himself in front of Rafe, before gently slapping his face. "Mr. Stone?" He repeated the name louder, the slaps harder. Lightning flickered, and Tyler looked over his shoulder toward where the monster had disappeared. Delilah's laboring heart skipped a beat, her panic over Rafe's injuries distracted slightly as she considered what had disappeared into the woods.

Rafe groaned, then started.

"Rafe, are you all right?"

He reached out and seized her arm, wrapped over his chest.

"It's me—Delilah."

"Deli . . ." He forced himself up, then cursed as he leaned

forward and wrapped both arms over his head. Delilah rubbed his back.

Tyler leaned closer. "Can you get up, boy? We need to get outa this storm."

Delilah felt Rafe's nod. Lightning intermittently illuminated the sodden night, but the thunder had grown fainter. He started to move, and she scrambled to her feet to help him. Tyler stood on his other side and pushed his hand under Rafe's arm, ready to pull him up. Rafe staggered to his feet, then careened onto his knees and threw up. After a moment, Tyler tried again. This time when he rose, Rafe managed to steady himself. Tyler supported most of his weight. Delilah glanced at the ink-black woods they were turning their backs on. She didn't know if it watched them or not, but they were silhouetted, easy targets, against the brightly lit interior of the Riverview Room.

"Will you stop fussing?"

Delilah blinked, and he immediately caught her to him. "I'm sorry, but it should be me taking care of you."

She kissed his bruised noggin, then pushed out of his arms and tossed the rag in the bowl sitting on their dinning-room table. Water sloshed the polished surface, and she snatched the bloody towel from his lap.

"What possessed you to do such a foolish thing?" she said, wiping up the mess before moving to the fireplace. Tyler had built a fire before he'd dried himself off and took his leave. Thank the Lord he'd been here.

"I was told he was harmless."

"Who told you that?"

"Simon."

Rafe watched her, soaked to the skin (he knew because he was, too), try to warm herself. He needed to get her upstairs and changed, but until his reprimand a moment ago, she'd continued to dab at the bloody knot on his forehead. Her concerned ministrations weren't helping matters, and his head still ached. Worse, he was embarrassed for allowing himself to be coldcocked and leaving her defenseless against a man who would, undoubtedly, have murdered them both. They had to catch this person.

"What makes you so sure it's Jubilee Parrish?"

"Honey, you heard Harry Tyler, he thinks so, too. The man has a special affection for the people at River's Bend."

"You call what he did here tonight showing affection?"

Lord she was beautiful, her damp hair, half up, half down, curling around her face. Tyler told him she'd charged out of the house on his heels, ready to fight to the death to protect him. Hell, she didn't have a lick more sense than he did.

"And that so-called affection goes back to Lorelei Ward's grandfather."

"Lorelei Ward's grandfather died in 1861. This Parrish person would have to be in his eighties today." She frowned, then clasped her hands in front of her. "Perhaps he's the ghost we hear walking—"

"He wouldn't have to be in his eighties, Delilah. He's probably in his sixties, and all we're hearing is this old house settling. Ghosts have no physical body, sweetheart. They have no weight to press against an old floor joist. They can't pick up tree limbs and whop people in the head either, and believe me, the body I knocked down out there was hard as stone."

"And the crying I heard?"

His battered brain was unable to come up with a quick response. He hadn't heard the crying. She blinked when he didn't answer and turned back to stare into the fire. "No, you haven't heard it. Maybe I'm the only one who can hear it, because it's coming for—"

"Stop it," he said. "Nothing is coming for you."

Momentarily she bowed her head, then raised her face to the ceiling. "I'm sorry for being so morbid."

She was scared, he was scared. Not of the person outside, but of tomorrow and what the doctor would say, and what the man would tell them needed to be done. Rafe watched her bank the fire and set up the screen. Dammit, he should be doing that.

"How is your head?" she said when she was done.

"It hurts."

"He knocked you out."

"I wasn't out for long."

"I don't care, you were still unconscious. I couldn't see what was happening, but I did see that thing had what Mr. Tyler says was a knife. You were on the ground, completely still—and after I forsook you, too." Suddenly, she covered her face with her hands. "Oh, God, Rafe, this has been such an awful night. Our world's turned upside down."

"It's just a little wobbly, kinda like you and me at the moment. And forsook is a bit of an overstatement. We did put that part of our world right, didn't we?"

She gave him a tear-filled smile, then rushed to his side when he started to stand. "You need to be careful," she said. "You've got a horrid egg on your head. You can't go to sleep yet."

He chuckled. "Neither one of us should be on those stairs."

"I haven't felt dizzy all afternoon."

He didn't tell her that Dr. Surrey said there was no way of predicting when the bullet might press against the vein. At any given moment, she could lose her balance and topple down the stairs, or be forced to sit and fight for breath. A given spell could last for seconds or minutes. It could ease off as it had been doing, or it could increase and kill her.

But there was one thing Rafe was certain of. Tonight he wanted her in his arms, cocooned in their bed, all night long.

"Come on," he said, "let's get up those stairs."

Chapter Forty-four

"In addition to myself, there were only four men who knew of my involvement with the heist," Henry Gifford said to Rafe when the latter opened River's Bend's front door. Gifford hadn't even prefaced his words with a "good morning."

"Charles Slade and your brother Jeremiah are dead," Rafe said. "Another was Morgan Ward. The fourth man was Mizer."

"Now answer me this, Mr. Stone, did you know that Micah Ziegler served under Charles Slade?"

Rafe stilled, then blew out a breath. "I did not."

"Saved his ass at Sharpsburg." Gifford's gaze moved from Rafe's eyes to his forehead, then back again. "Ship's complement saw Seth Abernathy's body in the water that night. It's his body that was never recovered."

"Did you know that Ziegler's widow received—"

"A watch in his personal effects with the initials S.A. engraved on it."

More relaxed now, Rafe smiled. "It wasn't his, but his wife said he wasn't above coming by such things dishonestly."

"It all fit yesterday, your telling me Mizer was the leader, not Slade. Slade owed Ziegler a lot, and he respected him. That's what it would have taken for an arrogant son of a bitch like Slade to team up with an enlisted man."

"And a need for a new career." Rafe moved aside. "Come in."

The newspaperman wiped wet leaves from his shoes, then hobbled across River's Bend's threshold. "Nasty night."

"It was indeed."

But that nasty night had given way to a crisp, clean, sun-filled day, if a bitterly cold one. Delilah was alive, he had woken up, and Dr. Surrey, he recalled, had been guardedly reassuring as to the outcome of the operation, his concerns being the precautions Delilah needed to take to prevent the bullet's shifting farther to the right and the urgency to get it out of her altogether.

Gifford glanced at his head again, graced him with a grudging smile, then took in the foyer with apparent interest. "Any leaks?"

"Not that we've noticed." Rafe closed the front door and led the way to the dining room. "Would you like some coffee?"

"I would, thank you. That storm last night left things colder than Sherman's grave."

"Let's hope he's warmer." Rafe stuck his head in the kitchen. "Belle, could you bring us some coffee?"

The girl winked. "I'll bring you cream and sugar, too."

By the time Rafe turned, Gifford was working himself into a chair. The man flexed his shoulders, then extended his bum leg.

"So Seth Abernathy is lying in Micah Ziegler's grave," Rafe said, taking the seat opposite Gifford.

"That's what I'm thinking."

"And Micah Ziegler is Mizer."

"Sounds right don't you think?" Gifford said.

It sure did. Why hadn't he heard it before?

Gifford straightened when Belle set the coffee service between them. "You're Simon Douglas's girl, aren't you?"

"Yessuh, I sho' am."

"Lord how the years have flown. Last time I saw you was your graddaddy's funeral. You must've been around six."

"He died on my fifth birthday."

"I recall that now. Your grandpa was a fine, fine man."

"Thank you, suh." She turned to Rafe. "I got hot biscuits."

"Maybe in a few minutes."

Gifford looked up when the door shut behind the girl. "What the hell happened to your head?"

Rafe reached for the knot. His headache was gone, but the thing still hurt to the touch.

"And where is the lovely Miss Delilah this morning?"

265

Rafe leaned back. "Well, you see, I was still able to subdue her after she hit me in the head last night. Once I caught her, I strangled her and buried her body in the basement."

Gifford took a sip of coffee. "I didn't know this place had a basement. Now, what really happened to your head?"

"I had a run-in with a fella named Jubilee Parrish."

"Jubilee Parrish?"

"Do you know him?"

The man's gaze returned to Rafe's injured head. "I do, or did. Years ago. Gentlest soul you'd ever want to meet. Did he tell you he was Jubilee Parrish?"

"He did not. My bride and Harry Tyler ran him off before he managed to beat me to a pulp. They said he had a knife."

"What was he doing?"

"Stalking my house, or my wife, I'm not sure which."

"Jubilee Parrish was in his thirties when old Richard died. He's seventy if he's a day. I hear rumors of him still traveling the river banks, but I've never heard of him hurting anyone."

"Well, I tackled him."

Gifford took another sip of coffee and one more glance at Rafe's head. "Guess he could be provoked if you scared him bad enough."

Scared him, hell. The old hermit had scared Delilah bloodless two times now, and he'd gotten Rafe's heart pumping pretty fast last night, too.

"Miss Delilah all right?"

"She wasn't hurt, if that's what you mean. She's resting. We got to bed late with her having to patch me up."

"I'll be damned. Chasing down Jubilee Parrish," Gifford said. "Seems all sorts of things are coming back to haunt River's Bend, Mr. Stone."

"Rafe, and was it old *haints* that brought you out here this morning, Mr. Gifford?"

"Hank, and you might say that. When you stood in my office yesterday studying the Seventeenth's colors, you told me a story without saying a word. Looking at you now, I see light at the end of my long, dark tunnel. I want to know what happened that April night over thirty years ago, and I think you can tell me."

$\mathcal{D}$elilah crossed the room to the open floor vent.

"*. . . was part of the plot, and he may have gotten Mizer, too.*"

"*Mizer's alive. At least he was in the wee morning hours after the heist.*"

Rafe's voice. Tinny, but Rafe none the less. The first voice she'd heard sounded like Henry Gifford's.

She'd been only moderately surprised when she stepped into her old bedroom and found no sign of Harry Tyler. Belle had told her he was in here, working on the gas, but too many of the soft groans and quiet squeaks seemed to emanate from the secret stairwell, not the bedroom. That suspicion had been eclipsed with the discovery of Rafe's and Henry Gifford's voices drifting up through the heater vent.

"*Mizer was a member of the detail. You were right, I refused to approach Jeremiah until Charles Slade gave me the details, but he always led me to believe he was the leader. I've had doubts for a long time as to Mizer's role in the double cross and whose plan it was to kill off everyone.*"

"*Mizer's. Though he may not have realized it, Slade was his hench-man. I think we both agree Ziegler's our man.*"

Rafe's voice again. Delilah was a tad short of breath this morning, but she wasn't dizzy, and that reassured her. Gathering up her morning gown, she knelt beside the vent.

Doubtless, adjacent vents throughout this house could be used in like manner—to eavesdrop on private conversations.

"*I've wallowed in this half my life. Do you know the origin of the sur-name Ziegler?*"

"*No.*"

"*It's German for a bricklayer, but more specifically, a roof—*"

A hand touched Delilah's shoulder, and her heart leaped into her throat. She twisted her head to see who had joined her.

Harry Tyler held an index finger over his lips, clearly indicating she be quiet. He closed the vent, then removed his hand from her shoulder and rose, motioning for her to rise, also. Wide-eyed, she did. He took her elbow and led her to the center of the room.

"What brought him back home was the money, Mrs. Stone. I knew who your husband was the moment I laid eyes on 'im."

Delilah stared at the gaunt little man.

"He's dangerous, honey. You've no business here with him."

"What do you mean?"

"I knew you didn't know who he was from the start. You couldn't answer one question I asked about him without giving each one some thought."

She didn't know enough about him even now to counter Mr. Tyler's sympathetic words. But did confirming this man's suspicions really matter at this point?

"Who do you think he is?" she whispered.

"Ain't no doubt," he said, lowering his own voice, "and you suspected, too. All those questions you kept askin' about the Merrifield boys."

"Raymond?" she said quickly.

"Yes."

That nagging fear clamped over her heart again and squeezed. Raymond, Raeford, Ray. He could have stolen his dead cousin's name because they sounded alike.

"Then who is this Mizer Rafe says is still alive?"

"He's a ruse. The man's name was Micah Ziegler, the brains behind the *Gilded Rose* raid, Mrs. Stone. But don't let 'em fool ya. Mizer's long dead. Morgan Ward murdered him that April night along with everyone else who didn't die in the firefight."

Delilah's heart raced. "How," she asked, "do you know that?"

His eyes widened. "Because I've been waitin', too. Waitin' for thirty years. Waitin' for Morgan Ward. My name's not really Tyler, it's Abernathy. I had a brother—"

Delilah grasped Mr. Tyler's arms. "Seth."

"Yes," he said, "Seth. You know he was killed during the raid on the *Gilded Rose*?"

"Murdered."

Tyler's smile was bitter. "You know then what happened?"

Delilah still held onto Tyler, but now allowed her gaze to drift away. "Like Mr. Gifford." She frowned and again found Harry

Tyler's eyes. "But why would Mr. Gifford be working with Raymond Merrifield?"

"'Cause he don't know that's Raymond. That Merrifield boy ain't nothin' but a confidence man and a ruthless killer. Ruthless. He murdered his family, then butchered his daddy's and step-mama's bodies to throw the sheriff off. Wanted 'em to think a madman done it. He could charm the feathers off a duck. He's made a fool out of you, honey, and he's makin' a fool out of Gifford downstairs this very moment. Gifford is graspin' at any-thing that will relieve his guilt. Blames hisself for his brother dyin' at the hands of Morgan Ward. Poor soul is lookin' less at justice than redemption."

Delilah dropped her hands from Tyler's biceps. "But what happened that Raymond should be searching for—"

"Boys found that gold. Figured their daddy wasn't going to share his wealth with 'em, and they wasn't going to share the gold with him.

"It was in strong boxes and heavy. Old Markham caught 'em tryin' to move it. He tossed 'em out of the house. But them boys knew ways into this house their daddy never did. Raymond snuck back in that same night and killed his papa and stepmama."

"And David?"

"My guess is he was already dead. Lord in heaven, you look awful pale, Mrs. Stone. Here." He took hold of her elbow and guided her to the foot of the bed, where she sat. "Better?"

She nodded. "You think Raymond killed David?"

"That'd be my guess, yes'm. Either he wanted all the gold for hisself, or else maybe David didn't agree with killin' the parents."

Delilah twisted her hands in her lap. She did not believe that of the man downstairs, she absolutely did not. "Why did he come back here?"

Harry Tyler looked at her as if she'd sprouted another head.

"Why, for the gold, of course."

"Why didn't he get it before—"

"'Cause he can't find it. Don't you see? For certain, Merrifield didn't have a chance to get it out of the house twixt the time he

269

found his sons with it and the time Raymond slipped back in that night and killed 'im. But he did have time to hide it somewhere else in this house. Naturally he'd have expected the boys to try and steal it. He wouldn't have expected them to kill 'im."

"And Raymond has just now come back after all these years?"

"After what he done, he couldn't stick around, could he?"

Delilah's fingers curled into the quilted comforter covering her old bed.

Tyler removed his hand from her arm. "I'm sorry."

"How do you know all this?" She stood quickly, and he stepped back, patting the air, but she refused to tone down her voice. "How could you?"

"Mrs. Stone, I know you don't want to hear this, but I've been watchin' this place for three decades."

"You are standing there telling me you knew everything that happened the night the Merrifields died and didn't say anything to the authorities?"

He drew himself up. "Yes, ma'am, that's right. You see, findin' justice for a selfish, thieving old man who would betray his own sons for a trollop was a lot less important to me than finding justice for my brother."

Delilah forced herself calm. "You actually saw Raymond kill his parents?"

He rubbed the stubble on his chin. "Not exactly."

His words were a reprieve, and more steady, she stepped to him and shook his arm. "You didn't hear him confess, either, did you?"

"No."

She knew it. Someone else, someone who knew, somehow, where Morgan Ward had hid the gold, came inside and killed them. Her Rafe, Raymond or whoever he happened to be, was after justice for more than his brother, and she would prove it. She stepped toward the closed vent, but Tyler took her arm in a loose hold.

"Come on," he said, "let's go down and hear what they're sayin'."

Chapter Forty-five

Henry Gifford laid his linen napkin next to his plate. "If you'd like, I can talk to Broderick about Parrish when I get back to town. Save you a trip."

"I'd appreciate it. I . . ." For minutes now Rafe had listened to the protesting floor joists above his head. He knew Harry Tyler was working in the house, and he assumed Delilah was up, but just now, he swore the creak he heard came from one of the ancient risers hidden behind the secret panel. "I won't be able to get in to town today."

"Has Miss Delilah talked to you about . . ."

Rafe rose, at the same time raising his chin in a silent "continue" gesture.

Gifford frowned, watching him. ". . . what she found in the Big Black Baptist Church Cemetery?"

Rafe stepped toward the fireplace, all the while curling his fingers toward him, indicating Gifford should keep talking. He pulled out the mantle, the brick, then lifted the catch. "No," he said, "what?"

The wall cracked, and he pushed the door open.

The sudden light produced a double impact of blindness and fright, and Delilah couldn't help but believe Harry Tyler had led her into a trap. They could have listened to the conversation through the vent upstairs.

"Sweet Jesus, Delilah, what are you thinkin'?"

Rafe just barely disguised the anger in his voice, and Delilah figured that was because Henry Gifford was there. She dropped

271

the hand protecting her eyes and stepped through the open panel. Rafe's angry gaze hardened when Mr. Tyler emerged behind her. The man took her left arm and pulled her with him into the room, out, she realized, of Rafe's reach.

"Your lovely wife almost stumbled upon me listenin' to you and Gifford plottin' the final distribution of the *Gilded Rose's* gold."

Rafe narrowed his eyes on Tyler before frowning at Delilah. "You followed him into that stairwell?"

"I could hear you through the heater duct in my old room."

Rafe turned slightly and glanced at the vent on the wall near the floor. "No one ever told me about that."

She stared at him and wondered who that 'no one' would have been, then on her right, Henry Gifford rose from his seat at the table, cluttered with used coffee cups.

Rafe looked back around, his attention focused on Mr. Tyler. "And you've been listening all along?"

Tyler snorted, and Delilah turned to look at the kindly little man—she thought—she liked. That would explain the creaking floors, and they'd given him free access to the house on any number of occasions.

Still, she couldn't imagine him weeping in the stairwell in the middle of the night.

He looked at her, watching him, then focused on Rafe. "I always thought somebody might come back one day. That was a lot of gold for one man to handle in a hurry."

The chair Henry Gifford had been sitting in made a noise as he pushed it back. "Evil is patient isn't it, Mizer?"

Delilah's stomach clenched, and she turned her head toward the newspaperman, at the same time raising her captured arm. Tyler's fingers tightened on her elbow. "I'm Michael Abernathy, Mrs. Stone. I've shadowed this place waitin' to mete out justice, nothin' more."

"His alias is Harry Tyler; his real name is Micah Henry Ziegler," Rafe said. He shifted his gaze from her captured arm to her eyes. "He's the last missing man from the *Gilded Rose* raid."

She shook her head. "Seth Abernathy—"

"Is lying in Micah Ziegler's grave in Ohio," Rafe finished for her.

"Miss Delilah," Mr. Gifford said, "Micah Ziegler was a member of the Union detail protecting that gold stolen thirty years ago. Seth Abernathy was also a member of the detail. He and Ziegler were the same rank. They wore the same uniform. In the confusion that night, Micah Ziegler murdered Abernathy and switched identification with him."

"I'm Michael Abernathy, and how would he know such, Mrs. Stone, unless he was part of the plot?"

"Because," Gifford said, "an excellent source has recently told me that immediately after Major Charles Slade, reputed leader of the Union thieves, shot Morgan Ward in the back"—Delilah heard Mr. Tyler's curse under his breath—"he bragged to him how he and Mizer had master-minded the entire plot."

Tyler leaned forward and whispered in her ear. "He's wrong. My name is Michael Abernathy. I came here right after the War and made a life for myself—"

"He's an obsessed thief and murderer, Miss Delilah. He's been waiting here for thirty years, sure Morgan Ward would return to River's Bend."

Delilah squinted at Gifford. The reporter had researched the raid on the *Gilded Rose* for years. Both he and the man beside her could be lying to her for their own purposes.

But what would those be? She was of no consequence in any of this. Slowly she turned to Rafe, stiff and silent, the length of two arms out of her reach. His eyes were cold and hard as he warily watched Tyler, but they warmed when his gaze found hers.

"He says you murdered your father and stepmother."

Rafe's mouth opened, then shut. "Delilah, sweetheart, I had a mother and a stepfather. They both died earlier this year of natural causes."

She blinked back tears. "In Brazil?"

"Yes. On our plantation near the Confederate colony at Santa Barbara."

273

"Who are you?"

"The name you know me by is my legal name, Raeford Gavin Stone. My stepfather adopted me." She watched the movement of his Adam's apple when he swallowed. "My real name is Raeford Gavin Ward. Morgan Ward was my natural father."

"Lorelei Richard is your mother?"

"Was. And yes, Lorelei Richard Ward Stone was my mother."

Rafe stepped toward Delilah. Tyler's grip tightened, and he pulled her farther from him. The tug hurt and she sucked in air. Rafe stopped cold.

"You said Slade shot Ward?" Tyler asked.

Rafe snapped his fingers. "That's right, all you found at Butler Lake was Charles Slade's body. Ward and the gold were gone. All these years you thought Ward killed Slade, then hid the money and disappeared, planning to come back." Rafe's laugh was contemptuous. "Good choice with Slade. You couldn't even leave him to shoot an unsuspecting man in the back and him not mess it up, could you?"

Delilah felt Tyler draw up behind her. He wanted to respond to Rafe, she could feel it in his touch, hear it in his labored breath. It occurred to her that Tyler had known the man who died at Butler Lake.

Rafe edged closer. His cautious moves and feigned ease were making her nervous. He was worried about her left arm and Tyler's hold on it.

"How did he get away from Slade?" Delilah asked.

"He murdered him," Tyler growled.

"He killed him, sweetheart, in self-defense after Slade shot him first." Rafe's eyes were watching her now. "But Charles Slade was a horse's ass. His bullet didn't kill Ward, who, as anyone not drunk on his own importance would have known, was still armed.

"Slade wanted to gloat, to rub it into the Johnny Reb, who he despised anyway, how he and all of them had been duped. How the five other men who had followed Ward that night had been betrayed and murdered during different stages of the robbery—

shoot, Morgan Ward had seen two of them fall during the raid—never suspecting in the dark, the fight silhouetted against the burning *Gilded Rose*, where the bullets had come from. Not until Charles Slade clarified everything." Rafe's gaze darted behind her to Tyler. "Sounds like him, doesn't it Ziegler?"

"Morgan Ward got off a shot?" she whispered.

"Two. The first hit Slade in the shin and brought him down almost to eye level. The second one got him in the head."

How could he? . . . "Rafe," Delilah said softly, "who told you that story?"

"My stepfather, the man I called Daddy."

On the other side of the table, Henry Gifford stirred, but Delilah ignored him.

"Raeford Gavin Stone? Your father's cousin?"

"Yes."

Tyler's breath accosted her neck, his body pressed against hers. "You see now? He's lying, he lied about everything."

"Miss Delilah," Gifford said, his voice cautious.

Delilah's eyes held Rafe's, but her head wobbled gently in confusion.

Rafe's gaze narrowed. "I'm telling you the truth."

God, he wasn't, but his eyes told her he was—*a confidence man who could charm the feathers off a duck.* Without warning, her own eyes filled with tears. Dammit, she doubted this man the night before, she would never, ever doubt him again.

"It doesn't matter, darling. I don't care. I know you have an honest reason for not telling me the truth."

"Honey," he said, his tone marked by desperation, "I am telling you the truth. Morgan Ward made it back to River's Bend and to my mother. She and Miss Annie and Miss Annie's man Gil got him out of here that night, to my great uncle downriver at Fort Adams. Uncle Will is a doctor. Morgan Ward lived two days, long enough to tell what happened."

"And Raeford Gavin Stone?" she asked softly.

"Uncle Will's son, Ward's cousin, Rafe. His mother had died in childbirth, and Uncle Will never remarried. The two boys were

275

the same age. They loved each other like brothers—in the case of some, maybe more.

"Lorelei Ward was pregnant with me. She was devastated when Morgan died and disgraced by the lie. She had no one to care for her, but Rafe wanted to, so he wed Morgan's widow and adopted his son, and shortly after, they left Mississippi, and the South, and went to Brazil."

Gently she shook her head. Mr. Gifford said her name once more, but Rafe looked so perplexed she didn't look the newsman's way.

"Rafe," she said, drawing in a breath, "I know that William Gavin Stone's son Rafe drowned in 1852."

Rafe's brow furrowed.

"I've seen his death certificate in—"

"Miss Delilah," Gifford said, loudly enough this time to cause her to turn his way.

"He doesn't know."

He doesn't know what? She snapped her head back to Rafe who was now staring at Henry Gifford as if the man had punched him.

"What do you mean?" he said, letting his gaze drift from Gifford back to her.

Oh God! Suddenly everything fit, right down to the ring Lorelei should have, *would* have, taken to her grave. In earnest, she pulled away from Tyler toward—

Her vulnerable left arm was suddenly free, then just as quickly Tyler's throttled her. Rafe, his right hand inside his coat, jerked forward at the same instant she grabbed for the restraint. Across from her, she heard Henry Gifford's chair scrape the floor.

Something hard and cold touched her temple, and she froze.

"Hold it, Stone, or I'll kill her." She felt Tyler stiffen, then pivot slightly. "You, too, Gifford. Now where's the gold?"

Delilah was having trouble breathing, Tyler pressed so hard, and she coughed. The crook of Tyler's arm squeezed tighter.

"You're choking her, Ziegler."

"I'll choke the very life out of her if you don't tell me where that money is."

"Do you really think I came back here for the gold?"

Next to her ear, an ominous click. She felt Tyler's chin brush the top of her head, and the buttons on his shirt pressed through her morning gown into her back.

"I could hope," Tyler said. "So could this little gal of yo'rn."

This was not the kind man who'd followed her around, easing her concerns and helping her upgrade the quality of living in this house.

"No," he said to Rafe, "your number one priority was the man who betrayed your daddy and your daddy's men."

"As well as his own."

"Fools, the lot of 'em, blue and gray. But everything Ward said about Slade was right. Biggest asshole that ever walked. More than one good man died following his sorry self, if one could accuse him of leading. And I'm talking about in combat. My last meaningful contribution to the Union army was meant to rid it of him. But Ward got him before me."

Tyler stepped back, dragging Delilah with him, and she whimpered, pulling on his arm with both her hands. This time, he relented, but only slightly.

"Get that Colt away from her head."

Delilah shivered with the chill in Rafe's voice. She didn't want to die. She had a lifetime in front of her to live with Rafe.

Tyler tightened his hold and pushed the muzzle into the skin covering her skull; it hurt. "I seen where he turned the wagon. Rain washed out the tracks after. Of all them lookin', no one but me knew he come back here for sure. Now what did he do with that gold?"

"You'll let her go?"

Scared though she was, even Delilah knew that wasn't going to happen.

"You tell me where the gold is, course I will."

Delilah could hear the hateful lie woven between Tyler's words, but what she saw was Rafe's visage harden. He wasn't looking at her, but above her head and, she knew, into the eyes of Micah Ziegler.

"It's in the basement."

"In the basement?"

"The hidden one beneath the central fireplace."

Tyler relaxed his hold somewhat and moved the cold nuzzle from her head. For a brief instant Delilah thought it was over.

"Beneath those loose bricks in the floor?" Tyler asked.

Rafe stared at him, and Tyler laughed. From the corner of her eye, Delilah saw the gun barrel level over her shoulder. It pointed at Rafe.

"Pity you'll never see what's beneath those bricks. If I can't have my money, I will have my vengeance by ending Morgan Ward's line right here and now."

She let go of Tyler's arm the same instant Belle burst through the kitchen door. Delilah deflected the barrel, and Belle let loose an ear-splintering scream in tandem with the discharge of Tyler's pistol. The young black woman threw her hands in the air, then disappeared into the kitchen, screaming for her daddy.

Tyler cursed and tried to fling Delilah away, but she clung to him long enough to get her fingers around the barrel, rendering it useless to him. To her left, Rafe, already moving, cried her name. In the blur that resulted when Tyler whirled, she saw that Gifford, too, was reacting to the opportunity. Tyler swung her farther, and her left side collided with the fireplace at the same instant James Dexter stepped from the secret stairwell. Burning agony engulfed her shoulder, neck, arm, and chest. Mind riveted on her pain, she clawed with her right hand at the scorching heat tearing through her left shoulder.

Her cheek was sliding down the rough brick. On her right, a gunshot split the air, then a second exploded behind her. She couldn't even manage a gasp. But her thoughts were of Rafe, and she tried to look for him as her bottom came to rest on the floor. Her world dimmed, worse still, it reeled. She called his name. She heard his voice say hers. Her heart sped up, and she groped away from the wall with her right arm. He was far away and for a moment she was terrified he'd been shot and was calling for her.

Deceptively gentle fingers wrapped around her right forearm, and someone pushed her up. She tried again to turn her head. A pleasant scent filled her nostrils. "Rafe?"

"I'm here."

"The room is spinning."

"Be still, honey, please be still."

Chapter Forty-six

"Ain't been any Federals round here on this case for nigh on twenty years," Sheriff Broderick said, glancing at the man Rafe knew as James Dexter.

"Lee," Henry Gifford said, "there was that other treasury investigator here right after the Merrifield murders."

"Oh, yeah." Broderick rose from beside the lifeless body of First Sergeant, United States Army, Micah Henry Ziegler, alias Harry Tyler, alias Mizer, and nodded at the 'alias' Dexter. "You know, I'm gonna miss this guy." He snorted good-naturedly. "Hell, I played checkers with him at least twice a month. He'd become so much a part of the community you'd have thunk he'd have been happy with that."

Gifford blew out a breath. "Probably had till Morgan Ward's son showed up and revitalized all those lost opportunities."

Rafe took two steps, stopped, looked up at the ceiling, then started pacing again. His gut had twisted into a dozen knots. He didn't want to be in this room; he wanted to be upstairs.

Broderick placed his slouch hat back atop his head. "And conjured up the worst part of his character, too, it would seem." The sheriff turned to Rafe, who'd stopped beside the table six feet from the corpse. "You shot him from where?"

Rafe moved away from the table and indicated where he'd been when Micah Ziegler had finally managed to get Delilah off him. Again, he raised his pocket pistol to show the sheriff.

"You got him through the heart," the sheriff said.

Gifford, his voice guarded, nodded to Rafe. "It was a good shot, son."

A 'just' shot is what he meant. Rafe couldn't credit himself much in the accuracy department. Killing the man that quick and only once wasn't satisfying retribution for those whose deaths he'd caused thirty years earlier. All he'd been thinking about when he squeezed that trigger was neutralizing the man and protecting Delilah, and all he could think about now was getting upstairs to her.

Broderick turned and surveyed the room, then looked at the faux James Dexter. "I'm assuming, Mr. Garrick, your people are going to want to take this?"

"We have it."

Broderick looked at Rafe, then at Garrick.

"Course, you still don't have your money back."

Garrick glanced at Rafe and grinned. "No, *they* don't. Such are the misfortunes of war. As for me, my daddy served with the Hinds County Defenders, 14th Infantry, C.S.A."

Rafe forced his attention on the man. "Treasury Department, huh?"

Dan Garrick sucked air through a lopsided grin. "'Fraid so, boss. Mama near disowned me. Daddy's more pragmatic."

And all this time he thought he'd been so careful.

"Where is James Dexter?"

Garrick pulled a watch from the inside pocket of his jacket and opened it. "Still at work in Jackson, I imagine."

"I have to assume—"

"When you telegraphed him of your interest in one alias 'Mizer,' he contacted Treasury, alerting us of your interest in the Carthage Point heist. Dexter was a Federal army officer. Settled in Mississippi after the War."

If he'd known that, he'd have never hired him. And as for this fella Garrick . . . ? Rafe squinted at the man. Hell, Rafe sided with the mom.

Garrick nodded to Henry Gifford. "Mr. Gifford's been cooperating with Treasury since '68." The agent shrugged. "On this anyway. We knew there was a 'Mizer,' but we didn't know who he was, and we'd given him up for dead. More people than not figured Morgan Ward made it out that night. We've been looking to hang him for a long, long time. As the son of a Confederate veteran, I'm proud to say I get to clear him—at least with Dixie."

"What were you doing here, this morning?" Rafe asked.

Garrick screwed up his face and cocked his head at Gifford. "Tailing him like you told me to." He grinned fully. "Of course, Gifford was a known entity to me. I was much more interested in what you had to say. I was sneaking around the house, trying to ascertain what was going on in this room, when I happened upon Mr. *Tyler* lurking about and trailed him instead."

Garrick's presence in that secret stairwell had been fortuitous. He'd have gotten Ziegler had Rafe missed, but, better still, he'd heard their whole conversation. Morgan Ward was still guilty (in U.S. government eyes) of armed robbery—but vindicated of the alleged treachery and murder of his own men that had shamed his name for thirty years. On the first count, he'd still be proud. On the second, he'd finally rest easy.

"I'll need written statements from you two and from that girl, Belle, and Mrs. Stone when she's able." Garrick frowned. "How is she?"

"Dr. Surrey's with her. Best he can tell her arm and neck on the left side have no feeling. But the worse part is the bullet is pressing against a vein leading from her lungs to her heart. Doc's afraid she's not getting enough oxygen."

"He's moving her to the hospital?"

"He's going to operate here. Moving her is dangerous, and time's critical."

Rafe turned to Broderick when the large man moved, but the sheriff was focused on Garrick. "We're 'bout done," he told the government agent. "All I need is to get Doc Surrey down here to certify Tyler, Ziegler, or whoever he is, is dead, and I'll move the body, if that's all right with you."

Garrick nodded, and the sheriff turned to Rafe. "Why don't you go up, son, and trade places with the doc for a few minutes."

Chapter Forty-seven

He touched her hand; she opened her eyes and looked at him. Rafe wrapped his fingers around hers, then maneuvered the rocker behind him and sat. "You felt that?"

"Yes," Delilah said.

"Dr. Surrey thought everything was okay." He touched her leg. "Where am I touching now?"

"My thigh never lost feeling."

He grinned and swallowed the lump in his throat. "I know."

She blinked back tears, at the same time trying to stifle a soft giggle. "Don't make me laugh, Rafe. Feeling in my shoulder is a mixed blessing."

Yes, she was in pain. He stood and kissed her forehead. From the time he'd found her in the stairwell until now an agonizing twenty-four hours had passed. The worst had ended three hours ago when she'd come out from under the chloroform. Rafe's sleepless night had finally elicited a rare invocation to a merciful and much-taken-for-granted God to bring them through this. Dr. Surrey's restless vigil had added to his anxiety, and when Delilah finally opened her eyes, she saw that his were red-rimmed.

The doc had operated for several hours. The location of the bullet had been precarious at best, situated as it was against the critical vein. The operation verified, as Dr. Surrey had feared, that over the course of its seven years, the bullet had become life-threatening. Removing the thing had been simple, repairing its damage, primarily to nerve and muscle in her shoulder, had not. The vein was bruised, but not broached. It would take her time to heal, Doc Surrey told him, but she should heal completely.

283

Then she'd taken hours to wake up.

"Doc told me he gave you laudanum a bit ago."

She forced her eyes open, but her lids immediately quivered shut. "You wake me up to tell me I'm going to sleep?"

He smiled.

"You're leaving me, aren't you?"

"Never, but I am going down to Fort Adams this morning. I've got to check on something."

"The man you called Daddy." Awkwardly, she turned on the pillow and studied him as best her heavy-lidded eyes would allow, then in a voice filled with remorse, said, "I'm so sorry. You may not . . ."

Want to come back is what she'd been about to say before the drug stopped her. She'd let a very old cat out of the bag and blamed herself for divulging something she feared would hurt him. Of course, it would have been only a matter of time, now that he was back in the United States. For sure he'd have found out when he went up to Warrenton to visit his Grandma Rachel's and Aunt Emmaline's graves, and, now, he recalled his uncle's request from days ago to go with him. No doubt, the existence there of Raeford Gavin Stone's grave was the reason.

"Did you ask Miss Annie?" Delilah said, her voice weak.

"Yes. She said it wasn't her place to tell. She told me I needed to talk to Uncle Will, and she's right."

Delilah gave him a small smile, and he kissed her quick. "I'll be back before dark."

"I want someone close all the time. Under no circumstances is she to be alone in this house. I should be back by nightfall, but if I'm not, promise one of you will spend the night."

Miss Annie pulled the rocker alongside Delilah's bed. "We'll be here, young massa, don't you worry."

"There are no plantation masters here now, Miss Annie. My daddy was never any such thing."

"No, but your grandpa was, and a fine one."

"And he freed you all, so you do not serve any master."

She chuckled. "You payin' me for this?"

"I am."

"No you ain't. Now you git, so you can git back. She's gonna want you when she wakes up, not some old negra woman. We'll all be here, Simon, too."

"Thank you," he said and saluted Lucianne, standing by the door. She smiled and followed him out of the room.

Chapter Forty-eight

"Uncle Will," Rafe said when the old man opened the door to the grand Victorian. "I'm here for that next visit."

Will Stone took one look at Rafe and nodded, understanding as potent on his face as his nose was prominent. "You went up to Warrenton without me."

"Delilah did."

"Ah, yes, the bane of your existence." The old man gave Rafe an apologetic smile. "I see what you mean, but at the moment, it's Morgan Ward's butt I could whip one last time." He moved aside. "Come on in here, boy. Sounds like the hardest part's over."

Rafe nodded. "I've got news to tell you, too."

Uncle Will looked up from where he'd bowed his head as the story of yesterday's encounter with "Mizer" unfolded.

"And her prognosis is good?"

"Very good."

His granduncle wiped his eyes on his shirtsleeve. In his hand, he held a letter he'd pulled from his roll-top desk when he and Rafe first entered the parlor fifteen minutes ago.

"So it's over," Uncle Will said. "He's cleared?"

"With those who mattered to him. Hank Gifford's planning a story for the paper, next he says he's gonna write a book." Rafe blew out a breath. "Uncle Willie, why didn't they tell me?"

The old man shifted in his upholstered patent rocker and with shaking fingers, took the letter from the envelope.

"They always meant to tell you eventually. You were a baby, then a little boy. You weren't capable of understanding any of

286

what happened then. They didn't want to run the risk of you saying something that might give them away in front of anyone. You were in what was, for all intent, a Southern colony. Someone there might have known or heard about the raid and the murders. What you didn't know wouldn't hurt any of you."

"You know, there were two questions I always had once I got old enough to understand the relationship between a man and a woman."

William Stone watched him expectantly.

"How could a man not be jealous of another fella, whom the woman he loved cared so strongly about—so much so that she filled that dead man's son, who this other fella raised as his own, with the determination to come back and clear his daddy's name? And how could one woman love two different men as much as my mother loved Morgan Ward and Raeford Stone?"

The old, gray head nodded knowingly. "He wrote me once, years ago now, that your mother's constant praise of Morgan Ward sometimes made him feel in competition with himself for your affection."

"Morgan Ward was legend to me, not flesh and blood. I loved the man who raised me as my dad. I hope he knew that."

William Stone tapped Rafe's arm with the folded letter. "He knew. And as for your mother, she loved your father. She gave up her name and heritage for him that night, but she did look back—far enough to see you walking the halls of River's Bend. Your family on her side goes back to the French Dominion."

Rafe took the offered letter and started unfolding it. "Yes, it does. I know every ancestor, every piece of dirt, every love affair, and every change made to that house up to the spring of 1865."

"He was gonna tell you after your mama died, but there's no predicting a heart attack. Wounds like the one he suffered that night at the hands of Charles Slade shortens a man's life."

"I think he lost the will to live after Mama died."

"He survived her by only three months. They had thirty-two years together, at least thirty were damn good ones, and they produced two beautiful children to carry on."

"I've got to tell Hannah she and I are full-blooded siblings."

"And she's lost a grandpa to boot."

"She nor I, neither one, have lost anything, Uncle Will. Y'all were the ones who made the sacrifices a long time ago."

The old man nodded at the letter in Rafe's hand. "That was his last letter to me. It will make you feel better, I think." He rose stiffly. "I'll leave you to it."

"Uncle Willie?" Rafe said, as the old man stepped away from where they were sitting. William stopped his measured pace.

"Is anyone in that grave I blubbered over not too long ago?"

"Young man, unidentified. Couple of fellas found him stabbed on the Woodville Road not too far from here. I was the closest doctor. He was dead by the time they got him to me. Lots of marauding going on at the time. Deserters, renegades. Always hoped he was one such, but I don't know. Lorelei helped get Morgan's uniform on him. Gil and I put him in the coffin, then the ground. No one knew how Morgan Ward was supposed to have died, and I wanted the Federals to find something in that pine box should they ever find the grave. Took 'em three weeks to track me here to Fort Adams, and they never found the grave. They didn't know they were supposed to be looking for one. They always assumed Morgan was alive, and that worried me. But they had to reestablish order with the end of the War. The nation had its hands full and findin' Morg and that money took low priority."

⋯⋯

. . . you know how she was, Uncle Will. If I told her once, I told her a thousand times to let Morgan Ward rest in peace. Firing Rafe up to go back and clear his father's name was push-ing the boy the wrong way, and Morgan Ward's name didn't matter. But she knew me well enough to know it did. And it still does, but not so much that I'd want Rafe to leave me and go back. Now that she's gone, I think sometimes I'll go back myself and find that no-good killer; but I consider Rafe and Hannah, who is married now,

*and figure simply growing old with my grand-
babies around me is enough.*

*So no, I haven't told him. He thinks his
daddy's cousin raised him, and believe me, I
know he loves me like I'm his father, as, of
course, I am, but I'm reluctant to tell him now. I
wonder if he'll be angry or hurt, but I know those
emotions will be short-lived.*

*What I fear most is that the truth will in-
vigorate him with his mother's zeal. The reason
he's still here is me. He's a good worker and
businessman, but he has no interest in ranching.
In many ways, he's his daddy's boy despite his
apparent contentment. He'd be happier losing at
the poker table and racing fine horses than with
these cows and sheep. He does show interest in
the mining, but I know once I'm gone, he'll be
headed back to Mississippi. But I'm afraid if I
tell him the truth now, he'll leave sooner. It's one
thing to seek vindication for a ghost. It's another
to want retribution for someone you love. So, I'll
keep my secret awhile longer.*

*Once again, Uncle, grief holds near. I can't
imagine living my life without her. I know you
understand.*

I do wish I could see you again.
Much love and affection,
Morg

Morg. Morgan. Rafe closed his eyes against threatening tears.
Grief holds near. His father, of course, was confiding in the man he
himself had loved as a father. Together they'd shared the loss of
the real Raeford Gavin Stone and then thirty years of separation.
For the man holding a small package to his chest as he made his
way back to Rafe, the separation had now proved interminable.

"He signed his real name."

289

The old man sat. "Didn't at first. For years he signed them 'the prodigal son.' I've got thirty years of letters from him and your mother, not one of which I should have kept. This past April it ceased to matter, but when I'm gone, I want you to take them. A person could write a history of that colony down there based on what's in 'em."

"You never saw Daddy again?"

Uncle Will placed the package in his lap and started peeling away the paper. Momentarily, he said, "We feared it was too dangerous, what with the government refusing to acknowledge Morg was dead. But he wrote often as I did. So did Lori." He bowed his head. "The day my Rafe died, the boat had capsized. Rafe was unconscious. Your dad got hold of him, but we were caught in the current. Morg couldn't hold him. He blamed himself, and I blamed me for not getting us off the water sooner.

"The loss was devastating for both of us. For months after Rafe's death, I feared Morgan would take his own life. You probably realize by now that your daddy had a wild streak in him. He was like his own daddy in that regard, one of the things that endeared the man to Rachel. It also led to his early demise. Morgan's need for a firm, but steady hand is the reason she asked me to raise him should anything ever happen to her. My nature was calmer, she said, than Cecil Sturgeon's. When Rafe died, Morgan became reckless and sullen. Hard to handle. I had my own grief, too. Then one night I caught him toying with my revolver. He was drunk. I near went to pieces right in front of him. He realized then I needed him even more than he needed me. He settled down a lot after that and finished school, and we got each other through that terrible time. But once he was out of school, he was rarin' at the bit, ready to go, and I knew to let him. He didn't go far. Won that little farm near Natchez. I couldn't stay in that house in Warrenton with Alice, Rafe, and Morg gone, so I moved here to Fort Adams, which had lost a doctor."

"I think Morg grew up the night Charles Slade shot him. The raid against the *Gilded Rose* had been, in my opinion, an insane gamble. He had a lot to gain, sure, but only when he was lying in his pregnant bride's arms, his blood soaking her nightdress, did he realize how much he had to lose."

From the wrappings in his lap, Uncle Will pulled out a small box and handed it to Rafe. "I've had little use for livin' these past six months or so. Then I opened the door six days ago and saw you standin' there." He nodded to the unopened box in Rafe's hand. "Ever so often, Lorelei wrote asking about that thing. Had a hell of a time getting it back from the Federals."

Rafe removed the lid, and his heart began to pound. Inside was a gold ring, not fanciful, neither embellished with jewels nor embossed.

"It was your grandmother Rachel's. Morgan's daddy gave it to her when they wed. When she remarried, she gave it to me to hold for Morgan. Morg gave it to Lorelei."

Rafe took it from its container and held it between his thumb and index finger. "This is what she left at the landing?"

"Yes. Your paternal grandfather had the inside engraved with his and Rachel's names and wedding date."

He saw. "The government wouldn't give it back?"

"Wasn't that so much. Investigators took it as evidence thirty years ago. I started requesting it five years back. They couldn't find it. They returned it to me earlier this year, shortly after your mother's death."

"I'll be damned." Rafe placed the ring back in its box and handed it . . .

"No, son, it's yours. She wanted you to have it."

So he exchanged the little box for the handkerchief in his pocket and blew his nose. Done, he looked at the letter in his lap, then at his uncle. "I always figured Daddy, who I believed to be Rafe Stone, ran because he had the money and didn't want to give it up. Now I know he was running from a hangman's noose, which makes me wonder if the money was worth the risk. It couldn't have been easy to hide." He frowned at the older man. "How the devil did they get out of here with all that gold?"

William Stone smiled. "All what gold?"

Chapter Forty-nine

Delilah woke to the rhythmic creaking of rockers against the pine floor. She smacked her lips, then swallowed the after-taste of laudanum.

Her left shoulder ached dully, but not nearly as bad as when she'd come out of the chloroform-induced stupor following the operation.

The rocking stopped when she moved, and Delilah opened her eyes. Miss Annie, in front of the window, was already rising from the cushioned chair, and momentarily she sat on the edge of the bed beside Delilah.

"How you feelin', missy?"

Delilah responded with a laugh that stopped just short of a bark. "I feel like all I want to do is sleep, but I hurt."

"Too much of them doctor's medicines. Miss Annie, she'll fix you something that will ease the pain and not put you to sleep."

"Thank you. What time is it?"

"'Bout two in the afternoon. Sun's good and bright now, but I can see clouds movin' in from upriver."

"Is Rafe back yet?"

The kerchief-covered head shook only once. "Fort Adams-Vicksburg packet will pass by here 'bout four. He'll prob'ly be on it."

She hoped so, and her stomach twinged slightly at the thought of what his mood would be. "Morgan Ward didn't die that night, did he?"

Miss Annie smiled sadly. "Not then. Six months ago now he died in South America. My Lorelei had died this past January.

292

Her heart was weak from rheumatic fever as a li'l child. Old Doc Stone down at Fort Adams, he come up and told me. We passed each other news when we got it."

"I'm sorry," Delilah said. Then she added, "You always knew he'd lived?"

"Oh, yes."

"Why didn't you tell me the truth?"

"Everythin' I told you 'bout that night was true. The lie was in what I didn't tell. The last time I saw my darlin' girl she was headin' south, skirtin' that river bank in that old skiff belonged to her granddaddy. My sweet Gil was with her. She held Morgan's head in her lap. Lorelei Richard Ward stopped bein' that night along with her Morgan.

"They made it safe to his uncle's downriver. Was Doc Stone who come up with the plan for Morgan to take his dead boy's name, so he became Raeford Stone."

"By the time they was safe and Morgan was healed, he had him a little baby and a wife not nearly as strong as she thought she was. They made a good life for themselves way down yonder. They had a lot of years together and two beautiful chillun, boy and girl. Man and woman shouldn't ask for mor'n that."

Delilah rolled her head on the pillow and smiled at the ceiling. "I knew Lorelei wouldn't have left her wedding ring for no reason. I knew it."

"You was right. She left it to throw the law off. Worked some, too, though there was always them that thought she'd left with him. Lawd, gal, you scared me when you asked 'bout her ring, and I thought I'd been so smart in my tellin' of the tale."

"Rafe didn't know."

"He knowed Morgan Ward was his daddy, but they didn't tell him Morgan Ward didn't die and Morgan was the man raisin' him. I was sure you didn't know nothin', and I didn't think it was my place to tell you the whole truth, when he didn't even know it. He had his reasons for not tellin' you why he was here."

Trust had been his initial reason, then fear for her safety.

"I fear the truth might have hurt him."

"Nah, ain't gonna hurt that man. Surprise him maybe, but not hurt him. Too much love in that family for him to be hurt."

"I wonder if he'll go back to Brazil."

The old Negress took Delilah's hand and looked around the bedroom. "A sweet sadness lays on me now. It fills my eyes and pulls the tears down my throat. Not long ago, I thought I'd take my soulful grief to my grave. Then three weeks ago I stepped through River's Bend's door once more. First time I laid eyes on your man, I knew Morgan Ward and my darlin' Lorelei done come home again." She set her gaze on Delilah. "No darlin', he ain't goin' back to Brazil. This is his home. He's gonna stay here and raise a fam'ly wif the woman he loves."

Delilah squeezed the old gnarled hand, and Miss Annie patted their entwined fingers with her free one, then pulled away.

"I'm gonna get you somethin' to drink, then I'm gonna make you some good medicine. Sent Belle out a little bit ago to find the ingredients. She should be back by now."

$\mathcal{D}$elilah dozed off and on. Belle and Lucianne took turns checking on her and bringing her cold well-water and coffee. She got up once to visit the bathroom and almost fell flat on her face, but she made it there and back, finally, with Lucianne's help.

The clouds moved in, and the afternoon shortened. The year waned as well. It would be good dark by five o'clock, and Delilah smiled at the thought of a Christmas tree in the front room. She hadn't had a Christmas tree at home since before her parents' deaths. She had spent four of those seven Christmases with Uncle Joe and Aunt Ophelia. They always enjoyed lovely holidays.

By four o'clock, the room had dimmed with the approaching clouds, and the house was getting cold. Lucianne brought her some chicken soup and cornbread and stayed by her side, making sure she ate at least some of it. Miss Annie was in the kitchen, trying to master that new gas stove in the process of boiling down herbs for her promised medicine. Air hissed through the heater vent, and Delilah's heart thumped madly, but it was Simon, Lucianne told her, not Rafe, feeding the furnace.

Of course. Rafe would have come up to see her first before starting any household chores.

Her arm ached more now, and she craved sleep, but only dozed fitfully amidst the creaks and groans of the old house. The wind had picked up with the oncoming storm. Delilah rolled a bit on her good right side, all the while wishing Miss Annie could speed the making of her herbal solace.

"You're prettier than she was."

Delilah started, then opened her eyes. The room had darkened, but she could make out the dingy wall in front of her. The smell of outside cold mixed with that of an unwashed human body. Delilah waited, afraid to move, staring at that wall.

"Much, much prettier." A male. At her back, the mattress gave, and a hand touched her injured shoulder.

"Don't," she said. Her heart throbbed against the base of her throat, and she rolled partially over so she could see him.

Braced on one knee, he loomed above her, hardly more than a dark silhouette against the dim ceiling.

"I'm hurt."

"How?" he said.

"The doctor removed a bullet from my shoulder yesterday."

She pushed herself up on the pillows and swallowed. Where was Belle with her promised coffee?

"Someone shot you?"

Delilah heard the veiled accusation in his voice — not directed at her per se, but more likely at her assailant. She scooted back as best she could. "My father."

"Oh, no." He sat down hard on the bed, and the jolt hurt her shoulder, but she didn't acknowledge it.

"It was years ago." She glanced at the closed bedroom door.

"Where is your father?"

Delilah swallowed and stared at the man's face in the dimness. She could make out a scraggly beard that touched his chest. His hair, long and loose around his face and down his back, was equally unkempt.

"Are you Jubilee Parrish?" she asked softly.

"Jubilee Parrish died a long time ago."

"A long time ago?"

"Years probably. Tell me where your father is."

"My father is dead."

"Did you kill him?"

Delilah hoped this person couldn't see the shocked expression she must have presented. "My father took his own life."

"I killed my father."

In the faint light, she saw him bow his head. "I wish he'd killed himself, though."

"Are you David?"

He jerked his head up. "David's gone," he blurted.

Raymond Merrifield.

"Papa killed David."

Delilah's breath caught. "Your father killed David?"

"She woke me screamin' like a banshee. He'd caught them in here. This was David's room. They didn't know I saw. Daddy was beating David with a poker. Are you going to have a baby?"

"N-no, I don't think so."

"Cecilia was going to have a baby."

She wanted to ask if that was the reason he'd killed her, but decided prudence would be the better course.

"David's baby," he said.

Sweet heaven, this story was getting worse with every word he spoke.

"I wish I hadn't killed her now, at least not then. I should have waited till after the baby, then part of David would have gone on."

Delilah closed her eyes and sucked in a steadying breath.

"All I have of him is a picture."

She opened her eyes and was able to make out his fishing something from his coat.

"Do you want to see?"

She did, and she told him so. He handed her the worn daguerreotype, but she couldn't see it well in the dark. He took it back.

"She told him David raped her. *Raped* her." He shook his head. "He loved her so, and she said that about him to protect herself. For two months, she'd been coming to David's bedroom when Papa was gone, and she fucked him."

Disgust swelled Delilah's gut, and she threw back the covers. Pain pierced her shoulder when he caught her arm. "No," he snarled and pushed her back.

Eyes closed, Delilah fought back the bile burning the top of her throat.

"You're not to go anywhere," he forced out between clenched teeth.

"Please," she said, not resisting his hold, "that's my injured arm."

He let go as if she scorched him.

"She always said there was something wrong with her, too. She made me want to puke."

Delilah could hear the sneer in his voice, and she almost asked him if he'd like to see her wound, but feared he might.

"I thought you were her when I first saw you from the river. Back, walking these halls again in that same white gown she'd always wear to David's room. Sometimes I think I hear her in this house, crying." His voice broke. "But it's only me."

Delilah remained still. "You've been living here?"

"I go up and down the river like Jubilee taught me, but this is my home. I come back whenever I want."

"You come into the house?"

He moved, and Delilah sensed he was trying to see her face. "I've been in since last night."

The house had been full of any number of people all night and all day today.

"But how do you get in?"

"From the old cookhouse. We used it as a larder when my mama was alive. Breezeway leads into the kitchen. . . .

The last of Charles Richard's eighteenth-century doors. "You have the key?"

"I forgot to put it back on the nail the night I left, so I kept it.

I've used it lots of times over the years. When David and me was little, we'd sneak in and out of the house using the old tunnel and the secret stairwell. Was us found 'em. Mama caught us sneakin' back into my room through the fireplace panel one mornin' and made Papa block up the tunnel. He liked the stairwell, though, and he wouldn't break the doors even though she wanted him to."

Delilah wanted to ask him about his real mother, but feared what she considered should produce a calming effect might as easily result in the opposite.

"I wish you were going to have a baby. I could keep you till the baby was born, then I could have the baby. I'd name him David."

She was shivering uncontrollably now.

"Why didn't I do that before?" he said into the darkness.

"The baby might not have been a boy," she said.

The bed moved, and Delilah had a feeling his entire body had become animated. "Wouldn't keep a girl. Girls are no good."

"But what would you . . . ?" Sweet Jesus, what was she thinking asking such a question?

"Put her in the ground with her damned mother."

"You could have given her to someone to take care of."

"I wouldn't want Cecilia's daughter to live," he said, and Delilah told herself to shut up.

"Do you want to see where he put him?"

No, she most certainly did not. She wanted someone rational to come through that bedroom door, and she wanted them now, and then she had a terrible, terrible thought that he'd already killed everyone else in this house.

"I want to show you."

"I don't want to see."

Delilah felt him rise, and she moved when he did, flinging herself from the bed. She heard him moving in the darkness, but she was halfway to the hall door. Then she was there. She found the knob. She turned . . .

A filthy hand covered her lips at the same time she felt the door strain against the stop. It was locked. The back of her hand scraped the key in its hole, then he yanked her back. She had only one good hand to work with—her injured shoulder felt as if it were being repeatedly struck by a hammer.

"Come on. I'm going to show you where my father's whore brought my brother."

"Ugh, I hope that's not supper you're making." Rafe draped his wet slicker over a ladder-back kitchen chair.

Miss Annie didn't even bother to look up from where she stooped over a cast-iron pot on the stove.

"Special medicine for your wife."

He held his hands over the warm oven and rubbed them together. "Is she awake?"

"Has been off and on most of the afternoon. She's hurtin'."

Rafe started for the laudanum in the cupboard over the sink.

"She's going to try my medicine, Mr. Ward," Miss Annie said.

He saw that she watched him and smiled when he pursed his lips, and he wondered what name *was* on his birth certificate?

"How long on that medicine?"

"Quarter of an hour."

He returned to the hot stove and lifted the lid from a pot on one of the back burners. "What is for dinner?"

"That's collards, Mr. Rafe." Lucianne scooted between him and Miss Annie and pointed to the other back burner. "Them's black-eyed peas. Cornbread is done."

Belle entered the kitchen via the dining room, a frown on her face. She looked around, then put her fists on her hips. "Where is Miss Dillie?"

Rafe stilled.

"Did you look in the bathroom?" Lucianne asked.

"I did."

Now, Lucianne turned to Miss Annie who had shown some interest in Belle's question. "I don't think she's up and around, Mama Douglas, do you?"

"No." Miss Annie stopped stirring.

"I looked everywhere she could be." Belle met Rafe's eye. "Even that room you two always go to at the end of the hall."

Rafe stepped toward Belle. "Has she been on her feet today?"

"Only once," Lucianne said. "Went to the bathroom, and she near fainted."

"And she'd locked her door from the inside too. I had to get a key from—"

Rafe bolted past Belle and through the dining room, foyer, then took the front stairs two at a time.

The lamp burned gently in their room, the bed mussed, but empty. Heart thumping, he moved to her old room. The coal oil lamp beside her bed burned in here, too. The panel was closed, but he reached out to touch it—to make sure.

"Both these rooms was pitch-black when I got up here."

Chest tight, Rafe looked across at the young black woman standing by the open door. So, Belle had lit the lamps.

"How long has it been since someone checked on her?"

"Fifteen minutes most, Mister Rafe," Lucianne said.

"Less," Belle said. "I'd taken her soup bowl back down. I was bringing her a piece of apple pie. She ate the soup good. I made her a cup of coffee she asked for while I waited for the pie to cool."

"Oh, Lawd!" Lucianne had bent at the waist and was staring at the floor near the threshold separating the two rooms. Belle immediately caught her skirts out of her mother's way, then squeaked and covered her mouth. With one stride, Rafe stood in front of them both, his racing heart now thumping against his sternum. He dropped to one knee and smeared the blood drops on the dark floor. Now he could see the blood trail to the panel.

"Get Simon," he said as he rose and headed to the fireplace mantle. "Tell him to check the attic."

He released the latch, then pushed the panel open.

The lantern was gone inside the second story landing, but after he'd stumbled down the first set of narrow risers, enough light emanated from below for his hope to rise.

Voices mumbled below him, and he had enough light at this point to speed his descent.

"She's hurt, now you let her go."

"No."

"You see that blood on that woman's gown? She ain't never done you no harm. Now you git out of her way and let her git back to bed."

"I have to make sure she sees."

"You can show me."

"*She* is like Cecilia, Miss Annie."

"She ain't like Cecilia."

"Yes," the voice shouted, "she is."

"Do you know how 'shamed your mama would be of you? What you doin' back here, anyhow? Ain't seen you in years."

"This is my home. I keep my eye on it during my travels. I know when people come in here, and I run the damn women off who try to take Mama's place. Cecilia wasn't nothin' but a nasty, lying whore."

Rafe heard stone hit stone. An arm's length in front of him stood Miss Annie, and he stopped at her back, then dipped his head to see who she was talking to in the dimly lit space below. Delilah, pale and disheveled, sat on the brick floor, the left shoulder of her white gown oozing bright red. Between her and the stairwell squatted a filthy, rumpled ghost of a man. Rafe balled his fists into hammerheads. He was gonna kill this lunatic with his bare hands.

Delilah's eyes, dark and frightened, but alert, met his, then softened. Despite her obvious misery, she managed a weak smile, and she placed her good hand flat against the wall behind her and started pushing herself up. A shovel, leaning against the wall beside her, slid to one side and fell.

The man, methodically pulling up and tossing away the loose sand-set brick, turned at the sound.

"Sit back down."

"No," she said.

"Git down, I said!"

On the landing, seven steps above the rough-hewn floor, Rafe stepped around Miss Annie.

"She said she wasn't going to."

The madman's head jerked around. "Who are you?"

"The owner of River's Bend, and that is my wife."

The man returned to the brick and cursed under his breath.

Rafe started forward, and the landing groaned. Instantly, the man looked up, his eyes wild. Miss Annie placed her withered hand upon Rafe's shoulder and whispered, "He has a knife." Then she stepped behind him.

The man grinned. "Yes, I have a knife, and I've used it before."

"On the dead?"

"On a murderer and a trollop."

"This is Raymond Merrifield, darling," Delilah said, her voice tired. "He killed his father and stepmother."

"Nice to meet you, Raymond," Rafe said, descending one step. "We are, as a matter of fact, cousins."

Rafe came down two more steps, but slowed when Raymond stopped his work and glared at him. Another step.

"I've no kin left means anything to me, and I don't need you down here. He's not deep."

"Who's not deep?"

The man went back to work, but Rafe noticed he no longer removed brick, but traced the dirt between the set stones or pulled a brick out partially, then let it fall back into place. Instinctively, Rafe became more cautious.

"We're digging up David," Delilah said.

Despite himself, Rafe grinned, but he never took his eyes off the madman between him and Delilah. "I told you, sweetheart, you've been doing too much digging. Look what you've uncovered now."

Rafe reached the floor, and now he eased forward, his gaze locked on Raymond, who watched his every move through veiled lids. The man's bony fingers tightened around a brick.

"Delilah, honey, can you walk?"

"I think so."

Shoot, she wasn't sure. "That's okay. Stay where you are."

302

Despite his talking to Delilah, Rafe remained focused on the sinister eyes of Ray Merrifield and the brick he held.

"I'll kill you, Merrifield, if you don't drop that brick and get away from her." Above him, on the steps, Rafe heard Simon talking in soft whispers to his mother. Well, they had the numbers if he could get Delilah safely out of this mad dog's reach.

"She's losing a lot of blood because of what you did to her."

"She's in my mother's house."

"On the contrary, she's in my mother's house."

Raymond wrinkled his nose as if he smelled something foul. "No, she's not welcome here. Cecilia wasn't welcome here either."

"She was your father's wife."

"She was a whore."

"Your brother slept with your father's wife. That was the ultimate betrayal, Raymond."

"No, marrying that whore and trying to let her take Mama's place was the betrayal."

"Is that why David seduced her, to get even with your father for marrying her?"

"That's a lie! She came to him."

"I don't think so."

Raymond roared like a wild animal and surged up, throwing the brick, but Rafe had expected the move and ducked. The brick smashed into the stairs behind him. Delilah bent, reaching for the shovel with her good hand. Raymond Merrifield, on his feet, must have heard her, dammit, because he whirled on her and pulled the knife from his waistband. Simon rushed down the stairs at the same moment Rafe recovered and lunged forward with a vicious cry. Like a trapped animal, the knife-wielding Raymond pivoted back toward Rafe and raised the knife. Rafe, arms open wide, stopped in mid-stride. Simon, like a wall, stood beside him. Wild-eyed, Raymond Merrifield stared at them both as if unsure which man to attack. Rafe lowered his right hand and reached inside his jacket. Raymond bent his knees at the same moment Rafe touched the butt of his pistol and pulled it from . . .

A thud ruptured the brief silence, and Raymond Merrifield

fell forward onto the brick floor at Rafe's feet. The knife skidded across the brick; Simon grabbed it.

Back against the wall, Delilah lost her balance and started to crumple. Rafe caught her before she hit the floor.

"You can let go of the shovel," he said softly. When she did, he lifted her in his arms. Simon, brick in hand, hovered over the groaning Raymond.

"Miss Annie," Rafe called and started toward the old woman on the stairs.

"Come on, boy, git her back upstairs. We'll stop that bleedin'. Ain't bad as it looks, I imagine. You should have seen the blood your daddy left behind."

Chapter Fifty

"Was David there?" Delilah asked.

Rafe had stopped at the doorway, not wanting to disturb her if she slept. Now, he entered the room. "There was a body. Sheriff and Doc Surrey seem confident it's him." He handed her a photo they'd taken from the unruly Raymond the night before.

What a difference the night had made. Between Miss Annie and the doc, Delilah's operation had been re-closed and bandaged up. This morning, she had color back in her cheeks.

She handed him back the likeness of David Merrifield. "Why, he doesn't look a thing like you."

He sat on the bed beside her and glanced at the photo. "No, he doesn't, and I trust you agree Raymond doesn't either. And to think you were worried about madness in your family."

"Who told you David seduced Cecilia?"

"I don't know that. The whole sordid affair probably happened the way Raymond said it did. Cecilia was the seducer. I was trying to make him mad. I wanted him after me and away from you. Oh," he said, and fished the heavy, cast-iron key from his pants pocket. He handed it to her. "We got that off him, too."

She weighed it in her hand. "Have you tried it?"

"That honor's yours. It is, after all, *your* treasured door." He winked at her. "I've already opened mine."

She smiled, then said, "What did you find out in Fort Adams?"

"Raeford Gavin Stone died in 1852."

"I'm sorry. I had no—"

"Idea Morgan Ward raised me?" He gave her a quick peck on the lips. "That makes two of us."

"Even when Mr. Gifford told me you didn't know, I couldn't figure out what he meant. You always knew everything."

He snorted.

"What are you going to do now?"

"We're filling in that tunnel," he said, searching his right pocket for the ring he'd secreted there. Ah, there it was. "It's gonna cave in on somebody. Then I'm gonna find a way to lock up that secret stairwell, and I'm replacing all the windows."

Ring in his palm, he reached across her lap for her left hand. "Then we're going to redecorate this entire house, starting with the Riverview Room, which will be our library."

He slipped the ring on her finger, and her gaze fell to the hand he held. She bent forward and, for a moment, sat there, staring at her hand. He wondered if she'd heard what he said about the Riverview Room. Then she placed the fingertips of her right hand against her lips and looked at him with tear-filled eyes.

"It's hers, isn't it? The one she left that night?"

"Yes," he said, "it was Daddy's mama's according to Uncle Will. My granddaddy gave it to her when they wed. Grandma left it for Daddy. Daddy gave it—"

Delilah unleashed a sob and threw herself against him. He felt her shudder and held her as she cried. "Sweetheart," he whispered into her hair, "you are pleased with the ring?"

She nodded against his chest, her hair tickling his chin. Momentarily she laughed and sat back, swiping at her eyes. "Oh Rafe, you could never have given me anything that made me feel more . . ."

"Wanted?" he finished when she didn't.

"Yes, wanted."

"I love you, Delilah."

She hugged him. "I love you, too."

"I knew that for sure when you reached for me the other morning in the dining room, despite the fact that you believed I was lying to you about the man who raised me."

He felt her giggle, then she pushed back to see his face.

"What?" he asked.

"Speaking of the man who raised you, can you tell me one more thing?"

"If I know the answer."

"Where is the gold?"

He smiled. "Oh, you're gonna like this, sweetheart. It seems that when Mama and Daddy arrived at Fort Adams they had one strongbox, only a fraction of the money. According to what Daddy told Uncle Will, and confirmed by Henry Gifford, once the gold was off the ship, the plan was to move it by skiff from Carthage Point down Old St. Catherine Creek to Butler Lake where the Confederates had stowed a wagon. From there they were to move it east, through the Piney Woods to the Pearl, then to the Coast and out of the country. Slade, who Henry Gifford believed was the ringleader, agreed to the plan."

"How—"

"The Confederates didn't have a plan to get the gold out of the country, but Gifford trusted Slade did. Slade was stationed in Vicksburg. He'd been in the area since the summer of '63, and he knew the immediate area pretty well, but not the Piney Woods, which was not only wild but lawless. The Seventeenth, on the other hand, was intimately familiar with the Pearl River area and had contacts there. For all intent, the Confederates appeared critical to the operation, but looking back, Henry Gifford says Slade's agreeing to move the gold into the Piney Woods was a sure giveaway that things weren't on the up-and-up."

"Why?"

"Gifford mumbled something about why would a cutthroat Br'er Fox allow wily Br'er Rabbit to lead him into that briar patch along with the gold?"

Delilah laughed. "He was referring to Joel Chandler Harris's *Uncle Remus* stories. They're popular here."

"Well, I knew the point Gifford was making is that those Yankees' venturing into the Piney Woods with the Confederates and all that gold would have been imprudent at best, and as you now know, the real mastermind behind the theft was Micah Ziegler. He had served under Slade and knew the kind of man he was. He contacted him at some point, probably after the gold left Virginia City. Gifford puts a lot of store in the fact that the *Gilded Rose* laid over in Vicksburg for six days. Whether that was when Ziegler first approached Slade or if he contacted him earlier, we'll probably never know, but we are confident they finalized plans for the heist, and double cross, while the ship was in Vicksburg. That included recruiting the Confederates.

"Gifford was a firebrand, a bitter, unrepentant Southerner. Slade had, as part of his duties, come into contact with him — in a conflicted way, not a friendly one — and he figured Gifford might be willing to help pull off the heist.

Slade approached Gifford four days before the raid. He told him he was working with a member of the Union detail and, at Gifford's asking, identified his point of contact as 'Mizer'. Slade told him several members of the detail were involved, as was the civilian pilot, a Southerner, who would run the ship aground for a cut. It was Slade who tipped the Confederates to the ship's departure schedule, and he was with the Seventeenth at Carthage Point during the attack.

"Once the conspirators got the gold off the ship, Daddy and Jeremiah Gifford were going to accompany Slade and James Penworth, another of the Federals, to Butler Lake with the gold. The rest of the group was to hang back and cover their escape in case they were pursued. Gifford and Penworth, however, were killed during the robbery — back shot as it turned out.

"Daddy and Slade arrived at the lake unscathed. Daddy had loaded the first strongbox onto the wagon in anticipation of moving it east as fast as they could. He had his back to Slade when the man shot him."

"You'd have thought Slade would have waited until your father helped him move all the gold from the boat to the wagon."

"A good point and one that supports my belief that Mizer and Slade intended to cross the lake and move the gold on down the creek to the Mississippi. Whatever their plan, it didn't happen. Slade bungled killing Daddy and got himself killed in the process."

Rafe purposefully stopped his tale and watched Delilah. Finally, she huffed. "Well, tell me what happened next!"

He laughed. "Daddy was in bad shape. The bullet missed his spine, but did tear up his right kidney pretty bad. The most immediate problem, though, was blood loss. There was no way he could have transferred the gold from the skiff to the wagon by himself. Knowing his men wouldn't be coming to help him, and Mizer would no doubt try to finish him off when he got there, Daddy fired two shots into the bottom of that skiff and set it adrift in the current where the creek runs into Butler Lake. By the time he'd struggled into the wagon with that lone strongbox in its bed and got the team turned around, the skiff was a good distance offshore and sinking fast. Daddy was four miles from River's Bend, and as you know, he made it home."

"All that gold is at the bottom of Butler Lake?"

"I believe so."

"Are you going to tell anyone?"

He gave her a crooked smile, then pulled her into his arms. "Our grandchildren."

Historical Note

I break precedent with *River's Bend*, placing the historical note after the story rather than its beginning. I feared the information provided here would give away too much of the novel's mystery early on.

Between the end of the War for Southern Independence and the 1880s, over three million Southerners left the South. Some went west and some to large northern cities, but many, mourning the loss of their way of life and disgusted with the abuse the Republican Congress inflicted on the South, in tandem with that body's clear violation and subsequent desecration of the U.S. Constitution, left the United States altogether to begin again in Canada, British Honduras (Belize), Venezuela, and Mexico, the latter an ill-fated venture to live as colonists/fight as mercenaries for Emperor Maximilian.

The presence in Mexico of Ferdinand Maximilian Joseph, archduke of Austria and puppet of the imperialistic Napoleon III of France violated the Monroe Doctrine, forbidding European interference in the Western Hemisphere. The French design came at the behest of Mexican conservatives determined to drive out the government of Benito Juarez, who had become President of Mexico in 1858. Maximilian accepted the offer of the Mexican "throne" in 1863 and was crowned emperor in June of 1864. By April of 1865, when the United States' conflict was ending, Mexico was embroiled in a bloody civil war of its own. French forces had driven Juarez and his followers to the Texas border. That same month, the United States government demanded the French withdraw from Mexico.

When Major General Joe Shelby, C.S.A., with perhaps as many as one thousand men, entered Mexico City in August 1865 offering service to the French, Maximilian declined, but did offer them refuge in one of the colonies he envisioned for American Southerners leaving their homeland. But though Mexican conservatives and French royalists were happy to have the Confederates (Americans) in their midst, the Juaristas were not. Not only were the French oppressive, the memory of the Mexican War (1848) had not faded, and when Maximilian fell in June 1867, so did the Confederate colonies in Mexico. Many Confederates died, as did Maximilian, others escaped back to the United States, but some moved farther south to the more-welcoming Brazil, home as it turned out of the largest and most lasting Confederate colonies.

Though maintaining neutrality during the War, Brazil had displayed sympathy for the Southern Cause and protected Southern blockade runners pursued by the U.S. Navy. The Federals' overzealous pursuit of Confederate ships into sovereign Brazilian ports strained relations between Brazil and the United States. I used this latter as a plot point in my story to explain the purpose of my fictional shipment of gold down the Mississippi.

Though a figurehead, Brazil's Emperor Dom Pedro was very popular both at home and abroad (particularly in the American South). He openly recruited defeated Southerners to his shores as cotton farmers, doctors, dentists, businessmen and engineers. Even a handful of freedmen immigrated to Brazil during the post-War years.

The number of Southern emigrants to Brazil is unknown; movement between nations did not suffer the restrictions applied in modern times, and Brazil did not keep immigration figures in those days. No passports or visas were required. Southerners simply caught a boat (many chartered for the colonists) out of New Orleans, Mobile, Savannah, Charleston, New York, and other cities and entered Brazil at any of a dozen ports, the most active being Rio de Janeiro. Popular estimates for the number of Southern emigrants to Brazil between 1867-1885 range from 10,000 to 20,000. Most made their way to the rich São Paulo province in south-central Brazil. Others, less in number, settled along the Amazon River much farther north.

I considered the Santarém colony in the isolated wilds of the

Amazon basin as the most appropriate refuge for a man on the run, but the lucrative potential of the much richer São Paulo province would have proved the ultimate choice of the alias "Rafe Stone." There he would have had ample opportunity to invest his small fortune, which, for the purpose of my story, grew exponentially.

For two generations the real *Confederados* maintained their dreams and memories of the Old South. Some eventually returned to the United States, but many more stayed, intermarried and are today Brazilian. For those of you interested in further study of the Brazilian *Confederados*, I refer you to Eugene Harter's *The Lost Colony of the Confederacy*, University of Mississippi Press, 1985.

The banner belonging to Morgan Ward's Seventeenth Horse Soldiers (company) is, like the Seventeenth itself, fictional. However, like the fighting companies that rallied in defense of the South in 1861, company banners were real. These colors identified the individual companies that made up Confederate regiments—and since it was a feature of the Confederacy that small localities formed up companies (with their local banners), which in turn supplied Confederate regiments (ten companies to a regiment), Southern regiments often carried multiple "colors" into battle.

Company banners were made with love and pride by the wives, daughters, mothers, sisters, sweethearts, friends, and neighbors of the men who fought for the Cause. Many banners were patterned after the First National Flag of the Confederacy (Stars and Bars) with their unit identification highlighted in bright colors and augmented by patriotic mottos. They were given to the companies in formal ceremonies prior to the company's "marching off to war." By the close of 1861, the plethora of "regimental" colors as well as battlefield confusion between the Stars and Bars and the Stars and Stripes prompted the Confederacy to adopt the single regimental Battle Flag still honored by true Southerners today.

313

The return of the Seventeenth's colors as narrated in my story by Henry Gifford follows a similar pattern for many real banners that were returned to Confederate societies by the Northerners who captured them and/or the U.S. War Department decades after the war ended.

Those who have read my first novel, *The Devil's Bastard*, will recognize River's Bend as the home of the pseudo-villain André Richard, albeit a century later. For the purpose of my story, River's Bend is located on the river roughly halfway between Natchez and St. Catherine Bend. Like many of the old plantation homes along any body of water, it had its own landing, and steamships routinely stopped at the private docks. The existence of an antebellum showcase that began life as a one-room French Dominion cabin might be stretching things a bit, though there are several houses in the area known to go back to the Spanish era (1780s) — including Hope Farm and Airlie — that began much smaller and more simplistic than they are today.

Most of the businesses and all of the people referenced as being in Natchez at the time of my story are fictional; however, the street names and a handful of the businesses, Natchez Gas Works, Rutherford & Dalgarn (Alabama coal), J.J. Cole & Co. and the Fisk Library were real. Natchez did have a hospital — on Cemetery Road, no less. I refer interested readers to an 1892 city directory published by the Banner Publishing Company in Natchez, which you can find at the Natchez Belle website: http://www.natchezbelle.org/adams-ind/1892directory.htm.

Today Old St. Catherine Creek and Butler Lake are the site of a 25,000-acre national wildlife refuge, the realization of a twenty-plus-year reforestation effort following two decades of clear-cutting the Mississippi River's bottomland forest for agricultural purposes. Since the area still abounded with hardwood forests and cypress swamp in the early 1960s, I assume it was wild and wonderful in 1895 and wilder still in 1865.

A little history, if I may, on Fort Adams and Warrenton, which along with Delilah's hometown of Rodney, are today little more than notations on a map. All are victims of the whims of the mighty Mississippi, which dictated their founding and subsequent importance (and they were all important), then moved away and left them in isolation, where they've all but faded away.

In 1698 the French missionary, Anthony Davion, under the auspices of the Seminary of Quebec, itself affiliated with the Seminary of Foreign Missions in Paris, established a Catholic mission among the Tunica Indians on a high hill overlooking the Mississippi River. The little mission was roughly six miles north of the 31st parallel. He called it Roche à Davion. Father Davion maintained his mission off and on (depending on how friendly the natives were) for twenty years. He returned to France in 1725.

At the close of the French and Indian War (1763), the site of Father Davion's mission fell to the British, who called it Loftus Heights. This region became part of Spain at the end of the American Revolution. In 1798, Spain surrendered the Natchez District to Captain Isaac Guion, representative of the United States government. Guion recommended Loftus Heights as the site of a fort to protect American interests in the region. Spanish Louisiana lay just across the Mississippi River and six miles to the south, across the 31st parallel. The stronghold, named Fort Adams in honor of then-President John Adams, served as the U.S. port of entry on the Mississippi River and boasted earthworks, a powder magazine, and a garrison of 500 U.S. regulars. In an 1803 letter to William C. C. Claiborne, governor of the Mississippi Territory, Commanding General James Wilkinson described Fort Adams as "the door to our whole western country." The little town that grew up around the fort was also called Fort Adams. This is where, many years later, my character William Stone lived.

With the purchase of Louisiana in 1803 and the United States' subsequent victory in the War of 1812, the Spanish threat disappeared, and Fort Adams was eventually abandoned. During the War Between the States, the Federals stationed the ironclad steamer *Chillicothe* at the foot of the hill upon which the fort had been built. The boat remained there one year, long enough, the story goes, for the drift of the water around its hull to cause the river to change course, moving more than a mile from the fort site.

Warrenton became the first county seat of Warren County in 1809. The region, originally part of the Natchez District, follows a pattern similar to Natchez. Here, Father Davion, the priest of Fort Adams' fame, named his mission St. Pierre. The military post the French called Yazoo Post. The Yazoo Indians slaughtered both in conjunction with the Natchez uprising of 1729.

During the Spanish era (1779-1798), the Spaniards built a fort in the area and called it Nogales (Walnuts). After assuming control of the region in 1798, the United States called this area Walnut Hills. This became the site of Vicksburg in 1825. In 1836, the seat moved from Warrenton to Vicksburg. In addition to usurping Warrenton's civic responsibilities, Vicksburg siphoned off the smaller town's commercial assets. But when the War Between the States started in 1861, Warrenton's inhabitants still numbered 500-600 people.

The Confederates fortified the town, and on 22 April 1863 its battery sank the Union boat *Tigress*, which had just escaped, unscathed, the mighty guns at Vicksburg.

In 1883, the Mississippi River changed course, leaving what was left of the town separated from the river by a huge sandbar, one mile wide. By the time of my story, Warrenton would have been no more than a small community south of Vicksburg. The Big Black Baptist Church and cemetery are fictional, but for my purposes are located to the southeast in a rural setting between Warrenton and the Big Black River (the Loosa Chitta).

Delilah's home, Rodney, has a very old history, appearing on early eighteenth-century maps as Petit Gulph, and is believed to be the site of a river crossing favored by the Indians. The town of Petit Gulph existed as of 1798. Residents changed its name to Rodney in 1814 in honor of Judge Thomas Rodney, the territorial magistrate.

It was in Rodney that Dr. Haller Nutt, a wealthy cotton and sugar-cane planter, developed the resilient Petit-Gulf strain of cotton, a disease-resistant cross of Egyptian and Mexican cottons and a primary contributor to the American South's Cotton Kingdom.

Rodney became a thriving commercial and cultural center and one of the busiest ports on the Mississippi, rivaling Natchez. On the eve of the War Between the States, the city had a thousand homes, 4,000 residents, numerous stores, newspapers, banks (with capital of one million dollars), and the first opera house in the state.

The misfortunes of war hit the town's interests hard; then in 1876, its lifeline, the meandering Mississippi, meandered two miles farther west. By the time my heroine Delilah Graff left it at the age of twelve (1888), the city would have been struggling, a shade of its former self. Still today, in the second decade of the twenty-first century, a small population continues to reside there.

As for sunken ships and missing gold—stories abound all over Dixie, and I'm sure I don't have to tell any reader who enjoys the type story I write how much fun it is to speculate about buried treasure. And to give the reader a perspective for what the raiders of the *Gilded Rose* were risking their lives at War's end, one hundred thousand dollars in 1865 would be worth roughly $1.5 million in 2011.

I hope you enjoyed *River's Bend*. Thanks for reading.

If you enjoyed *River's Bend* don't miss Charlsie Russell's award-winning first novel

The Devil's Bastard

Natchez on the river, 1793. The Spanish Fleet controls the Mississippi, and the Dons rule their rowdy British and American subjects with a patient hand. The location is strategic, the land fertile, and within two decades, cotton will be king. Into this web of international intrigue, the rich and powerful Elizabeth Boswell welcomes her orphaned grandniece Angelique Veilleux and introduces the impoverished beauty to a world of privilege. But power has enemies and wealth demands a price. Rumors state that Elizabeth's success stems from dalliance with a lustful demon that still prowls her family farm of De Leau outside Natchez.

At the center of this ominous legend is Elizabeth's grandson, the handsome and dangerous Mathias Douglas who saves Angelique from degradation and death near the end of her journey to Natchez. Mathias is the son of the doomed Julianna, Elizabeth's only daughter. Mathias's father, locals whisper, is Elizabeth's demon.

Despite the dark legend, Angelique cannot quell her feelings for Mathias, for whom she would make any sacrifice. An outcast, Mathias is cruelly tested by Angelique's affection. Determined not to dishonor her, he callously puts her aside. But Elizabeth has other plans and offers him the family farm at De Leau to marry the girl. Soon Angelique finds herself desperately in love with the man who has conquered her body and possessed her soul.

But something in the swamps surrounding De Leau stalks her, and nightmares invade her dreams. What she perceives as Mathias's indifference to the threat leaves Angelique isolated and afraid. She begins to doubt her grandaunt's motives for sending her to De Leau, as well as Mathias' role in Elizabeth's plan. Resolving her doubts means uncovering the secret of Mathias's sire.

From Mathias and Angelique's first meeting to Elizabeth Boswell's revelation at story's end, *The Devil's Bastard* is a splendid read. First and foremost a sensual romance, it is also a well-researched historical with a haunting mystery.

Don't miss Charlsie Russell's second award-winning novel

$\mathcal{W}olf\ \mathcal{D}awson$

Ten years after the Confederate army reported him killed in action, dirt-poor Jeff Dawson returns to Natchez, Mississippi, a wealthy man and purchases White Oak Glen, the once opulent home of the now impoverished Seatons, the aristocratic family that years ago shattered his own.

Burdened with her drunken brother Tucker and besieged by greedy relatives, Juliet Seaton struggles to hold on to what remains of her farm. Now she finds her family facing a new menace in the form of a marauding wolf, which slaughters valuable stock and assails the mind of her alcoholic brother. Tucker Seaton warns his sister that the man occupying White Oak Glen is a ghost, who in the form of that vicious wolf seeks to destroy what is left of the Seatons.

An infant when events occurred setting her family against the Dawsons, Juliet appears pitted against a neighbor hell-bent on avenging his sister, who died in childbirth after being violated by a Seaton male.

Jeff's grandfather was part Creek Indian. Local legend states he terrorized unfriendly neighbors with tales of his ability to shape-shift into a deadly wolf. Unidentified persons lynched the colorful old man following the savage killing, apparently by a wolf, of the Seaton who raped Jeff Dawson's sister.

But Juliet finds the handsome Jeff a living, breathing man. Hot-blooded to boot. His seductive touch weakens her resolve and blinds her to the danger he poses. Jeff, however, is no longer compelled to destroy the Seatons, if he ever was; they have destroyed themselves and left the vulnerable Juliet to his mercy — mercy he's quite willing to give, though he's not ready to let the feisty beauty know that.

Into this explosive mix of fear and distrust comes a sadistic killer, and what this fiend kills is not Seaton livestock.

With the countryside ablaze with suspicion directed toward Jeff, he and Juliet overcome mutual distrust and strip away a lost generation's hatred as quickly as the clothes covering their bodies. Old lies give way to new truths, lust to love, and together, the lovers set out to uncover not only a killer, but the identity of the spectral beast haunting the countryside.

Finally, don't miss Charlsie Russell's third award-winning novel

Epico Bayou

In the fall of 1897, a grand old gentleman of Handsboro, Mississippi dies a very wealthy man, and much to the chagrin of Lionel Augustus's siblings, he leaves the bulk of his estate to his estranged bastard son, Clay Boudreaux, and his beloved step-daughter, Olivia Lee. There is but one stipulation to Lionel's will, the two must wed.

For reasons of their own, the two young people agree to marry, sight unseen, but only days after her marriage by proxy to Deputy Sheriff Clay Boudreaux of Galveston County, Texas, Olivia learns her husband has died in a house fire and her extended family intends to contest the terms of the will. Exacerbating her situation, a mysterious stranger, claiming to be the dead Clay, but who her family warns is Clay's older brother Troy, invades Olivia's opulent home and accuses her of hiring Troy to kill Clay . . . and yet another henchman to eliminate Clay's killer.

Olivia and the handsome stranger, whoever he might be, both have sound reasons for confusing their roles in the plot to murder

Clay Boudreaux, reasons dealing with duty, justice, and survival. Neither is sure of the role the other plays in the Machiavellian plan of Lionel's siblings, nor is it clear if Lionel's brother and sister are the only subversives working to sabotage the terms of Lionel's will. So clear is the present danger it overshadows the dark secret driving Lionel's bizarre stipulation that Clay and Olivia wed.

Set on the Mississippi Gulf Coast at the close of the nineteenth century, Charlsie Russell's third novel is both a romantic charade and a compelling mystery, pitting the wit and will of one wary lover against the honor and sheer determination of the other, even while the sinister machinations of dangerous foes force them into a grudging alliance.

Though the tangled mystery sets this novel apart from her edgy Gothics, *The Devil's Bastard* and *Wolf Dawson*, Ms. Russell's *Epico Bayou* still features those tried and true elements of suspense, sensual romance, and historical setting that characterize her work. Pure escape. Don't miss this journey!

About the Author

Charlsie Russell is a retired United States Navy commander turned author. She loves history, and she loves the South. She focuses her writing on historical suspense set in her home state of Mississippi.

After seven years of rejection, she woke up one morning and determined she did not have enough years left on this planet to sit back and hope a New York publisher would one day take a risk on her novels. Thus resolved, she expanded her horizons into the publishing realm with the creation of Loblolly Writer's House.

In addition to writing and publishing, Ms. Russell is the mother and homemaker to five children and their father.

To learn more about Charlsie Russell and Loblolly Writer's House, visit www.loblollywritershouse.com.

Loblolly Writer's House

Order Blank
Tear this sheet out and

Mail order to:

Loblolly Writer's House
P.O. Box 7438
Gulfport, MS 39506-7438

Item	Price*	Qty	Total
The Devil's Bastard	$16.00	_____	_____
Wolf Dawson	$16.00	_____	_____
Epico Bayou	$16.00	_____	_____
River's Bend	$16.00	_____	_____
Shipping free:	0.00		

Total payment: _____

Would you like a signed copy?
Tell me how:_____
_____

Send to:
_____
_____
_____

*Price includes 7% Mississippi sales tax
For Bookseller rates visit: www.loblollywritershouse.com

CPSIA information can be obtained at www.ICGtesting.com
Printed in the USA
LVOW060906090112

262991LV00004B/1/P